Her Wicked Angel

Felicity Heaton

HER ANGEL SERIES

Her Dark Angel
Her Fallen Angel
Her Warrior Angel
Her Guardian Angel
Her Demonic Angel
Her Wicked Angel

Find out more at: www.felicityheaton.co.uk

CHAPTER 1

It was a black day in Hell.

Asmodeus stood high above the bottomless pit, his amber gaze locked on the tall obsidian spires in the distance. Screams and sobs rose up from below him on the hot air, the grunts of their tormentors a harsher note in a symphony he so often enjoyed. The demons were busy today. He had been busy too until he had felt the call of his master.

As much as he had wanted to keep the Devil waiting while he had finished his latest masterpiece, he had dropped everything and left his castle in the wastelands via a portal that had brought him to the plateau above the bottomless pit.

And there he stood, debating how long he could put off crossing the cragged, grim landscape to the Devil's fortress before his master lost his temper and called him again.

Asmodeus enjoyed pushing the male right to the limit of his patience. There was something satisfying about irritating his so-called master. The Devil would be able to sense his proximity and that he hadn't moved in close to twenty minutes. It was a game of wills he often played with him. Who would break first?

The call came again, stronger than it had been before, a tug he felt as a physical yank on his ribs, pulling him forwards towards the fortress.

A reminder that he was given freedom in Hell, but he was not master of it.

Asmodeus tipped forwards and plummeted towards the snaking wide ribbon of lava hundreds of feet below. Hot air rushed at him, sweeping his black hair back, battering his bare chest and ruffling his feathers. He stretched his obsidian wings to their full span, caught a thermal and levelled out just metres from the fiery surface of one of the principal rivers in Hell.

He gave a leisurely flap to keep his altitude and glided across the black, forbidding terrain.

Hell's angels stalked the land below him in their demonic forms. Dragon-like wings furled against their huge black bodies and their claws made quick work of the whimpering lesser demons they were dealing with for their master. Some demons were little more than pests in Asmodeus's eyes, and the eyes of his master. They caused more trouble than they were worth.

Asmodeus grinned, turned into a barrel roll and swooped down at one of the small scaly brown demons. He plucked it from the ground, had snapped its neck before it could even loose a shriek, and dropped it on the head of one of the Hell's angels in charge of cleaning up the area. The male snarled at him, exposing sharp red teeth, the fires of Hell burning in his crimson eyes.

Asmodeus flipped him off and beat his black feathered wings, resuming his course. He weaved as he flew, following the thermals that would carry him to the Devil's fortress without him having to expend any effort. What did his master want with him?

He didn't bother Asmodeus often. Normally, when he called upon him, it was to give him an important mission. Torture a captive demon for information on the angels. Track down a traitor in one of the more dangerous regions of Hell. Drown someone in a lake of lava.

Kill one of the angels who protected the plateau, Heaven's only sanctioned area in Hell.

Personally, Asmodeus couldn't see why they had access to any part of Hell. No creature of this realm was allowed to set foot in Heaven unless they were shackled and contained in the prison there. How was that fair? If Heaven could station a small contingent of angels in Hell, then Hell should be allowed to station some of its men in Heaven.

Asmodeus's grin widened.

He had sent his pet there recently. How had he fared?

Nevar had been a guardian angel until Asmodeus had found him snooping at the pool that recorded the history of the three realms. He had dealt with the curious angel, battling him until he was weak and then pushing him over the edge. The male was tainted now, turning as wicked as his new master. Asmodeus.

He had wanted Nevar to shake Heaven, but it seemed his wolf had failed to blow down the fortress as instructed. Perhaps he should have waited until Nevar had grown stronger, the darkness within him in full control, but patience had never been his strong suit. It was part of the reason he often lost the game of wills he played with the Devil and something he was working on. Now, Asmodeus had lost track of Nevar. What was he up to?

Asmodeus wanted to know, but since he had sent the angel to Heaven and he could not leave Hell, it was impossible for him to find out. He didn't doubt that their paths would cross again soon. Nevar had been hell-bent on killing him the last time they had seen each other. The male would be hunting him down soon enough and then Asmodeus would command him to return to Heaven and succeed this time, or die trying.

He beat his wings and shot over the spires of black rock that curved around the semi-circular courtyard of the Devil's obsidian fortress.

The tall twin black doors opened, revealing a crack of orange light and the silhouette of a figure that looked tiny in comparison.

Asmodeus lowered his feet and glided down to land on the black flagstones. He set down on his left foot and casually walked from there, furling his large wings against his bare back at the same time. The feathers grazed the gold-edged black strips of armour protecting his hips with each step and the longest ones curled forwards to caress his black knee-high leather boots and the metal plates that shielded his shins.

The Devil reached the top of the steps that led down from his fortress and straightened out the cuffs of his impeccable black suit jacket in a way that told Asmodeus he was on the verge of losing his cool.

The handsome black-haired male lifted his amber gaze and pinned Asmodeus with a glare that sent a shiver through him. A bolt of fire and lightning followed it, zinging through his blood and bones, a fierce reminder of the power this male wielded and a warning not to keep him waiting again.

The power flowing over him grew stronger and Asmodeus gritted his teeth as his knees trembled and fought to remain standing, refusing to succumb to the Devil's will.

He would never go to his knees unwillingly.

Never.

Asmodeus clenched his fists, every muscle tensing against the strain of remaining upright. Sweat broke out across his brow. His limbs shook and his breathing quickened, but he kept his gaze locked on the Devil's, holding it and showing him that he wouldn't back down.

He would not submit.

A curvaceous naked female stepped out of the fortress, wavering as she walked slowly towards the Devil, a distant look in her dark eyes. She draped her hands over his shoulders and rubbed herself against his back, mewling softly at the same time.

The Devil huffed and the pressure bearing down on Asmodeus lifted.

"Go back inside," the Devil muttered and touched the female's hand. She obeyed, turning away from him and plodding back into the fortress.

The Devil had been busy recently.

His Hell's angels had been bringing him female after female for him to seduce ever since his daughter, Erin, and the traitor Hell's angel had escaped his grasp. The Devil had even taken to keeping some of the mortal women with him at the fortress, creating himself a harem.

Attempting to bring another child into this dark world.

A difficult task to accomplish when there were few females strong enough to bring his child to term.

Erin was a rare success in a sea of failures.

The Devil had only managed to produce one single offspring in thousands of years of trying.

Asmodeus didn't think his current desperate tactic of sleeping with as many females as possible in an extremely short span of time would produce the result the male was looking for. Erin would birth her child soon and then she would be back to fight her father for his throne.

Asmodeus couldn't wait.

Hell was about to get very interesting.

Until then, Asmodeus was content with amusing himself watching the Devil grow increasingly frustrated and desperate. Weak.

He had never seen the Devil this weak before, not in the thousands of years he had lived.

"What business do you have with me?" Asmodeus casually preened his feathers, preparing them for the flight home, and ignored the Devil's scowl.

The male hated it when he spoke to him without an ounce of respect. Everyone else under his command simpered and scraped at his feet. As far as Asmodeus was concerned, the Devil had enough pathetic creatures kissing his expensive Italian leather shoes. Asmodeus wasn't about to join them. He was above them.

The Devil's right hand man.

A male created for destruction and bloodshed.

"You are to travel to the mortal realm and retrieve a female for me."

Asmodeus's black eyebrows pinched in a frown and it took him a moment to absorb exactly what the Devil had said and the connotations it contained.

One, he was ordering him to lower himself to the role of minion, retrieving him another female for his harem. Treating him like a servant. That irked him. He was not just another of the Devil's servants.

Two, he was offering him a taste of the mortal world, granting him leave to step outside the environs of Hell for the first time in his existence. That intrigued Asmodeus. He had always wanted to see the mortal realm with his own eyes and experience it.

Asmodeus stared at him, weighing his options. Swallow his pride and finally fly in the world above, seeing the buildings and the colours, and all the things he had only ever seen in the pool on the plateau, or tell the Devil to stick it and spend the next week in the cells, probably tortured, possibly maimed permanently for his disobedience.

Asmodeus swallowed his pride and it tasted bitter. "Fine."

The Devil grinned, revealing short fangs. "Good. You will find her in Paris, in the middle of the park near the base of the Eiffel Tower. She will be wearing crimson and black. Bring her to me."

Asmodeus nodded, took a step backwards and then turned away from the Devil.

He threw his hand out in front of him and a black vortex appeared, swirling like smoke. It had been many centuries since he had bothered practicing glamours and veils, having given up on ever leaving Hell and having no need for changing his appearance in this realm. He hoped he hadn't forgotten how to cast them.

Asmodeus focused on himself, casting a veil so none would see him when he stepped through the portal into the mortal realm.

"Bring her to me quickly, Asmodeus," the Devil said behind him and Asmodeus nodded again.

Perhaps he would dally just a little. Who knew when the Devil would allow him to leave Hell again?

He stepped through the black portal and tensed as he appeared in the mortal realm. His eyes watered and he blinked against the assault of strong light, leaning back into the shade of the tower that speared the blue sky above him.

Blue.

Asmodeus tipped his head back and stared up at it, and then looked at his surroundings. Green trees. Dark metal. Pale stone. Mortals dressed in a multitude of colours. The warm air carried strange scents. Dust. Something sweet. Smoke. Sounds came from every direction. Blasts of noise and distant rumbles of what he suspected were vehicles. Constant chatter. Laughter. Squeals of happiness. All alien to him.

All choking and closing in on him.

He didn't like it.

He took a step back towards the portal behind him and glared at everyone as they passed. Ants. Hundreds of them. Swarming. Shoving. Jostling each other. He wanted to kill them all. They were noisy. Brutal. Irritating.

Insignificant.

Powerless.

Asmodeus grinned, his golden eyes narrowing with it, and flexed his fingers. His fangs began to lengthen and his black claws followed them.

Prey for the hunter.

He would drown out the disgusting scents with the smell of blood. He would replace joy with fear, with screams and sobs and pointless pleas for mercy. He would bathe this colourful world in crimson.

Crimson.

A flash of that colour caught his eye and his gaze zeroed in on it. It was gone, lost in the sea of other hues. It flickered again, further off to his right, and his eyes shot to it. Wavy chestnut hair bounced against crimson ruffled material with each light step. He caught a sliver of black jeans. Crimson and black. The female the Devil wanted.

She turned and he glimpsed her face, and his desire to bathe his hands in the blood of these puny creatures slipped away, calm suffusing him, making him forget his irritation and dark desires.

She blinked, black lashes shuttering luminous hazel eyes, and turned away, continuing onwards towards a strip of green land to his right beyond the shadow of the tower.

Asmodeus felt a tug behind his breastbone, pulling him in her direction, but something told him it wasn't the Devil commanding him to follow her. It was something else that made him want to track her through the crowd.

He focused and altered his appearance as he walked, hiding his pieces of gold-edged black armour with a black dress shirt, black jeans and leather boots, and shielding his wings. He lifted the veil that concealed him from mortal eyes and stalked the female as she moved through the thinning crowd, keeping his distance but remaining close enough that he wouldn't lose her.

She stepped out into the bright sunlight on the vivid green grass and it cast golden highlights in her hair. Asmodeus's heart missed a beat and then thumped hard against his ribs. His palms sweated.

Why?

He had hunted thousands before for the Devil. This female was no different. He would capture her and take her to him.

He wouldn't.

Asmodeus shook his head and paused at the edge of the crowd, staring after her.

He wouldn't?

He had pushed the Devil to the limit of his patience a thousand times but he had never disobeyed an order. He would not begin now.

He would take the female to his master.

The female in question turned on the grass and peered up the height of the tower, using a slender hand to shield her eyes, and Asmodeus's heart missed another beat.

He slammed his hand against his bare chest and coughed. What was wrong with him?

Was the mortal world making him sick? He had never been sick before, but he had heard that demons could become ill. He wasn't a demon though. He had never heard of an angel growing sick. Was it possible?

All the more reason to grab the female and return to Hell.

He took a step towards her, and then another one. She turned her back on him and he closed in until he was only a few metres away.

He just needed to grab her and then deliver her to the Devil. It wasn't difficult, so why was he hesitating? He had never hesitated before. He had carried out his master's orders without pause or regret, spilling blood and carving flesh, destroying lives. This was easy. Grab. Deliver. End of mission.

The Devil would have a new female for his growing harem. Asmodeus would return to his castle.

His stomach turned at the thought of that male laying his filthy claws on this delicate, dainty female.

He stared at the back of her head, replaying how she had looked when she had paused to glance up the height of the Eiffel Tower.

Wide hazel eyes.

Soft rosy lips.

Delicate perfect features and porcelain skin.

Chestnut hair cascading over her shapely shoulders.

Beautiful.

Pure.

Asmodeus wanted to close the gap between them, gently lay his hands on her shoulders, and slowly turn her to face him so he could drink his fill of her beauty and purity all over again.

Instead, he took a step backwards, distancing himself from her. Foreign feelings and thoughts collided in his mind, filling it and sending him in circles, tearing him between completing his mission and doing something that astounded him.

He could leave her here, in peace, and come up with an excuse. He couldn't let his despicable master ruin her. He wouldn't.

He turned away and held his hand out before him, focusing on the air there to call a portal back to Hell.

"Where do you go, Asmodeus?" The soft female voice caught him off guard.

His shoulders tensed and his outstretched hand shook.

She knew his name. She recognised him. And she spoke in English, even though they were in France.

English was not the native language of this land.

He had never left Hell before.

How did she know him?

He looked over his right shoulder and found her standing where he had left her, but facing him, her hands clasped in front of her, over the point where her crimson short-sleeved gypsy-style top met her black jeans.

A serene smile curved her rosy lips and it was then that he felt the incredible power in her.

He had never felt power like this in anyone other than the Devil.

She was strong, but it was not evil that flowed through her veins. It was something else. She was something else.

He had never spoken to a female like her before, and he wasn't sure how to address her or whether he should even be concerned about such things. He swallowed the dry lump in his throat, steeled himself against his turbulent feelings, and told himself to get a grip. She was a target. He was here on a mission. He would not disobey his master. He would not allow this mere slip of a woman to affect him.

Asmodeus shifted to face her. "Who are you?"

"Liora," she said with a breezy smile and bright eyes, and held her hand out to him. He stared at it but didn't take it. She sighed and lowered it again. "You came for a reason… is it because of my cousin?"

He frowned. "Cousin?"

Perhaps he should have asked the Devil for more information about this mission before taking it. Why would he be here because of her cousin when he didn't even know who she was?

She knew who he was. That still bothered him. He wanted to know how she knew of him and why she wasn't running in fear.

The female called Liora nodded. "Serenity."

His guard instantly rose and his senses stretched out to map the area in case this was a trap. He scowled at her and his right hand twitched at his side, ready to call his blade should he need it.

Had she been awaiting his arrival, willing to play bait so they could catch him? How had Apollyon known his master would let him fly free of Hell?

Asmodeus drew in a deep breath to calm himself and pushed all his questions away. Apollyon could not know he was here and this was not a trap. There was no need for him to be on edge. There had to be a reasonable explanation for everything.

He stared at the female. Liora.

Apollyon's female, Serenity, was this beauty's cousin. That only made him more intrigued about why the Devil wanted her.

Did he intend to use Liora against Apollyon? Apollyon was the Great Destroyer, one of the most powerful angels in existence and the one who was destined to fight the Devil and keep him contained within Hell and the bottomless pit.

Apollyon was also Asmodeus's brother, or father of sorts. The first time the Devil had defeated Apollyon, he had tortured the male to the brink of insanity and had then drawn all that was evil out of him. The Devil had used that blood and a smattering of his own to create Asmodeus.

"You don't look much like Apollyon. I've met him and now I've also met you… and you seem very different." She eyed him, hazel gaze curious and intense as she cocked her head to one side. Her tone had a decidedly playful edge to it, soft and light, not exactly how he had expected a mortal to react to him. She was confident, calm, and a little bit teasing.

Asmodeus stared blankly at her. This was not normal female behaviour. He wasn't sure whether she was flirting with him. He didn't think it was a possibility, but she might be. He had no experience of such things.

His shock only increased when she raked her gaze over him, thoroughly inspecting him from head to toe, her stunning hazel eyes lingering on his bare torso. His palms sweated again and he swallowed hard as his pulse picked up.

Her right eyebrow quirked. "Why do you lack complete armour? Apollyon has all his armour. Why do you only have your hip pieces and armoured boots... are you incomplete?"

She could see his armour and his wings? His glamour wasn't working. Had he done it wrong after all?

Asmodeus cursed and swiftly glanced around him at the other mortals.

None of the ones milling around the park were screaming or praying for salvation, so he must have done it right.

"Glamours don't work on me," she said, as if she had read his mind and knew his thoughts.

Was he that transparent? He didn't like that she could see straight through him. He rose to his full height and glared down at her.

It didn't fluster her in the slightest. She flicked her hand upwards with only her right index finger extended. It pointed at the sky. "Factoid. I'm a witch."

Another first for him. He had never met a witch before.

Liora moved closer and looked him over again. "I've never seen cloning on this level. Normally something goes wrong. Did the Devil really create you from Apollyon's blood?"

She paused for air, frowned and canted her head the other way, her gaze rising to lock with his.

"Are you as powerful as Apollyon... or less powerful?"

"More powerful," Asmodeus barked and scowled at her. He was beginning to hate how she not only kept comparing him to Apollyon, but how she was making him feel inferior and broken, a mere shadow of a male.

False and unreal.

Not an individual.

He wanted to leave now.

He growled under his breath, his fangs itching to descend, and turned away from her, casting his hand out at the same time and calling a portal. The black swirling maelstrom formed before him. He'd had enough of this world. It did not live up to his expectations at all. It was noisy, bright, irritating and rude, and he didn't like how uncertain and off-balance he felt. No one respected him here.

They could all go to Hell.

Asmodeus grinned. Perhaps he could make this place Hell and teach them all a lesson they would never forget, because it would be the last thing they knew before they died. His claws sharpened. That sounded good.

"Wait!" Liora grabbed his left arm and tugged it backwards, her warm hands clasping it tightly. "Don't go... please... I didn't mean to sound pushy or upset you."

"I am not upset," he said gruffly and yanked his arm free.

8

He glanced over his shoulder at her. A mistake. She was so close to him, and so beautiful as she looked up at him with a strange mixture of fear and hope in her entrancing eyes. He should leave. He would if he could bring himself to move. He felt as though she had cast a spell on him and he was powerless to resist her. His fury melted away again, leaving him calm and docile, confused as to why he had been angry to begin with. His claws shrank back and his fangs ascended.

She wanted him to wait, and so he waited.

"I've been rude," she whispered and then tipped her chin up and a spark of confidence broke through the fear and hope in her eyes. "I'm sorry. It's a flaw. My mouth just starts running and I can't stop it. I'll tamp it down and think before I speak if you stay. It's just excitement."

"Excitement?" That had him turning to face her. What was she excited about?

His mind supplied that he was the reason for her excitement. A stupid idea. No one had ever been excited to meet him. Scared. Terrified. Having a near-death experience. Or possibly a pre-death experience since he was normally there to kill them. Not excited though.

He had caught the way she had glanced at his extended claws and the fear that had followed her seeing them. There was no possible way she could be excited by his presence.

Liora nodded again. "I was excited to meet you."

That was a definite first, and it only made him feel more out of place and confused by this world and this slight willowy female before him. "Most people are afraid to meet me."

She shrugged her slender shoulders. "I'm not most people. I've wanted to meet angels all of my life and I've studied them all I could, and then Serenity fell in love with Apollyon and I met one, but… and don't tell her this… he seems very stuffy."

Asmodeus smiled. He couldn't help it. The sight of it seemed to bring out her smile too. It was dazzling this time, as if she had found someone she could swap notes about Apollyon's faults with and was over the moon.

"So, when I heard about you, I really wanted to meet you… because I figured essentially you should be the opposite of Apollyon."

Asmodeus cocked an eyebrow. "Evil?"

She had wanted to meet him?

She laughed, the sound sending a pleasant shiver through his body. "No. Fun."

Fun? He really didn't think she would see him as that if she knew the things he had done that he had considered fun. The thought of massacring these irritating mortals swarming around him was fun. Watching a demon's head melt off in one of the lakes of lava while he held him fast, forcing him deeper into the fiery magma, was fun.

He had seen what mortals considered fun in the pool in Hell. Riding bicycles. Ponies. Playing various dull sports that didn't involve severed demon heads and spears. The closest thing that mortals considered fun that he had also found interesting was hunting animals, and even that had seemed tame and dull once he had realised it involved distance weapons, not hand-to-hand combat with feral creatures capable of maiming or even killing the hunter.

Everything mortals did seemed sanitised and harmless, designed to thrill without any real risk to the participants.

No, he did not think Liora and he were on the same page, or even in the same book, when it came to what was fun.

"Will you stay a moment, Asmodeus?"

He huffed. "Why?"

"Because I would like to know more about you."

He tipped his head back and frowned at the blue sky. Pale clouds spotted it now, adding interest. If he lingered, the Devil would want to know why. He would grow suspicious.

Asmodeus found he didn't care. The Devil couldn't leave Hell. He could only send his minions to find him, and they were no match for him. Besides, they were all busy clearing up the pests and bringing him other females. Perhaps those females would keep the Devil occupied while he entertained Liora long enough to understand why the Devil wanted her in particular.

"What would you like to know?" he said and slowly lowered his head, bringing his eyes down to meet hers.

She was far shorter than he was. As petite as her cousin, but as different as he was from Apollyon. He had seen Serenity in the pool, had watched her with Apollyon, trying to understand the complexities of relationships and what had attracted Apollyon to the female in the first place. Serenity was annoyingly good, sickly sweet, and came across as weak and in need of protection despite the immense power she could command if she put her mind to it.

Liora was nothing like her. In a handful of minutes, she had proven herself a little bit wicked, daring, confident, and a woman who knew she could handle herself. She didn't need a male to protect her.

Strange how that made Asmodeus want to do just that.

Liora nibbled her lower lip and then cast another glance over him. Her pupils expanded to swallow some of the colour in her irises and her teeth sank deeper into her lip, tugging on it.

What did she think to make her appearance change so dramatically?

He was not used to mortal behaviour or reactions, other than overwhelming fear. Their pupils expanded then, but he knew without a doubt it was not fear that caused hers to dilate.

"Why are pieces of your armour missing?" Her gaze darted up to his and then away, and he had the sense that she feared offending him again.

He much preferred her choice of wording this time.

He looked himself over, able to see beyond his own glamour to the gold-edged worn strips of metal that covered his black loincloth and the black leather boots and greaves that protected his shins.

"I have lost pieces in the years of my life, during battles in Hell against angels and demons." Asmodeus took hold of one of the pointed strips that covered his right hip and ran his thumb over the battered metal that had served him well in the many centuries of his existence. He would not deny that he missed his other pieces if she asked. He had often thought about finding a way to retrieve them and complete his armour. "There is no way for me to get those pieces back unless I fashion myself new armour… or the Devil sees fit to give me replacement pieces."

"Or you steal Apollyon's," she said and his eyes snapped up to meet hers, shock rippling through him. He amended his observation. She was more than a little wicked. She was positively mischievous. A blush of crimson climbed her cheeks. "They would be a perfect fit."

"True, but I do not think the male would allow me to simply take his armour. It would be a more interesting way to complete my armour though." He liked how she thought and how easy it was becoming to talk to her. He had witnessed mortals talking like this. Banter. He was making banter with her and he was enjoying it.

He also liked the idea of taking Apollyon's armour, leaving him appearing incomplete.

"You would have to fight him for it. Are you good at fighting?" She narrowed her gaze on his, as if trying to see the answer in it.

He nodded and held his hands out. His two golden curved swords materialised in his hands. Her eyes widened.

"You can do magic too!" She smiled and then did something he hadn't anticipated and that stole his voice so he couldn't tell her it wasn't magic as she knew it.

She reached out with her left hand and idly ran two fingers down the length of his right blade, stroking the metal and following the blunt curve. Her smile turned wicked and his heart missed another beat, and part of his anatomy that had never known a female's caress stirred beneath his armour.

Asmodeus cleared his throat, sent his swords away and took a step back from her. Her smile faded into a frown and he could see she thought she had done something wrong again.

He had the oddest urge to reassure her.

What was wrong with him?

Had she cast a spell on him?

The way he reacted to her fascinated and disturbed him at the same time. She had somehow calmed him twice now, erasing his dark hunger to maim and destroy, and had brought to the surface feelings and a part of himself that he had buried deep.

The longer he was in her presence, the more comfortable he felt around her, and the more he wanted to remain, but he also felt uncomfortable and wanted to leave too, and he knew why.

He had never felt his failings before meeting Liora, and the more time he spent with her, the more keenly he felt them. He was born evil, everything dark, cruel and deadly in Apollyon distilled into him. He had lived his life in Hell, doing as he pleased, trained by his master to embrace his darkest nature and inflict pain and terror upon others.

He had been happy with that life.

Asmodeus stared down into Liora's stunning eyes, losing himself in them all over again, forgetting his mission and feeling that part of him he had kept hidden for millennia stirring again.

There was no room for good in Hell. Good was weakness. Concern and care were faults. Affection was a sin. All of them made him a weak male, one undeserving of respect and the position he held. He did not need them.

He clenched his fists and struggled against them, battling them until they were subdued and he could shove them back into the place where they would remain secret, hidden from everyone. Hidden from his master.

The Devil would think him a failure if he knew of them.

Liora frowned and moved a step closer to him, stealing his attention and bringing it back to her.

What would she think of him?

She already thought him incomplete and false. A clone. Nothing but a shadow of Apollyon.

He tried to take a step back to keep some distance between them but his feet refused to move. He stood towering over her, his fists trembling at his sides, his thoughts running at a million miles an hour, bombarding him and threatening to unleash his softer emotions again. What was she doing to him?

She lifted her right hand and his heart set off at a dizzying pace, slamming against his ribs, making his limbs shake. *Weak.* She made him weak. He cast a nervous glance at her hand as she raised it towards his face.

He had never known a female's touch.

There had never been someone he desired.

"Asmodeus?" she whispered and stared up into his eyes. "What are you thinking in there? Your eyes are swirling like gold fire."

A product of his emotions. They were slipping beyond his grasp and he had the strangest desire to embrace them and the sliver of good he held locked deep within.

Because of her.

What did the Devil want with her? He had a feeling it wasn't to breed with her. She was Serenity's cousin. A witch. She would produce powerful offspring and might be strong enough to bring a child to term, but she would also be likely to fight the Devil just as Erin had and refuse to surrender her babe.

Her soft hand cupped his cheek.

His eyes closed against his will and he inhaled sharply. Heat spread outwards from where they touched, surging through his body and setting his feelings free and his blood on fire.

Whatever the Devil's plans for her, they would not come to pass.

Asmodeus would not let him have her.

Liora would belong to him.

12

CHAPTER 2

Liora stared deep into the incredible swirling gold depths of Asmodeus's eyes. She had countless reasons not to trust him, but she couldn't bring herself to listen to them or her head where he was concerned.

The moment she had set eyes on him, loitering under the Eiffel Tower, looking as though he was contemplating tearing through the crowd with claw and fang, a current had run through her, setting her heart racing. She could sense the darkness in him, the incredible evil that flowed in his veins, but in the background, she could feel a faint glimmer of good. That tiny sliver had given her the courage to speak with him.

She had wanted to know him.

Her picture of him had been as incomplete as his armour before today. She had found out about him when she had overheard her cousin talking with Apollyon and they had realised she had been hiding in the hallway of their apartment, listening in. She had pressed Apollyon to tell her about Asmodeus.

Apollyon had painted a bleak picture of his counterpart, telling her that Asmodeus was pure evil, without a shred of good in him. Had he lied to her and to Serenity?

Liora looked at Asmodeus again, recalling how Apollyon often referred to him as a creature, as if he didn't deserve angelic, demonic or even human status.

As if he were an animal.

Something below their level.

There was darkness in him, she couldn't deny that or the fact that the evil he harboured had come to the surface at times and the strength of it had shocked her enough to make her reconsider her desire to know more about him.

He wasn't an animal though.

She couldn't view him like that. He was as real as Apollyon and her too.

He was intelligent, powerful, and felt warm beneath her fingers. She had caught the flickers of true emotions in him. He had been shocked, dismayed and even offended by her questions and her observations so far. Her behaviour had intrigued, and possibly confused him.

He felt things.

He wasn't as Apollyon painted him at all. Did Apollyon really know Asmodeus?

Had he never witnessed this side of his twin?

It was likely that Asmodeus had never had reason to reveal this side of himself to Apollyon. They had probably ended up locked in battle whenever they had come across each other.

He had revealed it to her though. She wasn't sure why, but she knew that she liked it. She liked being around him and seeing how she affected him. It fascinated her.

"Rose?" The heavily-accented male voice jolted her and her heart skipped a beat, shock running through her blood at the sudden intrusion into her quiet moment with Asmodeus.

A young man offered a bunch of plastic-wrapped single red roses to her and then to Asmodeus and she lifted her hand from Asmodeus's face, meaning to refuse the street vendor.

"Rose?" The man smiled at Asmodeus and then held his free hand out in her direction.

All Hell broke loose.

Asmodeus growled, his top lip peeling back to reveal short fangs, and her stomach turned. The rise in the flow of power he constantly emitted was swift and startling, a crushing force that pressed down on her. His hand shot out and he grasped the vendor by his throat, yanking him away from her.

Liora's eyes flew wide as Asmodeus's golden irises brightened and then turned red. Not a normal colour and she wasn't sure he could hide that change with a glamour.

The man choked and dropped his roses. He smashed his hands against Asmodeus's bare arm and clawed at his fingers. Asmodeus grinned, his eyes narrowing darkly on the man, and began to squeeze. The man gasped, his eyes watered, and the veins in his temples popped to the surface as he turned red.

Liora pushed through shocked and straight into horrified. She leaped between them, shoving Asmodeus back and seizing his arm that held the man at the same time. Asmodeus snarled when she sent fire to her palm, singeing his flesh, and pinned her with a black, vicious glare as he released the man.

The man collapsed onto the grass.

"I'm so sorry." Liora dropped to her knees and tried to check him over but he swatted at her, his fear and panic spiking.

He scrambled around, grabbing his roses, and she tried to lay her hand on him so she could heal his throat, but he shoved her in the chest and caught her off balance. Her backside hit the dirt and she could only stare as he broke into a dead run in the opposite direction to her and Asmodeus, heading for the towering trees that lined the edges of the park.

The oppressive wave of Asmodeus's power only grew worse and wind gusted against her, the longest of his black feathers appearing in the edges of her vision as he beat his wings. Hell, no. She was not about to let him fly after the innocent street vendor and terrorise him. Not on her watch.

Liora shot to her feet, turning at the same time, and threw everything she had into her swing. Her palm connected hard with his left cheek, the slap ringing loudly across the area and drawing more attention to them than Asmodeus had when he had attacked that poor man for no good reason.

His head snapped to his right, his wild black hair falling down over his brow. The dark slashes of his eyebrows met in a scowl and his jaw tensed as he growled.

"You deserved that." Liora drew in a deep breath to steady her racing heart and hoped she hadn't just pushed this immense, extremely powerful male over the edge. The force of the power he emanated wasn't growing weaker. If anything, it was getting stronger, and darker.

His red eyes slowly opened and locked on her, and he rose to his full height, towering a good eight inches taller than she was. He spread his black wings and bared his fangs at her, and it took every ounce of her will to stop her from backing off a step. She stood her ground, her knees trembling, and reconsidered her whole opinion of Asmodeus.

He was evil and dangerous, and as violent and cruel as Apollyon had said.

But there was still good in him.

The red in his eyes faded as he stared down at her, his bare chest heaving with each deep breath, and his expression slowly changed at the same time as the pressing force of his power lessened. Gold broke through crimson, his eyebrows relaxed, his jaw slackened and his breathing slowed to a steady tempo.

"Never strike me again, Female." Those words were a vicious growl that told her he was serious and that there would be a dire consequence if she ignored his warning.

"Noted." She brushed imaginary lint off her black jeans, unable to bring herself to look at him while he was staring at her as if he was still considering punishing her for raising a hand against him. "You were being an arse though. He only wanted to make a couple of euro selling you a rose for me."

He huffed. "Noted... I am not accustomed to people selling me anything."

Liora tried not to smile inside at that. "Where have you been all your life that no one has ever tried to sell you anything?"

"In Hell." His deadpan tone made her lift her gaze from her jeans to his to see if he was serious.

He had never looked more serious.

"You're telling me you've never left Hell?" Liora knew she sounded a little backward having to ask that but she wanted to be sure she wasn't mistaken.

He nodded and preened his huge black wings. "I have never left Hell before now."

Her eyebrows rose high on her forehead. "Am I the first mortal you've met?"

He shook his head and kept his eyes downcast, his long black lashes shuttering them so she couldn't read them at all. She didn't need to see them in order to know why he was only offering her a shake of his head as a reply, rather than an explanation.

He had lived in Hell for his whole life. Any mortals he had met must have been taken there for some terrible reason and Asmodeus had been the one to deal with them, or had at least watched someone else do the work.

Liora looked him over, trying to see him for all that he was and telling herself all the terrible things he had probably done in the years he had been alive, in Hell, working for his master.

Apollyon had told her that Asmodeus shared his blood, and that he himself had been created for destruction and violence. If Apollyon had been brought into this world in order to rain destruction down upon mortals, and everyone could view him as good and kind, then she had to at least try to give Asmodeus the chance his twin had been offered.

She had to discover whether there was good in him or whether she had been imagining it.

"Would you have killed the street vendor if I hadn't stopped you?" She managed to keep the tremble out of her voice as she asked, afraid of what his response would be because part of her already knew the answer to that question.

Asmodeus drew in a deep breath, his broad bare chest expanding with it, tipped his chin up and stared down at her, no trace of guilt in his eyes. "Yes."

"Why?" She swallowed to wet her dry throat and shift the lump from it.

He had to have a reason. He wasn't a mindless killing machine for the Devil, not like Apollyon said he was. She had seen his keen intelligence and his feelings playing out in his eyes. There was good in him. There was reasoning and calculation behind his every action. He had a reason for attacking the man. He had to have one.

Asmodeus lifted his hand between them, flexed his fingers and then lowered it back to his side. He stared off to his right, into the distance beyond her, and was quiet for so long that she feared he would never answer and she would never know the truth of him.

She wanted to see beyond the name and the stories, and the things she had been told, to the real Asmodeus. The one she had glimpsed earlier before he had locked it down and brought his guard back up.

He closed his eyes and lowered his head a fraction. "I thought he meant to harm you."

Her hazel eyes widened.

Asmodeus frowned and clenched his fists at his sides. "I felt you tense and heard your heart jump, and your power flared. You were scared. I only meant to remove the source of your fear."

He had been protecting her.

Liora glanced skywards to give herself a moment to absorb the revelation. This powerful male that everyone told her was cruel and evil, and had no good in him, had wanted to protect her. It was all the proof she needed that there was a sliver of good in him and it reinforced her desire to know more about him.

The sun was setting though and that meant more rose sellers and people around the Eiffel Tower to see it as it lit up. If she wanted to continue her time with Asmodeus, she would need to take him somewhere it would get quieter, not busier.

She dropped her gaze to his. "Will you fly me somewhere?"

He looked beautifully startled, his eyes going round and falling to her body. A touch of colour crept onto his cheeks and his pupils expanded, gobbling up the gold in his irises. Was he thinking about carrying her when he looked so flushed with desire?

A warm shiver raced through her blood and she swept her tongue across her lips, not even bothering to deny that she felt that same burst of desire whenever she raked her gaze over him, even when she knew she shouldn't.

He nodded. "Where?"

Liora turned and pointed towards the basilica of Sacré-Coeur where it stood on the hill in the distance, the three white domes of the grand church illuminated by golden light. "There. It will get quieter there as night falls."

His throat worked on a hard swallow and he opened his thickly muscled arms to her. "I will fly you there."

Liora slipped the strap of her small black bag over her shoulder so it fell across her front and took a deep breath as she stepped into his arms. Serenity was going to kill her for this but she didn't care. Something about Asmodeus had her going against convention and everything she knew she should do. She felt a connection between them, a link she had never experienced with another, and she felt as if she could be wild and free around him and he would never judge her or tell her what to do.

He would let her be herself.

He would be right there with her.

He dipped his body, slipped one arm beneath her knees and the other behind her back, and effortlessly lifted her into his arms. She settled her right palm against his chest and stared into his eyes. They were even more beautiful up close.

Flecks of black and rich amber swirled amongst liquid gold. His heart thundered against her palm and his breathing quickened as she continued to look deep into his eyes.

Awareness grew within her, stealing her focus away from the world until it was all settled on him. She could feel his large hands pressed into her ribs and clutching her knee. She could feel his powerful body pressing against her side, shifting with each heavy breath. Each of those breaths washed over her, moist and sweet, bringing her heart to a gallop.

His power flowed around her, a protective shield that allowed hers to recede for the first time in what felt like forever.

She had never felt so safe, not since her parents had died.

Asmodeus would protect her.

Her gaze drifted down the straight slope of his nose to the firm line of his lips, and they parted to reveal blunt white teeth.

"Hold on," he murmured, his deep husky voice sending a shiver of heat across her skin, and she couldn't resist snaking her hands around his strong neck and teasing the ends of his short black hair. He gritted his teeth, his jaw tensing, and a quiet growl escaped him.

His fingers flexed against her, drawing her closer, and she felt wicked because she liked how he clutched her as if he was never going to let her go.

She was playing with fire.

The Hell kind.

The problem was, she didn't care if she got burned.

Asmodeus spread his glossy black wings, bent at the knee and pushed off. She clung to him for a whole different reason as each powerful beat of his wings carried them higher into the warm evening air. She hadn't exactly thought about what she was asking.

Flying had sounded charming and fascinating. Now it was beginning to look frightening.

It was already a long drop to a very painful death.

"You will not fall, Liora," Asmodeus whispered against her ear and she melted in his arms.

Someone so evil shouldn't have a voice that could do wicked things to a woman like his did.

Or perhaps it was perfect for him, made for seducing and getting his way. Was he a seducer?

She drew back to look at him and his grip on her tightened, his scowl re-emerging at the same time. His golden gaze shifted to her and then back to the distance. She studied his face as he flew, trying to figure him out by replaying everything that had happened. He had never left Hell but he had met mortals, and there were plenty of demons who looked human. She didn't think there was a Mrs Asmodeus waiting for him back in Hell though.

She had made him blush by touching his cheek, had sparked desire by touching his sword, and had caught the passion that flared in his eyes whenever he looked at her.

He didn't have a steady relationship but that didn't mean he wasn't a seducer. He could be playing her right now, performing perfectly to lure her in with practiced reactions designed to get him what he wanted from a woman.

"Why do you stare at me?" Asmodeus said and she tapped into her power, channelling it into him in the hope of discovering whether his awkwardness was real or an act.

She could sense no falseness in him. Her staring genuinely confused him.

"I'm trying to figure you out." There was no point in hiding her intentions. The more honest she was with him, the more liable he was to be honest with her.

"And?" A playful edge entered his eyes and she wasn't surprised to find the corners of his lips curling into a wicked smile.

"I'm getting nowhere." She cocked her head to one side and narrowed her gaze on him. "Are you evil?"

"Yes."

A very blunt and honest answer. "Evil because everyone expects you to be evil... or because you really are that way?"

He frowned at her and then switched his focus back to the skies ahead of him. "I was born evil."

"I know the story," she said and he flicked another glance at her, a touch of surprise in his eyes now. "You're everything evil in Apollyon... blah, blah, blah... but I'm not convinced that you're only evil."

His golden eyes darkened and crimson edged them. She was pushing his buttons again. He didn't like her mentioning Apollyon or comparing them in any way. She could understand why. She hated it whenever her coven mentioned how she should strive to be more like Serenity—all good and graceful. Serenity had never lived through hell as she had. Serenity had no reason to have darkness and hatred inside her.

Liora looked down as he glided around the top of the beautiful white domes of the church of Sacré-Coeur with her and then brought them down in the square below. She expected at least a bump as they landed, but it was smoother than any touch down she had ever experienced.

He carried her to the iron fence edging the square and stared out over the city. Dusk turned the elegant stone buildings and the ribbon of the river pink and gold, making them more beautiful than ever.

Asmodeus gently set her down.

"You've really never left Hell?" she said while watching him absorb the view of the city with wide eyes.

He looked like a man who had never witnessed such a view. She had asked Apollyon about Hell. His answer had been that it was black and grim, and that the only colours in the bleak landscape were the boiling rivers of lava.

"Never." Asmodeus narrowed his golden gaze and shifted it down to her. "Have you ever left the mortal realm?"

She shook her head, the loose tangled waves of her chestnut hair brushing her shoulders. "Never... what's it like where you live?"

"I have a castle I built."

"A home." She looked out over the city, enjoying the view even though she had come here often during the first two weeks into her stay with Serenity and Apollyon. It was nice to escape them sometimes, finding her own space so she could think and be herself.

"I do not think of it as a home."

Liora frowned and looked across at him. He stood with his profile to her, his eyes drifting over the city, the sinking sun bringing out their colour but not warming them. They were cold and empty again. Where had his thoughts taken him?

The more she looked at him and thought about what he had said, the more she felt he was lonely but didn't realise it. He had never left Hell and he refused to view his castle as his home.

Did he have no love and light in his life?

"So what are your friends like? Are they all bad-ass demons or are you mates with the Devil?"

Asmodeus's gaze locked on a distant point and then flicked straight to her. "I have none."

He had no friends.

He had no home.

What sort of lonely life was he leading in Hell? She was beginning to wonder how there was even a sliver of good in him. He had no reason to feel that or any positive emotions at all.

Liora placed her hand over his on the black metal railing and he looked down at them, his eyes slowly widening in that way that made her feel that there was something about Asmodeus that would surprise everyone who saw him if they knew about it.

He had always been alone.

No one had ever shown him compassion or care.

No one had ever touched him like this, as a friend would, offering comfort and support.

He was a clone of Apollyon, everything evil distilled into its purest and most vicious form, but he was a product of his environment too.

He had been starved of good and driven to do bad. He had never been given a chance to be anything else. The Devil had moulded him into this man before her and for some reason she wanted to be the one to show the world that they were wrong about Asmodeus, and he could be something more than they believed him to be.

"Do you have no companions at all?" She looked up into his eyes, her eyebrows furrowed and a tiny flicker of hope in her heart.

He lifted his gaze to lock with hers and his thumb brushed hers, causing her heart to leap and race.

He swallowed hard and hesitated, and she thought he wouldn't answer as he averted his gaze, fixing it far below them at the base of the hill and the street there. His eyes tracked something, turning distant at the same time. She looked down and frowned when she saw an old woman walking two miniature poodles.

"I have Romulus and Remus," he said in a gruff voice and she raised her eyes back to his. He looked at her out of the corner of his eye. "They are not quite like those canines. Hellhounds are larger, and live far longer."

He had dogs. Companions. Hellhounds were an evil angel's best friends.

"What are they like?" She couldn't picture hellhounds at all. Images of Cerberus, the three-headed hound sprang into her mind. "Do they only have one head?"

He smiled and her heart lifted at the sight of it and the way the cold edge left his golden eyes. "Yes, they only have one head. They are black and very large, coming to stand with their shoulders around here."

He held his hand palm down just above his hip and Liora's gaze disobeyed her direct command and drifted across to the taut ripped muscles of his stomach and the sexy dip of his navel, and the dusting of dark hair that led her eyes downwards. Her pulse picked up again and it took all of her will to drag her gaze back to his hand.

It was trembling.

Her eyes shot up to his and he looked away again, but she caught the flicker of desire that still darkened his gaze.

"What do they look like? Are they hairy?" Curse her voice for shaking. She had been around men she felt attracted to before and had never reacted like this whenever they had flirted with her or shown their interest. She sidled closer to Asmodeus and butted her hand up against his to measure their height against her own body.

According to his measurements, these hellhounds would reach shoulder height on her if she included a modest addition for their heads.

"Hell is hot and rather filled with fire. Hair is not a good thing in that sort of environment. They are shorthaired and somewhat resemble a canine of this world... a Great Dane. Do you know of it?"

"Scooby Doo? You have demonic Scooby Doos?"

"Scooby Doo?" He frowned. "I am not familiar with this Scooby Doo."

"He's a cartoon... like moving drawings with sound." She wasn't sure he knew what a cartoon was. She doubted you could pick up satellite or cable in Hell. "But he's brown. The right breed though..."

She measured Asmodeus's guide height against her again.

"I'm guessing yours are bigger than our version." She waved her hand around the height she imagined them to be.

"And broader… and they have red eyes."

"I could have guessed." She really could have. It didn't surprise her at all. Even Asmodeus had red eyes whenever he was losing his temper.

When coupled with the way she could feel his power rising or ebbing with his emotions, she had a barometer for Asmodeus.

At least she could tell when he was about to unleash Hell on the poor unsuspecting population of Paris.

"And I can talk to them."

That, she hadn't guessed possible. "They talk?"

Asmodeus casually shrugged, causing his black wings to shift against his bare back. "They communicate with each other in their own language using telepathy, but I do not have that ability so I have taught them to understand me and I can understand their responses. They are clever creatures and picked up an understanding of the demonic language quickly."

So he could communicate with his two hellhounds. Romulus and Remus. Who no doubt lived at the castle that wasn't a home.

Something came back to her, something she had heard Apollyon say to Serenity when she had been listening in on them and Serenity had asked why Asmodeus had given him information he could use against the Devil.

Asmodeus was complicated.

Liora stared at him.

Complicated and gorgeous, and she wanted to unravel the mystery that he wore like a protective cloak.

She wouldn't stop until she knew the truth of Asmodeus.

Until she knew the real him.

The one he was fighting to hide from her.

CHAPTER 3

Asmodeus was on edge. He stared out over the darkening city of Paris, his senses stretching around him, mapping everything that moved and was therefore potentially a threat to the female beside him.

He didn't like the mortal world.

Already one male had attempted to harm her and others in this area kept glancing her way, and he did not trust any of them.

In Hell, no one would have dared try to harm her while she was with him. He had half a mind to cast a portal and take her down to his castle and keep her there, only the other half of his mind wasn't sure why he felt such a fierce need to protect her.

She was a witch and could most likely take care of herself, without his assistance.

Asmodeus idly rubbed his left cheek. Her strike had caught him off guard and had stung for long seconds afterwards, while she had thrown verbal barbs at him that had confirmed he had done something wrong.

His gaze lost focus as he replayed what had happened, trying to understand what he had done wrong and why she had been angry with him.

He turned his back on the city and watched the mortals milling around the square instead, snapping photographs of the white domed church on the mount above him or pictures of the city at sunset behind him. They interacted with each other, using a series of facial expressions and touches, neither of which he truly understood or could decipher.

Even here, the mortal world was a bombardment of scents, sights, tastes and sounds, and feelings.

He had never felt so out of place and unnerved, and unsure of himself.

He didn't know how to function in this world and found it impossible to behave as expected of a mortal because he wasn't one. He didn't understand how they worked.

He didn't understand how Liora worked.

Men glanced her way as they passed, disgusting eyes lingering on her shapely form without her knowing, possessing curves that were not theirs to study.

He scowled at them all, feeling a growing urge to lift his glamour and reveal his true appearance to them in order to scare them away. The only reason he wasn't surrendering to that wicked desire was because he had already frightened Liora with his violent behaviour near the tower.

He had only been trying to protect her.

Asmodeus rested his elbows on the black railing behind him, tilted his head right back and stared at the colourful cloud-strewn sky, trying to figure out why he had received a hard slap as payment for protecting her from the male.

He wanted to understand this world and the protocols, and somehow find a way to learn the right reactions to situations.

He didn't want to scare her away.

His senses shifted entirely to her, locked and focused, feeling her close beside him, her power wrapping around him like warm arms. She had felt soft and light when he had carried her, warm against his flesh. She had stared at him until he had been intensely aware of her gaze on his face.

On his lips.

He had wanted to kiss her.

He still wanted to even though she was full of light and purity, and she was so warm and friendly, filled with beautiful concern about everyone. Even strangers.

Even him.

He had never witnessed such good in anyone before.

It left him feeling there really was no good in him and made him wish more than ever that there were.

He had told her that he was evil and she had seen the darkness in him, the violence he was quick to embrace and the cruelty, but she had remained with him, asking him to take her somewhere else, somewhere quieter.

He had expected her to leave and she had wanted him to stay.

He didn't understand her at all.

Asmodeus raised his left hand above him, stretched his fingers out with his palm facing the sky, and stared at it.

He had told her that he had no friends and she had held this hand, squeezing it against the railing and showing him compassion. Why?

There was no room for friendship in his life. It was a weakness. Good was a weakness. Affection was a sin. Compassion and care were flaws.

So why did he want to feel these things?

He didn't. He clenched his teeth and his fingernails transformed into sharp black claws and his fangs lengthened. He had no weakness. No soft emotions to leave him open to attack. No vulnerabilities.

He felt Liora's gaze on him and ignored her, struggling with his feelings and trying to subdue them again. He was wasting time here. He should take her down to the Devil and be done with it. All he was doing was worsening the punishment his master would deal when he returned with her, and he would return with her. The Devil would see to that.

He was weak.

Vulnerable.

Unable to fight his master's orders.

The Devil had absolute power over him and eventually he would tire of waiting and command him to return, and Asmodeus would not be strong enough to fight that order.

"How long have you had Romulus and Remus?" Liora's tone was soft and soothing, calming the growing tempest within him until it subsided and he forgot his fear and lowered his gaze to her.

New fear grew in its place.

He had never talked about himself to anyone before. No one had ever wanted to know about him, but she was genuinely interested and for some reason he was finding it hard to deny her. It was strange to talk to her about his life. Strange and dangerous.

It left him feeling uncertain and more on edge than the males who loitered in the square and were potentially a threat to her.

If she knew the things he had done and the person he was, she wouldn't want to know about him anymore.

"Several centuries." He kept his response short and before she could ask another question, he changed tactics on her. "Have you been a witch all your life?"

This was new to him too. He had never wanted to know about anyone before, but he wanted to know all about her.

She nodded, her chestnut waves bouncing against her shoulders. "Ever since I was born. I've lived with a coven the whole time."

The area began to empty, the single males dwindling in number and the couples moving away into darker corners. Asmodeus tried not to look at them as they embraced or kissed.

Liora ran her fingers along the metal railing and her arm brushed his, sending a thousand volts jolting up it and through his body. His gaze whipped around to her and found her looking out at the city, not at him. He could have sworn she had been watching him a second ago.

"Are you as powerful as Serenity... or less powerful?" He couldn't resist turning her earlier question against her, or staring at her. The streetlights illuminated her face, softening her features further. Her beauty entranced him.

She smiled, rosy lips curling slowly into it, and a light entered her eyes, a twinkle that he knew he had put there. He had never made anyone smile like that before and he found he liked it and wanted to make it happen again. He just wasn't sure how. He had zero experience of being amusing or entertaining, unless you were the Devil. He could entertain his master no end by torturing demons for his viewing pleasure.

Asmodeus didn't think that would entertain or amuse Liora.

"More powerful," she echoed his earlier words and he found himself smiling at her.

Liora turned to face him, her left arm remaining leaning against the black railing, and held her right hand out in front of her.

She snapped her fingers and a glowing black rose made of light appeared in her hand.

She held it out to him and when he went to take it, she evaded his hand and brushed the soft warm petals over his bare chest. His heart thudded hard and the smile that had been working its way onto his lips dropped away. The air around him sizzled and the awareness of Liora he felt at times came back full force, flowing through him like electricity, coursing through his blood and making him hot all over.

Liora looked up at him, the action of tilting her head back causing her lips to part invitingly.

Asmodeus swallowed and fought the dark instinct to claim those lips and devour them.

Unless she wanted him to kiss her.

Was that possible? He had studied the couples in the area, and how they courted with smiles and laughter, and light touches that seem designed to arouse and excite the interest of their partner.

He wanted to kiss her.

No good would come of it though. It would only increase his desire to keep her from the Devil and fight his master's orders, and it would only cut him when he failed and delivered her to that wretched male.

The black rose disappeared and her hand settled against his bare chest. It was shaking. She was nervous too, afraid of whatever this was that zinged between them whenever they were close.

Asmodeus raised his hand to cover hers and froze when a shiver bolted down his spine, hot and fierce, and the ground trembled.

"Conceal yourself," he barked and she stared blankly at him. He cursed and cast a veil over her, and pushed her behind him at the same time, shielding her with his body and his black wings in case his spell failed.

A bright orange spot formed on the pale stone slabs before him and then forked outwards into a glowing fault line. The ground trembled again and the fiery line cracked open, becoming a fissure. Steam and smoke rose from it and the mortals in the area screamed and ran.

Liora shook beneath his hand that clutched her wrist but he could feel her power rising, growing in the face of her fear.

A Hell's angel burst from the earth and beat his crimson wings. He drifted down to stand a few metres from Asmodeus and furled his feathered wings against his back. Whenever they travelled to the mortal realm, Hell's angels preferred to use an angelic appearance, looking human for the most part. The dark-haired male's red-edged obsidian armour gleamed in the light from the fiery streak at his feet.

Asmodeus had never liked the colour of their armour pieces. It was the only reason he hadn't defeated one and stolen the breastplate and black plate that covered their upper torso or the vambraces that shielded them from wrist to elbow.

"Report," the male said, voice gravelly and thick as the smoke billowing behind him.

Asmodeus straightened to his full height, his anger spiking over being spoken to without a shred of respect. He bared his fangs at the fallen angel and unleashed a fraction of his power, enough that the male would feel it bearing down on him but not so much that he would harm Liora.

"I meant to say… our master would like a progress report, King of Demons." The fallen angel pressed his left hand to his black breastplate and lowered his head.

"Tell him that I have not yet located the female."

The male lifted his gaze to him and a wary edge entered it. Asmodeus prepared himself, sensing the male was about to make a grave mistake and insist that he had found the female and demand he take her to the Devil.

The Hell's angel slowly lowered his left hand to his side and a short black rod tipped with two curved red blades the length of his forearm appeared in his grasp.

A declaration of war.

The fallen angel's eyes flashed red and the skin around them turned black.

He meant to take Liora to the Devil.

Asmodeus would not allow this male or any other to lay a single claw on her.

Asmodeus's claws and fangs extended, his eyes blazed crimson and he snarled as he called his golden blade to his right hand. He released Liora, gave a powerful beat of his wings that tore a shriek from her, and shot towards the male. The man didn't have a chance to block him.

He swung in an upwards diagonal arc with his curved sword and sliced straight through the male's sword arm. It dropped and before it could hit the pavement, Asmodeus had spun around behind the male and decapitated him.

He came to a halt with his blade extended out at his side, blood rolling down its length and dripping to the ground, and breathed hard.

What had he done?

Bright light burst from the sky, the golden shaft encasing the dead angel. The body disappeared and the light faded, and Asmodeus continued to stare at the pool of blood that remained.

Something moved on his senses. He jerked his head up and had his sword at the ready before he had realised it was Liora. He lowered his weapon and sent it away, still reeling from what had happened.

Liora moved another step forwards and he moved his gaze from the blood to her. Shock filled every beautiful line of her face and it echoed within him.

"Why did you do that?" she whispered and stared down at the blood on the ground between them. "Was the female you mentioned me... are you supposed to take me to the Devil?"

Asmodeus's shoulders slumped. There was no going back now. There was only going forwards. He had killed one of the Devil's men and sent him back to Heaven. The Devil wasn't a fool. He would know that it had been his doing and that it had not been the act of an angel of Heaven who happened to be in the city. There was no way of concealing what he had done.

He stared at Liora. It would be so easy to lie to her and say he had meant another female, and it was what he would have done with anyone else, but he couldn't bring himself to say false words to her.

Even if the truth would drive her away.

Perhaps it was better that way.

She was safer away from him.

"The Devil sent me to the mortal realm to capture you and bring you back to him."

Her eyes slowly widened with each word he spoke and her anger rose at the same pace, together with another emotion he found he didn't like feeling in her.

Hurt.

"You were allowed to come to this world for the first time... because he wanted you to take me to Hell?" Liora's hazel eyes narrowed on him and her power increased in strength, until it flowed around him, buffeting him like a strong wind, jabbing at him and shocking him. The ground beneath him shook but it wasn't the impending arrival of a Hell's angel this time. It was Liora.

The trees swayed, leaves breaking free of their branches to swirl around him.

The sky darkened, black clouds blotting out the early stars.

The streetlamps lining the square flickered and buzzed.

"You meant to take me to your master?" she hissed and her eyes darkened. Red ribbons curled around her fingers and up her arms, twining with black and purple. Lightning forked across the sky and slammed into the ground in the distance. He decided he was glad he had never met a witch before meeting her. He hadn't anticipated the level of her power would be this strong and it was still growing stronger, and he had a feeling she was intending to use every ounce of it on him. She breathed hard, each one laboured, and struggled to speak. "This was all a sick game to you... lies and deception... a cruel and vicious... twisted game. You bastard... I thought... I wanted to see the real you and I guess I just did."

She raised her hands to attack.

Asmodeus raised his in an act of surrender. "Liora... I have no intention of doing as the Devil bids. I swear it. I have not deceived you. These hours with you have not been a game. I do not want to let the Devil have you."

He knew she had no reason to trust him or believe a word he had said, but a quiet, hidden part of him hoped that she would listen and wouldn't hit him with everything she had. He wasn't sure he could survive such a blow and he didn't want the first female he had ever desired to kill him when he had done nothing wrong and had not yet tasted her lips.

Her magic faltered and her frown lessened. "Why not?"

Asmodeus laid it all on the line without hesitation, knowing it was the only way to halt her attack and convince her that he only wanted to protect her from the Devil, even though he was far from a white knight. He would be that for her if he could though. He would somehow find a way to show her that while he was born of darkness and evil, he was deserving of her light and good. Somehow.

He held his right hand out to her and focused hard on it, materialising something he had never created with his power before and never thought he would create either.

A black rose that he offered to Liora.

"Because I want you for myself."

CHAPTER 4

Liora reacted to Asmodeus in the same way she reacted to everything. She embraced her impulses and was in his arms before she could reconsider what she was doing or even contemplate how far south of crazy she was about to go. She tiptoed, slid her right hand around the back of his neck and dragged his mouth down to hers. The moment her lips meshed with his, he froze, going stock-still and as stiff as a board.

Either he didn't want her quite as much as he had just said or the impossible was possible after all and he had never done this before.

"Relax," she murmured against his lips and was pleasantly surprised when he obeyed her and the rigidness left his shoulders and his neck, and his mouth fused with hers.

She moved her lips across his, gently grazing them and easing him into it, and he began to mimic her. She liked the firmness of his lips and how his hands settled possessively on her hips, drawing her front against the full delicious length of his. She tilted her head back further, not wanting to break the kiss for any reason.

Asmodeus dug the points of his fingers into her back and pulled her closer still, a low growl rumbling in his throat, thrilling her. The strips of armour protecting his hips pressed into her stomach and each ragged breath he drew caused his chest and stomach to heave against hers. She slanted her head and opened her mouth, and flicked her tongue across his lower lip. That earned her another low, huskier growl and he angled his head, fiercely claimed her mouth and ripped a moan from her. The man was a natural.

Liora's hands slipped to his shoulders and she lost herself in the kiss. It was gentle and soft, and everything she hadn't expected. It overwhelmed her and she couldn't help melting into it, letting him take the lead because she liked how this powerful, sexy male kissed her with tender reverence, as if he was afraid of hurting her.

As if he was worshipping her.

She didn't feel as though she was kissing an evil angel, but Serenity would be the first to remind her of what he was if she ever found out about this, and Apollyon would likely have some harsh words to say about her choice of male.

She couldn't help herself though.

She couldn't help her feelings.

She had felt attracted to Asmodeus from the moment she had noticed him back at the Eiffel Tower and had been struggling to resist the urge to kiss his wicked lips ever since.

He was dark, but handsome.

Evil, yet sweet.

Protective.

Passionate too.

She could feel it in him, bubbling beneath the surface, held back by his inexperience.

He was exactly the sort of man she had always felt drawn to but had never been with before.

He tightened his grip on her hips and deepened the kiss, his tongue thrusting past her lips to tangle with hers. His moan was wanton and erotic, full of undiluted hunger and pleasure that echoed within her. She tackled his tongue with her own, taking the lead, pulling another groan from him and joining him this time.

When breathing became a serious issue, she reluctantly pulled back, breaking apart from him. He breathed hard, his swirling golden eyes bright in the darkness and locked on her lips. That hungry look thrilled her. He wanted more and she wanted to give it to him, but they really needed to pace themselves, and perhaps get away from an area that now looked like a murder scene.

She guessed it was in reality.

Asmodeus had killed one of his master's men because that fallen angel had wanted to take her from him.

She broke her own rules and kissed him again, silently thanking him and fearing he would get into trouble with the Devil now because of what he had done. Would the Devil send more men to claim her? Why did he want her?

Was the Devil the presence she had felt watching her at times during these past few weeks?

It couldn't have been Asmodeus. When he had been watching her at the Eiffel Tower, she had sensed his eyes on her but it had felt different. Not a dark threatening feeling like the other times.

She had to speak with Serenity and Apollyon. They might be able to help her figure out why the Devil wanted her and would be able to protect her. She would pay a high price for asking them for assistance though.

Asmodeus had made his dislike of Apollyon clear during the short hours they had known each other. Apollyon hated Asmodeus too. Putting them together in the same room would be asking for trouble.

She drew back to ask him to come with her to Serenity and Apollyon's home but the words fled her lips when she looked at him. If she asked him such a thing, he would leave her. He would return to Hell. She would lose him, and probably one of her best shots at remaining out of the Devil's hands. Apollyon could protect her, but she had felt the power in Asmodeus and had seen him deal with that fallen angel, effortlessly killing him. He was stronger than Apollyon, whether Apollyon wanted to admit it or not.

He was her best shot at surviving whatever was coming.

That and she didn't particularly want to let him go now that they had rocketed past that awkward 'I want to kiss you but I don't know how to approach it' phase.

"Come, we must move." Asmodeus scooped her up into his arms and beat his wings before she could even form a response, taking off into the crisp night air.

It was getting chilly.

Liora used it as an excuse to cuddle up to his bare chest and was thankful he only had partial armour. It was much nicer curling up against hard hot flesh than it would have been rubbing against cold metal plates.

"You're going to be in trouble, aren't you?" she said and the breeze carried her voice over his shoulder.

He beat his shadowy black wings and took them higher, until they were gliding above the city and she couldn't take her eyes off how beautiful it was. All the lights twinkled in the darkness and cars streamed down streets forming bright slashes of red and white. Boats caused the wide river to glow in places. The Eiffel Tower sparkled in the distance.

"Perhaps," he whispered and she felt his gaze shift to her, boring into the side of her face. "But I have a feeling that you may be worth it."

She smiled at that. How could anyone think this man pure evil? She had only had to speak to him to know that while he held darkness inside him, and was capable of great cruelty and violence, there was still some good in him, hidden away beneath the vicious exterior he wore like a shield.

She turned her head to look at him but he moved his gaze away from her, looking down at the city as they flew over it instead. She drank him in, studying the nuances of his expression as his golden gaze flitted around, taking in the scene stretching below them. The wind ruffled his wild black hair and she ached to brush her fingers through it, combing it back and feeling its silkiness just as nature was allowed to do.

"Will the Devil send more men for me?" She feared the answer to that question even though she already knew it deep in her heart.

The black slashes of his eyebrows met in a frown and his golden eyes darted to her. "Yes."

"Will you fight them?" Her voice trembled and she hoped he would think it was the wind that caused it, not the fear growing in her heart. She had never been this afraid before, had always faced things head-on and without flinching, even as a child. The thought that the Devil wanted her for some nefarious reason and had sent his best man to retrieve her, marking her as important to him, made cold steal into her veins and sent a shiver through her soul.

Asmodeus hesitated and something surfaced in his eyes, something that set her on edge. He looked uncertain.

Over a year ago, Serenity had called and told her that they had to cancel their get together because something had happened to Apollyon. Heaven had exercised its will on him and had controlled him, forcing him to do their bidding against his will, and it had shaken the powerful male.

If Heaven held that power over Apollyon, did that mean Hell and the Devil wielded it over Asmodeus?

"I will try." He looked away again, the sombre note to his deep voice and the fraction of his emotions that she could sense with her power conveying that he meant it but he didn't believe he would be able to defeat whatever force the Devil sent after him.

All the more reason to ask Apollyon and Serenity for help, but she still couldn't bring herself to raise it with him, not while everything felt so tentative and liable to fall apart if she mentioned the other angel.

"Perhaps you would be safer away from me."

Liora stared at him, shock rippling through her. "No. I'm safer with you."

"Do not fool yourself, Liora. I feel your fear. I thrive on that emotion. It gives me pleasure as much as anger and rage, and pain." His voice gained a dark edge that echoed within his power and she frowned when she realised what he was doing. He was driving a wedge between them. He meant to make her leave. "You are safer away from me."

"I am safer with you. If anyone has the power to protect me, it's you, Asmodeus."

"Or Apollyon. He would be the better choice. He is always the better choice." The darkness in his voice turned to bitterness that she could feel lacing his power and she held on to him.

"How do you know he's the better choice for me? Isn't it my choice?" She glared at him now and then it faded away when she caught the tiny almost imperceptible grain of fear hidden beneath his other emotions.

Fear that he would fail her?

Or fear that he would end up doing as his dark master commanded and would hurt her?

He thrived on seeing others hurt and their suffering. He was afraid that the Devil would make him harm her and that he would end up enjoying it. She had thought the Devil would be sick and twisted, but this was taking sick and twisted to a whole new level.

"Asmodeus," she whispered and he looked at her, his beautiful golden eyes void of any warmth. She wished she could touch his cheek and reassure him somehow, but she didn't want to loosen her grip on him when they were so high above the city. "You will not fail me."

He looked away again and uncertainty filled his eyes for a brief few seconds before they cleared again.

"Apollyon will not fail you. I am only a shadow of that male."

It struck her that he was having one serious existential crisis and she was in part to blame for it. Her careless words when they had first met had dealt blows and wounded him, and now he couldn't shake the doubts that she had placed in his head. She wished she had the ability to turn back time and relive that moment all over again with the knowledge she had now, but even she wasn't that powerful.

All she could do was try to smooth things out and heal the wounds she had unwittingly inflicted with her words.

"You're not a shadow... not any more than I'm a shadow of my cousin. She's so damn good and caring, and I'm reckless and wild, and liable to go off demon hunting without telling anyone, and I'm forever getting into scrapes. Everyone tells me I should be more like her... but I'm not her. We share blood but we're not the same person. We couldn't be more different." Liora leaned in and pressed a kiss to his cheek, lingering with her lips against his cool flesh.

He paused, beating his wings to keep them steady in the night air high above the glittering lights of Paris.

"You won't fail me, Asmodeus. I'm choosing you," she whispered against his skin and then settled her head on his shoulder, waiting for him to rebuff her.

He didn't.

She looked down at the quiet world below them,

"Do you like the view?" she said to fill the silence.

"It seems alien to me… bright and colourful… strange… unsettling." He didn't sound as if he liked it. "Hell is a black cavernous ceiling above a forbidding harsh landscape. Rivers of molten lava and lakes of fire provide the only natural light. It is… different to this world. You would think it bleak, desolate and dangerous."

Everything Apollyon had told her it was.

She frowned and looked at Asmodeus. "Then you've never seen the stars?"

His golden gaze drew away from the world below them and rose to meet hers. "No."

"Will you take me somewhere?"

He nodded. "Where?"

Liora bravely took one hand away from his neck and Asmodeus's grip on her increased, drawing her closer to him, filling her with a sense of safety that felt strange considering he was apparently made of pure evil. She didn't think a male with nothing but evil in his heart would care much about whether she fell to her death or not. A male who was only evil and nothing good would have laughed as she fell and ensured he was close enough to get a good view when she splatted against the pavement.

She pointed to the distance, to the darkness beyond the city boundaries. "Take me out there. Take me to the stars."

He held her against him and beat his broad black wings, carrying them over the city to the outskirts and then into the countryside. The air grew colder as they flew and she moved as close to Asmodeus as she could get, seeking his warmth. His skin heated hers but it didn't chase the chill from deep within her.

The Devil wanted her and Asmodeus wanted to protect her.

She didn't want to think about the reasons why his master might want her or what would happen to Asmodeus because he had disobeyed him, but it ran around her head, taunting her, mingling in with her thoughts about the man holding her.

He hadn't been lying when he had told her that he took pleasure from terrible things, and her initial reaction had been the one he had probably sought to evoke with his words. He had wanted her to feel she shouldn't be around him and that whatever this was that was happening between them would never have a happy ending. She had felt that for a split-second before she had rallied and had seen beyond his harsh words and hard expression to the trace of fear in his heart.

She had grown up in a world filled with love and light.

Asmodeus had grown up in a world made of darkness and death. A savage realm where horror and bloodshed were a part of daily life. What was normal there was terrible in her eyes but it was all he had ever known.

He had no friends to speak of and no sense of home.

Apollyon had called him evil, but Liora could see the good in him, buried deep.

Hidden.

"Is there good in you, Asmodeus?" she whispered and looked at him. It was getting too dark to see him clearly now that they were beyond the city lights.

"No." The bluntness of his reply didn't surprise her.

"Are you lying to me, Asmodeus?" Liora shifted her right hand to his cheek and tried to make him look at her but he tensed, making it impossible. Refusing her.

She sighed and frowned at him, trying to make him out in the darkness, wanting to see whether he was lying to her or not. If she couldn't get him to confess there was a seed of good in him, then perhaps she could get him to admit that he viewed it as a weakness. She suspected that was the reason he denied its existence.

"What do they do to good people in Hell?" She tried to say it in a light and conversational tone so he would answer her but wasn't sure she had succeeded when silence greeted her for almost a full minute.

"You do not want to know." He beat his black wings and swooped lower, carrying her over fields towards a low hill in the distance.

"I do want to know."

He glanced at her. "We make them realise that it is a flaw. We... remove it for them."

That sounded like a polite and coded way of saying that they tortured the good out of people.

"In the same way that the Devil removed the good from Apollyon... torturing him until he lost his mind and held only evil in his heart?" Her voice shook and then she shrieked as Asmodeus dropped her and she hit the grass a few feet below, the impact jarring her spine.

Asmodeus growled and his eyes glowed in the darkness, as bright as the pools of lava in Hell that he had mentioned. He landed and stalked towards her, until he towered over her, his power increasing and pressing down on her. Her own rose in response, coming to protect her from his wrath.

"Yes," he barked and grabbed her by the front of her crimson short-sleeved gypsy top and hauled her onto her feet. "I torture the good from fools who think that side of themselves makes them strong. I show them how weak it makes them... and I relish it."

He shoved her away from him and stalked down the slope, a dangerous immense shadow in the darkness.

"Would the Devil torture the good from you if he knew there was some inside you?" she said without a trace of fear in her voice even though her hands were shaking. "Would he punish you, Asmodeus?"

"There is no good in me. You only believe there is. You want to see it, and so you do." He turned back to face her, his golden eyes verging on scarlet.

"So you're telling me you're all bad... and nothing good?"

"To be good or bad you must believe the mortal concept of right and wrong... there is no right or wrong in Hell, Liora, not in the way you think of it. It is a human belief." He took a step up the incline towards her and clenched his fists at his sides. "In Hell, there is only strength... and that strength is measured by the blood we have spilled, the bones we have crushed, and the pain we have dealt and endured. It is not measured by the good we do. It is measured by what you mortals believe is bad. In Hell... bad is good... and I am second only to the Devil."

Liora collapsed to her backside on the grass and stared down at him, her heart aching for him. He denied the seed of good in him and now she understood why.

The Devil had conditioned him to resort to violence without a moment's pause if he felt threatened, to eradicate any shred of positive emotions in himself and in others, to torture and maim, and destroy, because in Hell that was what made you strong.

His master had probably beaten it into him from the moment he had been born into that dark world, moulding him into the powerful male before her, one worthy of being the Devil's right hand man.

One capable of doing the Devil's dirty work and strong enough to command the respect of every demon and Hell's angel in that realm.

A king of demons.

He had to be strong or face losing his standing, and the gods only knew what would happen to him if that happened. What use would the Devil have for a right hand man who had a sliver of good in his heart and knew compassion and caring, affection?

The Devil would kill him.

Asmodeus was something he had created and he would likely view the tiny seed of good in him as a fatal flaw that made him a failure. If a manufacturer found a fundamental problem in one of their products, they simply scrapped it and began again, working harder to ensure the next one didn't fail.

Asmodeus didn't want to die so he denied the good in his heart.

Liora held her hand out to him. "I don't want to argue with you about right and wrong, or good and evil, Asmodeus. If you say there is no good in you, then I accept that. Come, look at the stars with me."

He heaved a sigh, stalked up the hill, and set himself down beside her on the grass, spreading his black wings. One stretched out behind her, shielding her from the cold breeze washing over the brow of the hill, and the other rested on the grass to his left. His hands settled behind him, propping him up, and he tipped his head back and looked at the dark sky.

She wasn't sure what to say to him. She'd had a head full of colliding thoughts before she had learned more about him and now she had a whole new bunch of thoughts knocking around in her skull. Apollyon needed a better word than 'complicated' for his apparently evil twin.

Liora looked across at him and held her sigh inside.

He had said that Paris seemed alien to him but she had the feeling that it was more than the city that had him constantly on edge. It was everything, from his surroundings, to her, and to the things that she had said to him, that had him questioning himself and all he knew.

This entire world was alien to him.

She worried that it was too alien and he would find a way to leave her whether she wanted that or not.

Liora set her hands behind her to prop herself up and intentionally laid her left hand over his right one. He tensed beneath her.

She tipped her head back, stared at the stars scattered across the black velvet, and said a silent prayer to the gods of nature that Asmodeus would stay because she thought she needed him, and not only because her survival potentially depended upon him.

The gods had never answered her before.

She hoped they would this time.

They owed her for taking her parents.

CHAPTER 5

Asmodeus's head was tied in more knots than ever and every inch of him felt tense, and he couldn't convince his body to relax, not while he was drowning under the tidal pull of his thoughts. He wanted to get them straight and figure everything out, and come to understand this world and Liora, but the more he spoke to her and the more he saw of this realm, the more on edge and overwhelmed he became.

He hadn't meant to lose his temper with her, and he regretted dropping her from even a short height and shouting at her. Another first for him. He couldn't remember ever regretting anything before. He couldn't remember experiencing guilt before he had met Liora.

Her hand covered his, warm and slight, her light weight pressing it into the grass. She had fallen quiet and he wished that she hadn't. He liked the sound of her voice and the sharp note it had at times, a tone that told him she wasn't going to just back down and let him have his way.

He had felt powerless to leave her and had wanted to convince her to leave him, because he feared that the Devil would force him to obey his command to bring her to him. He had tried to draw a line between them, hoping to force her into seeing that he didn't subscribe to her mortal concepts of right and wrong, and that there was no good in him as she would view it. Rather what she viewed as bad, he saw as good.

She had been afraid at one point, he felt sure of it, but had rallied and refused to leave him, instead telling him that she knew he could protect her and she was safest with him.

Asmodeus didn't believe that, so he wasn't sure how she could. He had done nothing to prove himself worthy of her belief and she barely knew him. She probably knew Apollyon well, and together with Serenity and perhaps their friends, that male would be better able to protect her from the Devil.

He stared up at the stars, trying to ignore the creeping fear at the back of his mind. He refused to feel that emotion. He had feared the Devil in the past, scores of centuries ago, when he had been young and weak, and unsure of himself. With every decade that had passed, every victory on the battlefield and captive that had cracked from his torture alone, he had grown stronger and more confident, becoming fitting of the title the Devil had given him.

King of Demons.

A title he had to live up to or risk losing.

The Devil would strip him of it if he discovered that he had already met the female and was refusing to bring her to him.

He had to return to his master and learn more about why he wanted her, but he didn't think Liora would allow him to leave without a fight. She wanted him to stay.

Why?

His heart supplied that perhaps she desired to kiss him again.

He wished.

Asmodeus tried to focus on the stars and failed when his thoughts turned to Liora and when she had kissed him. He could still taste her. The kiss had made him feel strange, fuzzy and unfocused, and he wanted to do it again.

He wanted the petite female sitting beside him with her beautiful eyes on the stars and her hand covering his, even though she was full of light and purity.

For the first time in his life, he wished there was more good in him in the human sense of the word, not less. He wanted to be worthy of her and right now he wasn't. A beautiful, noble, and caring female like Liora deserved a male of equal character.

She would never truly desire someone only capable of violence, cruelty, and darkness. Everything she viewed as bad.

His gaze slid to her against his will and traced the outline of her profile. Starlight bathed her skin in pale tones that his eyes could see. They were accustomed to the dark and marked another difference between them.

She was mortal.

He was immortal.

She glanced across at him and he averted his gaze to his wings. The wind played in his black feathers. It had felt good to fly with her in his arms, held close against his chest, and to feel her hands on his skin.

Asmodeus slipped his right hand from beneath hers, leaned to his left and brought his wing forwards, between them. She frowned and a flicker of hurt crossed her face. He hadn't meant it as a barrier or an act of pushing her away.

He nimbly preened his ruffled feathers and she relaxed again, and went back to gazing at the stars. Asmodeus focused on tending to his wings. Some of the feathers were out of place from flying and he needed something other than Liora to concentrate on so he could free up his mind. Working on a task that was second nature to him often allowed him to clear his head and caused his thoughts to fall into better order. He hoped it was the case today.

Cleaning his weapons normally produced the same effect.

One of his swords did need cleaning, but he didn't think that Liora would appreciate him tending to the blade. It would remind her of what he had done, and that the Devil wanted her, and it would spoil this quiet moment of calm.

"Do you not like the stars?" she whispered, her gaze returning to him.

Asmodeus paused at his work and looked over his wing to her. He did like the stars and he liked her too, and he thought she was infinitely more beautiful than they were. What would she say if he told her that?

He shoved that thought away and nodded. "I do, but my feathers are misaligned. They irritate me."

"Can you put your wings away?" Her hazel eyes lowered to his wing and, before he could answer that he could if he desired it, she had reached over, laid her palm on the curve of his wing, and was running her hand down it.

Holy Hell, that felt good.

A shiver bolted through him, hot and fierce, reigniting his blood and making it burn for more. He wanted her to stroke his wing again, to caress it and tease him, driving him wild with need for her.

His fangs lengthened and he sensed the moment his irises brightened and began to verge on crimson. Her eyes widened and her fingers paused against his feathers.

She sounded breathless when she uttered, "You like me touching them?"

Asmodeus told himself not to nod and not to let on that her touching his wings had him hurtling towards the edge of bliss and had him rock hard in his loincloth.

He tried.

Failed.

He nodded and swallowed hard when she resumed her stroking, sending hot little shivers tripping over his flesh, stoking his hunger up degree after degree until he couldn't take any more.

His red eyes narrowed on her lips.

He wanted to taste them again. He wanted to shove his fingers into her fall of soft chestnut hair, grasp the back of her head and yank it back so he could devour her mouth and master her.

He would do just that.

Asmodeus reached for her.

His head turned, his stomach twisted, and his fingers shook. A wave of weakness crashed over him and he trembled and pressed his hand to his stomach. His heart raced.

"Asmodeus, what's wrong?" Liora's hand settled against his cheek and he lifted his wide eyes to hers.

"I do not know." Admitting that sent shame sweeping through him and he cast his gaze away from her. He focused on his body, his pulse spiking and skin prickling. What was wrong with him?

His vision blurred and his stomach cramped, violently this time, turning in on itself until he came close to vomiting.

"You're shaking." Liora pressed her palm to his forehead. "Tell me what you're feeling."

Asmodeus swallowed and nodded, and tried to focus again. It was harder now and took much of his remaining strength. That was fading fast, leaving him shaking worse than he had been barely a second ago.

"Dizzy. Nauseous. Weak. Ailing... I have never felt like this before." He lifted his gaze to hers again and clutched his bare stomach. "At the tower... I felt strange... I feared I was growing sick."

"Maybe you are sick." She pressed her hand harder against his forehead and he caught the flicker of panic in amidst the concern brightening her eyes. "We need to take you somewhere safe and find a way to treat you."

He nodded again. He didn't want to be sick. He didn't like this feeling of weakness invading him.

She rose to her feet and offered her hand to him. He refused to take it and lumbered onto his feet, staggered a few steps down the hill, and finally found his balance. A growl slipped free of his lips and he straightened to his full height, unwilling to let whatever was affecting him get the better of him. He was not weak. He was strong, powerful, and immortal.

He would defeat this sickness.

Liora came to stand opposite him and grasped both of his hands in hers. She looked up at him, her fine eyebrows furrowed with the concern that shone in her eyes, and gave him a short smile.

"We'll get you better. Just… trust me… okay, Asmodeus? Trust me."

He wasn't sure he knew how to trust because he had never tried to place that sort of faith in anyone before, but he was willing to try for her. He nodded and she closed her eyes, and sudden warmth flooded his hands and raced up his arms. He tried to take them away from her but she tightened her grip until it felt as if she was branding his bones with fire.

The dark countryside disappeared and a pale room took its place, filled with elegant matching furniture.

Asmodeus glanced around the expansive living room. It was light and airy. Was this Liora's home?

"What the hell are you doing here?" The male voice crashed into his ears a split-second before a fist slammed into his jaw, snapping his head to his left and knocking him off balance. His head turned violently and he stumbled, reaching blindly for something to grab to stop himself from hitting the polished wooden floor. The male growled again. "Get behind me, Liora."

Liora ignored that command and held on to Asmodeus's wrists, keeping him upright.

She had betrayed him.

Asmodeus snarled and tore free of Liora's grip, and came to face a male he hated with every drop of blood in his body.

Apollyon's blue eyes flashed in warning and his black wings erupted from his bare back. The male beat them hard and slammed into Asmodeus, sending him flying backwards against the cream wall. He tried to evade the vicious swing of Apollyon's right hook but he wasn't quick enough in his weakened state. The male's fist smashed into his mouth and blood flooded it.

Asmodeus growled and exposed his bloodied fangs, his anger rising and obliterating the weakness that had been invading him, driving it to the back of his mind.

"Apollyon," Liora snapped and the large black-haired male paid her no heed as he pushed her behind him.

Apollyon sent his loose black cotton bottoms away, replacing them with his gold-edged black armour and Asmodeus hated him all the more.

Before him stood a completed version of himself, a male worthy of the notice of the female bravely advancing on them. He despised Apollyon for having what he lacked and therefore being able to possess what he could never dream of having.

Liora.

Asmodeus's black claws sharpened and he swung at Apollyon. The male easily evaded the weak blow, grasped his shoulders, and shoved him hard against the wall, pinning his wings and knocking the wind from him.

Defeated.

How the demons would laugh if they could see him now. Weak and pathetic. Unable to fight. On the verge of collapse.

Only the wall and Apollyon's unforgiving grip was keeping him standing.

"What are you doing here, Wretch?" Apollyon shoved him harder against the wall, his fingers pressing deep into his shoulders, and narrowed his swirling blue gaze on him. The male's long black hair was wild and ruffled. He had been asleep. This was not Liora's home.

She had brought him to Apollyon.

He had grown weak, sick, and she had taken it as a chance to bring him here to this male. Why? Because she desired him to see his failings? She had asked him to trust her. He would never trust her again.

Asmodeus's lips peeled back off his fangs and he glared as he spit blood at his superior twin.

Apollyon released one of his shoulders to wipe the blood off his face and Asmodeus snarled and struggled again. He managed to crack his left fist across Apollyon's jaw, knocking the angel away from him. It cost him.

His head turned, the world wobbled out of focus, and his balance left him.

"Asmodeus," Liora shouted and was there before him in an instant, shoving Apollyon aside and wrapping her arms around his chest to support him.

Asmodeus growled, pushed her away, and stumbled to his left. He hit a small white wooden table in the corner of the room and the china lamp on it toppled onto the floor and smashed. Asmodeus shot his left hand out, pressed it against the wall in front of him and braced himself, breathing hard as his stomach rebelled again and the terrible weakness returned.

"I made a vow to deal with you if you ever left Hell," Apollyon said, his voice pure darkness and malevolence. "I will do just that."

"No," Liora barked and when Asmodeus looked over his shoulder, he found her standing between him and his twin, her arms outstretched and blocking Apollyon's way to him. "Please... he's sick."

The petite blonde Asmodeus knew to be Serenity appeared in the doorway behind Apollyon, a cream satin robe covering her slender frame. She finished tying the belt to keep it closed and frowned at him and then Liora.

Apollyon straightened and advanced a step.

Liora tensed.

Asmodeus growled and bared his fangs.

If the male dared to lay a finger on her, he would use the last of his strength to protect her. He would not let the bastard harm her.

Apollyon's blue gaze shifted from Liora, to him and then back again.

"Explain why you have brought this creature to me." Malice dripped from Apollyon's deep voice and Asmodeus hated how alike they sounded even though they had been raised in different realms.

"Do not tell him." Asmodeus pushed away from the wall before him, turned to face his enemy, and leaned against the other wall beside him, using it for support and hating that he needed to.

Liora looked over her shoulder at him and he knew she wasn't going to obey that order. Foolish woman. She might believe that telling Apollyon and her cousin why he was here would help them trust him, but in reality it would do the opposite. Apollyon would want to remove his head.

She drew in a deep breath, lowered her hands and flexed her fingers at her sides. Her palms faced him and a tiny flicker of black, red and purple magic twirled in her hands, hidden from Apollyon and Serenity.

She would fight for him?

He pushed himself up until he was standing with only his right palm against the wall, and slowly straightened to tower behind her, eyelevel with Apollyon.

"The Devil sent him to take me to Hell, but he isn't going to do that." Liora's voice didn't wobble in the slightest and pride filled his heart. His little witch wasn't afraid of Apollyon or her cousin. She would fight them if it came to it. "He wants to help me."

"You believe him?" Serenity's French accent strongly laced her English. "You are a fool... he is lying."

"She is right, Liora. What reason do you have to trust his word? He is evil, despicable, and I have seen what he is capable of... he will deceive you given the chance. It will sweeten the satisfaction he will feel when he hands you over to his master." Apollyon glared over her head at him and Asmodeus stared right back, his anger rising as each vicious word about him left Apollyon's lips.

"If he is evil and despicable and takes pleasure from doing horrible things... then you are too... because all of that comes from you." Liora tipped her chin up and squared her shoulders and Asmodeus grinned behind her, enjoying the brief flicker of shock in Apollyon's eyes.

"Liora," Serenity snapped and Liora held her left hand out to silence her.

"Stay out of this, Cousin." Liora lowered her hand. "You want to know why I can trust him? He killed a nasty looking fallen angel to protect me when the Devil sent him to take me to Hell."

Apollyon's blue gaze shot to him. "Is this true?"

Asmodeus didn't answer him. He lowered his gaze to the back of Liora's head and fought off another wave of sickness. It was stronger this time and the room wavered so badly that he feared he would pass out.

When everything stopped whirling, Liora was before him, her hands against his bare chest, supporting him. The concern in her hazel eyes touched him deeply and his black eyebrows furrowed. He didn't deserve such a tender, caring female.

"Please, Apollyon... he's sick and I don't know what's wrong with him." Liora looked over her shoulder at the dark angel. "I didn't know who else to bring him to."

She hadn't meant to betray him. She had brought him here because she had feared for him and had thought that Apollyon would know how to treat him, and she had known how he would react to it. That was why she had asked him to trust her.

Apollyon heaved a sigh, sent his armour and wings away, replacing them with the black loose bottoms he had worn before, and padded barefoot across the wooden floor to him.

41

Liora stepped aside.

Asmodeus bit back a growl when Apollyon roughly inspected him, checking his eyes, mouth, and throat and prodding his bare stomach.

Apollyon shoved him back against the wall. "He is hungry."

The male stalked from the room, passing Serenity and heading into a dark area beyond an opening opposite Asmodeus. He returned with a clear plastic pack with some brown crescent-shaped items in it and threw it hard at Asmodeus. It hit him square in the face and dropped to the floor before he could catch it. Asmodeus growled at him.

Liora bent and picked up the pack of brown things, and frowned at them and then at him, and then at Apollyon.

"Hungry? Who doesn't know when they're hungry?" She looked back at him, an incredulous look on her face that he hated because it made him feel stupid.

He cast his gaze down to his boots and growled under his breath at her.

"Asmodeus has never left Hell. In Hell, he would never feel hunger or thirst, and would never feel the need to sleep. In the mortal world, he will." Apollyon scoffed and Asmodeus looked up at him through his lashes, narrowed his gaze on him and snarled.

Apollyon grinned at him and Asmodeus wanted to rip it from his face. He was mocking him and making him feel like a fool, and he was doing it on purpose.

Asmodeus didn't want to look like an idiot in front of Liora.

He didn't want her to think he was weaker than Apollyon and less intelligent.

A shadow of Apollyon.

"Why are you really here, Wretch? You might fool her, but you do not fool me. You are up to something and, in this world, I am king and you are nothing more than the court jester. Answer me, or I end you here and now." Apollyon's derisive tone cranked Asmodeus's anger into the red.

Asmodeus shoved away from the wall and came to face him, using all of his remaining strength to keep upright, refusing to allow his twin to mock him in front of Liora and refusing to show any weakness.

"I don't have to explain myself to you," he snapped and squared up to Apollyon, staring straight into his blue eyes. "If I wished it, I would be king of this realm and you would kneel at my feet. Remember that."

Apollyon smiled and Asmodeus sensed the rise in his power. It swept over him, too much for him to handle in his weakened state, pressing down on him and making his knees threaten to give out. He would not allow it. He would not have Apollyon make a fool of him.

He would not unwillingly go to his knees.

"I will remember it… and I will remind you of it in a few minutes time when you pass out because you were hungry and thought you were sick." Apollyon's smile widened into a vicious grin. "I will drag you back to Hell where you belong."

Asmodeus stepped back, edging towards a closed door that had many locks.

He glanced at Liora. She stared at him, disbelief still colouring her expression, mocking him as much as Apollyon's words had been. Serenity stood a short distance behind her, her expression dark and threatening. His head turned again, spinning and sending him stumbling backwards. He was too weak to fight Apollyon and he wouldn't stand here and let the male mock him and make a fool of him. He was no court jester. He was king.

King of Demons.

A king without a queen.

His gaze drifted to Liora and the look she still wore cut him to the bone. She thought him a fool. They all did. His fangs descended again and darkness rose within him, obliterating and crushing the weakness, the softer emotions he had foolishly allowed to take control of him because he had wanted her affection and attention. He didn't need a queen.

"Burn in Hell," Asmodeus barked, turned and grabbed the door handle. He yanked it open, breaking the locks, and stormed out of the apartment and down the dimly lit staircase.

"Asmodeus," Liora called after him but he didn't slow.

He didn't need her.

He didn't need anyone.

CHAPTER 6

Liora was madder than the March Hare.

She turned away from the staircase, stalked back into the pale spacious apartment, and glared at Apollyon.

"Have you been with him the whole day and night?" Apollyon said in his usual dark commanding tone that demanded an answer and she continued to stare at him, funnelling her fury into it so he could sense how angry she was with him. "Serenity has been worried sick… and you have been out with that wretch!"

"Don't call him that!" Liora's power curled around her fingers before she had even uttered a command to call it forth.

It swirled black and purple with flashes of red, a sign of her growing rage, and left her feeling invincible. If she wanted, she could put Apollyon on his backside before he could even attempt to defend himself. Serenity would be angry with her if she did such a thing though.

Liora found she didn't care, but she wasn't in the habit of making enemies of her friends.

She tamped down her anger and dialled back her power until magic lazily circled her hands, there if she needed it but not liable to spin out of control and harm her friends without her really desiring it. Whenever she lost her temper, her magic had a tendency to act without her consent. It was the danger of being in possession of such strong power, and something she'd had to live with ever since her parents had died and she had gained their magic on top of hers.

She drew in a slow deep breath to calm it further, bringing it firmly under her control, and exhaled, releasing her tension with it.

"He has a name, Apollyon," she said in a low voice. "He is not a creature or a wretch or something despicable. He has feelings."

"There is evil in him. Great evil. I could feel it. Can you not feel it too?" Serenity whispered and Liora looked her way and then back at Apollyon where he stood closer to her.

"You're right. There is evil in him, but there is also good. I have felt it." She waited for Apollyon to say something but he remained quiet.

She stared at him, seeing the similarities between him and Asmodeus, but also the differences. It wasn't just their eye colour and hairstyle that set them apart. It was everything and nothing at the same time. They weren't as different as Apollyon wanted to believe, and he had shown that tonight. He wasn't as good as he acted. Asmodeus wasn't as evil as he acted.

"You've felt it too, haven't you?" Liora took a step towards Apollyon. He opened his mouth and she didn't give him a chance to voice the lie she could see coming. "Tell me the truth, Apollyon. You have seen the good in him."

Serenity looked at her dark angel, a frown creasing her brow.

44

Apollyon closed his eyes and lowered his head, causing long strands of his mussed hair to fall down and caress his sculpted cheeks. "You are right. There is good in him, but that does not mean he is worthy of your trust."

"He protected me when the Devil sent that angel to bring me to him. He killed him and light took the body. He did that to stop the Devil from having me." She neglected to mention that Asmodeus had stated that he had done it because he wanted her for himself.

Her heart said to go to him before he left her. He needed her. He was weak and hungry, and she wanted to take care of him and make him strong again, and not just because she believed he could protect her from the Devil.

"Why does the Devil want you?" Serenity said and she shrugged.

"I don't know. Asmodeus doesn't know either. He was only told to grab me and bring me to him."

"I have seen what that fiend does with females and the lengths he will go to in order to get what he wants. It is highly likely that the Devil will attempt to sire a child on you." Apollyon's tone lacked warmth and his words left her cold to the bone.

The thought of being used in such a way turned her stomach and she knew from the way that Asmodeus had looked when he had told her that the Devil wanted her and he wouldn't let him have her, that it didn't sit well with him either.

She had to go to him, but there was something else she had to say first.

She stared straight into Apollyon's rich blue eyes.

"You were mean to make him look foolish because he had never experienced hunger. It was cruel." She held her hand up when Serenity went to speak and frowned at Apollyon, unafraid of the way the paler flecks in his eyes started to swirl and his power rose, beginning to press down on her. "It was cruel and you took pleasure from it."

Liora shook her head. She had expected Apollyon to be angry with her for bringing Asmodeus to his home, and had even expected him to turn on Asmodeus, but she hadn't expected him to be so nasty.

"I can see where Asmodeus got that trait," she said and turned towards the door.

"Liora!" Serenity snapped and she braced herself on instinct, expecting her cousin to lash out at her with magic for her vicious verbal attack on her lover. When she spoke, her tone had softened and the power Liora felt in her faded. "Where are you going?"

Just like her good cousin to forgive her so swiftly. If their positions had been reversed, Liora would have at least shot a warning spell across her bow.

"I have to speak with Asmodeus." Liora looked over her shoulder at Apollyon and Serenity.

"You cannot trust him," Serenity said and came to stand beside Apollyon in the middle of the room. They made a good couple. Both of them were powerful, virtuous and held the respect of their peers.

Perhaps Liora and Asmodeus looked that good standing beside each other. She would have to look in the next window or mirror they passed and find out. Both of them were powerful, a bit wicked and dangerous, and didn't give a damn what others thought about them.

"I can trust him. I've felt the good in him and I know he will protect me."

"There is good in him, Liora, as well as evil, but that does not mean you can trust him. He works for the Devil. He was created for that purpose, to be the Devil's right hand man, a powerful ally. He serves that dark lord, Liora." Apollyon took a step towards her, his black eyebrows pinching tightly together and his blue eyes narrowing with them. He looked like Asmodeus when he did that, and it made her want to see her angel even more.

"I need to speak with him. I can handle myself and I will be careful, but I have to go." She stepped out of the door and raced down the stairs, taking deep breaths with each step, feeling the oppressive weight of being around Apollyon and Serenity lifting as she neared the ground floor and hopefully Asmodeus.

She didn't just want to talk to Asmodeus about what the Devil had planned for her. She wanted to talk to him about the weird feelings she'd had recently, the sense that someone was watching her and had been close to her several times. She needed to know if he thought it was the Devil or someone else.

Liora muttered another prayer under her breath that when she reached the main doors of the building, Asmodeus would be there.

She bolted across the marble floor of the elegant foyer and shoved the brass and glass doors open. Her heart lifted and her tension melted away when she spotted Asmodeus standing on the pavement in the quiet narrow street, his head tipped back, causing the longer strands of his black hair to fall away from his handsome face.

Liora took the three stone steps down to the pavement and stopped beside him.

He looked stern and his golden eyes had gone cold. She didn't like it.

A chill crept through her when his irises brightened, the flakes in them beginning to swirl, and he wavered on the spot, as if in a trance. His gaze slowly inched down to her, bringing his head down with it, his eyes focused on her like a hawk eyeing prey and then he visibly relaxed. His shoulders settled and his frown disappeared, as if whatever had been bothering him was gone now.

"Is something wrong?" She couldn't get her voice above a whisper while he was staring straight at her, the black and amber flakes in his eyes settling and his pupils narrowing.

He shook his head. "Go back inside and leave me alone."

Well, that was rude. She placed her hands on her hips and glared at him.

"No," she said and he raised a single black eyebrow at her. She could see straight past his cool but dark façade to the reason he wanted her to leave him alone and she wasn't going to let him have his way, because he had no reason to feel hurt or upset. She reached out and laid her left hand on his forearm. "You're new to hunger. It isn't unreasonable that you would mistake it for sickness."

Asmodeus huffed and stalked away from her, heading down the street, the long feathers of his black wings fluttering around his ankles. Liora frowned now. She wasn't going to let him leave her, not when he was still starving and not even after she had somehow managed to get him to listen to her.

She hurried after him, adjusting her small black bag so it was behind her and wasn't hindering her strides.

"Go away, Liora," Asmodeus tossed the words over his broad shoulders and she shook her head even though he couldn't see it.

"Not going to happen. There's a nice café this way. We could get something to eat." She looked up at the sky. It was getting light but it was still early. It would be at least thirty minutes to an hour before the café opened for the morning rush.

He cheated.

He spread his black wings and beat them hard, forcing her to stop to avoid being struck by them, and shot into the air. He landed on the edge of the building above her and strolled along it.

Now he was really pissing her off.

Liora focused on his position and called her magic. It was going to take a lot of her remaining power to get her up there. She had used a vast amount of it to bring Asmodeus to Apollyon and had left herself weak.

The world darkened and then a different view greeted her. Rooftops stretched around her, lower than she had expected.

Her coordinates were off.

Liora shrieked and dropped to the tar roof several feet below her, landing awkwardly on her right foot. Her ankle blazed, fire shooting up her leg, and she cried out again and her backside hit the roof. Her shin and foot throbbed as she rolled onto her back and clutched them, gritting her teeth against the pain.

Asmodeus appeared above her, his golden gaze darting between her eyes. The concern in it touched her. He shifted back and she wanted to ask him not to leave her and then realised that he wasn't going further than a few feet.

He eased her hands away from her leg and carefully removed her black leather ankle boot. He placed it down on the roof beside her, kneeled and set her foot down on his bare thighs. She stared at him as he gently inspected her ankle, feeling the bones, a beautiful frown of concentration on his face.

It hurt like a bitch.

"Is it broken?" she said, afraid that she had pushed her luck too far this time. She had never broken a bone outside of a battle before and in those circumstances adrenaline kept the pain at bay until long after she had claimed victory.

He shook his head, settled her foot in his lap, and frowned down at her. "You were a fool for following me."

That wasn't very nice. "I had to… I need to speak with you about everything. I need to know why you didn't take me to your master… I need to hear you say it again."

He looked away from her, his focus fixing on the roof beside her. The sun was rising behind him, casting his face in shadows but giving him a glorious golden and pink hued backdrop. His black wings shifted and he drew in a deep breath that had her pain melting away as her gaze dropped to his bare chest and she watched his muscles ripple.

"The Devil is only my master in name. He does not rule me. We are equal in power and standing."

She could see he truly believed that.

Liora didn't. If the Devil commanded him to bring her to him, Asmodeus would fight the order, but she feared he would fail. Part of her said that she was safer away from him, with Apollyon and Serenity. The rest overruled it and told her to stay and not let him slip out of her grasp.

"Why didn't you take me to him?" she whispered and his eyes finally came back to rest on her. They lost their darkness and the cold edge they had gained, and softened, revealing the emotions he tried so hard to hide from the world.

"I will never let him have you. You will never belong to him… because… I desire… something foolish. Pointless." Asmodeus stood and raked his fingers through his hair. He tipped his head back and sighed.

"It isn't foolish and pointless to desire something, Asmodeus… not if the object of that desire feels the same."

His gaze sharply dropped to hers and widened. She smiled and held her hand out to him.

"Help me up?"

He nodded and slipped his hand into hers. The moment they touched, a jolt ran up her arm, causing her fine hairs to stand on end and her heart to race. She stared up into Asmodeus's beautiful golden gaze, catching his shock and awe, feeling the same inside.

He eased her onto her feet and bent before her. She laid one hand on his shoulder to steady herself when he carefully slipped her boot back onto her injured foot and didn't let go when he stood.

Asmodeus paused, his gaze holding hers, filled with the conflicting feelings that she could sense in him through her touch. His eyes drifted down to her mouth and her lips parted, anticipation stealing her breath and leaving her trembling. She ached to feel his mouth on hers again, reaffirming everything he had told her before, making her feel that she wasn't going crazy and that things would somehow work out between them.

He bent and scooped her up into his arms, turned and beat his wings. They lifted off into the air and Asmodeus beat his wings again, carrying them over a gap between the buildings. He wobbled and she snapped her head around, catching him with his eyes closed and a frown pinching his eyebrows.

"Asmodeus?" She clutched his cheeks.

He growled, twisted awkwardly and dropped. She threw her arms around his neck and held on, screwing her eyes shut. He landed hard, stumbled forwards a few steps and eventually righted himself.

Liora opened her eyes and smoothed her thumbs across his cheeks, her fingertips resting along his jaw. "You need to eat. Your blood sugar will be hitting rock bottom."

He frowned, lifted his eyelids, and stared at her. Red ringed his irises.

"I am fine."

Liora sighed and stroked his jaw, searching for a way of making him see that she wasn't mocking him and she didn't want to make him feel weak. She wanted to make him strong again. She cursed Apollyon for acting the way he had towards his twin, putting it in his head that he was weak because he needed to eat and hadn't realised that hunger was making him sick.

She had to get him to eat. How?

She smiled.

"Well, I'm hungry and I'm going to eat, so you might as well come with me and eat too." Before he could respond, she tapped the last of her power to teleport them to an alley behind the main street where her favourite café was located.

Asmodeus frowned at her and set her down.

She looked him over. "Am I seeing you as everyone else will be?"

He nodded. That wasn't good. She couldn't take him to the café when he was sporting wings and partial armour.

"You'll have to change your appearance," she said and he stared at her, his gaze focused and intense. After half a minute, she added, "Done?"

He shook his head and his handsome face twisted into a black scowl. His hands clenched at his sides, the toned muscles of his forearms following them, giving her a brief flash of how sexy his body could be, exuding strength and power.

"I do not want to go with you." Asmodeus turned away from her and folded his arms across his chest.

Liora's eyebrows rose high on her forehead as it dawned on her that he was too proud to admit that he had tried and had found he didn't have the strength left to change his appearance.

"That's cool. I'll just go and get some stuff and bring it back here. I hate how crowded it gets there. It's nice here." It wasn't nice at all but her only other option was to call him on his problem and have him mad at her, and then he would try to leave her again.

She left before he could say anything, hobbling out of the side road and into the main avenue. Her ankle was killing her and she wished she had kept a sliver of magic, enough to take some of the pain away and kick start her body's natural healing ability.

There were plenty of people coming and going along the Champs Elysees. She looked further up the wide tree-lined street to her right and smiled. The café was open, the cream awning stretching out from the beautiful old sandstone building. Parasols covered elegant black wrought-iron tables and chairs on the wide pavement in front of it. She would have liked to sit there with Asmodeus, enjoying sweet pastries and the early morning sun. Maybe they could do that some other time.

Liora brought her black bag around and rifled through it for her purse. Asmodeus would need something sweet, and something substantial. The café wasn't likely to have all the baguettes made for the day at this early hour. Savoury was probably off the menu. She hoped Asmodeus liked sweet things.

She entered the small café and made her way to the long counter that was covered in tall curved glass that showed off the beautiful array of sweets they offered. Her gaze darted from one delicious pastry to another. One of the staff asked her what she wanted and she ended up ordering more than she needed, and two bottles of orange juice to go.

She wasn't sure what sort of pastries Asmodeus would like, or whether he would like them at all. He had never left Hell before and she presumed that meant he had never eaten before too. He had some serious catching up to do and she couldn't wait to see what he made of the things she had bought. Introducing him to the pleasures of food was going to be interesting.

Liora paid for her purchases and made her way back to the alley. Asmodeus was sitting on the step of one of the buildings lining the narrow street, his wings carefully placed so the longest black feathers curled around his ankles. He looked pale, his skin almost milk-white against his wild black hair and thick dark lashes. He lifted his head and gazed at her as she hobbled towards him, his golden eyes warming and then burning like fire as they took her in. Heat chased in the wake of his eyes, setting her body aflame and stirring a different sort of hunger.

She wanted to drop her things beside him, settle herself astride his lithe muscular thighs, and run her fingers through his hair, raking the satiny black strands back from his sculpted face. She would force him to tip it back and look up at her, and the action would cause his lips to part. She would swoop on them then, feeling their firmness beneath hers, waiting for him to hit that point where he found the courage to take the lead and showed her a hint of the passion he held locked beneath his incredible exterior.

His gaze dropped to the bag she carried, reminding her that he had to eat before she could do anything with him or he was liable to pass out. She sat on the step below him, took the white box of pastries out of the carrier bag and carefully untied the ribbon. She pushed the lid up to reveal the neat rows of sweet treats and her mouth watered.

Asmodeus stared.

"What are those?" He looked curious. That was good. Maybe he would eat some for her.

"Pastries." She plucked a strawberry mille-feuille out of the box and offered it to him.

He took it from her and peered at it, turning it this way and that and getting cream and icing all over his hand.

"It's my favourite." She picked up the other one she had bought and bit into it. The layers of fine crisp puff pastry, custard-cream and strawberries were delicious and she moaned and took another bite, unable to resist the tempting allure of the sweet heavenly confection.

When she risked a glance at Asmodeus, his pastry was gone and he was licking his fingers. She moaned for a different reason, her head filling with thoughts about what he could do with that tongue and some cream, and he looked at her.

There was a spot of cream at the left corner of his mouth and she couldn't resist. She reached up, swiped it off and sucked her finger clean. His gaze darkened and zeroed in on her lips. Her heart fluttered in response, shivery heat washing through her and making her want to keep sucking her finger and giving him wicked ideas.

Food first. Fun later.

She finished her pastry and offered him the box.

He took a small rectangular slice of chocolate gateaux and devoured it in two bites before taking a pain au chocolat, and then a wedge of tarte au citron. He pulled a face on eating that one, his nose wrinkling up.

"Not into the citrus fruits?" she said and he shook his head. She pulled the bottle of orange juice from her bag and smiled apologetically. "You might not like this then."

He took it anyway and inspected the plastic bottle. Rather than taking the bottle from him and twisting the cap off, something that would probably make him feel foolish again, she took her own bottle from the bag and opened it intentionally slowly.

Asmodeus mimicked her, acting like a pro and snapping the cap off his bottle. He drank half the contents in one go and then frowned at the bottle.

"It is not as bad as the sweet thing." He set the bottle down beside him on the stone step and took the other slice of chocolate gateaux, and then paused when her gaze lovingly followed it towards him. "Would you like some?"

She had bought the pastries, so she deserved at least a portion of the gateaux. It was her second favourite item.

Asmodeus held it out to her and rather than taking it, she leaned over and bit into it, her gaze on his the whole time. His golden irises darkened again, his pupils expanding to relay his desire. They only darkened further when she licked her lips.

"Delicious," she whispered and he growled, his gaze boring into her mouth, robbing her of her breath and making her silently beg him to kiss her.

He hesitated and she cursed him when he sat back, taking the remains of the gateaux slice with him. He devoured it and set the paper case back in the box.

Liora stuffed her face with a piece of tarte tatin. It wasn't as sweet as kissing Asmodeus would have been and it didn't satisfy her in the slightest.

"I enjoy these pastries," Asmodeus said and licked his lips clean, enticing her into kissing him if he wouldn't kiss her.

He finished his orange juice, leaned back and sighed. He was looking better already, his skin no longer a sickly hue and his strength returning. She could feel his power rising again, coming back to the level it usually rested at when he was around her.

"Are you feeling better?" She screwed up the paper her tarte tatin had been on and tossed it back into the box.

He should be feeling sick after eating that many pastries but, then again, she had seen Apollyon devour an entire chocolate cake in one sitting without it giving him an upset stomach.

He frowned. "My head still hurts."

"It'll pass." Had he never had a headache before either? What else was new to him?

He lowered his eyes to the road and stared at it, his gaze turning distant and cold again. He stayed like it for so long that the worry that had faded on hearing he was feeling better began to return.

"Are you still unwell?" she said.

He blinked and his attention snapped to her, a flicker of surprise in his golden eyes, as if he had lost track of the world and was shocked to see her sitting beside him.

He sighed, pinched the bridge of his nose and closed his eyes. "I am being compelled to return."

The Devil was ordering him to return to Hell. Liora's worry returned, worse than ever. If he went back to Hell, would the Devil punish him for killing the angel and lying to him about her?

What if he didn't go back?

"Will the Devil send another bad angel after you if you don't go to him?" she said and his eyes opened and slid across to her.

"I am a bad angel... the baddest."

Liora blushed at that, wicked scenarios running through her mind. He quirked his right eyebrow at her reaction and she could understand why it had confused him. He had meant to place distance between them, warning her away from him, and she had the terrible feeling she knew why.

He stood, brushed the crumbs off the strips of armour around his hips and stepped down onto the pavement.

"Return to Serenity and stay with them. You will be safe there. I must go."

The ground bucked and cracked, a glowing fiery fault line stretching thirty feet across the road in front of her. The jagged line widened and lava dripped down into the dark crevasse, hissing as it disappeared from view.

A gateway to Hell.

"Wait." Liora shot to her feet and reached out to him.

Asmodeus looked over his shoulder at her and then dropped into the darkness.

His wings caught her arm as he spread them and she tipped forwards, flailed her arms in a desperate attempt to right herself, and shrieked as she fell over the edge and plummeted into the abyss.

CHAPTER 7

Asmodeus's heart missed a beat, slammed painfully hard against his chest and began to race as Liora dropped past him, perilously close to the sharp ragged black cliffs of the crevasse.

He pinned his obsidian wings back and shot after her, reaching for her with both hands at the same time, stretching as far as he could, until his muscles burned and joints ached.

Her chestnut hair streamed upwards, fluttering around her face, and her legs and arms flailed above her as her back took the brunt of the hot air blasting upwards from Hell. Magic sparked around her hands, hitting the rocks and sending shards of black basalt exploding over him.

"Liora." He beat his wings and pinned them back again, closing the gap between them.

She thrashed her arms and legs and then her hair cleared from her face and she stared up at him, her eyes enormous and flooded with fear. That emotion struck him hard, beating within his heart and driving him to break the limits of his power and his body in order to bring her into the safety of his arms and take away her fear.

He growled and flew harder, using all of his strength because hers had failed her. She had used it up teleporting him to Apollyon and then to a place where they could eat.

Liora reached for him, her fingers stretching, and he reached for her, his heart pounding at a sickening pace against his chest. Hers rushed in his ears, her fear flowing over him, calling to him. He took no pleasure from it.

The walls ended and opened into the cavern of Hell, and the plateau loomed before him. He had only a few hundred feet left in which to catch her or lose her forever.

Asmodeus snarled, his fangs descended, his claws lengthened and his eyes burned red.

He would not lose her.

He flapped his immense wings and then pinned them back as far as they would go. It still wasn't enough.

His eyes widened.

He knew what he had to do.

He focused and sent his wings away. They shrank into his back and his velocity increased as he became more streamlined, sending him rocketing towards Liora.

"Spread your arms and legs," he called to her and she did as he instructed.

The second she had formed a cross before him, she shot upwards, straight into his arms.

He wrapped them tightly around her and focused on his wings again, calling them to emerge. The ground came at him fast, quicker than his wings were forming. He growled and threw his right hand out, casting a black vortex before him.

Liora screamed as they hit it and he twisted with her as they appeared on the other side, above his castle in the plains. His wings erupted from his back but too late for them to be of any use. They only made the crash landing worse on him.

He hit the black grounds of his castle hard, taking the brunt of the impact for Liora. Her body slammed into his, knocking the air from his lungs, and he held her with both arms, clutching her against his chest.

Fire tore through his wings as they twisted and bent beneath him. He skidded across the harsh, polished pavement of his garden and came to a halt near the pillars that supported a balcony that ran around the front of his black castle.

Asmodeus closed his eyes and let his head fall back. It smacked against the black slabs beneath him. He breathed hard, fighting to subdue the pain ripping through every inch of him and still clutching Liora close to him.

"Asmodeus?" Liora's soft voice called to him, soothing some of his pain, and she moved in his arms.

He opened his eyes and looked up at her. Her hands pressed against his bare chest, burning into his flesh in the most delicious way.

"Are you okay?" she whispered and brushed the hair from his brow, concern lighting her hazel eyes. They searched his and he basked in her worry and the compassion and affection she showed him.

"I will live," he said to alleviate her concern and then grimaced as a wet tongue slapped at his cheek.

Liora squealed and shot backwards, straight into the bulky black body of Romulus. The hellhound growled, exposing twin rows of deadly sharp black teeth. Remus stopped licking Asmodeus and lifted his head too, his red gaze locking on Liora.

"Heel," Asmodeus commanded in the demonic tongue and the two hellhounds whimpered and moved to him. They lay beside him and nuzzled his cheeks, whining low in their throats.

It was difficult when he was lying on the ground, but he managed to twist enough to pet them on their muzzles and soothe them.

They sat up when he pushed himself up and moved closer, crowding him. Romulus trod on one of his wing feathers, pulling on it. Asmodeus grimaced and pushed him away. Foolish mutts. They always had wanted to sit on him rather than beside him, and were forever accidentally catching him with their claws or treading places that hurt.

Liora stood and offered her trembling hand to him, earning her another growl from both Romulus and Remus.

"Quiet," he snapped in his native language again and the hellhounds lowered their heads and settled down to lie beside him, resting their jaws on their large paws.

He took Liora's hand, lumbered onto his feet and ran his gaze over her. She had a few scratches on her bare arms but other than that and her pale complexion, she seemed unharmed by her fall.

He wanted to take her back to her realm but he couldn't yet. The Devil would know he had entered Hell and would become suspicious if he didn't report in. She would be safe here at his castle in the wasteland, far from the Devil's fortress and his army of Hell's angels. Romulus and Remus kept the area clear of demons too, hunting and devouring any who strayed too close to the spire of rock on which his castle stood.

Romulus and Remus would protect her while he went to the Devil.

The two black hellhounds sat up and Liora moved closer to him, eyeing them warily.

"Come," he said and the two got to their paws and trotted over to him.

Liora tensed and clutched his arm in both of her hands, and he liked the way she did that, using him as a shield, relying on him to protect her even though she wasn't in any danger.

The hellhounds sat in front of him and started panting. Remus's left ear drooped and then perked up again. He never had been able to keep it fully straightened. It somewhat spoiled his vicious, deadly appearance when it drooped and refused to stand again, giving him a lopsided look.

"Liora, this is Romulus and Remus." Asmodeus pointed to each hellhound in turn and they both looked up at her, their ears pricking and their panting halting.

"They look the same to me." Liora moved closer to him and the hellhounds, but remained slightly tucked behind him.

Her breasts pressed against his bare arm, wrecking his concentration. They were soft and warm, and he wanted to palm them.

"Will they be upset if I call them by the wrong names? Will they eat me?"

Asmodeus laughed. "No. They always travel together, ever since they were pups seven centuries ago and I found them in an empty den."

"Where were their parents?" Liora emerged from behind him, her curious gaze fixed on the two hellhounds, a spark of sympathy emerging in it.

"The mother was dead a few metres from the den. I am not sure what killed her," he said casually, remembering the day he had gone out to survey his realm and had spotted the butchered carcass from the air, and had found the twin pups nearby.

"So you brought them home?" There was a twinkle in her hazel eyes that he didn't understand. She looked almost pleased.

He nodded. "I brought them to the castle and took care of them."

She smiled at him.

"What is wrong? Did I say something strange?"

She shook her head, causing her tangled chestnut waves to brush across the crimson shoulders of her gypsy top. "No. I think it's good that you took the hounds in and raised them… protected them. You must have spent hours each day taking care of them… feeding them… cleaning them… teaching them. It was very sweet of you, Asmodeus."

Ah, he could see why she had smiled at him now, and it left him feeling uncomfortable and unsure what to say. He didn't view what he had done as an act of charity, not as she did. He hadn't even thought about it at the time. He had seen the pups alone, their mother gone, and knew they would die. He hadn't been able to leave them.

He had done just as she had said. He had raised them, weaned them, fed them and trained them. He had taken care of them and they had taken care of him.

They both whined and looked up at him, their red eyes bright in the low light. Asmodeus petted them, rubbing the spots between their ears, feeling they knew his thoughts.

He crouched and they moved to sit in front of him.

He stared into their eyes and spoke to them in the demon tongue he had raised them to understand.

"Take care of Liora. She is precious to me. I am counting on you to keep her safe. Understand?"

They nuzzled his hands and nipped at his palms and he knew what they were telling him even though he didn't have the power of telepathy so he couldn't hear their reply.

"Is that the language you taught them?" Liora said from behind him.

He looked over his shoulder at her, stood, and nodded. "They will do as I bid and protect you."

Liora toyed with a small silver pentagram around her neck, twirling it in her fingers and then clutching it in her right palm. He hadn't noticed it before now. It must have been tucked beneath the frilled elastic neck of her crimson top the whole time they had been together, hidden from view. Between her breasts. He swallowed at that thought and stared at them.

She stopped playing with the pendant and he felt her gaze on him. When he finally dragged his away from her small pert breasts, she was blushing and there was that darkness in her eyes again, the one that said his staring had affected her, stirring passion that echoed within him.

"Thank you," she said and then looked down at Romulus and Remus. "Thank you, too."

They stared blankly at her. Asmodeus relayed her gratitude in the demon tongue and they began panting again. Remus's left ear drooped. Asmodeus sighed and straightened it for him.

Liora hid her smile well.

Asmodeus turned to her. "You will be safe here. No one dares venture close to the castle and my hellhounds will protect you. Wait for me."

Her relaxed air dissipated and she caught his wrist. "You're leaving?"

He nodded. "I must report."

Her nerves increased and he sighed and stepped closer to her, until her body brushed his and she had to tilt her head back to hold his gaze. He lifted his right hand and swept his knuckles across her cheek, marvelling over how soft it was beneath his caress and how she let him do such a thing. She closed her eyes and he opened his hand, laid his palm against her face, and she leaned into it.

He had never had anyone seek comfort from him before. The experience was incredible and overwhelming, and ignited a fierce need to stay and protect her. He wanted to make her feel safe.

Liora opened her hazel eyes and looked up at him, a soft needful look in them. His heart raced, anticipation stealing his breath and making it hard to focus. He wanted to fulfil that wish he could see in her eyes. He would, but not right now. He would do so later, when they had time, because once he began kissing her, he wouldn't want to stop.

"I will not let anything happen to you, Liora, and neither will Romulus and Remus." He stroked her cheek again, savouring the silky warmth of her skin and how she sought comfort from him.

"Those angels—"

"Cannot enter this castle or the grounds around it," he interjected and she looked up at the tall towers of his black castle that rose above them, tipped with spiked roofs.

"Your home," she whispered and he nodded, conceding that it was just that to him.

His home.

"You will be safe here, in my home. The Hell's angels cannot enter here and the Devil cannot travel this far from the bottomless pit. No one will bother you. I swear it." He dropped a brief kiss on her forehead and stepped back from her.

Before she could convince him to linger any longer, he threw his hand forwards and a portal appeared. He stepped into the swirling black vortex and through it, coming out close to the Devil's obsidian fortress.

It speared the sky in the distance, black and forbidding, each tower taller than the last until it melted into the darkness. Black sharp spikes almost seventy feet tall curved around it and the expansive courtyard, forming a vicious wall intended to keep most demons out as they couldn't fly and scaling the spires was impossible. Part of the wall was lower than the rest, the result of the Devil's battle against his daughter, Erin, and Veiron, a traitorous Hell's angel. The shards were slowly repairing themselves, bleeding lava from close to their newly forming peaks, but it would be many months before they towered as high as the rest.

Asmodeus took a few deep breaths to settle his nerves. He would not let the Devil have Liora. No matter what happened during this meeting with his master, she would be safe.

Even if the Devil killed him.

He casually strode towards the fortress, buying himself time to get his nerves under control and extinguish them together with the pain that still ebbed and flowed through his body. He would not show any weakness in front of the Devil. If he did, the male would realise that he already had Liora and would exploit the weakness that came from his feelings for her. He would play on them and taunt Asmodeus, and then he would probably command him to bring her to him.

He was regaining his strength, but was still weak. In his current state, he wouldn't be able to resist if the Devil used the full might of his power on him.

He had to try though. He had to do what he must to keep his promise to Liora and keep her safe.

He crossed the cragged black landscape, following a wide path that wound through the short columns of rock that belched smoke and magma. The lava hissed as it rolled down their bumpy faces, cooling despite the fiery heat of Hell. He had never realised before now just how hot this realm was, the air thick with the scent of sulphur and other chemicals that turned it acrid.

Small brown and grey scaly demons scurried away as he approached, disappearing into the harsh terrain.

When he reached the formidable wall that encircled the Devil's fortress, he spread his large black feathered wings and flew up the spires. His wings ached with each beat, sending fire along their bones and down his back. He gritted his teeth and flew higher and over the top of the wall.

From above, it was easy to see the damage the Devil's battle against his daughter had done to the courtyard. The polished black flagstones had cracked and buckled in some areas, fused together at vicious angles by cooled lava. The place was a mess. Only a few sections of the paving had survived intact, most of them close to the imposing fortress.

It had been his home once, many centuries ago, when he had been happy living under the same roof as his master.

The Devil had not been pleased when he had decided to leave the fortress and set about building his own castle in a wasteland far away, miles beyond his reach during the times when he was limited to the bottomless pit. He had accused Asmodeus of plotting to create his own realm, one that would challenge his reign.

Asmodeus had scoffed at that. He had no interest in running Hell. He had merely wanted a place of his own where he could do as he pleased.

He landed on a smooth section of the courtyard near the steps that led up to the fortress.

The tall twin doors opened a crack and the Devil stepped out, dressed impeccably in a sharp black suit with a patterned black tie.

Sometimes when Asmodeus looked in one of the tarnished mirrors in his castle, he could see this male in him. Those same golden eyes looked back at him, framed by the same long black lashes, from a face crowned by the same wild short black hair.

Asmodeus hated it. It was worse than seeing Apollyon staring back at him.

He was a clone of neither of those males. He was his own man, with his own history and his own destiny.

He was not a shadow.

"Asmodeus," the Devil said, his smooth baritone filled with warmth that Asmodeus knew was false and placed there to make him feel the male was pleased to see him. "I half expected you to disobey my order again and remain in that mortal realm. I trust you found it to your liking and enjoyed the brief moment you had there?"

"I did. I will return to it when I see fit."

"Will you now?" The Devil's mouth curled into a wicked smile and his amber eyes flashed. "And how will you do that?"

The male meant to taunt him but it wouldn't work. The Devil could restrict his power to use a portal to reach that realm all he wanted, attempting to control him and keep him in Hell against his will, but it wouldn't stop Asmodeus.

"Under my own volition. I have discovered that I share another power of Apollyon's that you failed to mention before." Asmodeus allowed himself a small smile of victory when the grin on his master's face faded and his expression soured. "I see you were aware of it. I can apparently create the rift between this realm and the mortal one, just as he can. I do not have to rely on the power of creating portals that you granted me."

Discovering that power had led Asmodeus to consider what other ones he possessed that the Devil had kept hidden from him. It had only been a brief consideration. Liora had dropped into the rift he had created just as he had thought it and his focus had shot to her instead. When he returned to her at his castle, he would ask her about Apollyon to discover what she knew of his powers and he would ponder whether he could use them too.

"Very well. You may come and go as you please... when you have brought the female to me." The Devil brushed the sleeves of his suit jacket and picked at something with his black claws.

"What do you want with her?" Asmodeus advanced a step, coming to stand at the bottom of the steps that led up to the fortress.

"That is my business. You have never questioned me before and it is unwise to begin to do so now. What I desire the female for will remain my business."

Asmodeus lowered his hands to his sides and his fingers twitched, eager to feel the hilts of his blades in them. "If you want me to retrieve her for you, then you will tell me."

The Devil smiled again, exposing short fangs. "You think to threaten me?"

He did. It was insane, but it was his only choice. He needed to know why the Devil wanted Liora so he could better protect her.

Something dawned in the Devil's golden eyes. "Ah... I had wondered what had happened. You have been busy, Asmodeus... killing one of your own."

"The male you sent was not one of my own. I have no kin. He showed me no respect and so I taught him a lesson. I removed his head." Asmodeus straightened to his full height, flapped his black wings and furled them against his bare back, allowing none of the pain it caused him to show on his face. "He will not make the same mistake again."

"And because of your impertinence, I am down a man. You know I should punish you for the crime you committed."

Asmodeus laughed. "Crime? You taught me to gain the respect of those beneath me through showing them what would happen should they disappoint me, and you taught me well. I will not tolerate the disrespect of your men."

"And I will not tolerate your disrespect." The Devil flexed his fingers and black fire chased over them, fluttering across his knuckles. The power he constantly emanated grew in strength, washing over Asmodeus and pressing down on him.

Asmodeus's power rose to meet it, shielding him from the full force of the Devil's. He wouldn't be able to match the Devil's strength if the male went all out on him, but he would do his best, for Liora's sake. She was expecting him to return to her. If he didn't, she would be stuck in this realm until Apollyon came for her.

That didn't sit well with Asmodeus.

He would not allow his twin to be her saviour.

"You do not know what you are dealing with, Asmodeus." The Devil straightened to his full height and black ribbons of smoke twined around his fingers, streaming from his obsidian claws.

"Then tell me what I am dealing with. Tell me what you want with the female." Asmodeus wouldn't cower before his master. The Devil meant to keep him in the dark and he would never allow that to happen. He needed to know why the Devil wanted Liora and what he would do to her if he got his hands on her, not that Asmodeus would ever allow that to happen.

"I told you, that is my business. I will only tell you that she is dangerous in the wrong hands."

Dangerous? Liora was powerful but she was mortal. Her magic was strong, but her body was weak. It wouldn't hold out in a battle against a strong demon or angel, and definitely not against his master.

"Dangerous in your hands, perhaps." Asmodeus held his master's gaze, unflinching even when the Devil narrowed his eyes on him and his power rose, the air growing thicker around him. "Tell me why she is dangerous and I will consider bringing the female to you."

"Lies. You dare lie to me? I created you, Asmodeus, and I can destroy you just as easily. Remember that."

Asmodeus glared at him and spat out a vile curse in the black language of Hell.

"Tell me, Asmodeus, is she worth the pain you will suffer?" The Devil's tone dripped venom and his gaze gained a cruel edge, his wicked smile conveying his black thoughts and the pleasure he felt from thinking about torturing Asmodeus.

That pleasure would increase a thousandfold when he actually carried out the terrible acts he was envisaging.

"I have withstood torture before. Whatever you do to me, I will not break." Asmodeus tipped his chin up and stared the Devil straight in the eye.

The male flashed his fangs in a grin. "Who said I would torture you? I have a feeling you will break when I take her from you and torment her before your very eyes while you are under my orders to watch in silence."

Asmodeus stood his ground, unwilling to show fear to his master. His power rose in response to the anger beginning to boil in his blood, fuelled by thoughts of this wretched male harming his Liora.

"You cannot control me," he said and advanced another step, closing in on the Devil where he stood at the top of the steps, looking down on him. "Not as Heaven can control their angels. I do not belong to you."

"You do belong to me, whether you want to admit it or not. I own you. You will bring her to me, Asmodeus."

He felt the tug of those words in his chest, yanking him to his right in the direction of his castle, beyond the rough jagged black spikes that enclosed the courtyard. He fought the command but he still wasn't strong enough to deny the effect it had on his body. He shifted his right foot to brace himself as it pulled him towards Liora.

The Devil's grin turned twisted and pleased, and Asmodeus's stomach dropped. "I see. The female is already in Hell."

Asmodeus called both of his curved golden blades to his hands and growled at the Devil. "I will not bring her to you."

"Bring her to me." The Devil raised his hands at his sides, black fire chasing over them, and the oppressive weight of his power increased, pushing down on Asmodeus.

Asmodeus readied his blades and drew in a fortifying breath. "I will never let you have her."

"It is not a question of let, Maggot. You will obey whether you like it or not."

The tug came again, stronger this time, pulling him towards Liora. Asmodeus ground his molars together and fought it, focusing all of his strength on denying the Devil's command.

"Never," Asmodeus roared and launched himself up the steps at the Devil.

The slender black-haired male flung his left hand forwards and shadowy tendrils shot from his fingers and slammed into Asmodeus's chest.

Asmodeus flew backwards through the air, his wings streaming before him, the velocity of his flight so great that he couldn't move them. The impact with the jagged basalt spires that lined the curved courtyard tore a scream from his throat. Fiery heat lanced his flesh and branded his bones. The rock shattered under the force of the impact.

An ominous crack echoed around the paved area.

Asmodeus's head spun and darkness encroached.

He slid down the curve of the wall, shards of basalt spearing his back and his thighs, and fell forwards. The pain stole all feeling, leaving him numb and weak, his mind whirling and vision distorting. He rolled onto his back and a shadow loomed above him, growing larger. Unconsciousness?

His vision aligned again and his eyes widened.

Death.

He rolled onto his front and scrambled forwards, kicking hard at the fragmented pavement and beating his aching wings.

The enormous piece of one of the spires crashed into the ground behind him base first and shattered. Asmodeus flew harder, grimacing with each painful beat of his black wings, fire blistering his skin where each needle of rock penetrated his flesh. Small fragments of the falling spire caught his booted feet and his wings, but he pushed on, the thought of being crushed under the weight of the broken rock driving him onwards.

He made it beyond the fallout zone from the shattered spire and turned towards the Devil.

Another blast of black took his legs out, sending him face-first into the pavement.

Asmodeus growled and pushed onto his knees, and then cried out as claws grasped the back of his neck, digging into his flesh like fiery acid. He arched forwards, yelling his agony at the black vault of Hell, tears streaming from the corners of his eyes.

The Devil lowered his mouth to Asmodeus's ear. "I had expected a better fight than this. My daughter and her consort gave me a harder time than you have. You disappoint me."

The male shoved him forwards and released him and Asmodeus hit the flagstones again. He lay on his front, breathing hard and struggling to shut down the pain blazing through every inch of his flesh and his bones. If he could just lay here for five minutes and catch his breath, he could give the Devil the fight he desired. He was sure of it.

His master didn't even give him five seconds.

He stepped around Asmodeus, slid his right foot under his left shoulder, and flipped him onto his back, twisting his wings beneath him. Asmodeus groaned and held his right hand out, willing one of his blades to come to him. The Devil stepped onto Asmodeus's throat and pressed down. He choked, all of his agony focusing in that one spot, driving him close to the edge of oblivion again.

Asmodeus gave up trying to call his blade as darkness encroached, crowding like shadows at the corners of his vision. He wheezed, desperate for air, and weakly lifted his hands to the Devil's foot. He fumbled with it, too tired and dizzy to grasp it and push it off his throat.

His master stood over him, cocked his head to one side, and stared down at him.

"Such a disappointment. Bring her to me, Asmodeus." The Devil's eyes brightened, a corona of crimson encircling his golden irises. "Do not disappoint me again."

Black shadows streamed from the Devil's shoulders, rising and shifting, becoming dragon-like wings. His eyes burned red, his lips twisted in a sneer that exposed his vicious fangs, and he shoved his foot down hard onto Asmodeus's throat.

Darkness claimed him.

CHAPTER 8

Liora strolled through the black-walled corridors of Asmodeus's castle, enjoying the cooler air inside and tailed by his hellhounds.

Well, she was hobbling and snooping, but it made her feel better if she pretended she wasn't doing anything wrong.

When he had left her, disappearing through the black vortex that she presumed teleported him elsewhere in Hell, and closer to his master, she had pottered around the grounds of the imposing castle. Romulus and Remus had tracked her every move, keeping close to her heels. Clearly, they took their duty seriously and were determined not to fail their master. She had tried to lose them, but they were quicker than she was in her somewhat battered, bruised and shaken state, so she had given up.

She had actually begun to feel safer with them around. Hell wasn't a particularly quiet place. Every few seconds there was a distant shriek or piercing cry of something that sounded big and armed with rows of sharp teeth and even sharper claws.

Romulus and Remus snapped to attention whenever the call echoed around the distant black mountains that surrounded the featureless basin below her. Sometimes they bared their own black fangs and closed formation, pinning her between them. Remus had even licked her hand when the cry had sounded closer and she had tensed, her heart beating wildly, sending adrenaline rocketing through her veins.

Differentiating between the two immense black hellhounds hadn't been hard once she had realised that Remus had a floppy ear. She smiled again at the memory of how Asmodeus had corrected it for him, his air that of a doting but frustrated father. It did wreck the hellhound's deadly and frightening appearance, and that had softened her initial feelings towards them both, making them less scary and threatening.

When she had reached the far end of the walled grounds, she had peered over the edge. Her head had turned and her stomach somersaulted at the sheer drop to the valley far below. Romulus had moved between her and the wall and nudged her backwards, forcing her away from the frightening drop. The hellhound hadn't stopped nudging her until she had been a good five metres from the wall.

Liora had turned then and paused, frozen by the sight of the black castle. It was strangely beautiful and enchanting, made of tall cylindrical towers topped with conical roofs that reached high into the thick hot air. She had drawn such castles as a child. It had a fairy tale air about it.

The enchanted castle of a dark prince.

Where was her dark prince now?

Liora ran her gaze over the black walls inside his home. They were unadorned. She had walked through several empty rooms and through endless bare corridors. She could hardly call it snooping when there was nothing to peek at.

Romulus and Remus stalked behind her and she had the feeling that she was slowing them down. She hobbled on and focused on her magic. It was still weak and it would be a while before it was strong enough for her to use on her sprained ankle.

"Maybe I could ride one of you?" She looked over her shoulder at her two dark guardians. They were as large as she had pictured, their ears easily reaching her shoulder, and were thickly muscled too. "Could you support my weight?"

They stared blankly at her, red eyes not giving away if they could understand her or not. Asmodeus spoke English. She shook that thought away. He had said they understood him when he spoke a demonic sort of tongue. They hadn't understood her earlier. She should have pressed Asmodeus to teach her a few commands, just in case she needed them. They seemed complacent and hadn't shown any sign of wanting to attack her, but she still couldn't bring herself to trust them one hundred percent.

They had dark auras and unnaturally strong energy. It set her magic on edge and she was having a hard time convincing herself that they wouldn't harm her so it would relax and she could focus on recuperating.

She doubted they would obey her even if she did speak their language.

Romulus trotted on ahead, loping down the dark dimly lit corridor. Remus huffed and followed, and they turned left and disappeared from view. Growls filled the silence and she hurried forwards, afraid that Asmodeus had been wrong and there was an intruder. Her limited magic sparked around her fingers, draining her strength as she tried to use her natural energy to enhance it.

She rounded the corner and sighed, her magic fading again.

The two hellhounds rolled around in the corridor ahead of her, growling at each other and trying to grab each other's scruff.

It wasn't the first time they had done this.

They acted like puppies sometimes, bounding ahead of her and shouldering each other, snarling and growling at the same time. It made it difficult for her to believe they were several hundred years old.

Liora smiled as she watched them playing and her thoughts turned back to Asmodeus. He had raised them from puppies, saving them from death. It was proof of the good in him that he hid so well from others. If Apollyon were aware of what Asmodeus had done, he wouldn't view his twin as evil at all.

Romulus and Remus got to their paws and came to her. Surprise claimed her when they pushed under her palms, causing her to rub their heads between their tall pointed ears.

Liora petted them as Asmodeus had, stroking their short satiny black fur.

"Do you love your master?" she whispered and they both lifted their heads, looking up at her with bright red eyes, and wagged their whip-like tails with enthusiasm. Liora smiled at them. They definitely loved their master and she had a feeling that he loved them in return.

They moved off as one, scouting the corridor ahead.

Liora followed them, allowing them to lead her deeper into the castle and up a set of stone steps to the next floor.

It was a whole different world.

The stairs ended in a large rectangular room filled with ornately carved black stone furniture. Shelves lined most of the walls, crammed with books, some of which were tomes and many of which looked extremely old and worn. Long low cupboards filled the gaps between them on the wall to her left.

She rounded the large rectangular table in the middle of the room, drawn to the cupboards and the incredible array of knickknacks on top of them. None of them seemed to go together. Everything on the main table at her back was the same, and on the smaller tables dotted around the expansive room and the mantelpiece of the huge fireplace behind her. It was a bizarre and colourful collection of random items, and many of them were antiques, dating back thousands of years if she had to guess.

On the cupboard before her was a small black and gold statue of an Egyptian cat that she knew was a goddess, a very simple candlestick that looked as if it had been fashioned from ivory, and countless other things, including coloured glass bottles, cutlery, shells, dolls and toys. She picked up an old, worn brown bear. One of its eyes was missing and the left arm was about to fall off.

Liora moved on to the bookcase that stood between the cupboard and the next one, and ran her fingers over the spines of the books. He had so many of them. She plucked one that had been bound in green scaly leather from the shelf and leafed through it. She didn't know the language written on the crinkled paper. The ink was faded too, almost impossible to make out in places. Elaborate and beautiful illustrations filled some of the fragile pages. One of them was of a dragon.

She ghosted her fingers over the lifelike image and then closed the book and set it back on the shelf.

Further along, she paused again, her fingers resting on the spine of a large tome. Power. It flowed through her fingertips and up her arm, gifting her with some of its strength. Liora grabbed the black leather-bound book from the shelf and flipped it open. Familiar writing greeted her. A spell book.

She closed it and held it to her chest, and looked at the others around it. She touched them each in turn, feeling the power they contained. Some of that power felt familiar to her, but others were different, new and exciting. She wanted to tear each book from the shelf, curl up beside the fireplace and devour them. She could learn so much from these books. Ancient spells that had been lost in her world.

Remus whined behind her and she looked back at him. He wagged his tail and she took the hint. She set the book back on the shelf. When Asmodeus returned, she would ask him if she could read them. Maybe he could help her with them. Her grasp of languages wasn't exactly extensive and something told her that not every witch would write in the ones she knew. Asmodeus was old, probably as ancient as these tomes. He might be able to speak the languages and help her decipher them.

The hellhound moved off to play with Romulus. The way the other canine snapped at his heels and Remus bent his head made Liora feel that Romulus was the older of the twins. The leader of their small pack.

Liora moved on to the next cupboard and frowned at the collection of items crammed on every inch of the black surface.

The more she looked at the items, the more she felt that Asmodeus had tried to make his castle a home by filling it with things that a normal person would have in theirs.

The books, the statues, toys and dolls.

The pictures in front of her.

The frames were a mishmash of modern and antique, in colours ranging from blue and white through to solid silver. Many of the old photographs and pictures they contained didn't fit the frames, and some of them looked like photos taken from people's wallets. Two or three of the frames just contained the sample picture that had come with them.

Liora touched the silver frame closest to her, staring at the small wonky faded photograph of a seascape it contained.

A sense of sorrow rose up within her and the longer she stared at the picture, the stronger it grew.

Asmodeus had tried so hard to make this place feel like a home, yet he had said it wasn't his home. He didn't feel that it was. He was filling it with things that weren't his, a bizarre collection of broken, faded, worn items.

More than ever, she felt he was missing something.

Companionship.

He tried to fill the void within him with these objects and with his hellhounds, but he still felt alone.

She had seen it in his eyes at times and could sense it in him.

He struggled to be around her during those instances, turned uncertain and awkward, and it was normally then that she had a sense of hope or positive feelings inside him. Warm feelings. Good feelings.

She felt sorry for him when he struggled with himself and his emotions, so unsure of himself and afraid of what he was experiencing, driven to fight it because he feared it made him weak and he would pay in blood if the Devil knew he harboured good within him.

Liora had only known him a short time, but there had been many instances when she had felt that he was trying to be normal and that he wanted to be like others. He wanted to be good, even though it wasn't in his makeup. The Devil had distilled evil in his blood and moulded him into a violent, cruel man.

She had felt that evil and darkness in him when they had first met, an aura of danger and malice that had warned her away. The good in him had been so small, barely noticeable. Now, the good in him was something she could sense with ease, and she knew it was growing, nurtured by however he felt about her and how hard he was trying to change.

For her?

She wasn't sure.

Was it just exposure to her world and the people in it that was changing him, or was he changing himself because of the desire that zinged between them whenever they were together?

He wanted her, just as he had told her after he had protected her from the Hell's angel and had turned on his own kind, and he was willing to go against everyone, his master included, to have her.

He had saved her when she had fallen into Hell, taking the impact and shielding her in his arms.

He had gone off to face his master and had ordered his hellhounds to protect her and keep her safe in his absence.

He cared about her.

She cared about him too.

He didn't need to change in order for her to feel something for him. She desired him as he was and could see the good in him, and she wanted to be with him. Screw convention and what everyone else thought about him. She wanted him.

Liora turned away from the cupboard and frowned at the long rectangular stone table that stretched across the room before her.

In the middle of it was organised chaos.

Scraps of parchment mingled with pencil stubs, crayons, pastels and paints. There was a hotchpotch collection of scraggly paintbrushes that had seen better days in a stained glass jar.

Next to them was a large black bulging folder held closed by an elastic strap around the middle.

A portfolio?

Liora's heart thumped as she reached for it. She was going too far now, probing too much, but she wanted to see this side of Asmodeus. She had wanted the truth about him, and she had heard that an artist's work was often a reflection of their mood and inner self.

She wanted to see beyond the veil of darkness he wore like a shield to the man beneath.

Romulus and Remus whined as she drew the portfolio across the table to her and slipped the elastic off. She glanced at them where they sat beside her, their red eyes almost level with hers.

"I just want a peek. Don't tell him, okay?" she whispered, her fingers paused at their devious work.

The hellhounds settled, lying at her feet, and she took it as them giving her their consent.

Liora's heart set off at a pace again, spreading prickly heat through her veins. She shouldn't do this. What if Apollyon was right and there was only darkness in Asmodeus?

Asmodeus had told her that he took pleasure from inflicting pain, inciting fear and being cruel. His drawings were likely to be a reflection of that and his environment, images of demons and mutilations, of torture and bloodshed.

She hesitated, afraid of what she would find now, unsure whether she had the strength to look inside Asmodeus's soul through his drawings.

Liora took a deep breath, closed her eyes, and flipped the portfolio open.

She sucked down another breath and quickly opened her eyes, settling them straight on the first sheet of paper.

Her eyebrows shot up.

It was Romulus and Remus, sleeping curled together beside a fireplace that she recognised.

Liora lifted her gaze from the charcoal drawing to the ornate black fireplace opposite her. Her eyes drifted left, towards the end of the table. A tall-backed black throne stood there, close to the fireplace.

Asmodeus had sat there and drawn his faithful friends.

She looked back down at the picture. It was good, done with a skilled hand and far better than she had expected. He had talent. Then again, he had probably been drawing for thousands of years. He'd had time to hone what natural talent he might have had, especially if what Apollyon had said was true and he didn't need to sleep when in this realm.

Liora carefully eased the drawing aside to slowly reveal the one beneath, taking her time in case it was a gross image and one she didn't want to see.

It was another painting of his hellhounds, done in shades of grey. Beneath it was another one and then another. Were they all of Romulus and Remus?

She skipped forwards and paused once again, her breath leaving her.

Before her was a beautiful colourful painting.

A lush green landscape with rolling hills, a sparkling river that snaked through the scene, and a rustic stone bridge. The detail was amazing and she could see that he had taken great pains to create something close to real, even though he only had second-hand equipment.

He had never left Hell yet he had drawn a picture of the mortal world.

Liora moved to the next picture. It was a bustling square in what appeared to be a European city, with elegant pale stone buildings, packed cafés with colourful parasols, a beautiful white marble fountain with a statue of a nude powerful male in the centre, and a stretching blue sky.

Liora quickly shifted it aside so she could see the next painting and then the next. It was scene after beautiful vivid scene. From pirate ships on wild seas populated by mermaids embracing sailors in the frothy dark waves, to ancient ruins deep in the rainforest with a jaguar prowling through them, to frosty forbidding and desolate mountains, and all manner of scenes with people in them.

Festivals and celebrations, all of them buzzing with life and bursting with colour.

The more she saw, the more she felt how deeply Asmodeus had longed to see the mortal world, so much so that he had painted it so he could see it whenever he wanted. Because he couldn't see it for real?

Was it that he had never left Hell before meeting her or that he had never been allowed to leave Hell?

Liora traced her fingers over a painting of Paris from the air, a scene that she had seen from his arms.

How had he truly felt when he had seen this image with his own eyes?

When she had asked him whether he liked the view, he had told her that it felt alien to him and colourful, and had made her feel that he didn't like it. She wanted to ask him whether he had really felt that way or whether he had been excited to see it, but she feared how he would react if he knew she had been snooping at his private things.

She carefully stacked all of the pictures, closed the hard black cover over them and snapped the elastic strap into place.

Liora stroked her hand over the portfolio, staring at it, lost deep in her thoughts of Asmodeus. Complicated was definitely an understatement.

She turned away, went back to the books on witchcraft, and selected the one she knew she could read. She set it down on the long stone table and thumbed through it. Her coven would kill for this book and probably go to war for the others Asmodeus owned.

Romulus and Remus perked up. They whined and she looked down at them. Both of them had their ears pricked, as if they were listening to something.

"What is it?" she whispered, afraid it really was an intruder this time.

Black smoke swirled at the end of the room and the hellhounds rose to their paws before her, their focus locked on the shifting shadowy ribbons.

Liora's eyes widened as a leg appeared through the portal, covered in blood and laced with dark gashes. A hand followed it, groping forwards as if looking for support, equally caked with blood.

Her heart stopped dead.

Asmodeus.

He stepped through the portal, stumbled into the table and grasped it. The black ribbons behind him dissipated and he slumped, barely remaining upright.

Romulus and Remus trotted forwards, lowering their heads and pinning their ears back as they moved, whining to each other.

Liora rushed behind them, cursing her ankle when it slowed her down. "What happened?"

Asmodeus growled and looked up at her through the wild black lengths of his hair, his eyes glowing crimson. Dirt and blood covered almost every inch of him. He rolled his shoulder, grimaced, and reached under his left arm with his right hand, supporting all of his weight on his left. She gasped when he roared, his face twisting in agony, and his hand came away coated in fresh blood. He opened his fingers and a three-inch black dagger-like shard fell from it, clattering on the table.

"Asmodeus," she whispered and swallowed hard when he moved around the table ahead of her and she saw the state of his back and his legs. More of those spikes of black rock stuck out of his skin, rivers of blood leaking from the wounds.

The two hellhounds followed him and she followed them, rounding the table.

"Asmodeus... tell me what happened," she said in a firmer tone, losing her patience. He was a mess. He had gone to the Devil to report and he had come back like this, and something told her she was lucky he had come back at all.

He paused, wavered on his feet and slammed his left hand onto the stone table, leaning heavily on it. A grunt left him. His black wings shrank into his back and disappeared, revealing the full extent of his injuries. Magic spiralled lazily around her hands, brought forth by her concern and her deep desire to heal him. It would use what little power she had managed to regain, but she owed him. He had been hurt because of her. She knew it.

"I failed. I was not strong enough," he husked, his voice raspy and thick, gravelly. She could barely make out the words. "I could not defeat him."

He had fought for her.

Liora shoved past Romulus and Remus, earning a dark growl from both of them, and laid her hand against an injured spot on Asmodeus's right shoulder.

"Asmodeus," she whispered and he looked over his shoulder at her, pain in his red eyes.

She had never had a man fight for her before. Even in the battlefield against demons, the male witches of her coven had always let her handle herself, never moving to protect her as they would some of the other females.

Asmodeus had been fighting for her since the moment they had met, and it touched her deeply, leaving her feeling shaken for the first time in decades. Her heart whispered that he was a man she could depend upon, could lean on when she needed strength and count on to protect her.

She didn't have to stand alone anymore.

She could trust someone to have her back and keep her safe.

Her hands shook and her heart ached, a deep dull throb in her chest.

The last time she had relied on anyone like that was back when she was a child. She had depended on her parents, and they had died, and she hadn't depended on anyone since then. Part of her wanted to give Asmodeus that trust and that duty, but the rest of her feared that by doing so, she would give all of herself to him and be left with nothing. She would weaken herself by relying on him so much.

He swallowed hard and his gaze narrowed, the pain in it increasing, causing golden flickers to break through the red until his irises burned like fire.

Liora steadied her breathing and fought for the words, words she found difficult to voice because they had meaning. They resonated with echoes of her past, of a time she didn't want to remember, and threatened to bring back all the pain. She had long ago given up saying things that allowed another to see a part of her she hid behind bravado and fearlessness.

Asmodeus deserved to hear them though. He deserved to see that what he had done had touched her because no one had fought to protect her in what felt like forever.

"You didn't fail me. I'm safe because of you... because you fought for my sake. Let me heal you."

He snarled, flashing vicious fangs, and shoved away from her. He only made it a few stumbling steps before he quickly grasped the table again. She gasped when his knees gave out and he hit the floor hard. He leaned forwards, his left hand clutching the edge of the table and his right one pressing into the black tiles beneath him.

Liora raced to him and kneeled behind him, placing both of her hands on his back. "Asmodeus, please."

He didn't respond, but he didn't push her away either. She took it as a sign that he was willing to allow her to help him.

She sat back and looked him over, inspecting the full length of his back. She wasn't sure where to begin. It was going to hurt like hell no matter which splinter of black rock she chose to remove first. She decided to begin at his shoulders, where the wounds didn't look as deep. He growled with each sliver of rock she removed, his big body tensing as she tugged, wriggled and eased each one out of his flesh and then quickly used her magic to stem the flow of blood from the hole.

His claws extended, black sharp points digging into the stone beneath him and the table top, scratching the hard surfaces and leaving vicious grooves.

Liora moved down his back, flinching with each splinter she carefully removed, unsure whether it was better to pull them out quicker or slower. Either way seemed to pain him greatly and unsettled his hellhounds. They growled each time he did, snarling close behind her, their breath hot on the back of her neck.

She swallowed when she reached the last shard of rock. It stuck out of his back above his right hip, as thick as her wrist and jagged, piercing him in several places at an upwards angle, as if he had slid onto it.

"How did this happen?" she murmured as she stroked the area around the wound, building up the courage to pull it out. It was going to hurt worse than the previous ones and she didn't want to inflict that sort of pain on Asmodeus.

She focused on the area, funnelling her magic into his skin, numbing it to take at least some of the pain he would feel away.

"Weak," he grumbled and her heart went out to him, not only because he hadn't been strong enough to defeat the Devil for her sake, but because she knew that her helping him made him feel weak too, unable to take care of himself as he was used to. He had to learn to rely on others too and lean on them when the time was right. They both needed to learn that it wasn't a crime to depend on someone.

Liora closed her eyes, curled her hand around the shard and yanked it out in one swift stroke.

Asmodeus arched forwards and roared.

Romulus and Remus snarled right behind her, closer than before.

Asmodeus barked something dark in his demonic tongue and the two hellhounds backed off, allowing Liora a moment to swallow her heart back down from her mouth.

He tightened his grip on the table and hauled himself up. There were deep wounds on the backs of his thighs too. She reached out to touch them, to heal them, and he moved beyond her, slowly working his way forwards.

Liora remained kneeling, shocked by the state of him and what he had endured.

Romulus and Remus followed him.

Asmodeus trudged to the end of the long table and grimaced as he settled himself on his black throne. Even with his wounds, he looked like a dark prince, noble and wild, and dangerous. Romulus and Remus went to him and laid at his feet on either side of the throne, completing the picture for her.

No. As he sat there with his muscular thighs spread and hands curled over the ornate ends of the arm rests, battered and bloodied, fresh from a fight, with that fire smouldering in his eyes, he was every bit a king and he knew it.

She could see the confidence in him at last. Here in this castle, in his domain, he was finally sure of himself and she had never seen anything as sexy as Asmodeus when he was sure of himself.

It was alluring and enticing.

He had seemed powerful to her in Paris but in this hellish realm, he was king and she had the damnedest urge to kneel at his feet and kiss her way up his thighs until her king knew the pleasures of a woman's mouth on his flesh. She ached to show him carnal delight and see this confidence blossom into something more—the sexy self-assuredness of a man who had power and someone to share it with.

Liora got to her feet and approached him slowly, her magic still curling around her hands, itching to heal him because it was her heart's true desire. He wearily lifted his right hand and raked the black hair from his face, his eyes closing as he leaned back into his throne.

Her desire to heal him increased when she noticed the reason why his voice was rougher than before.

Black bruising banded across the entire front of his throat. The Devil had crushed it.

Asmodeus opened his eyes and stared at her, and the sudden fear in them frightened her. She had never seen him so afraid and vulnerable. It made her want to lift his spirits somehow and reassure him that this would never happen again. He would heal and grow stronger, and if he crossed swords with the Devil again, he would defeat him.

She stopped before him and dropped her gaze to his bare chest and the wounds that peppered it.

"Let me heal you." She wasn't going to give him a choice but he would feel better about it if he thought that he was getting one.

He nodded, shifted on the seat and settled his arms back on the ornate ones of the throne, and curled his fingers over the ends. His grip on them tightened, his black claws digging into the stone. Bracing himself.

It would hurt, and she wished that she could do something so it wouldn't, but she had only a fraction of her power left and she would need it all to seal the worst of his wounds.

She could distract him though, talk to him and take his mind off what she was doing.

Liora stepped between his knees and lowered her hands to his throat. First, she needed to make sure he could speak without hurting himself. Asmodeus closed his eyes, frowned, and then opened them again and looked up at her, straight into her eyes.

"Ready?" she whispered and he gave a curt nod.

She channelled her power through her hands, focusing on healing and soothing, on giving him relief from his pain. He grimaced, his handsome face distorting into a dark expression, and she silently apologised to him. She didn't want to hurt him. She wanted to help him.

The bruising around his throat gradually faded and she could feel him healing, feel the flesh knitting back together beneath the surface and his body mending.

She drew her hands away, leaving her magic to continue working on that area as it faded, and moved on to his chest. Her head turned and fatigue crashed over her but she held on, refusing to succumb to the pressing need to sleep. Serenity had told her that healing immortals was a huge drain on her magic and Liora hadn't believed her until now. She could feel her energy dropping faster than she had ever experienced before today and she had only healed a few of his wounds. She had to hold on until she had closed at least the major ones.

"You have a lot of stuff," she said, trying to keep her voice light and airy so he didn't see the toll that healing him was taking on her.

He didn't take his eyes off hers. "The Devil used to bring me things during the times when he could leave Hell. Not all of the items are from him. Some are from Hell's angel captains, and some are belongings of people and demons left in Hell after their deaths."

She was glad his voice was back to its normal delicious gruff baritone.

He had been a very busy collector. He must have taken the items whenever he had come across them, scouring the land for them to bring back to his home.

"You're like a magpie," she said with a smile and glanced behind her at the Egyptian cat on the far cupboard. "Some of these items are hundreds or thousands of years old. How old are you?"

"Ancient," he said and then grimaced as another of his wounds closed.

Liora moved on to the next, a particularly nasty gash down his left biceps. "Thousands of years old?"

He nodded.

She shifted her gaze from his incredible body to his face. It was hard to think that he was thousands of years old but had only just experienced his first kiss and had his first trip to the mortal realm and his first taste of food. She couldn't believe all that, especially the kissing part. She also couldn't resist finding out for sure whether her suspicion was correct.

"Have you ever kissed before?" She finished healing his arm and realised that only minor wounds remained. She would have to leave them or tend to them in a more conventional manner, or she was going to pass out.

"No." That was a very blunt and brusque reply.

Liora held her smile inside and snuck a glance at him out of the corner of her eye. "Would you like to do it again?"

His gaze darkened, his pupils gobbling up his gold and crimson irises. "Yes."

She couldn't contain her smile now. She liked his short, snappish replies and the way desire flared in his eyes as he looked at her lips.

She had never had a man look at her like that before, as if he wanted to devour her and possess her. It excited her.

Liora ran her hands over his thighs, earning a low growl for her efforts. She wanted to curl up on them and fall asleep until her magic had replenished itself, but she couldn't. She had to find a way back to her world, far away from this one and the Devil. Right now, she didn't have the strength to teleport out of Hell, and wasn't even sure if it would work if she tried. She knew how to teleport in her world but the rules were different here. This wasn't her world and she would probably need to learn the trick to bending space in this realm before she could teleport.

"Can you take me home?" she said and knew from the way his eyes darkened that he didn't like that request.

"No, not yet." He leaned back again and stared up at her as she stepped back, trailing her hands off his thighs and coming to stand a few feet away from him. She frowned at him, taking in the number of injuries that remained on his body and how weak he had been when he had first returned through the portal.

He wasn't in any condition to transport her out of this realm and neither was she.

"It is not safe right now," he said and Romulus sat up beside him. Asmodeus stroked him between his ears, his gaze still locked on her. "Later."

The intensity of his gaze on her and her awareness of him increased, until the world around her fell away and she was aware of only him and the feelings flowing through her, lighting up her blood like firecrackers and reigniting her desire.

Before her sat a powerful male, bloodstained and beaten because he desired to protect her, a dark and wicked angel capable of incredible evil and absolute good. A king of demons on his throne.

He was everything cruel and vicious, dangerous and deadly, and the tiny sensible part of her heart said that she should fear this man. She was in his world now, a land of shadows and terror, and he wasn't going to let her go. He wanted to keep her here in his castle and that alone should scare her and make her want to leave.

Funny, but all she could think about was crawling onto his lap and satisfying her need for him.

"Will you kiss me again, Liora?" he husked and a hot shiver went through her, causing fire to pool in her belly. "I would like that."

It was all the confirmation her remaining sensible part needed. He could take her home if he wanted to, but he was enjoying having her here in his castle, all to himself, away from her cousin and his twin.

Sensible Liora said to demand that he take her home.

Wicked Liora crushed that tiny voice, obliterating it.

This beautiful deadly male before her was such a contradiction, a mixture of innocence and experience. She liked the way he looked at her as if he wanted to devour her. She liked that he didn't want to let her leave now that he had her in his home. She loved that he didn't care about anyone, but he seemed to care about her.

She liked that she could tease him and he would find a way to compromise and please her.

He would do anything to keep her.

"Unlike you, I do need to eat when I'm in Hell. I'll starve if you keep me here."

He frowned and folded his arms across his chest, causing his muscles to bunch and tense in a way that stoked the fire in her belly, making it overflow into her veins again, heating her to a thousand degrees.

"I enjoyed my first experience of food. It was interesting. Sweet. I would like to eat more. I want to experience other food."

"We can do that." She was tempted to mention that he would have to leave Hell to procure said food and therefore he could take her with him, but resisted. She couldn't resist teasing him a little more to get a reaction from him though. Proof of innocence, as it were. "I know what caffeine does to angels so we'll keep away from that."

His frown deepened. "What does it do?"

Liora motioned a rising action with her rigid right index finger, swinging it slowly upwards, and pointedly looked down at his black loincloth and the worn strips of armour covering it.

Asmodeus's eyes went wide and a blush darkened his cheeks, visible even through the blood and grime. He looked down at his crotch and then up into her eyes.

"It will make me hard?"

Liora blushed worse than he was from the blunt way he said that when she had been too afraid to say it aloud. It wasn't like her. Normally, she was forward and spoke her mind without blushing. She had been blushing like a maiden around Asmodeus though, as if she was the one verging on her first time.

"Get me food then… if you want me to stay here for a while." She cursed under her breath as those words left her in a stuttering unsteady manner.

Asmodeus nodded. "I will feed you and take care of your needs."

Liora bit her lower lip and tried not to jump on that one, but she failed dramatically. "All of my needs?"

He blushed again but quickly recovered. His golden gaze darkened with desire and she shivered under the intensity of it.

"All of them," he growled and swiftly stood and closed the gap between them.

He brushed the knuckles of his right hand across her face, tunnelled his fingers into her chestnut hair and grasped it tightly. Liora gasped when he tugged her head backwards and banded his other arm around her, holding her immobile and powerless. His hungry gaze fell to her lips. He growled again, a husky feral sound that thrilled her, dropped his head and kissed her hard, devouring her mouth and dominating her. She melted into him, helpless against the force of his kiss and the pleasure that swept through her in response.

Liora ran her palms down his bare chest and pressed her short nails into his pectorals. He growled into her mouth and kissed her harder, his tongue tangling with hers, stoking her own passion until she battled him for dominance and could think only of satisfying her incredible need for her powerful wicked angel.

Asmodeus tightened his grip on her long hair and snarled as he deepened the kiss, taking all of her, driving her into submission. She went willingly, allowing him to master her and take the lead, letting him pour out his passion and feeling it flow over her.

This was the passion she had felt locked within him.

Passion she had awakened.

Passion she would unleash.

CHAPTER 9

All Liora wanted to do was keep kissing Asmodeus until her lips went numb and every inch of her tingled, but the longer he kissed her, clutching her possessively against his chest, the more she could taste ash and blood.

His blood.

Liora reluctantly pressed her palms against the rock-hard muscles of his chest and eased him back, breaking the kiss. He growled and tried to pull her back to him, but she sighed and stood her ground, barely.

Asmodeus drew back, righting her in the process and setting her back on her feet, and narrowed his gaze on her. He wasn't pleased. Maybe she could do something about that.

She walked her fingers over his dirty chest. "I don't suppose you have water in Hell?"

The fire that had been dying in his irises sparked right back up into an inferno and the corners of his lips tilted into a wicked smile.

"There is a pool in which I regularly bathe, sheltered by rocks. It is akin to what you mortals think of as natural hot baths." His grip on her loosened and he looked her over, a frown marring his handsome face. No doubt she looked like a mess too now, spotted with blood from his wounds. His gaze roamed back up to devour her lips and then ventured onwards, meeting hers. "You wish to bathe?"

She nodded and then let out a wicked smile of her own. "I wish to bathe you."

His heart slammed against her palms and his pupils expanded, blotting out the colour in his eyes and turning them dark with passion that she was surprised he managed to wrestle into submission. There was a fleeting moment where he looked as if he was on the verge of tugging her back against him and kissing her again, and then he was taking another step backwards, beyond her reach.

Asmodeus stared hard at her for long seconds, his breathing coming quicker and quicker, and then tipped his chin up, squared his jaw and exhaled. The picture of calm and confidence once more, he threw his hand out behind him, casting one of his portals there.

Romulus and Remus got to their paws and panted. Remus's ear flopped and his tongue lolled out of his mouth, hooking on his black fangs.

Asmodeus petted Romulus and then righted Remus's ear for him, and gave them both a grave look. "Protect the castle while I am gone."

"Will they understand you if you speak in English to them?" Liora studied the two hellhounds. Asmodeus had mentioned that they could speak telepathically to each other. She would love to find a spell that would allow her to talk with them. She was sure they would have countless stories to tell her and would dish up the dirt on their master.

"They will learn." Asmodeus caught both hellhounds under their jaws, cupping them in his dirty palms and tipping their heads up so their eyes locked on him.

He spoke in the dark tongue of his world and Romulus and Remus began panting again. Liora took that as a yes, because Asmodeus grabbed her around the wrist and pulled her into the portal.

There was a horrible rush of cold darkness over her skin that made her shiver and made her magic tremble in her veins, and then she was standing at the edge of the black plain she had seen stretching below the castle. Steaming pools dotted the cragged ground before her, at least seven of them and all of them different in temperature and depth judging by how some were boiling viciously and black as tar. A rocky jagged wall curved around the pools, shielding them from view on one side. The open side faced the fortress and the plain. Beyond the wall was a rough, hilly landscape that rose almost as high as the spire of rock upon which the castle stood.

Liora looked over her shoulder at it. From a distance, it was magnificent and imposing, a black bastion that had a horror movie vibe that could make even the bravest demon think twice about dropping in for a visit.

Now that she was on the ground, she could see that it wasn't as flat as she had imagined it from above. She frowned at the regular lines scored into the black basalt, intersecting each other, and paced the length of one of the rectangles they formed. Liora looked back up at the fortress.

"It's a quarry," she whispered.

"I needed stone from a local source." Asmodeus's voice was so close to her shoulder that she jumped at the sound of it and looked over at him. His golden eyes roamed the fortress above them, a hint of pride in their beautiful depths.

Her eyes widened. "You built it?"

He looked down at her, his expression turning perplexed. "Of course."

"No 'of course'. I figured you had an army of demon slaves build it for you." She really had. It hadn't once crossed her mind that Asmodeus might have constructed this fortress.

Alone.

Always alone.

Even a project of this magnitude was handled alone. It must have taken him centuries to carve each stone and place it, gradually building up the incredible towers and the walls of his home.

"Things are rarely as people figure." He turned away from her.

She supposed he was right. Everyone figured Asmodeus was evil incarnate and she could certainly prove them wrong about that now.

Liora bit her tongue before she could ask where he had slept while building it. He didn't sleep. He didn't eat. He had probably worked tirelessly, toiling non-stop, to build the castle towering above them. His home. A place designed to keep others out. Did he want to be alone or did he want company but found Hell lacking in the variety he desired?

He certainly seemed to be embracing the thought of having her stay with him in his immense empty fortress.

"It is only safe to bathe in one of the pools. Come." He grasped her wrist and tugged her with him, leading her through the narrow strips of lumpy black ground between the rocky-edged bubbling pools towards the largest one at the back. It steamed gently, mist curling and rising, dancing across its placid surface, and was paler than the others too, a milky quality to the water.

"Is it really safe?" She eyed it suspiciously. It did look a little more inviting than she had imagined water would in this inhospitable land, but she still couldn't bring herself to trust it.

"It is safe, Liora. I would never allow anything to happen to you." Asmodeus released her hand, bent at the edge of the pool with effort and a serious grimace that she pretended not to see, and ran his hand through the water. He rose to stand before her and held up his hand, a smile teasing his lips. "See, it has not melted off my fingers or done me any harm. Come."

He held his hand out with his palm facing her and she sucked down a breath for courage and then pressed her fingers against his wet ones. Nothing happened other than a jolt of electricity shocking every nerve along her arm as they touched. Asmodeus's eyes darkened again and her pulse picked up, nerves kicking it into overdrive.

If she bathed him as she had said she wanted to then she wasn't going to stop there. Once she laid her hands on the delicious six-foot-plus of sexy before her, she wouldn't be able to resist the temptation to take things to the next level. Once she pushed him over that ledge, there would be no coming back. He wouldn't settle for just a taste of her. She knew that. He would want all of her and she would be powerless to deny him.

"You're sure people can't see us here?" She cast a glance around at the hills above and the plain behind her.

"The only people in Hell are in the Devil's prisons... but demons do not come here, and nor do Hell's angels. We are alone, Liora."

And he liked it. She could hear it in his voice and the way it dropped to a sultry growl. He had her all to himself and he was in his element, and there would be no stopping him now. He wanted her. She shivered at the thought of him touching her, teasing her flesh with his warm tongue and scraping fangs over her breasts, her thighs. Her belly fluttered and heated.

"You think wicked things," Asmodeus drawled in a gruff, thick voice heavy with hunger and passion.

She nodded and bit her lower lip. She thought very wicked things indeed, and now that she had him all to herself and he was in his element, there would be no stopping her.

Liora stepped towards him and trailed her fingers down his bare chest and over the hard ridges of his stomach. She lingered close to his navel before running her fingertips over the waist of the armour that protected his hips.

"You can't bathe in this," she whispered, shocked by how breathless she sounded. "It'll get rusty."

His lips quirked again and fire filled his eyes, hunger that echoed within her. He captured her hands, held them a moment, and then moved them away from his waist.

Liora stepped back so she could fully admire him as he stripped off the metal armour around his hips, revealing the black loincloth he wore beneath. If she had sounded breathless before, she could barely speak now. He stole her voice as he moved, his powerful cut muscles bunching and relaxing, enticing her to stop him so she could trail her lips over each and every one of them and moan her approval. He bent and removed the armour that protected his shins, and then his black leather boots.

He placed them carefully near the pool and she bit back a smile. He valued what little armour he had and she could understand why. He had already lost vital pieces of it, leaving him exposed and vulnerable. If she could, she would hire the best blacksmiths in the world to craft armour of his liking and give it to him so he felt complete again.

Asmodeus turned his back to her and all rational thought fled at the sight of his delicious backside wonderfully cupped by tight black material. Liora wanted to rip it off with her teeth.

He ran his hands around the waist, paused, glanced back at her and then lowered his hands to his sides. She allowed a small smile to break free at the brief display of nerves and uncertainty. She had meant nude bathing but it seemed he wasn't quite ready to take that step. If she hadn't thought him innocent in that department before, she would have thought it now. He had never been naked before a woman, and she wanted to be his first.

He stepped into the pool and the milky water covered him to his knees. It was deeper than she had expected it to be. On her, the surface would be somewhere around mid-thigh and stepping down into it was going to be a challenge.

Asmodeus moved to the edge of the pool opposite her, casually sat down and ducked his head under the water. Liora wanted a slow-motion replay of the moment he surfaced, droplets of water racing over his dirty skin, pushed his wet black hair back with one hand and pinned her with his intense, fiery eyes.

The confidence in them wavered as she crouched and tested the water for herself. It was hot, maybe a degree or two too much for her taste, but it didn't eat her hand like acid and she really was itching for a bath.

Liora straightened and hesitated only a second before grabbing the hem of her crimson top and pulling it off over her head. She felt Asmodeus's gaze on her stomach the second she revealed it and the intensity of his eyes on her and the way she always felt aware of him made her belly flutter again.

She held it together, refusing to show her nerves, and dropped her top on the ground behind her. Asmodeus's gaze remained rooted on her stomach, darkening by degrees, verging on red again. Clearly, anger wasn't the only emotion that triggered a change in his eyes.

She tackled her belt and was popping the button on her jeans when he caught on and caught up, and his eyes darted down, following her every move as she unzipped her jeans and then pushed them down her legs. It gave her the courage to keep going even as the confidence was draining from his eyes, his nerves surfacing again. She toed off her boots, stepped out of her jeans and straightened so Asmodeus could get a good view of her. She had ogled him after all. It was only fair she let him do the same.

He growled low in his throat, his eyes burning crimson now, swirling with gold fire.

Liora blushed.

It was the first time a man had growled his approval of her slender build and she wasn't going to deny that there was something wicked and sexy about the way he chose to let her know that he liked what he saw. Dangerous.

His confidence was clinging on for dear life though. She could see it in the depths of his eyes and the way they flickered between hers and her body, and the water.

Liora decided to have mercy on him.

He had remained in his underwear-of-sorts. She would remain in hers. Small steps. It wouldn't do to push him too far and make him feel mocked. She had seen how violently he could react to feeling belittled and shamed and she didn't want anything to spoil this moment. She would play things cool, take her time, and let it all progress at a natural speed. Asmodeus was used to being in control. Liora wasn't averse to letting him take the lead. It would be a nice change.

She stepped down into the pool and rather awkwardly ended up almost falling in face first because of the difference in height between the plain and the bottom of the hot spring.

Another blush crept up her cheeks and she masked it by cupping some water and pouring it over her hair, and then slicking it back from her face. Asmodeus didn't seem to notice her embarrassment at all. He was too busy staring at her breasts and the beads of water trailing down her skin and soaking into her black bra.

Liora waded towards him. His expression turned uneasy and he leaned back against the side of the pool and rested his arms along it in what would have been a casual way had he not looked half scared out of his wits.

She held back another smile and sank lower in the middle of the pool, letting it lap at her hips.

A moan escaped her, tugging another husky growl from her dark angel. She wouldn't have been able to hold it in even if she had tried.

The water felt wonderful, hot and steamy, and fresh. The air around the pool didn't smell as much as that around the castle and she breathed deep of it, savouring the slight salty tang that laced it. Minerals? She had done a couple of mineral soaks in her life and had always felt wonderful afterwards. The barely leashed passion in Asmodeus's eyes said she would feel wonderful after this bath too, but it wouldn't be because of the minerals.

"How can you stand the stink in this place?" She remained in the middle of the pool and dipped lower, sinking down to her shoulders, giving him time to build his confidence back up and vanquish his fears.

Asmodeus looked beyond her, towards the fortress, and then off to his right, his gaze distant. "It is far worse near the pit, where the Devil resides and several of the primary lava rivers of Hell converge."

"Lava rivers... how nice. Is this the only water in Hell?"

He shook his head, causing his jet-black hair to spike in places and droplets of water to spill onto his forehead and roll down. Liora wanted to lick them off his skin.

She edged closer.

He bent his right leg, his knee breaching the surface, and tipped his head back, captivating her. She paused again. He was beautiful and wicked, his eyebrows black slashes that cut above his incredible fiery eyes, his jaw strong and straight, and his lips profanely sensual and firm, made for kissing and wicked things. He was beautiful and he didn't know just how handsome he was, and she liked that.

He was nothing like Apollyon. They were similar enough that anyone who met them would think them twins, but they weren't the same. Now that she knew Asmodeus, she could see just how different he was to Apollyon.

It was strange looking at Asmodeus and knowing her cousin was in love with his twin. Liora had never felt attracted to Apollyon. He was too stuffy and haughty, too dull and focused on avoiding trouble, and that took something away from him that even his good looks couldn't make up for.

He lacked the vital spark that Asmodeus had—the instant fire that had ignited the moment she had set eyes on him and now burned between them like an inferno, sweeping through her every time their gazes met or bodies touched.

It wasn't just that fire that attracted her to him though.

She preferred Asmodeus's wild hair and golden eyes, and his wicked personality.

She loved his fearlessness and how he would fight the Devil himself in order to protect her.

He wasn't one for diplomatic solutions and thinking things through before acting.

He was reckless, brash, dangerous and a little bit crazy.

Just like her.

Liora moved silently through the water and settled before him, kneeling between his feet.

He tensed when she reached for his right knee where it breached the surface of the opaque steaming water. Liora held back, fingers hovering an inch above his skin, giving him a chance to become accustomed to this because she had a suspicion this was another first for him.

A suspicion she wanted to hear him confirm.

"No one has ever bathed with you before?" She kept her voice even and calm, betraying none of her nerves or the jealous thoughts slowly surfacing at the back of her mind.

Those black thoughts made her realise that her question was about more than confirming suspicions. She needed to hear him tell her that no other female had been given the pleasure of touching him. She needed it with a ferocity that shocked her. She had never been inclined towards jealous fits before, but then she had never been with a man like Asmodeus, a man she wanted to be all hers and no one else's. She wanted to covet this powerful male sitting before her. She wanted to possess him.

He seemed more relaxed now, his power flowing around her at a sedate level, mingling with her own returning magic. She liked how their powers did that at times, twining together, as if they were lovers.

Asmodeus finally shook his head.

Liora smiled and squashed a few jealous notions. "Would you like me to wash you, Asmodeus?"

"Yes." His tone turned gravelly again, edged with barely restrained hunger. He very much wanted her to wash him.

Her smile widened and then faded when his face fell and his eyes turned cold and empty.

"Have you washed many males?" he bit out, a harsh snap in his voice that made her smile inside although she would never dare let him know that she was on to him.

She liked the jealous hiss in his tone, the dark glowering look on his face, and the possessive way his eyes held hers, as if he was her master now and he would not allow her to refuse to answer. She liked that she wasn't the only one becoming a victim of that snake that lived inside all sentient beings and the vicious words it hissed in their ears.

Liora laid her hand on his right knee and felt a glimmer of his pain and how much waiting for her answer was tormenting him together with other questions he had yet to voice, but she could guess at.

"No, I have never bathed with a man." She slid her hand down his shin to the water, cupped it and brought it up over his knee, gently washing away the grime.

His expression warmed again and she felt him relax beneath her hand.

Liora really couldn't help teasing him. "Does that please you?"

"Yes." Very gruff. She smiled now, unafraid to show that his jealousy pleased her.

"You like that I've only done this with you?"

"Yes."

"Why?" She ran her fingers in expanding circles around his knee, growing outwards from the centre of his kneecap, teasing his fine dark hairs and taking care not to apply any pressure to the black bruise on the left side.

He narrowed his heated gaze on her and the possessive edge it gained thrilled her.

"Because you are mine."

Her heart did a ridiculous fluttering thing over that. She swallowed to stop it. He looked so serious that she felt like teasing him further but her voice failed her.

Liora focused on washing the blood off his thighs beneath the water to quell the urge to kiss him breathless and it wasn't long before he was breathless anyway, leaning back against the edge of the pool with his eyes closed and lips parted, and nostrils flaring as his body tensed with each sweep of her hands. He liked this. He enjoyed how she touched him and being cleaned by her.

She suspected it was more than that though. Everything always had a deeper meaning with this man. He liked what they were doing because she was caring for him, and she knew without a doubt that no one had ever cared for him before, tending to his wounds and washing the blood of battle from his tired body. No one had ever shown him this affection, the softer side of mortal and immortal nature.

Liora ran her palm down his thigh beneath the surface, feeling the strength in his toned sinewy muscles, enjoying this moment too.

The milky water hid everything beneath the surface from view but Liora was a betting woman and she had good odds that if she moved her hands a few inches east, she would find him steel-hard and straining against his loincloth.

She cursed the water. She wanted to see just what sort of weapon this man concealed down there.

Liora moved closer and he spread his thighs to accommodate her, inviting her in. Her knees hit his backside and she moved to his left thigh, cleaning it with the same care as she had his other one. The water began to turn muddy with blood around them. She didn't care. She was entranced by how fiercely Asmodeus reacted to every innocent sweep and stroke of her palms.

He would look at her one moment with such fire in his eyes that she felt she was going to get burned, and then tip his head back and growl the next, exposing his short fangs and causing every muscle of his honed delicious torso to tense and delight her.

She finished with his legs and carefully washed his face, giving him a moment to get his breathing back under control and slowing things down. He was used to her touching him here, brushing his sculpted cheeks with her fingers, tracing the firm curve of his lower lip with the pad of her thumb. His lips parted and his breath was cool on her overheated flesh, teasing her and sending goose bumps rushing up her arms.

Mother Earth, she wanted to kiss him. The hunger for it twisted her stomach into knots and heated her belly.

Liora forced herself to finish her work first and swept her hands down his neck, careful to keep her motions lighter whenever she was cleaning where the heaviest bruising had been. She stroked his Adam's apple and stared at it, lost in her thoughts and feeling her magic come to a rolling boil in her veins.

"You are... annoyed. Why?" Asmodeus's deep voice pulled her up from the quagmire of her thoughts and she raised her eyes to meet his. Confusion shone in them.

"He crushed your windpipe, didn't he?" She skimmed her fingertips over his throat, remembering how black the bruises had been, and how badly he had been hurt.

Annoyed was putting it mildly. She had rarely felt this angry. It was dangerous for her to let her emotions rule her like this. Her power could easily slip beyond her control, her feelings taking the reins and driving her to let go of all reason and fight without restraint. It had happened a few times, most notably when her parents had been taken from her. She had destroyed many lives that night in the maelstrom of her rage and pain.

"Yes." Water splashed as he lifted his hand from beneath the surface and caught hers, gently holding it to his throat. The touch soothed her, calming her rising magic until it simmered back down to a steady undercurrent in her blood. "It is nothing I would not have healed."

"How can you say that... as if it was nothing?" she snapped and snatched her hand back, her rough sudden movements sending small waves rippling outwards across the pool's surface. Her magic spiked again, blistering her blood, her fury demanding she unleash it and make Asmodeus's master pay for his sin of harming her angel. "He tried to kill you... he's a bastard... a vicious, evil, conniving bastard, and I want his head for what he did to you."

Asmodeus caught her hand and gently drew her back to him. He kissed her fingers one by one, the action calming her and settling her heart in her chest, soothing the rampant magic in her veins.

"I would endure far worse to keep you safe, my sweet little mortal. Besides, the punishment he meted out for my disrespect and disobedience has had its own rewards." The wickedness of his smile told her that he meant what they were doing now.

He had been beaten, bruised, and stabbed multiple times by shards of black rock, and then had his throat crushed, and he took it in his stride because she was bathing with him as a result of the pain his master had inflicted upon him? She couldn't be as forgiving. She wanted the Devil dead for what he had done to Asmodeus.

"I still want his head," she grumbled and he sighed.

"It would not be wise. To collect his head, you would have to seek him out. It is what he wants. He wants you, Liora, and if you go to him to seek out retribution for what he did to me, he would have you. Do not doubt that. You are not powerful enough to defeat him." Asmodeus released her hand and smoothed his palm across her cheek. "Do not give him what he desires. Do not make what I suffered worth nothing."

Liora stilled and absorbed what he had said. He was right. If she tracked down the Devil, she would end up his prisoner, and everything Asmodeus had gone through would have been for nothing.

She lowered her gaze to his chest and then lifted it again, meeting his.

"He still wants you to take me to him, doesn't he?"

Asmodeus hesitated and then nodded. "I will resist... but I believe it is the reason he allowed me to remain alive rather than killing me once I had fallen unconscious. He still has a use for me."

The earnest look in his golden eyes spoke to her heart, telling it that he would do his best to go against his master's orders, resisting his command to take her to him. She brushed her fingers across his throat, her gaze falling there.

The Devil had rendered him unconscious and must have left him then, leaving him exposed and vulnerable, at the mercy of any passing demon or Hell's angel. She tried to calm her anger but it spiked back up again, burning fiercer than ever as she pictured Asmodeus laying bloodied and beaten, out cold.

Alone.

What if he hadn't come around when he had or hadn't been left with enough power to create a portal to take him to his castle? What would have happened to him then?

Asmodeus captured her hand, brought it to his lips and pressed a long kiss to it.

"Sweet Liora..." he murmured against her fingers and closed his eyes. "It touches me that you desire to punish my master for my sake, but bothers me too. Let go of this desire... it is what he wants you to feel and how he wants you to act. Do not give him the satisfaction."

She nodded, drew their joined hands towards her and kissed a gash on the back of his.

"Sorry," she whispered and sighed, pushing out all of her anger and irritation, and letting it go. Here she was with a gorgeous man, almost naked, in a hot spring, and she was thinking about spilling blood. Something was very wrong with her. "I won't do anything stupid… but I can't help how I feel."

Asmodeus smiled at her, as if she had given him a beautiful gift with those words, and she blushed and dropped his hand and her gaze at the same time.

She set back to work on cleaning him, taking her time as she washed his chest, slowly revealing his bronzed skin beneath all the blood and black dirt. She luxuriated in running her fingers down his stomach and feeling his muscles quiver beneath her touch, a sign of his returning nerves, and found her willpower lacking once again when she reached the waist of his loincloth beneath the water.

She accidentally brushed the extremely impressive bulge in his loincloth.

Asmodeus moved faster than she could see, snagging her hands and pulling them free of the water, holding them away from him.

She was ready with a false apology when she lifted her gaze to his, expecting to see brooked desire in his eyes.

There was only endless darkness.

His grip on her wrists tightened, crushing her bones together, and she flinched.

"How many males have you touched like this?" he barked, his voice loud as it echoed around the steep hills surrounding the black plain.

The edge to his eyes said that he didn't really want to know. She could see he was running numbers through his head, numbers that he didn't like, males he felt he needed to compete with and best.

Liora extricated her hands from his grasp and rubbed her sore wrists before gently taking hold of his hands. She looked deep into his eyes, seeing his need to know what he was up against, how experienced she was, and how much that set him on edge.

"I have touched men like this, but I have only had one lover."

He didn't look relieved to hear that. Liora moved closer and released his hands. She ran her palms up his chest, leaned in, and softly captured his lips with hers. His large hands claimed her waist and he slanted his head and kissed her, delving his tongue between her lips. She met it, tangling them together, losing herself all over again.

Asmodeus pulled her against him and her breasts pressed into his chest, her knees hit his backside, and his rested against her hips. His hands slipped over her hips and clutched her bottom, his fingertips pressing in so hard that it bordered on painful. Were his claws out? The thought of him using them to shred her knickers had moisture pooling between her thighs.

"I love the way you kiss me," she whispered against his lips, teasing him with flicks of her tongue over them. "It's as if you can't get enough of me. Can't you?"

His voice dropped, low and serious, heart-meltingly sexy. "No. *Never*. The more I taste these lips… the more I hunger for them."

Liora smiled against his mouth. "No man has ever talked to me like you do… and I love it too."

He pushed her back and searched her eyes, his all swirling red and gold, as on fire as she felt inside. He looked as though he thought she was wonderful for saying such a thing.

If he thought that her honest words were wonderful, he would think her a goddess and be screaming her name at the top of his lungs when she showed him what other things she could do with her mouth.

CHAPTER 10

Liora was mistaken.

She might be the one screaming his name at the top of her lungs.

Asmodeus had a wicked way of kissing, palming her backside in time with each hard flick of his tongue across her lips and playful nip with his teeth. She moaned when he caught her lower lip between one short fang and his lip, and pulled it into his mouth before thrusting his tongue inside hers and dominating her once again. The man was a quick study, growing in boldness as his hunger slipped its leash and took control.

Liora leaned into him, her breasts mashed against his hard chest, feeling his heart pounding at the same crazy rhythm as hers. He clutched and squeezed her bottom, fingers inching slowly lower, coming to graze her groin. She moaned and undulated her hips, aching for him to touch her where she needed him most, wanting to feel his fingers on her at last.

He released her mouth, panting hard, his eyes blazing crimson fire that burned her. His chest heaved, delicious and hard, muscles straining and delighting her eyes. She couldn't help herself. She raked her short nails down his pectorals and he hissed in pleasure, his eyes going hooded as he flashed fangs.

She squealed when his hands shot to her waist and he lifted her from the water as if she weighed nothing, and then groaned when he brought her back down astride his hips and she sank down to rub against his hard length. Asmodeus growled and gritted his teeth, the muscle in his jaw flexing as he stared into her eyes, cranking her temperature up with the intensity of his gaze.

Liora grasped his shoulders and rubbed herself along his length, her own hazel eyes going hooded. Mother Earth, she wanted him inside her.

Asmodeus slipped his hands over her thighs and she shivered when he skimmed the inside of them, close to her underwear. He continued downwards to her knees and pushed her back, breaking contact between their bodies. She mewled and tried to get close to him but he held her firm, keeping the distance between them, his gaze commanding her to obey. She didn't want to behave. She wanted all of him.

He released her, swallowed hard, and moved his hands beneath the water. Doing what?

She found out when he took hold of her hand again, pulled it to him, and wrapped it around his naked hard shaft. Mercy. A shiver went through her, hot and achy, spilling bliss through her veins and making her moan. He gripped her hand with his right one, keeping it on his flesh, and began stroking.

Liora hadn't expected him to be this forward but she loved it. She liked how tightly he held her hand around his rigid cock, moving it up and down the full length from crown to root, showing her how to pleasure him.

Asmodeus closed his eyes and tipped his head back, grunting as the rhythm built and she began to move with him, stroking him hard but at a measured pace, one that would give him the most pleasure. His arms tensed, muscles bunching beautifully, and his torso followed, every ridge pronouncing itself. Her heart fluttered and belly heated, and she wanted to find her own pleasure. If he wasn't afraid to show her how he liked to be touched, then she shouldn't be afraid either.

His eyes snapped open when she took hold of his free hand, slowing the tempo of her strokes, keeping him hard but not pushing him towards the edge.

His red gaze followed her as she led his hand under the water towards her. He swallowed hard, throat flexing with it, and stared at the point where their joined hands entered the water, his breath coming faster again.

Liora stroked him hard to take his mind off it and he screwed his face up and rocked his hips, growling as he thrust through the ring of their joined fingers.

She waited until he was deep in his pleasure and then pushed aside her black panties and slipped his fingers into her folds.

Asmodeus stilled right down to his breathing.

Liora didn't stop. She gently held his hand from behind, keeping his palm facing her body, curled his ring and little finger over, and stroked her pert nub with his other two fingers.

His gaze narrowed, burning like an inferno now, and he growled, flashing fangs.

She started stroking him again, slower now, moving their hands in time with each other. Asmodeus was a very quick study. Quicker than she had anticipated. He moved his hand against her, gaze intent on the water, as if he could see through it to her and what he was doing. He wanted to see. He wanted to watch their joined hands touching her.

She could do that.

Liora reluctantly took her hand away from his shaft, earning a growl from him. She wiped the angry look from his face by rising to her feet, coming to stand before him, and shimmying out of her knickers.

Asmodeus stared.

Growled.

His hands shot up from the water, spraying it everywhere, and clutched her hips. He drew her closer, his eyes locked on the thatch of curls between her thighs. Liora took hold of one of his hands and guided it to her, curling his fingers over as before so only two remained. She lifted her left leg, her heart pounding, and settled it on his shoulder, pinning him back against the edge of the pool and revealing herself to him.

He groaned now, the sound desperate and rough, as if she was killing him.

"Touch me," she whispered, and slipped his fingers between her moist folds, bringing them back to where they had been before. "Like this."

She moved his flattened fingers up and down, and then swirled them around. Asmodeus's crimson eyes burned into her, studying everything she did. Her heart pounded, heat rushing through her veins, tingles spreading outwards from her core.

He licked his lips and began mimicking what she had shown him, moving his own fingers, teasing her closer to the edge. She breathed hard, lost in the pleasure rippling through her, aching for the next step. Asmodeus was ahead of her. He dipped his fingers down, found her slick core and growled low in his throat.

"Claws," she uttered before he lost his head and he snatched his hand back, looking for all the world as if she had just told him to back the hell off and get away from her. Liora rocked her hips, too far gone to stop herself, her body demanding release. "No... don't stop... just... keep those bad boys in check... yeah?"

He grunted in response, honed his gaze on her groin and brought his fingers back to her. He swirled his fingers around her nub, bringing her back to a crescendo again, teetering on the edge of bliss, and then eased them downwards. She smiled at how beautifully intense and focused he became, and could almost hear him mentally chanting to keep his claws away. He hesitated. Damn it. She hadn't meant to put him off completely.

"Like this," she murmured and took hold of his hand again, sliding it downwards. She shifted her hips forwards and moaned as she eased two of his fingers into her hot sheath. Asmodeus snarled, his gaze burning her, locked with such intensity that she shivered. He slowly withdrew his fingers and carefully moved them back inside, stroking her sensitive flesh. "Yes... like that. Mother Earth... just like that."

Liora arched her back, tangled her hands in her hair and clutched it to her head, her elbows pointed skywards.

She bit her lip and undulated her hips, riding the slow steady thrust of his fingers, losing herself in the hot shivery pleasure burning through her with each one.

Asmodeus built the pace, gaining confidence, taking her higher. Liora screwed her eyes shut and groaned, her knees trembling and threatening to give out. Not before she climaxed. She just needed a few more seconds. A few more strokes.

The intensity of his gaze on her magnified.

She shrieked when he pulled his fingers from her, grabbed her hips and yanked her forwards. It ended in a moan when her back hit the hot ground next to the pool and Asmodeus buried his head between her thighs, his tongue delving between her plush petals and licking the length of her.

"Oh gods," she moaned and arched her back, rocking her hips against his face, riding that wicked tongue of his.

Oh, he was a natural. A god amongst men.

Liora dug her fingers into his hair, clutching him to her, and settled her legs over his shoulders. He raised her hips and devoured her, stroking and teasing her nub, driving her out of her mind with a need for that one final push. She reached for it, straining and moaning, rocking her hips in search of it.

Asmodeus slowed his attack on her and she wanted to curse him for it until he obliterated her ability to speak by easing his fingers into her.

She was done for.

Liora lasted two long strokes of his fingers before she shattered, crying out as a wave of pleasure so intense that she felt hazy from head to toe crashed over her, sending her thighs quivering against the sides of his head and her mind spinning.

Asmodeus growled between her thighs and she smiled lazily, trembling around his fingers, glad he liked to feel her coming because of his touch.

He withdrew his fingers and lapped the length of her, tasting her flesh and her desire, the release he had wrought from her. She melted into the black basalt, shaking all over, spent and lost, feeling too high to move.

Water splashed over her and she opened her eyes to find Asmodeus above her, his gaze near-black with arousal.

"You taste divine." He rested all of his weight on one arm and stroked her cheek, the light caress tickling her in her sensitized state. "I want to do that again."

"Let me catch my breath." She smiled when he looked disappointed and wiped that expression from his face by curling her fingers around the rigid length of his cock. His eyes turned hooded again, lips parting on a sigh as his nostrils flared. "How about I steal your breath like you did mine?"

He frowned and growled, and she pressed her other hand against his chest, forcing him back as she sat up. He kneeled before her, completely nude and beautiful, his long shaft straining for her attention.

Liora leaned in and licked from root to crown, eliciting a husky moan from him. He was going to be doing a lot more than moaning quietly before long. She swirled her tongue around the thick head and ran her tongue over the slit, tasting his essence. His hands leaped to her shoulders and he clutched them. They were trembling. She smiled at that. He would be shaking all over when she was done with him. She was going to rock his world.

She closed her mouth over the crown and he jerked forwards, thrusting further inside, grunting darkly.

Liora wrapped one hand around his impressive length and let the other drift over his stomach and thighs as she sucked him gently, giving him a moment to get accustomed to the feel of her mouth on his flesh. She eased off him and fluttered her tongue around the dark head, tearing another groan from him, sharply followed by another. He clutched her more tightly, his big body tensing, and she couldn't resist gazing up the height of him.

The sight of his face twisted in pleasure, his eyes screwed shut and fangs sinking into his lower lip, made her quiver inside and reignited her desire. She flexed her pelvic muscles and took him back into her mouth, moaning at the brief aftershock of pleasure. She moved her hand on his length in time with her mouth and he rocked into her, short thrusts that she knew he couldn't help, just as she hadn't been able to stop herself from riding his fingers. He was lost.

Her other hand skimmed downwards, ready to join in the fun now that she had him close to the edge, skirting ecstasy.

She cupped his sac and rolled it gently in her fingers, and he bucked forwards, a harsh moan leaving his lips. That moan turned fierce and guttural when she gave his balls a gentle squeeze and tug, and he thrust through her fingers, rocking his cock into her mouth. His right hand moved to her head, guiding her on him, controlling her movements.

Liora alternated between sucking him and swirling her tongue around the crown, driving him wild, until he had his fingers tangled in her hair and was grunting with each thrust into her mouth and each squeeze of his sac.

He uttered something in the demon tongue and she hoped it was complimentary.

His thrusts hardened, his breathing quickened and his balls tightened. Liora sucked him harder and moved her hand quicker on his flesh, stroking it as he had shown her he liked it, combining it with her hot wet mouth to propel him firmly over the edge.

He growled what might have been her name, every inch of him went as taut as a bowstring, and she looked up the length of him, wanting to see his first climax with her as it claimed him body and soul.

He tossed his head back and roared in a vicious yet sexy way as he shot his hot seed into her mouth and she swallowed around him. His fangs extended, his claws pressed into her skin, and his wings erupted from his back.

Delicious.

She sucked him softly, drawing out his climax, feeling him throb and jerk, continuing to spill himself in short bursts. He breathed hard, body straining and muscles covered in a fine sheen. Liora released him and ran her hands over his trembling hips.

His eyes slowly opened and dropped to her, blazing red and filled with an explosive combination of satisfaction and need, hunger for more.

She liked that look in them. The one that left her feeling that he would never get enough of her. The one that backed up his earlier words.

Because you are mine.

She believed in equality, and if she were a little braver, she might have voiced the words that echoed in her heart. Because you are mine.

His gaze narrowed on hers and he captured her jaw with his right hand, lifted her chin, leaned down and kissed her. It was soft and sweet, tender, and it melted her inside. She savoured it and this side of him, the one that he showed only to her.

He broke the kiss, stood and pulled her up onto her feet, wrapping his wings around her. Shielding her from any prying eyes.

He didn't want anyone else to see her like this. She didn't want any demon bitches getting a good look at her man all naked and sated either.

Liora snapped her fingers, using a fraction of her returning power to get his damp loincloth back in place. He raised an eyebrow at her, his red eyes silently questioning her.

She found her voice.

"Because you are mine."

CHAPTER 11

Mine.

Asmodeus sat on his throne, dressed in his armour again, watching Liora drying her beautiful chestnut hair using the fire he had built for her as she sat on the rug between the fireplace and the table. Romulus lay beside him on the floor, curled up. Remus had chosen to settle close to Liora and was sleeping on his side, a contented air around him. The hellhound had blocked Asmodeus's way to Liora when she had sat by the fire, stealing her from him, demanding her attention. She had petted the foolish irritating creature for twenty minutes straight before he had fallen asleep.

Liora ran her fingers through the unruly strands of her hair, her head tilted towards the flames, her body wrapped in the finest black silk robe he had been able to materialise for her to wear.

His female deserved the finest things.

"What are you thinking while you stare at me like that?" She opened her hazel eyes and locked them on him, a playful smile tugging at her rosy lips.

Lips he had kissed and tasted at his leisure. She allowed him to sample them whenever he desired. Because she was his now.

Her words drifted around his head, bringing out his smile, making him feel strangely light inside. Warm.

She viewed him as hers too.

She had placed a claim on him.

She had allowed him to do intimate things with her, and he wanted more. He couldn't stop thinking about every lick, kiss and caress that had happened at the bathing pool.

"I am thinking wicked things," he murmured in a low voice and ran his eyes over her, taking in every inch, recalling how she had looked when she had stood before him in the water, her body partially bared for his gaze and his touch.

She smiled. "Very wicked things?"

"The wickedest." He ground his teeth as his loincloth pinched, too tight against his straining length. He wanted her again and wanted more this time. He wanted to claim her fully and sheathe himself in her hot body, taking her as his fingers had.

The feel of her quivering around him, her juices flowing hot and fast, and the sound of her cries of pleasure ringing around the hills, had driven him mad with a need to take her. He had wanted to part her milky thighs and thrust to the hilt, ripping another cry of bliss from her sweet lips.

"Very wicked indeed, judging by how dark your eyes have gone." Her smile teased him, her hazel eyes twinkling with it. She liked that he couldn't hide his desire from her or how fiercely he wanted her at all times.

Asmodeus leaned back in his throne and watched her dry her hair. Her eyes remained on him, pupils growing larger, desire affecting them just as it had affected his.

"You think wicked things too," he said with a smile.

"The wickedest," she parroted and then tilted her head the other way and let her hands fall into her lap. "I like it when you smile like that."

"Many do not like it when I smile." He turned his gaze away from her, disliking the abrupt change that came over him, washing away the warmth and leaving cold behind.

"It's not the same smile." Her voice softened, soothing him and battling the rising tide of darkness in his veins.

"It is born of the same lips belonging to the same male." He silently cursed her for ruining the moment, or had he been the one to do it? She had only mentioned that she liked the smile he had given her. In truth, it was not the same smile that he wore when carrying out the Devil's orders, enjoying bloodying his hands and hearing the tormented screams of his prey.

He wasn't sure he could take any joy from that sort of act now that the softer emotions he had long denied had gained ground within him, pushing back the darkness and beginning to form a sort of balance with it.

"It's not the same smile," she said in a firmer tone and he looked at her, seeing the belief in her eyes.

He didn't want to argue with her. He had been enjoying their time together.

Asmodeus searched for a different topic of conversation. His gaze fell on the pendant she wore, a silver pentagram, intricate in design.

"It is very beautiful." He lifted his eyes to hers and they turned cold before she cast them down at her knees.

"It was my mother's." A sore subject judging by how frosty she had become. Was he destined to ruin their time together?

He decided to leave that topic alone and search for another one. If she wanted to tell him why speaking of her mother upset her, then she would in her own time. He wouldn't force it from her.

Asmodeus paused.

Just how much had she changed him already?

In the past, he would have demanded an answer, not giving the person a choice, forcing it out of them if that was what it took. She was softening him. Weakening him.

Good was a weakness. A sin. A fault.

A death sentence.

"Asmodeus?" she whispered and he focused on her, frowning at the trace of fear in her eyes. "You went cold again... I don't like it when you look at me like that."

He shook his head, hoping to shake away his black thoughts with it, and then dragged his right hand down his face and sighed.

"Was the Devil calling to you?" she said in a voice so small that he barely caught her words over the crackle of the fire and Remus's snoring.

Another shake of his head. "No. I... it was nothing."

She frowned. "Let me guess... it was something and it was along the lines of... you like being with me... you like who you are when you're around me... and then you remembered where you were, and who you're supposed to be, and you went off on that whole…" She cleared her throat and deepened it, and he surmised she was attempting to sound like him. "Good and bad are a mortal concept. In Hell, bad is good. Good is a weakness."

Asmodeus huffed and looked away from her.

"Good is not a weakness, Asmodeus. You don't have to be who everyone expects you to be. You can be whoever you want to be."

Part of him wished that were true. The good part.

"You do not know this realm, Liora. Do not act as if you do. Do not pretend you understand it and how I feel. Perhaps I am not acting as expected of me. Perhaps this is who I am and who I want to be."

His sensitive hearing picked up on her stomach growling. A perfect excuse to get some air.

He stood, the force of his swift action causing his throne to move backwards, scraping across the floor. Romulus and Remus shot to their paws.

He cast a portal beside him and didn't give her a chance to say a word before he stepped through it, coming out in the middle of Paris near the alley where he had first tasted food.

It was dark again. Did that mean the place where she had purchased food for him would be closed? He knew that mortal shops had hours in which they were open and ones in which they were closed.

He focused to put his wings away, feeling them shrink into his back, and then cast a mental command to bring him mortal clothing from his fortress. He had a small collection of clothing that fit him and suited him too. He liked to think so anyway. He replaced his loincloth and hip armour with black jeans, his boots and greaves with heavy biker boots, and donned a black shirt. He buttoned it and rolled up the sleeves until they were tight around his forearms.

Asmodeus raked his fingers through his black hair, tousling the longer strands, and then stalked out into the main avenue in search of food for his female.

Mortals scurried before him, fewer in number than there had been at the tower and far less irritating. Some females glanced his way and glanced again, lingering the second time. He glared at them, displeased by how they stared. He was not theirs to gaze upon. He belonged to Liora.

He flashed fangs, scaring them off, and began his hunt.

It was not fruitful at first. No store selling edible goods was open along the long stretch of tree-lined buildings. He walked the length of the avenue until he came to a pointed column and a large square, with an illuminated glass pyramid in the distance.

Asmodeus sniffed, trying to detect the scent of food. Two male mortals passing him carried plastic bags laden with boxes and bottles. Liquids came in bottles. He could ask for directions.

He stiffened at that thought.

He did not need mortals to show him how to find the place that was open and selling goods. He could find it himself. It couldn't be far. Possibly around the corner. Yes. Around the corner. He would look there.

He turned left, sniffing and trying to follow the trail of the two males. It led him into a narrower street and then ended. Asmodeus huffed and frowned, scouring the buildings and glowing signs for an establishment that might offer food.

Liora needed food.

He had sworn to provide for her and take care of her every need.

He would not fail her.

"What are you doing here, Asmodeus?"

He refused to turn and face the owner of that voice. Now that he had rested, he was strong enough to fight him. The male was no longer a threat to him.

If Apollyon dared to attempt to fight him, he would prove the male's earlier words wrong. He would destroy him.

Asmodeus settled on a direction and casually walked in it, heading deeper into the side street, using all of his keen senses to guide him. The smell of the males returned. It was spicy and strange. Unnatural. Did the males wear some sort of fragrance? Did females find that attractive?

Apollyon stalked behind him, an unwelcome shadow, earning them glances from more females. Did they look like twins to them? Asmodeus despised that thought.

He flashed his fangs again, snarling this time, ensuring they would look at him no more.

"Asmodeus." Apollyon's tone held a note of warning. "I will not ask you again."

Asmodeus would not ask for directions, not from this male, not even for Liora's sake.

She was hungry though.

If he returned empty-handed, she would weaken. She would want to leave his castle and return to this world. He did not want to fail her.

"I am hunting," he said, finding it a reasonable thing to say. It was neither asking for directions nor not asking for them.

Apollyon grabbed his shoulder, spun him around and slammed him against a pale stone building so hard it cracked under the force of his impact. Asmodeus growled and bared his fangs, snatched his irritating twin's wrist and twisted it viciously, causing him to drop to his knees. Apollyon rolled, breaking free of his grasp, and came to his feet.

"I will not allow you to harm these mortals," Apollyon growled, his blue eyes flashing dangerously and his power rising, swamping Asmodeus.

Asmodeus unleashed a fraction of his power, combating Apollyon's, driving it back and showing him that he was stronger now, able to fight him. If they fought in this world, in the open, they would cause mortal casualties.

Asmodeus hesitated. Liora would not be pleased if she learned he had fought his twin and had harmed mortals without feeling any remorse.

But he did feel it.

And it shocked him.

He stepped back, glaring at Apollyon, and swallowed hard. What was she doing to him? She had unleashed one emotion in him after another, bringing them all out, tempering his darker ones with light, creating balance within him.

Weakness.

He clenched his fists and shoved past Apollyon, his mood darkening and Liora's words ringing in his mind. Good was not a weakness. Liora was strong. Was it the good in her that made her that way?

She had been brave around him, had shown him compassion and tenderness, and affection too. She had taken care of his wounds and bathed him, all with warmth in her eyes and in her touch. Her desire to do good had given her the strength to weather his snarls and his fury over being defeated so easily, and had given her the courage to reveal herself to him, letting him see that she cared for him and would tend to him whether he wanted her to or not.

"I warn you, Asmodeus. Lay a hand on these mortals and I will end you."

Asmodeus lifted his right hand above his shoulder and flipped Apollyon off. "I am not here to hunt mortals."

He felt his twin's confusion, a sickening side effect of sharing his blood.

"What is it you hunt then?"

"Sustenance." He continued onwards, studying every mortal that passed him, picking out any who carried a bag.

Many of them did not contain food.

He huffed again, growing impatient and bored of this hunt. He would not ask Apollyon though. He would sooner die than give the angel the satisfaction of having yet another thing he could do better than Asmodeus.

"You are hungry again?"

Asmodeus closed his eyes and asked the Devil to give him strength so he wouldn't kill his twin just to make him shut up. The mission was what mattered. Liora would be happy if he found her food and returned with it to her. They could feed each other again and he could try new items. Perhaps savoury things that he had witnessed mortals eating while watching the pool on the plateau.

Perhaps caffeine.

He smiled to himself and was tempted to ask his shadow whether Liora had been telling the truth and caffeine was indeed a stimulant of that nature.

His shadow chose that moment to grow even more irritating. "Where is Liora?"

"Safe." It was all the wretched annoying male needed to know.

"With you?" Apollyon laughed. "I hardly think she is safe."

Asmodeus growled at him over his shoulder and frowned. Apollyon meant business. He had changed into his gold-edged black armour and had his curved golden blades sheathed at his waist.

"I have no interest in fighting you. I am on a deadline." A self-imposed one, but a deadline nonetheless. A female walking towards him had a bag similar to the one the two males had carried. He glanced into it as she passed. Food items. Notably things in a clear bag similar to what Apollyon had thrown in his face. He was close.

He sniffed to catch her scent and kept walking, following the rather pungent trail.

"Because you are hungry? That means you are hiding somewhere in the mortal world. I have not sensed you in Paris since over a day ago. You hide her somewhere else."

"She is not hidden and I am not hungry." Irritating angel. Asmodeus frowned. He supposed she was hidden in a way, but not from Apollyon and Serenity. He was hiding her from the Devil.

Apollyon grabbed him again, took his leg out and sent him crashing to the ground with him on top. His twin pinned him, using all of his weight and his power to keep him on the pavement. Asmodeus glared at him.

"She is in Hell?" The wild look in the death angel's eyes warned Asmodeus that Apollyon would beat the answer out of him if he dared to ignore the question.

"She is safe there... and hungry... and that is the only reason I am not ripping your throat out with my fangs, Brother."

"I warned you never to call me that." Apollyon grasped his throat and Asmodeus snapped, the memory of having his windpipe crushed by the Devil's shoe sending fury burning through his blood.

He smashed his right fist into Apollyon's jaw, knocking him to one side, enough that he could tip the male off balance and escape. He came to his feet and kicked Apollyon hard in the gut before he could defend, winding him.

"And I warned you never to underestimate me." Asmodeus backed off a step and breathed hard, fighting to quell the urge to bloody his claws. "Luckily for you, I have more important matters that require my time."

He scanned the route ahead. The road forked. Asmodeus cursed in the demon tongue, choosing the foulest one available to him.

Apollyon picked himself up, dusted himself off and frowned at him. "Serenity would kill me if her cousin went hungry and ended up stuck in Hell. That is the only reason I am not killing you right now. You will return her, Asmodeus. You had no right to take her."

Asmodeus smiled wickedly. "I did not take her."

Apollyon's blue eyes widened, shock rippling across his face, a face Asmodeus wanted to beat into a bloody pulp until they no longer resembled each other.

"She followed me. I told her to remain. She fell into Hell after me."

"That changes nothing. You could still bring her back."

Asmodeus stepped up to him, staring straight into his eyes. "It changes everything. She is *mine*. She chose to be with me."

"Asmodeus," Apollyon growled and Asmodeus shook his head, warning him not to even try to fight him. His twin clenched his fists, squared his jaw and then relaxed. "Tell me she is at least far enough from the pit that the eternal pain in my backside cannot reach her."

"She is safe." He would not say it again. He was tired of his twin questioning his ability to protect what was his.

"Swear you will return her to her cousin soon."

"I will do no such thing. Liora will return when she chooses it. I have promised her I will bring her back to this world once she is ready... but I will not do so before I know she is safe from my master." Asmodeus stepped away from Apollyon and looked up at the sliver of inky sky between the buildings.

No stars. The city lights drowned them out. He would have liked to see them again. Perhaps after everything had ended and he knew Liora was safe, they could gaze at them together again.

He had to keep her safe first and protect her from the Devil, a man who had easily defeated him and had commanded him to bring her to him. It wouldn't be long before the Devil lost patience and did something foolish, like send Hell's angels to find him and Liora. He needed to stop the Devil. He needed to win this time.

"Apollyon," he said, voice as distant as his gaze and his thoughts.

"What?"

"When you fight the Devil... how do you defeat him?"

Apollyon fell silent and tense. Asmodeus closed his eyes, lowered his head, and opened them again, settling them directly on his twin.

"I need to know." It was hard for him to ask for his twin's aid and Apollyon had to know that, and therefore know how important it was to him. "I need to protect her."

Apollyon stared at him. "You are serious about her."

Asmodeus cast his gaze at his feet, wishing he could see beyond the paving slabs, rock and earth to his beautiful Liora.

"I give it my all and do not give up, even when it feels I am on the verge of death and I am defeated, unable to go on," Apollyon said in a quiet voice. "I keep fighting because I want to live. Have a reason to live and you will have a reason to fight."

"Liora," Asmodeus whispered, his heart expanding in his chest, aching to see her again. "I would slay anything for her. I would die for her."

"You are missing the point," Apollyon said and Asmodeus looked at him, surprised to catch warmth in his blue eyes, a touch of compassion and understanding. His twin had never looked at him with anything other than disgust before. "Liora is your reason to live. You will live for her... even when you feel you cannot go on and your end is near, you will not give up because you want to live for her."

"With her." Asmodeus wanted to be with her right that moment, looking into her hazel eyes and hearing her soft melodic voice caressing his ears, bathing in her smiles and tender touches, and savouring the sweetness of her kiss.

Apollyon shook his head, a look of pity in his eyes. "She has you well under her spell."

If only he knew. She had cast it upon Asmodeus the moment he had set eyes on her and had held him under her thrall ever since, powerless to fight her, unable to resist her, desperate to win her against all the odds.

"You get a pass this time, but the next time I sense you in Paris, you had better have Liora with you. I would not leave it too long either. Serenity has a temper and no one messes with her family. She will geld you if you keep her cousin from her much longer." Apollyon unfurled his black wings and spread them, cast him one last look filled with confusion and concern, and took flight. His voice drifted down from the darkness. "And the supermarket is down the road to your left, just around the corner."

"Fuck you," Asmodeus growled. "I had that."

Apollyon laughed.

Asmodeus was tempted to unleash his wings, call his sword and chop his twin's head off to shut him up. He hadn't needed his help. He had been handling everything. He trudged onwards, pretending he hadn't heard the directions and feigning surprise when he found the supermarket around the corner.

He approached the doors and leaped backwards when they swished open without him touching them, flashing his fangs at the unholy invention. A male walked out, cast him a look that asked if he was deranged, and walked on. Asmodeus cautiously approached the doors as they closed and they slid open again, allowing him entrance.

He stepped inside and squinted, the bright lights hurting his sensitive eyes.

A woman bustled past him with a small person in tow. A child. Offspring. The female had mated and borne a boy. Asmodeus plastered on his best smile when the boy looked up at him. Clearly, it was not the one Liora liked as the young fair-haired boy gasped, grabbed his mother's hand and hid behind her skirt.

The mother didn't seem to notice her offspring's fear and picked up a green plastic box that had one open side and a handle. She proceeded through a rotating device of four bent metal poles, dragging the boy with her, and unleashed the hellhound to wreak havoc. The boy immediately began picking things up and prodding holes in colourful round items. His mother noticed that, scolding him in French.

She called them fruit.

Asmodeus knew fruit. He had tasted fruit. He did not like citrus ones, although the orange juice had tasted sweeter than the one called lemon.

He picked up a basket, cautiously edged through the rotating device that allowed him into the main area of the shop, and avoided the citrus area of fruit. He picked up apples and strawberries, knowing for certain that Liora enjoyed those. There was a display of wrapped rectangles of chocolate nearby that seemed rather popular with the female shoppers too. He took many of those and then proceeded to walk up and down every aisle, feeling it wise to scour every inch of the large shop. He filled the basket with a mixture of sweet and savoury, and avoided anything chilled. It was sure to turn rancid in the heat of Hell.

Unfortunately, it placed many of the items he had already tasted and enjoyed off his menu. He settled for trying other items instead. There were things called crackers, peanuts, biscuits, cakes that looked interesting, and drinks in many colours and variations.

A woman at the end of the drink aisle offered him a tiny paper cup and a smile.

He peered at the black contents but didn't take it so she offered him a different one, this one creamy in colour. Asmodeus still refrained, uncertain of what it was. He looked at the display next to her that had many more tiny cups.

Coffee.

Caffeine.

He backed off a step and glared at the woman.

She meant to seduce him with the aphrodisiac qualities of coffee.

This mortal world was far more dangerous than he had thought. Females openly sought to lure males into their honeyed traps.

Asmodeus growled at her, flashing his fangs in warning, showing her that he would not fall for her ploy.

She shrieked and called out a word he didn't recognise as she ran from him. He frowned in the direction she had gone, wracking his brain for the right translation. The female returned, two burly yet pathetic males in uniform behind her. Asmodeus smiled as the word came to him. Security.

Puny mortals.

He grinned wickedly and unfurled his huge black feathered wings, letting them rip through his shirt at the same time as he unleashed a fraction of his power, causing darkness to wash across the store. The woman shrieked again and leaped behind one of the men, pushing both wary males towards him. They leaned back, trying to keep their distance and fumbling with whatever weapons they had holstered at their sides. Asmodeus bared his fangs and threw his hand towards them, earning terrified screams that echoed around the store as the portal opened before him.

Everyone scattered when he took a single step forwards, the supermarket erupting into chaos.

Asmodeus sighed and casually walked into the portal, and stepped out into the main room of his castle.

Liora greeted him with a vicious slap across his left cheek.

Not the victorious hero's greeting he had expected.

CHAPTER 12

"Where the hell have you… ooh… food." Liora pounced on the basket, yanked it from Asmodeus's hand and carried it to the table, her long black robe swishing around her ankles. She paused before reaching it and frowned at him. "I take it from the mode of transport that you neglected to pay for this food?"

She held the basket up.

Asmodeus shrugged.

Liora sighed in a manner that made him feel she was thinking she had to teach him right from wrong when it came to honest behaviour when in the mortal world, and then went to place the basket down on the table and froze again. "You're wearing clothes."

"Very observant. Blending in tends to work better when you look like the rest of the population. I did not want to draw attention to myself while searching for food for you."

She set the basket on the long black stone table. "Why not just use a glamour?"

"I am still recovering my strength. Materialising clothing is far less taxing on my power than using a glamour to conceal my true appearance, although forcing my wings away does drain me." He slid the basket across the table to him and frowned at his portfolio. He hadn't left it at that angle.

"I have to say, mortal clothing looks very good on you." Liora gave him a wicked smile and rifled through the basket. A grin formed when she spotted the chocolate.

Asmodeus's frown darkened.

She slowed down and stared at him, and then followed his gaze to the black folder on the table near them.

"Ah… I might have taken a tiny peek at your drawings and paintings. They're very beautiful."

Asmodeus turned on her. "Very private."

"Don't be angry with me." She tiptoed and brushed her fingers across his cheek, and his anger faded, unable to stand up to the calming effect of her touch. Under her spell indeed. "Did you draw the pictures from books?"

He looked back at his portfolio and wondered just how much of a peek she had taken. It sounded to him as if she had gone through the entire thing from start to finish. Hardly a tiny peek.

"No." He shook his head and she lowered her hand to his chest, and he liked the feel of it there, settled on him, connecting them. "There is a pool that records the history of the mortal world. It is guarded by angels, but sometimes they are not around. When they are not around, I use the pool to see into your world, and sometimes I draw what I see."

He hoped she didn't ask why the guards weren't around for long enough for him to draw and paint the scenes he paused in the pool.

"How did you really feel when you saw Paris from the air for the first time? It was your picture come to life."

Relief flowed through him, relaxing his body beneath her warm hand. He felt comfortable enough around her now to tell her the truth.

"It awed me, but I think it was more than the view that took my breath away." He lifted his hand and smoothed his palm across her cheek, cupping it and stroking it with his thumb, tilting her head back so she was looking up at him and he could bathe in her beautiful hazel eyes. "You took my breath away."

She blushed and a shy smile curled her rosy lips, tempting him into dropping his head and kissing her.

"There you go again… saying things that most women would die to hear."

"You are not most women." He remembered her telling him something similar before and she was right. She wasn't one of many. She was unique. Perfect. *His.*

"That look in your eyes is silently telling me something you said to me earlier, and I like that too." She tiptoed, wrapped her slender silk-covered arms around his shoulders and kissed him.

Asmodeus banded his arms around her waist, holding her to him, savouring the softness of the kiss and the feel of her in his arms. It felt right to have her in his embrace like this. It felt as though she belonged there.

As if they were meant to be like this.

Together. Not alone.

She pulled back before he was ready for her to and smiled up into his eyes. "So who did you get into a fight with in the mortal world?"

He frowned at her and she touched his cheek. It stung. The bastard Apollyon must have grazed it.

"My not-so-evil-twin."

"Apollyon?" Her eyes widened and she released him. "What did he want?"

"Me to return you. I denied his request of course. He decided to make it into more of a demand. I decided to show him that I do not kneel to anyone." He claimed her waist and pulled her back to him, not stopping until her front was flush against his and he could feel her heat through his clothes.

"Did you tell him why I'm here?"

He nodded. "I did… eventually. He found me when I was tracking down an adequate source of sustenance for you. As always, he opened with various accusations and misguided beliefs, and then flexed his muscles. I flexed mine back. We argued, came to an understanding, and parted company."

She touched his cheek again, anger shining in her eyes. "I hope he came off worse."

Asmodeus smiled, captured her hand and brought it to his lips. He kissed each of her slight fingers, feeling her power rising to the fore, brought out by her fury.

"I did come close to breaking his arm and definitely bloodied his lip."

She beamed with pride. Asmodeus kissed her again, silently thanking her for her belief in him and that she had chosen to side with him over his twin.

Her lips played with his for too brief a moment and then she was pulling back again. "Did he mention Serenity?"

"Repeatedly." He tried to pull her back to him but she resisted. Stubborn little mortal. He did love it when she fought him.

"Is she pissed?"

Asmodeus had lost her. "Drunk?"

She laughed, the sound like music to his ears, sending a delightful shiver through him. "No. Angry."

"Apparently. She is under the impression I have kidnapped you."

Her look soured. "I wonder who could have made her think that."

"Someone dashingly handsome, but too good for his own good with an evil twin who is far superior in every way?" Asmodeus tugged her back to him, settling his hands on her bottom. He palmed it, his body instantly growing hard for her. He wanted to end this dull talk of his twin and her cousin. He wanted to feed his female and satisfy her. He could see the next question rising to the tip of her tongue. "Yes, I corrected his view, confirming you were safe and had chosen to accompany me to Hell, where you are probably far safer than you were in the mortal world. I have also informed him that you will be allowed to return when you so choose, as long as I have dealt with our mutual problem."

"Your boss?" Her face fell further. "You aren't seriously thinking of fighting him again?"

"I must." He lifted his shoulders in an easy shrug. "It is either fight him or hand you over, and I have decided I will do the former. I will defeat him this time. I swear it."

"Forgive me if that doesn't reassure me in the slightest. At least wait a while, rebuild your strength, and strategize with me about it. We could fight him together."

That was not going to happen. He would not allow Liora anywhere near the Devil.

"I do not have time. Apollyon mentioned that your cousin has a tendency to fall foul of her temper. Are all of your family like her?"

"I am... I can't vouch for the rest. I don't remember that much about my parents."

"They are gone?" The sorrow that entered her eyes when he asked that confirmed that she had lost them, and a long time ago judging by what she had said. "I am sorry."

She offered him a watery smile. "I guess I'm like you. No really close family. Just Serenity. I lost my parents when I was twelve... during a demon attack on my coven in London."

Asmodeus growled at the knowledge that she had come under attack by Hell's minions and that the Devil had likely ordered that attack himself. He held her closer, pinning her against his chest, and vowed to protect her even as he suddenly felt as though they were never meant to be.

He would be alone again before long.

Demons had taken her family from her, those she loved. How long before she began to see him for what he really was, realised that this was his world and he had done terrible things?

He had killed people, destroying families just as the Devil had destroyed hers.

"You've gone all quiet," Liora whispered and emerged from his embrace, looking up at him. He stared over her head at the far wall of the long black room, unable to bring himself to look into her eyes while he was wrestling with his fears. "Asmodeus? Look at me."

He couldn't ignore her command. He dropped his gaze to meet hers and she brushed her knuckles across his cheek.

"I know your thoughts." She stared into his eyes, hers soft with understanding and reassurance.

"How?"

"I'm psychic?" She smiled but he saw no warmth in it this time. "Because I know you, and I know what you fear."

"I fear nothing."

"I know what you fear," she repeated, ignoring him. "Because I... I fear it too."

He stared down at her, confused and uncertain, wishing he could believe that they did share the same fear. What reason did she have to fear though? She was good and pure and beautiful, and he would lay down his life for her.

No. He would live for her.

Liora cupped both of his cheeks, keeping his eyes on her, and he could see the fear she spoke of in her hazel eyes. She hesitated, swallowed, and her fingers trembled against his face, confirming the nerves he could sense in the tremulous beat of her heart.

"I'm afraid that I'm going to lose you... one way or another. I don't want that to happen."

Asmodeus wrapped her in his arms and curled his black wings around her too, shielding her completely and blocking out the world. "You won't lose me. If I had the power, if my pledge to the monster who created me wasn't eternal and unbreakable, I would swear fealty to you, Liora... if I had the power, I would make that binding contract between us in a heartbeat... but I do not and cannot. All I can do is offer you the heart that beats for only you."

Liora shot back and stared up at him, her eyes so wide he could see white all around her irises. "You mean that?"

She liked his pretty words but couldn't believe them?

"I am born of evil... vicious and cruel... have the blood of thousands on my hands... can kill without regret and take pleasure from violence and suffering... it is understandable that you would not believe a foul creature like me could ever feel an emotion born of good." He released her and stepped back, his heart stinging in his chest, spreading poison in his veins.

"I didn't mean it like that!" Liora grabbed his wrists and held him firm. "I just... I have to know this is serious... that you're serious and this isn't just a game."

Asmodeus sighed. "I would never do such a cruel thing to you, Liora. Apollyon says you have me under your spell. If this is a spell, then I hope it is never broken... not as my heart feels."

"Asmodeus," she whispered and squeezed his hands. "I don't intend to break your heart. I'm just surprised. Wait. You told Apollyon about this?"

"He questioned me, after I asked him how he defeats the Devil when he fights him." Perhaps too much information to have given her judging by her widening eyes. "I needed to know. He asked if I was serious about you. I am... but how you lost your family... I could come to understand if you could not... no. I am nothing more than a creature born of evil and Hell, a demon in many eyes, but I vow I will never harm you as other demons have. I will not let you leave me. You are mine, Liora. I am yours. And so it will be until the end of time."

She smiled. "For a moment there, I thought you were going to go a little bit beta on me just when I had gotten used to you being all alpha."

Alpha? Beta? He wasn't sure what she meant by that but he didn't let on. He took it as a good thing that he had remained alpha. Greek. Did it mean he was first? Or like a captive wolf pack? The leader. Top dog.

He glanced at Romulus and Remus where they slept curled together in front of the fire. He was the leader of the pack in a way. Their alpha. He looked back at Liora. Her alpha.

"Do you believe me now?" he whispered, slowly easing her back into his embrace, folding his wings around her again.

She nodded.

"And will you take the black heart I offer you?"

She smiled. "It's not that black. More... really dark red."

He frowned at her, wondering if she could see how much he had already changed because of her.

She teasingly patted his cheek. "You went easy on Apollyon didn't you?" She paused and he shrugged as his reply. Her smile broadened. "You went easy on him because of me. You were thinking I might not be happy if you beat him to a pulp, weren't you?"

She had him there. For the same reason, he had stayed his blade several times and resorted to merely terrifying the mortals to amuse himself. He had even attempted a kind smile at the boy, although he had frightened him instead.

Asmodeus looked down at Liora. He knew not whether angels could create life. Could he plant his seed in her and see it blossom? Would she ever want such a thing?

Would it be born evil like him or good like her?

Or perhaps a mixture of both of them?

"What are you thinking?" She prodded his chest and he blinked, coming out of his thoughts.

"I saw a boy in the place called a supermarket. He was small and frail. Weak. I do not quite understand why mortals procreate." A lie, but a good way of getting an answer to his questions.

"I guess some people just want to make a family. I don't think anyone makes kids to continue the human race anymore."

"Does your cousin Serenity intend to make herself such a family with Apollyon?" Another cleverly constructed question, as long as she overlooked the fact that he was asking things about her cousin and his twin, two people he really didn't give a damn about.

Her expression shifted, revealing a sliver of confusion. "I don't think so... I mean... how? Angels are sterile."

And that was the answer to most of his questions.

Now came the tiebreaker.

"Do you want a family to replace those you lost?"

She stared at his chest for the longest time and then lifted her eyes back to his. "I can't say I've ever thought about it. I don't really go crazy over babies like some witches at the coven. I don't particularly feel compelled to pick them up and coddle them, or even play with them. Most of the time they seem to get in the way."

"So you don't want a baby in your belly?"

She giggled. "Is that your rather childish way of asking whether I'll be pissed if you don't knock me up somehow?"

Asmodeus glared at her and set her away from him, furling his wings against his back. He folded his arms across his chest.

Romulus perked up and drowsily checked on him, having evidently sensed his rising anger, and then yawned and went back to sleep.

Liora ran her hands over Asmodeus's folded arms, separating them easily, and took hold of his hands again. "No, I won't be upset. Babies really aren't on my agenda."

"Because you fear demons will take them from you?"

She laughed now. "Seriously? If you were the father, I could hardly see that happening. You fought the Devil for me. I can't imagine who you would fight to protect your offspring."

"I would tear down Heaven to protect them and you." That earned him a bright smile.

"There you go again... saying beautiful things. So... yes."

"Yes?" He couldn't remember asking her a question other than whether she feared demons would take her babies.

She tiptoed, kissed him, and whispered against his lips, "Yes, I'll take the heart you offered me."

Asmodeus recaptured her lips, seizing control of the kiss and showing her just how much that meant to him. He curled his wings around her again, shielding her from the inquisitive gaze of Remus, and gathered her into his arms. Her palms pressed against his chest, burning him through his ruined black shirt, and his heart beat against them, eager to leap into her hands.

She nipped his lower lip with her blunt teeth and then swiftly ducked out of his arms, muttering something about food.

He furled his wings and found her at the basket, tipping everything out onto the stone table. The contents scattered everywhere and he snatched a bottle as it rolled over the edge.

Liora frowned at it. "What's that?"

"Not edible, I think. I hope." He held the small white plastic bottle out to her. "It washes clothes... I think. My French is a little lacking, but the picture on the front made it look as though it will clean material things. True?"

He hoped she said yes.

She nodded. "Why did you want it?"

She had to be very hungry if her brain was no longer functioning. He had been there. It was not a pleasant experience or one he had any desire to relive.

"I intend to wash your clothes for you."

Her smile was brilliant, as if he had just given her something as dazzling and precious as a diamond ring, and she tore open a packet of biscuits.

"Evil angels make the best boyfriends."

Boyfriend?

Asmodeus dropped the plastic bottle, grabbed her and kissed her hard, tasting only creamy biscuit. It was good. He kissed her harder. She shoved him back and stuffed a biscuit in his mouth.

"Food first. Sex later."

CHAPTER 13

Asmodeus choked on his biscuit.

Liora's eyes turned wild and panicked and her hands fluttered in front of her, spilling biscuits on the black stone floor of his home. Remus was there in a shot, snaffling them and licking the crumbs up.

"Too forward?" Liora said and he shook his head and pounded his fist against his chest, coughing hard.

"Unexpected," he wheezed and grabbed the nearest bottle. The glass was cool beneath his fingers. He twisted the metal cap off and swallowed a mouthful of the clear liquid. Fire. His throat burned and his stomach was on fire. He coughed worse than before and scowled at the bottle. "What in three realms is vodka?"

Liora grabbed it from him. "Alcohol."

She screwed the lid back on and hid the bottle behind her.

"Another aphrodisiac? Does it contain caffeine like the coffee the female offered me in the market to seduce me?"

"No, it'll just make you lose your inhibitions and get you really drunk, and probably sick if you haven't had it before... what the hell did you say?"

His head felt funny so he laughed. "Woman... in the market... she offered me coffee... wanted me."

Were his words slurring together?

The entire room turned, wavered, spun until his eyes couldn't focus.

Liora slapped him again, righting the world and bringing her into vivid detail. She was not happy.

Because the female had attempted to seduce him?

"I did not drink it. I bared my..." He flashed his fangs at her as he had the woman. She did not look impressed. "She screamed... called security..."

Asmodeus grinned.

"Oh, mercy, what did you do?"

He waved away her horrified look, dismissing it. "Nothing bad. Just frightened them a little." He pinched his fingers together to show her how little and grinned again. "Should've seen their faces. Then they ran. I thought... people... found angels... awful?"

"I think you mean people are awed by angels, not people find angels awful... although in your case, clearly what you said is more appropriate since you scared the ever living crap out of them!" She huffed and shook her head. "Aren't there rules about public exposure?"

He laughed. "I didn't flash that. I flashed these."

He grinned at her, showing his fangs. She wobbled in his vision again. Either he needed another mouthful of the vodka or he needed to keep the hell away from it. He couldn't decide which.

"No, I mean, revealing yourself to mortals."

Asmodeus shook his head. "Not for me. No rules for me. Rules for the wretches under the yoke of Heaven and the fools under the yoke of Hell."

She gave him a look that said she was dearly tempted to point out that technically he fell under the fools heading.

He reached around her for the vodka. She moved it away from him so he growled at her. The threat didn't work. Asmodeus sighed and leaned his backside against the edge of the table.

Well, he leaned where he thought the edge of the table was, which was behind him even though he remembered it was actually beside him when his backside hit the floor with enough force to jar his spine.

"Fantastic. You're a lousy drinker to get drunk on this tiny amount." She held the bottle out in front of her and measured how much he had taken from it in that one mouthful and her eyes widened. His did too. Apparently, he had a big mouth. Nearly half the bottle was gone.

He laughed.

She scowled at him as she would a naughty child.

Asmodeus had a sudden urge to eat the cake he had bought for Liora. All of it.

He groped for the edge of the table, pulled himself onto his knees and scoured the scattered food for it. When he spotted it near Liora, he reached for it but she was there before him, snatching the box up against her chest.

"No, you don't. Apollyon can put away a whole cake in one go and I'm not sitting here watching you do the same."

Same. Apollyon.

Same.

Asmodeus erupted from the floor, growling at her and the way she had compared him to his twin, making out they were the same.

Apollyon liked a whole chocolate cake. Of course he would too. He was just a shadow of that male. A copy. He would want and like everything that male did because it was programmed into him. Everyone thought it and who was he to deny it?

"Chocolate cake... witches... what else do I have a penchant for according to the wise Liora? Maybe I should be wanting to fuck your cousin, not you?"

Liora punched him. When his brain stopped rattling around his skull from the force of the blow, he was staring at the ceiling, flat on his back, his legs hanging awkwardly over his toppled throne.

That was a hell of a mean swing his little mortal had on her. Magically reinforced judging by the blood he could taste and how far she had sent him flying across the room.

She appeared in view above him and he tilted his head, trying to keep her straight in his vision.

"You shit." She kicked him hard in the ribs and he groaned and curled up in a ball on his side.

He had said something wrong. Liora must have knocked a few brain cells loose with her punch because it took him a second to remember what had made her lash out.

He cringed.

Smooth. Very smooth.

"Liora, my sweet." He reached for her and she slapped his hand away.

"Don't sweet me. I take it back. You're a shitty drunk."

He didn't think he was drunk anymore. She had punched him right through drunk to stone cold sober.

Asmodeus sprawled out on the floor, letting her glare at him, defeated by a girl.

"I swear I will never drink again," he muttered, staring at the ceiling, watching it lazily spin. Not sober after all.

"Tell me why you said it."

It took a lot of effort to get his eyes to move to her without the contents of his stomach attempting to crawl back up his throat.

"Shadow." The moment it left his lips, her shoulders sagged and a defeated look crossed her face.

"You are not a shadow of Apollyon." She kneeled beside him and brushed his black hair from his brow, and he closed his eyes, amazed by how soothing her touch was and how it calmed his raging head and tumultuous stomach. "Have I not told you that?"

He nodded.

"Just because you're both pigs, and I mentioned that, doesn't mean I think you're like him. I have it on good authority that all angels are pigs."

He opened his eyes and she smiled at him.

"You look like hell." Her smile turned a little bit awkward and guilty. "I think I might have lost my temper a little and my magic tends to control me then…"

She touched his chin and white-hot fire burned along his jaw. She flinched for him, as if she had sensed it, and then the pain dulled, fading away, and he knew she was healing him.

He wanted to heal her too.

He had hurt her.

"I did not mean it," he whispered, barely moving his lips, afraid that she might fuse together the wrong parts if he moved while she was healing him. She looked at him, a flicker of confusion breaking through the concern in her bright hazel eyes. He spelled it out for her. "I do not desire to have sex with your cousin."

Her lips trembled.

Either she was about to cry or she was trying hard not to smile.

"What about the woman in the supermarket who was trying to seduce you?" She managed to stifle her smile and scowled at him.

"I refused her advances."

"Was she offering this wicked cocktail of coffee in a small, possibly paper cup, while wearing a big stupid fake smile?" Liora said and stroked his jaw. He nodded. She smiled now and it was not reassuring. It was teasing and had a faint mocking edge to it. "It was a sample. Supermarkets sometimes offer samples of items they want to sell lots of. The French love coffee almost as much as the Italians do. She wasn't trying to seduce you."

He held back his own smile, knowing she was likely to hit or kick him again if she saw it. "She was persistent, and now I think back, her smile was… flirtatious."

Liora ground her teeth. "Keep it up and you will have bruised balls and you'll be taking me back to the mortal world so I can do some terrorizing of my own."

Asmodeus caught her wrist, pulled her down to him and kissed her. He expected her to pull away and slap him again, either physically or verbally, but she melted into him, settling her breasts against his chest and curling up beside him.

"Forgiven?" he whispered against her lips and peppered them with kisses.

She scrunched her nose up, wriggled her lips and then smiled. "It depends. Are you sober?"

Asmodeus did a mental body check. "I don't know. It is hard to tell through the throbbing in my head. It may be the result of the alcohol or my girlfriend's wrath."

She smiled properly at last. "You called me your girlfriend."

"So? You called me your boyfriend first."

"I did?"

He nodded. "You said evil angels made the best boyfriends... and then you said we could have sex later."

"And then you wrecked your chances by getting drunk and being a shit."

He frowned at her, tried to prepare a defence to counter her accusation, and failed. "No sex?"

"You are still drunk." She kissed the tip of his nose. "If you weren't drunk, you wouldn't be so forward about this or so relaxed."

"I would not?" He edged his hands down to the small of her back, inching towards her bottom.

She shook her head. "Nope. Not a chance, Buster. You blew it."

"You blew me." He grinned.

"Mother Earth! See, this is why I know you're drunk. You're vulgar and crass. Like every other male in the world."

Asmodeus scowled. "Not like every man."

She didn't agree with him. She walked her fingers across his chest and then pressed her palms against it and pushed. She was getting up. Asmodeus tightened his grip, pinning her against him.

"Stay." He held her even when she wriggled and frowned. "Stay, sweet little Liora."

"It's not very comfortable." A reasonable rejoinder.

"Then I will take you somewhere more comfortable and we can lie together."

She didn't look as though she was going to go along with that one. "I'm still hungry. Someone got drunk and raucous, and got himself into trouble with his woman, and that woman is still hungry."

Asmodeus relented and loosened his grip on her. She wriggled out of his arms, the action brushing her breasts across his chest in the most tormenting way.

Remus whined and gave him a sympathetic look. Asmodeus spoke to him in the demon tongue, wishing him better fortune when he found a female of his own. They were complicated, temperamental creatures.

He hauled himself onto his feet, straightened his wings and tore his wrecked shirt off. Liora glanced at him and then her eyes drifted back to him, lingering on his bare chest. Not that complicated at times. His female liked his body and the way she was staring told him that she would reconsider her refusal of his advances if he remained this way for long enough.

He was feeling like a spoilsport today though.

He called another item of clothing to him, a shirt he had altered, focusing so it fitted perfectly over his wings. He considered buttoning it but liked the way Liora's gaze kept zipping to the slice of bare chest and stomach she could see between the two open sides of the black shirt.

She bit into an apple in a way that left him feeling she wanted to take a bite out of him.

He moved to the table, sat on it, crossed his legs, and picked up a small black sketchbook he had acquired in the supermarket. He took up a pencil stub and studied Liora as she picked through the food, sketching her in a moment when she tucked her long chestnut hair behind her ear and her lips parted, her gaze cast down at something on the table. Beautiful. His fingers made swift work of capturing her and by the time she had selected her next item of food, he had finished the sketch.

She looked over at him, frowned and tiptoed, attempting to peer at the drawing. He held it against his chest.

"Private," he said and peeked at it, teasing her.

She sidled closer, rolling another apple along the table beside her, and her dire attempt to look casual and uninterested brought a smile to his lips. She was a terrible actor.

Liora lunged for the small book with her free hand but he saw the attempt coming before it had even formed as an idea in her head. He beat his wings and shot backwards, far beyond her reach, and landed in the corner of the room.

He leisurely perused the drawing, going so far as to hold it out before him, comparing it to her.

She planted her hands on her hips and glared daggers at him.

"I will let you see it," he said and she brightened. "If you pay me."

"Pay you how?" Her glare turned suspicious but darkened with unmistakable desire at the same time. Wicked girl. He wasn't asking her to offer that much in return for the drawing.

"A kiss." He held it out to her.

"That all?"

"Feel free to bargain for a higher price." He waggled the book. "If you want to pay more, I could be convinced."

"A kiss it is." She crossed the room to him and he held the book above his head, not convinced that she wouldn't try to steal it and leave him down a kiss.

She sighed, grabbed the collar of his shirt in both hands, dragged him down and captured his mouth with her own. It was more than a kiss. The way her lips danced against his and her tongue teased, flicking over and swiping at his lower lip, luring him into wanting to taste her in a similar fashion, intoxicated him more than the vodka had. He groaned and closed his eyes and claimed her mouth, kissing her harder and eliciting a moan from her that burned through him, making him forget what they were doing. The only thing that mattered was this kiss.

He wrapped his arms around her and she was gone, twirled from his embrace, her high giggle ringing around him.

Asmodeus huffed.

Tricked.

"Witch," he muttered and she mimicked him, waggling the book as she danced back across the room to her food stash.

She opened the book and her laughter died, her actions ceasing. She stared down at the drawing with a blank expression on her face and his heart beat hard against his chest, uncertainty creeping through his veins and taking hold of him, leaving him with a head full of doubts. Did she not like it?

She had admired his other drawings and paintings. She had to admire this one too. He had drawn it for her. He had never drawn anything for anyone before, had kept his passion a secret, something private and for his eyes only. Her praise had given him the courage to draw for her, to show what was a rough sketch rather than a finished perfected drawing to her because he thought she might like it.

He stepped towards her, intent on taking it back and cursing her, and she looked up at him and blinked.

"It's beautiful," she whispered. "This is really how you see me?"

He shook his head. "It is how you are, not how I see you. You are beautiful. I am afraid my skill does not do you justice."

She smiled. "Flattery like that might earn you another kiss."

Asmodeus rounded the table to her and picked up the apple she had discarded. He rolled it between his palms, careful not to damage it with his strength, and studied her as she alternated between looking over the food and looking at the picture he had drawn. Sometimes she glanced at him too, a blush touching her cheeks. At least she was no longer angry with him.

And he was no longer drunk.

Liora opened a different drink and swigged from the bottle between bites of apple, biscuits and other savoury items he had brought her. She offered him a strip of dark chocolate. He had no need to eat right now, didn't feel hunger as she did, but he wanted to taste the food with her. He stepped up to her and she held the chocolate higher, closer to his mouth. Asmodeus bit the strip in half and savoured the slightly bitter yet sweet taste.

He sampled the other items she had opened. Something she explained was a fried potato chip that tasted salty, various nuts that all tasted vaguely the same to him, and more biscuits. He decided he liked sweet things. Like Liora.

He stood behind her, slipped his arms beneath hers and settled them around her waist, holding her with her back pressing against his front. She continued eating, working her way through most of a packet of pale creamy biscuits and finishing her apple and a bottle of water.

Asmodeus leaned down and rested his chin on her shoulder. She fed him a strawberry and made a click of chastisement when he took her fingers into his mouth with it.

"You're still in the doghouse." She pulled her fingers from his lips and poked his nose. "Besides, I'm full and now I'm tired."

He had no idea how mortal bodies worked. It didn't make sense that she had eaten her fill and now she was more tired than before, when she had been hungry. He also wasn't sure how long a mortal could live without sleep before their body began to shut down and became useless to them.

Liora had been awake for what mortals perceived as days, and she had been through much in that short span of time. It had likely taken its toll on her and now that he was close to her and was aware of her tiredness, he could sense her weakening.

"You really don't sleep?" She tilted her head and pressed a kiss to his cheek. He shook his head. She sighed. "I can't imagine what it would be like to never sleep... never dream."

Asmodeus felt as though he was dreaming now, with her in his arms like this, trusting him to keep her safe. He felt extremely protective of her and it had been one hell of a long few days. He couldn't imagine what would happen next. Whatever happened, he needed to think before he spoke. He needed to take more care or she would end up smashing the heart he had given to her.

"Do you have a bedroom?" she whispered and his body ached, growing hard at the thought of laying her down on a sumptuous bed and sending her off into good dreams by worshipping every inch of her.

"No." Not anything he could definitely call a bedroom anyway.

"All these rooms and no bedroom?" She sounded as if she was teasing him again now.

"I can make one for you, but it will take me time. I will need to return to the mortal realm and acquire necessary items." He didn't mind the challenge of hunting for a good bed and comfortable mattress for his Liora, but he didn't want to leave her when she was tired and vulnerable, weak from fatigue.

What else could he do though? She needed to rest and he had no comfortable bed to offer her.

"How comfy is your throne?" She looked towards it where it lay toppled on the black stone floor.

"Moderately."

She yawned. "Could you sit in it for a few hours?"

He arched an eyebrow, unsure where she was going with her questions. Was she meaning to sleep in his throne? It was not that comfortable. She was petite and soft, unaccustomed to the firm seat.

"Possibly." He had sat in it for hours before with no negative effect on him.

"Good." Liora twisted out of his arms, took hold of his hand and led him to the throne. He righted it for her so she could sit on it. She moved around in front of him and pushed him backwards, towards the seat. "Sit."

Asmodeus obeyed, settling himself in the chair, ensuring his wings were comfortable.

Liora surprised him by sitting down on his thighs and curling up against him, pulling her knees close to her chest.

He liked this.

He wrapped his arms around her and then his wings, tucking her in and ensuring she would be warm and would feel safe enough to sleep. He would watch over her. The fire crackled in the grate. Remus shifted restlessly and poked one paw in Romulus's right eye. Romulus growled sleepily.

Liora was sound asleep.

Asmodeus watched her, studying her face as she slumbered. She was beautiful in sleep, her features soft and dainty and her long chestnut hair curling around her black silk robe covered shoulders. He couldn't believe how much she trusted him, giving him the honour of protecting her when she was at her most vulnerable.

He had never protected anyone before Liora had come into his life, turning his world upside down, shaking his carefully constructed image to reveal the side of himself he had always hidden because he had believed it made him weak and would make others turn on him.

It had drawn Liora to him.

A familiar tug yanked his chest and Asmodeus held Liora closer to him. Her head settled against his chest, her warm breath skating over his skin. He refused to heed his master's command. The Devil had never been able to break his will as he could with his Hell's angels, easily forcing them to do something against their desire.

He looked down at his sleeping beauty, focusing everything on her, shutting out the Devil.

She couldn't be very comfortable in his arms, in his home, in his realm of demons.

Demons like the ones who had killed her parents.

The sliver of good in him said to take her back to her cousin, where she could be with what remained of her family and sleep in a soft warm bed. He crushed it. She wasn't safe in the mortal world. Serenity and Apollyon weren't strong enough to protect her there, where Hell's angels could easily reach them.

Asmodeus drew her even closer, closed his eyes and pressed a long kiss to her brow, breathing in her subtle yet sweet fragrance.

With her like this, he didn't feel that the good in him was a weakness. He felt that the emotions he harboured that were born of that side of him, the way he felt about this willowy, challenging and beautiful female, made him strong and gave him the strength to do whatever it took to protect her.

He would never let the Devil have her.

Because she was his.

CHAPTER 14

Asmodeus wasn't sure how long a male resided in the doghouse before their female decided to let them out to play again.

Liora had been her normal teasing and amusing self around him for the past two mortal days in his castle. They had finished all of the food he had acquired for her on the first day and she had given him a list of other foods that she liked and had sent him on a mission. He had inquired whether she had wanted to come with him, a small part of him fearing she would want to and would then prefer to remain in the mortal realm where she truly belonged. Liora had kissed him and had told him that she had no intention of leaving his castle for the time being because she was enjoying being alone with him.

He had taken that as a good omen, one that said if he returned from his mission with the bounty she desired, they could perhaps spend a few hours being intimate.

He had returned with everything she wanted, and she had kissed him as a reward, but nothing more. When he had tried to take things further, she had poked him in the chest and told him he had to do better than that to get out of the doghouse with her.

Asmodeus had upped his game then, leaving her while she played with Romulus and Remus, and returning to the mortal world to hunt for a bed. She had caught him constructing it in one of the larger rooms that had a balcony overlooking the courtyard of his castle and her smile had been brilliant.

That night, when she had grown tired, she had asked him to come and sleep with her in the bed. He had held her close to him, her head resting on his chest and warm body pressing against his side. Neither of them had been nude but it had been wonderful. He hadn't bothered trying to sleep. He had spent hours focused on Liora and thinking over everything, wrestling with himself.

Whenever she slept, he slipped and his darker emotions gained ground again, driving out the good. His fears easily took hold of him in those long hours, filling his head with doubts about what would happen if he fought the Devil again and what was in store for them. With each minute that passed, he grew more restless, his fears increasing their grasp, tightening icy claws around his heart. The threat of the Devil hung over his head, invisible but oppressing, marring his time with Liora.

She sat on the long black stone table, dressed in her crimson top and black jeans, thumbing through a magic book. She had explained that contact with them boosted her power even if she couldn't understand the words on the pages. He had helped her translate a few spells written in dead languages, gaining more kisses as his reward.

Asmodeus shifted his wings behind him, so they cleared the arms of his throne and lay more comfortably, and crossed his black jeans-clad legs. The dark stone seat was cool against his bare back and arms. He petted Remus, stroking him between his ears, and studied Liora in silence.

She flicked a page, bit into another strawberry, and then wrinkled her nose. She reached over, picked up a dark plastic bottle, flipped open the cap and squeezed the equally dark rich syrupy contents onto another strawberry.

Liora paused and looked at him with wide eyes, her eyebrows high on her forehead.

"Want some?" She offered the strawberry coated with the dark sauce.

"What is it?" Asmodeus stood, furled his black wings against his back, and crossed the room to her. Remus stuck close to his heels.

Romulus was already beside Liora, resting his head on the table, his ears back and eyes constantly following the food she held. A pool of drool covered the table surface around his jaw. Both of the hellhounds had discovered a love of mortal food and had taken to sampling it all with him and Liora, but then Liora had told him that chocolate was poisonous to canines.

Asmodeus had immediately removed it from the list of food they were allowed, gaining him angry red glares from the twins.

"Chocolate sauce and strawberry. Very decadent." She waggled it and some of the sauce ran down her finger.

"Very wicked?" he asked and a blush coloured her cheeks.

She nodded, her pupils dilating.

Asmodeus stopped before her and opened his mouth, accustomed to her habit of feeding him now. She seemed to enjoy it.

She placed the strawberry in his mouth and he sucked her fingers in with it, swirling his tongue around to capture every molecule of chocolate sauce.

Her hazel gaze darkened, locked on his lips. She pulled her fingers free, her eyes lingering, burning into him. Her breathing accelerated, driving his to do the same, anticipation making his pulse rise until his heart slammed hard against his chest.

Liora's lips parted.

Asmodeus swooped on them.

She met him halfway, grabbing him around the back of his neck and dragging him down to her. She pulled him off balance and he crashed into her, knocking her backwards onto the table. Her legs were around his waist in an instant, her feet locking them together behind his backside, and she pulled him on top of her.

Asmodeus growled and kissed her harder, slanting his head and taking her with his tongue. She moaned and arched beneath him, pressing her breasts against his chest. He snarled and swept his hand across the table, shoving all of the books onto the floor and clearing some room.

Liora wriggled backwards and he mounted the table, kneeling between her thighs, his groin pressing against the heat of hers.

He moaned and kissed her again, tasting strawberry and chocolate. Decadent. Wicked.

Romulus and Remus whined and trotted out of the room.

Liora moved beneath him, undulating her hips in a maddening way that had him as hard as steel and straining to be inside her. Her delicious heat stroked him through his own jeans. He needed her closer. Needed to feel her skin-to-skin, feel her rocking her wet core against him.

He wanted all of her this time.

He focused and sent his jeans away, leaving him naked on top of her. A switch in his thoughts and she was naked too, her clothes strewn across the room.

She gasped. "Cheat. You do that so easily."

There was a smile in her voice. If he could show her how to do it, he would, but it was a talent all angels possessed and even he wasn't sure how he made it work.

Asmodeus peppered her throat with kisses and groaned as he rubbed himself against her. She worked her body against him, rocking in time, pushing him closer to the edge. He shut out the voice at the back of his mind, the one that had plagued him when he had been with Liora like this before. He would make it good for her. They were meant to be together. What he lacked in experience, he would make up for with effort. He would give her pleasure as he had at the pool and she would cry his name again as she came.

He wanted to feel her quiver around his cock as she had trembled around his fingers.

He wanted to claim her.

"Out of the doghouse?" he whispered against her neck between kisses.

"Out and waving you in." She giggled and rubbed her bare breasts against his chest.

He presumed that was a sexual reference.

She wanted him inside her. Just the thought had him rock hard and ready to explode. He gritted his teeth and focused on other things. Breasts. Her breasts were bare. He hadn't seen them yet.

Asmodeus pushed himself up on his palms and looked down at her, taking in her perfection. Firm creamy mounds topped with pale pink buds called to him. He dropped his head and pulled one nipple into his mouth, sucking on it as he had sucked on her fingers. Liora moaned, clutched his hair with one hand and threw the other above her head, grasping the edge of the table.

He growled. He wanted to take her while she lay like that, holding on to the table, bared for him and at his mercy.

"Asmodeus," she moaned and he added the sound of her uttering his name in an ecstasy-drenched voice to the things he loved about her.

No one had ever said his name in the ways that she had. With affection. With concern. With pleasure. With passion.

He groaned when she released his hair and ran her hand down his neck to his wing.

She stroked the feathers, teasing him and putting him off what he was doing. He realised the moment he stopped swirling his tongue around her nipple. She pressed her feet into his backside and spurred him on. It was hard to concentrate while she was teasing his wings, sending waves of shivers through him. He suckled her nipple and rested on his elbow so he could toy with her other one at the same time. She liked that. It made her rub her core against him. Another groan escaped him and he countered her, thrusting the length of his cock against her moist heat. Too much. He rocked harder, curling his hips, needing more.

She moaned his name again and tugged on his wing, using her feet to keep him thrusting into her. Did she want him inside her too, filling her sweet body with his?

He grunted and kissed over her chest to her neck, licking and nipping at it as he flexed his hips, losing himself in how good it felt to do this with her.

This was the closest he had ever been to a female.

Liora wanted him closer.

She skimmed her hand down his side and then around it, dipping it between their bodies. He closed his eyes and exhaled hard as her fingers brushed the head of his length. His hips jerked forwards, his body eager for more.

She slackened the grip of her legs, allowing him to shift backwards to let her reach him. He groaned and swallowed, breathing hard against her throat as she closed her fingers around his length and slowly stroked him. Much more of that and he would climax before he was inside her.

"Let me taste you again," she murmured, voice low with passion and desire that burned through him. He wanted to deny her, knew that if she placed her mouth on him he wouldn't last, but he equally wanted to experience that again.

He moved back to kneel between her spread thighs and frowned, his nostrils flaring with it, when he looked down at her glistening curls. He swept his hands over her milky thighs and down between them, brushing the petals of her groin, teasing her. She giggled and then it turned into a moan when he slipped his fingers between her folds and found her sweet nub. He rubbed it in circles, swirling his fingers around it, and lowered his other hand to her sheath.

Liora tipped her head back and clutched the edge of the table with both hands as he eased his fingers into her. Her legs fell further open, spread by his knees, and she raised her hips towards him. He frowned and stroked her nub while stroking her inside too, feeling her hot sheath grip him as she flexed her muscles and groaned.

She looked wanton like that, bared for him and lost in her pleasure. Pleasure he had given her. He wanted to keep her like this for hours, balanced on the edge, teasing her close to falling and then slowing down again, until she begged for mercy. He could spend days watching her in this sensual haze, intoxicated by his touch.

Her grip on the stone table tightened and she shifted her hips, rocking herself on his fingers. "Asmodeus."

Her face screwed up, breathing turning ragged and heart accelerating, pumping as wildly as his was against his chest. Her breasts heaved, the dusky buds tight with need, calling for his attention. He denied them, was too transfixed by the sight of her wound tight with pleasure and the feel of her under his hands. Her hot sheath gripped his fingers, drawing them deeper into her, and he pumped her harder, giving her what she desired.

More.

He swirled his fingers around her nub, teasing it and bringing her close to the edge, and then backed off again. She mewled and screwed her face up, tipping her head back and thrusting her breasts high in the air. Delicious.

"Please," she whispered, husky and raw, desperate.

Asmodeus gave her what she needed, plunging two fingers deep into her and brushing his other fingers over her nub at the same time. She shattered before him, crying out as her body quivered and convulsed, pulling his fingers in deeper and saturating them in warmth.

He wanted to taste her.

He growled, withdrew his fingers and slipped from the edge of the table. He caught her hips, dragged her to the edge and kneeled between her legs. She gasped at the first flick of his tongue over her flesh and then moaned and raised her hips as he lapped at her, tasting her pleasure.

His cock throbbed, hungry for a taste of her too. He couldn't stop himself from rocking his hips as he pushed his tongue inside her. Liora moaned and shivered, trembled anew around him. He licked and then sucked, wanting more from her.

"Asmodeus," Liora uttered and he lifted his gaze and looked up the length of her body. She lay propped up on her elbows, her smile wicked. "My turn."

He wanted to deny her but the way his length went as rigid as steel and ached as it never had before shut down that denial before it could leave his lips.

"Stand." She moved to kneel on the table and he rose before her, wondering what she had planned.

Liora leaned forwards onto her hands and knees and crawled towards him, giving him a glorious view down her back to the peachy globes of her bottom. He growled at the thought of being on the other side of the table, seeing her from that angle, her body on display for him, tempting him into taking her.

Her tongue flicked over the crown of his cock and then she took him into her hot mouth and all of his thoughts derailed. He groaned and grunted, hazy from head to toe as she licked and sucked him, lavishing his length with attention. She cupped his sac again, toying with it as she had near the pool, each little tug sending hot shivers blasting outwards and heightening his pleasure.

Asmodeus clutched her shoulders and tried to fight his desire to rock himself into her mouth, taking it. He stared at her bottom, imagining himself behind her, thrusting into her body like this. He grunted again and pumped into her mouth. She moaned, the noise vibrating along the length of him, adding to his pleasure and making him moan along with her.

She sucked more greedily, pulling hard on him once more and then softening her approach the next. Driving him mad. Was she getting him back for what he had done to her? It felt as though she wanted to torture him for hours, bringing him to the edge and then refusing to push him over it.

His knees trembled and he held her tighter, trying to keep himself upright. She squeezed and tugged his balls, wrenching another groan from him, and stroked his length in time with her sucking. Was this how she would feel when he was inside her?

The thought tipped him right over the edge and he grunted as pleasure shot through him and he spilled himself into her mouth, shallowly thrusting through the ring of her fingers. She lapped at him as he had her, licking up his spending and sending another shivery hot wave crashing through him.

Asmodeus's hands slipped to the table. He grasped the edge, closed his eyes, and breathed slowly, trying to bring himself gently down.

Liora released him and he glanced down at his softening cock. He had wanted to be inside her this time. She kneeled and ran her hands up his stomach to his chest, rising before him. His heart pounded against his ribs, the rhythm still too fast, making him feel dizzy and hazy. She looped her arms around his neck and he moaned as she kissed him.

He twitched. Stirred.

Grinned.

The more she kissed him and stroked his wings, the harder he became, until he prodded her belly and she gasped and looked down.

"Angel stamin—"

Asmodeus caught her behind her knees and flipped her onto her back, knocking the words from her lips. He growled and spread her thighs, staring down at her feminine core and then slowly raking his eyes up over her beautiful body to meet hers.

Liora stretched her arms above her head and curled her fingers around the edge of the table again. Her eyes darkened with arousal.

He grabbed her hips and yanked her closer, tearing another gasp from her and making her eyes go even darker, and narrowed his gaze on her glistening curls.

He took hold of his rigid length and bent at the knee, bringing him down to level with her. His hand shook. He crushed the nerves that made it tremble and ran the head of his flesh through her folds. She moaned and writhed, and he didn't want to wait any longer.

Asmodeus edged further down and lost his breath when the crown nudged inside her. Hot. She felt hotter around it than she had around his fingers. He eased forwards and she arched, moaning and straining, incredibly tight around him.

He froze. Too tight.

"Don't stop... go slow... okay?"

He groaned. He could do slow. It would kill him, but he would do it for her, so he didn't hurt her. He wanted this to feel good, the best she'd had. Better than the male who had dared touch what was his.

Asmodeus slowly entered her, inch by excruciating inch, swallowing hard to resist ramming forwards and seating himself to his hilt. He planted his hands on the table and then grasped her hips and raised them as he straightened, coming to stand between her thighs. She moaned now, this time one of pleasure not pain.

"Keep going," she whispered, as breathless as he felt.

He eased forwards, throbbing from how tightly she gloved him and how hot she was, scorching him with her wet heat. The end of his length hit something.

"Oh, bingo," she muttered. "Mother Earth, you're big."

"A bad thing?" He hoped not. He intended to do this often with her. As often as she allowed and then more.

She shook her head. "Remember. Slow and steady wins the race."

This was a race?

He stared at her. She cracked her eyes open and smiled. "It's a metaphor. It means you don't need to rush."

"Easier said than done... every fibre of me wants to claim you and I want to claim you hard."

She moaned and flexed around him, and he choked. She could go tighter?

"I love it when you talk dirty."

He wasn't sure whether she was teasing. He grasped her hips and stared down at the point where their bodies joined, fascinated as he slowly withdrew and then thrust back in, watching his cock disappear into her body. She felt good. Incredibly good. Insanely good.

He struggled to set a slow and steady pace as she had instructed. He held her firm when she kept trying to wriggle and gently increased his speed as she began to loosen around him. Asmodeus watched their bodies joining, his hard length pumping into her, filling her completely and ripping a moan from her each time it did so. He hadn't imagined that sex itself would be so arousing.

If she watched them coupling, would it thrill her too?

He wanted to know.

"Would you feel more pleasure if you could see my cock entering you?"

She choked and stared at him with wide eyes. "You're embracing the dirty talk, aren't you?"

He nodded and slowed his pace, decided he liked how she seemed to lose her ability to concentrate when he did that, thrusting in long leisurely strokes, and watched her. "I was curious."

She looked thoughtful and then moaned.

"The thought arouses you?" he said and she blushed, then gave a tiny nod. He looked down again, shifting his hips further back this time, until the head of his cock almost left her, and then easing back in. "It is rather wicked."

"I want to see." She crooked her finger.

She wanted him to mount the table while inside her? That was a rather impossible feat and he didn't feel like withdrawing from her completely.

She made the decision for him by pulling up with her arms, tugging herself free of him. He growled and mounted the table, and then groaned when she pushed him onto his back and mounted him.

Asmodeus lay beneath her, his wings stretched across the black table top, staring up at her. She grasped his cock, positioned it and then twirled her hair up and pinned it using one of his pencils. He held her hips and she pressed her hands against his chest as she looked between them. He watched their joining with her, moaning in time with her as she inched down onto him.

"Very wicked," she whispered breathlessly and began moving on him, faster than he had dared, long strokes that had him grasping the edge of the table as she had, at her mercy as she rode him.

The sight of her rocking on him was far more wicked than just the sight of him thrusting into her and then withdrawing. He lay beneath her and lost himself in it, amazed that she was doing this with him, wanted him like this. She grasped his hips and tipped her head back, arching her breasts towards him and moaning each time she thrust down onto him, taking him deep into her body. She moved faster, wilder, rotating her hips and moaning louder.

His little hellion.

"Asmodeus," she groaned and he countered her thrusts, plunging his cock hard into her every time she bore down on him. It still wasn't enough for him. He needed more. She needed it too.

He growled, flipped her onto her back and grasped her shoulders, thrusting deep. She groaned and grabbed his wings, tugging them and pulling him down to her, undulating her hips beneath him and flexing around him, clenching his length. It seemed the time for slow and steady had passed and she was too far gone to care about any pain. It had all become pleasure.

Asmodeus curled his hips, grunting each time their bodies met and she clawed at his shoulder or clutched one of his wings and groaned. He gritted his teeth and pumped her harder, using the full length of his rigid shaft to feel all of her, and make her feel all of him. She belonged to him. He was claiming her and when he was done, she would be his forever. He would never let her go.

She moaned hotly into his ear, craned her neck and bit the lobe, ripping a growl from him. "Harder."

Holy hell. He could do that.

He held her tighter and thrust harder, shorter strokes that had her rocking in his arms. His balls drew up and his shaft swelled, aching inside her. She tightened around him, choking him in her heat, drawing him closer to the edge. Not yet. She would have her bliss first.

"More," she whispered and he complied, holding back and giving her what she desired, letting her feel every inch of him as he took her, giving her pleasure. She dug her nails into his bare backside, clawing at him, forcing him to move faster. He grunted into her neck, bit down without thinking, and she screamed at the top of her lungs.

She went so tight he grunted in pain this time, and then she convulsed into him and her whole body shook as she quivered around him, her sheath milking his cock.

Asmodeus growled into her neck and kept thrusting, drawing out her climax as he sought his own. She clung to him, still pushing his backside, making him take her hard and fast. He tasted blood on his tongue, tasted heat and life, and power.

The moment he swallowed to clear the taste away, his blood lit up like lightning and he jerked deep into her body and came hard, his climax wringing his seed from him over and over again until he trembled and collapsed on top of her, breathing hard against her throat. His cock continued to pulse inside her.

"Mother Earth…" she muttered into his ear and he grunted in response, unable to form words to express how that had made him feel but agreeing with her and the awed tone she had used. She poked his arm, nudging him. "Asmodeus?"

He grunted again.

"You okay?"

Shrugged.

He felt dizzy. Drained. High.

He tried to look at her and closed his eyes again. "Spinning."

Her hand knocked against his face and then touched her neck. "You bit me."

It took him a moment to remember that. He nodded. "Did not mean to."

"Blood. Sex. Magic." Her tone made those three words sound significant and he managed to push himself up and drowsily looked down at her. His length still throbbed, sending pleasant aftershocks tripping through him.

"Huh?" he mumbled and her eyes darted between his. She cupped his cheeks and pulled his lower eyelids down with her thumbs, inspecting his eyes, and then checked his teeth and he was beginning to feel mildly concerned. Only mildly though. Panic had no chance against the hot hazy bliss consuming him. "Huh?"

"Witches are forbidden to exchange blood during sex."

He was glad she still sounded breathless and her voice hitched at intervals during her explanation, her pupils swallowing her irises in time with each one. Aftershocks. She had them too. He could feel her quiver when they happened.

"Why?" he said.

"Normally it has a bad side effect... like... death."

"Death by sex?" Not a good side effect at all. "We did not exchange blood. I had a tiny taste of yours. It tastes like lightning."

"Really?" Curiosity replaced any shred of fear in her eyes. "I guess we didn't exchange blood... and you're not a witch... and you're immortal and rather powerful... but... you had me worried there."

"Felt good though." He tried to stifle his smile, knowing she would detect the touch of pride in it.

She blushed and said in a small shy voice, "It did."

Asmodeus grinned. "Want to do it again?"

Her blush deepened.

He took that as a yes.

He dipped his head to kiss her.

The entire castle shook.

CHAPTER 15

Liora was one hundred percent certain that shaking had not been a pleasure aftershock like the ones rocking her body.

Asmodeus growled, pulled out of her and was clothed in an instant in his pieces of gold-edged black armour. Liora hastily hopped down from the table, grabbed her clothes and pulled them on. She had just managed to get her bra fastened when Romulus and Remus bounded into the room, growling and snarling, their crimson eyes bright with death and fangs dripping blood.

Asmodeus spoke in his dark tongue to them and then his golden blades appeared in his hands and he rose to stand on the table, his black wings furled against his back and his eyes burning red.

"What's happening?" She looked up at him.

His crimson gaze shifted to her and his black eyebrows met in a scowl.

"We have company. I shall turn them away." He walked the length of the table and dropped down from the end, landing silently on the stone floor.

"Wait." Liora raced after him. "I'm not letting you go out there alone."

He strode down the steps to the next level. "Go to the bedroom, Liora, and remain there with Remus."

"No!" She damned well wasn't going to let him order her around like that and treat her like a damsel in distress, a woman unable to protect herself and fight. "You don't have to do this alone. I won't let you do this alone. We're a team. We do this together."

He paused and looked back at her, the dark expression on his face warning her that he wasn't in the mood to argue. She wasn't in the mood either and there was no argument. She was going with him whether he liked it or not.

"Return to the bedroom," he snapped and began walking again. The castle rocked and dust rained down from the black ceiling of the corridor.

Remus whined behind her as she followed Asmodeus. He might not want to anger his master by disobeying his orders, but she wasn't going to let him boss her around.

"I've fought countless demons, Asmodeus."

He stopped again and turned to face her. "When you were twelve and your parents died? What did you know about fighting at that age?"

She shook her head and swallowed her nerves. "No... after that. I've participated in countless demon hunts and I have killed hundreds of them."

He frowned at her and her stomach squirmed. He must have caught the flicker of guilt in her eyes because he sighed, stepped towards her and sheathed one of his swords so he could stroke her cheek.

"You do not have to apologise for what you have done, Liora. It is how you were raised and you were protecting your world and your people. The demons likely deserved to die." He settled his palm against her cheek and stared down into her eyes, his shining with the guilt she felt in her heart.

He looked away from her and frowned at the floor, and his hand fell from her face.

She knew that look. He was comparing her actions to his own. She had killed countless demons and he had killed countless humans, but they had killed for different reasons.

"I am no good for you, Liora. I had hoped that the more time I spent with you, the more I would see I could be good for you... but I only see how bad I am for you and that we are not right for each other." He closed his eyes and she took hold of his hand, curling her fingers around to brush his palm. He was about to head out into battle against who knew how many adversaries, all so he could protect her, and he still couldn't see the good in himself without ending up doubting his actions and feelings.

"You are good for me, Asmodeus, and I'm good for you. We're good for each other. Right for each other. Tell me why you feel we aren't."

"Because you have killed demons, but you had a reason for taking their lives. There has never been a reason behind the things I have done. I killed because I was told to or because I enjoyed it."

Liora bit her lip. "I, uh, might have done that too."

He opened his eyes, incredulity filling them.

"Okay, so we're not so different after all. You just can't see it because you have this image of me in your head that is more suitable for a fantasy princess than who I really am. Look at me, Asmodeus, because I'm telling you the truth." She squeezed his hand and looked deep into his crimson eyes. "I've killed demons for fun. I've killed them because I was angry, because I was scared, because I wanted revenge and because I was bored. I'm not a saint. I've fought demons I had no reason to fight. I've gone out of my way to hunt down demons who weren't even on our naughty list because I was itching for a fight. I'm a reprobate. I'm bad. My coven made me take a trip to Paris to cool off because I went nuclear on a few demons and almost got someone from my coven killed in the crossfire."

He stared at her.

"Now, tell me we aren't so different," she whispered and hoped he didn't find another excuse to tell her otherwise.

He slipped his hand free of hers and brushed his knuckles across her cheek. The hard planes of his face softened and his gaze narrowed on hers, the darkness in it fading to reveal warmth. The faintest smile curled the corners of his sexy mouth.

"We are not so different," he murmured and tipped her head up, lowered his mouth and pressed a soft kiss to her lips.

When he released her, she smiled. "So I'm in... I can fight too?"

"No." He turned on his heel and she scowled at his back.

"Coming anyway." She ignored his huff and followed him.

Remus gave up whining and moved alongside her, his head almost level with hers. Romulus had gone on ahead but was waiting at the end of the corridor, where it turned and led down to the courtyard. The walls shook again. What was out there?

Asmodeus stopped at the end, pressed his back against the wall and peered around the corner. The next second, she was on her back with Asmodeus on top of her, his hands over her head to protect it. Romulus and Remus were beside them and heat washed over her, blistering in temperature, and bright gold filled her vision.

Fire.

A mighty roar shook the castle.

"What the hell is out there?" She stared at the ceiling and the smoke lazily curling along it. "A freaking dragon?"

Asmodeus pushed himself up onto his elbows and gave her another incredulous look. "You are familiar with the creatures of Hell."

Not incredulous. Impressed.

"I was joking!" She pushed him off her and tried to sneak to the end of the corridor to see if it really was a dragon tearing up the courtyard. Asmodeus grabbed her arm and pulled her back to him.

"Wait here."

"Wait here? While you what? Slay a dragon?" There was no way she was letting him outside the do that. It sounded big, and it had fire and who knew what else in its arsenal.

He nodded.

"No. No way. You are not fighting that thing." She pulled him away from the end of the corridor, back towards the interior of the castle. He stopped dead and she grunted with effort as she tried to convince him to keep moving. He didn't budge an inch.

"It is not my first dragon."

"But it might be your last," she grumbled and she wasn't about to let him go off and get himself killed after he had given her the most fantastic sex of her life and she was still shivering with small aftershocks from it. "I plan to keep you in one piece for as many years as I can."

He stumbled forwards and she looked back at him, catching the goofy smile on his face before he schooled his expression. He liked it when she talked about keeping him. She could work on that.

"I need you in one piece... whole... because you owe me more fantastic sex."

He grinned now. "It was good."

"I said fantastic, didn't I?" She pulled on his arm. "Now, move."

"I am not accustomed to fleeing." He stood his ground again and she sighed.

"It isn't fleeing if you technically haven't started fighting." She wasn't banking on that one to work. She was running out of ways to keep him distracted and keep him from fighting. She had to do something.

"It is so." He twisted free of her grip. "I am the King of Demons. I do not flee from dragons."

Magic began to lazily spiral around her hands as her panic and anger rose. It was stronger than before, fed by the books in Asmodeus's library. Hell was a different realm but it was still part of her world, just as Heaven was. Could she teleport?

She looked at Asmodeus as he drew his second blade and prepared himself, and then at Romulus and Remus.

She had never teleported more than one person before and she was leaving no one behind to face that dragon.

"Liora!"

The world exploded around her. Pain blasted every bone in her body. Her ears rang and dust choked her lungs. Darkness invaded and swirled around her. Heat licked her hands.

Doggy heat. One of the hellhounds was licking her hand.

Liora frowned and cracked her eyes open, and squinted as they stung, the acrid smoke making them water. Something heavy pressed down on her. Something whined, sounding pained.

Liora choked and felt around in the darkness. Asmodeus. He had shielded her again, using his body to take a violent blow that would have easily killed her. She blinked away her tears and saw through the smoke. Half of the castle had fallen down, nothing but rubble a few metres further along the corridor where the entrance had once been.

"Asmodeus," she whispered and shook him. He didn't respond. Her heart leaped into meltdown mode and magic crackled along her arms. The hellhound licking her hand yelped and she silently apologised. "Asmodeus?"

He still didn't respond. Was he breathing? She fluttered her hand over his throat and found a weak pulse. Her relief bloomed and died within a heartbeat.

Through the clearing smoke, she saw bright green eyes the size of car windshields, surrounded by iridescent blue scales that shone green and pink in the light of the fires blazing around her.

Dragon.

It hissed and sharp teeth the length of her arms and legs came zooming towards her.

Liora wrapped her free leg around Asmodeus, grabbed the mutts by whatever she could reach and closed her eyes, praying to Mother Earth for a helping hand. Heat and the stench of smoke wafted over her, a sharp spear lanced her side and then cool air surrounded her.

Someone swore in French.

Romulus and Remus shot to their paws, snarling and snapping at her cousin, protecting her and Asmodeus even though they were injured too. Blood spotted their black fur, making it glisten, and she could see red gashes in places on their muscular bodies.

Apollyon cursed and metal scraped along leather as he drew his sword.

Liora rolled Asmodeus off her and leaped between him and the hellhounds. Well, she attempted a leap. She fell flat on her face between the two canines, one arm reaching out in front of her.

"No," she mumbled into the wooden floor.

"Liora?" Serenity said and then made the stupid mistake of rushing to her. That set the two hellhounds off again. Serenity shrieked and leaped away from them. Apollyon rushed forwards and shielded her, waving his sword at Romulus and Remus.

"Ungh," Liora grunted and pushed onto her hands and knees, and clumsily shoved Apollyon's sword away from Remus.

Remus's ear flopped but quickly perked up again. Apollyon didn't seem to notice. He was too busy staring at her.

"What happened?" he demanded and didn't he sound just like Asmodeus when he was feeling stroppy and temperamental?

She sighed, coughed to clear the smoke from her throat, and looked over her shoulder at Asmodeus.

"Dragon," she said and wrapped her arms around Remus's neck. He kindly stayed put as she pulled herself onto her feet. Her right leg screamed in pain and she cursed it. Was she destined to be forever hobbled?

"Dragon?" Serenity parroted.

Her cousin clearly had hearing difficulties.

"Big scaly thing. Green eyes. Huge fangs. Tendency to breathe smoke and fire." Liora cast a hand down herself to emphasise the smoke and fire part. Her crimson top was singed in places and black soot covered her.

"Liora," Apollyon warned and she ignored him.

She turned and hobbled to Asmodeus. Remus remained with her, acting as her crutch, and then sat beside his master, allowing her to gently ease down his body to kneel beside Asmodeus.

"Asmodeus?" she whispered and gently patted his cheek. Still no response. She checked his pulse again. It was stronger this time.

Liora closed her eyes, placed her hands on his cheeks and focused. She had tapped a lot of magic to transport him and his hellhounds all the way to Paris but it was quick to come to her, as if it had reserved some of itself for this task, knowing she would need it.

She let out her breath and gently pushed her magic into Asmodeus, seeking his wounds, healing him from the inside. His bones cracked back into place and healed, and his heart beat harder, growing stronger. Organs repaired themselves and the burns on his back and his charred feathers disappeared.

Her head turned and her heart missed a beat, and she reluctantly severed the connection. She curled up on his bare chest and listened to his heart beating, strong and steady again, a heavy comforting rhythm against her ear.

He groaned. She smiled.

"Liora!" He shot up, knocking her awkwardly off him, and she bumped into Remus. She cursed and Asmodeus's red eyes darted to her, the panic in them faded, and confusion replaced them shortly followed by something close to fury when he realised where they were.

"You saved me... again," she said, hoping to distract him from the angel standing behind her, towering over them both. Romulus and Remus closed ranks, coming to protect him and her, growling whenever Apollyon or Serenity looked as if they might move. "You really have to stop doing that."

Asmodeus managed a smile and slowly lifted his hand. He grimaced and frowned, and she could almost feel him forcing himself to keep moving. She took hold of his blackened bloodied hand and brought it to her face for him, and kissed his palm.

"I swore to protect you," he husked and she smiled now, closed her eyes and savoured how good it felt to have him touching her again, alive and well, when she had feared she was going to lose him.

Remus snarled.

Liora lowered Asmodeus's hand to her lap and petted the hellhound. He looked ready to eat Apollyon but confused at the same time. Remus's gaze shifted to her.

"This is your master's not-so-nice-twin... Apollyon. He won't seek to harm us. Will you, Apollyon?" She looked behind her at the angel and he glowered, sent his swords away and folded his muscular arms across his broad chest. "Will you, Apollyon?"

He said something in the demonic language. Remus got to his paws, lowered his head and snarled, revealing his black fangs.

Asmodeus growled too.

"I don't know what you just said, but take it back or we're leaving." She petted Remus but he didn't calm this time. The black fur down his back stood on end.

"He said we dogs of Hell will return there or he would send us back in pieces." Asmodeus hauled himself onto his feet and wavered.

Liora got to hers and pressed her hands against his chest, steadying him.

"I will not remain here." Asmodeus tried to move a step and collapsed against her.

"You're really in no condition to argue. Neither of you. Serenity, I *will* leave."

"Apollyon will not harm Asmodeus... or his... ah... chiens?" Serenity threw her a desperate glance.

"Hellhounds," she supplied and nodded. "There, see. The big evil angel won't harm us."

She stroked Remus to soothe him, keeping hold of Asmodeus with her other hand so he didn't fall.

"You need to rest," Liora whispered to him and he said nothing, just glared at Apollyon over her head. "Asmodeus?"

He dropped his gaze to her, stared at her for the longest time, and then subtly nodded. She was glad he wasn't going to fight her on it. She didn't want to make him feel weak in front of Apollyon, but he did need to rest. He was still injured. Her magic had only quickened the healing process for him.

"We can go to my room." She pointed across the living room to it.

He would have to navigate past Apollyon and Serenity, and the cream couch, but she would be behind him every step of the way in case he needed her. What she really wanted to do was sling his arm around her shoulders and help him walk there, but like his counterpart, he had an overabundance of pride and was liable to snap at her if she made him feel weak.

Asmodeus managed to reach her temporary room with only a few wobbles. Remus and Romulus tried to squeeze through the narrow doorframe at the same time and ended up snapping at each other. Liora sighed, grabbed Romulus by his scruff and pulled him through first. She swore the hellhound had as much pride as his owner. He always wanted to be first before Remus.

She closed the door and Apollyon immediately muttered something to Serenity. Her cousin would handle him and his concerns. Liora was only planning to remain here as long as it took Asmodeus to regain his strength and then they would need to find a new home. She had no doubt that if the Devil had sent a dragon to kill Asmodeus in Hell, he would gladly send the same one to kill him in the mortal realm.

Asmodeus flopped down onto the bed, wrecking the cream bedclothes with his soot-covered body.

"You dare bring me back here?" he grumbled and she didn't quite hear the usual level of anger and indignation in his voice. It seemed more like grousing to keep up appearances. Was he secretly glad they were safe and she had brought them here, to Apollyon and Serenity? Her cousin and his twin were powerful, more than able to keep them safe for the time being.

"Consider yourself lucky my spell worked and we're still alive and not toast. It was a pretty close call." Liora pressed her hand to her side and flinched. The bastard had got her. She had feared as much.

Asmodeus's eyes darkened but not with anger. Concern filled them. "You are injured."

He held his hand out to her and she went to him. "Let me see."

Liora lifted her top up and revealed her left side where the dragon's tooth had pierced her. Asmodeus sighed and relief filled his eyes. He touched the wound, fingers gently brushing her skin.

"It is not deep. You are fortunate, my little mortal. A dragon has a poisonous bite when it intends to wound and toy with its prey, able to inject a nerve toxin into the veins with a single scratch of its fangs."

Her heart shot into her throat and she leaned her hip outwards so she could see the wound. It was nothing more than a small red crater on the fleshy part of her side. "I've been poisoned?"

"No. Hence, you are fortunate. The dragon feared my master. His mission was to capture you unharmed. He did not dare poison you." Asmodeus bent his head.

She gasped when he sucked the wound, the feel of his mouth latching onto her flesh taking her back to making love with him and his biting her, and sending another shivery aftershock rocking her.

Asmodeus drew back and smiled. "You think wicked things even at a time like this?"

His voice had gone thick and gravelly, raw with passion, just the way she liked it. Liora stepped between his legs and raked her fingers through his short wild black hair. He tipped his head back and looked up into her eyes.

"I do, but you are in no condition."

He frowned. "But I owe you more fantastic sex."

There was that flicker of pride in his eyes again, the one that made her smile in spite of her attempts not to. He liked that he had pleased her.

"Rest now. Making love later."

"Making love?" he whispered, huskier than before. "I like the sound of that."

"It'll give you something to look forward to while you rest." She gently pushed his shoulder and he fell backwards onto the bed.

"You must rest with me too." He tried to catch her hand and she evaded him.

"I need to speak with my cousin and warn them about what they might be in for. Besides, I have the feeling that if I crawl into this bed with you, we will do anything but rest."

He growled and his eyes darkened.

Liora leaned over him, pressed her hands into the mattress on either side of his head and kissed him slowly, drawing it out and pouring her feelings into it, relishing being able to do this with him. She pressed her forehead against his so their noses touched and sighed.

"You do need to take more care of yourself."

"Why?" he whispered and she shook her head.

"Because you're not alone now. You have a responsibility to be more careful, because I don't want to face a world without you. It would break the heart you stole from me." She kissed him again before he could respond and his hands claimed her waist, keeping her on top of him. He kissed her softly, far more gently than she had anticipated, as if he wanted to savour it too.

He settled back against the bed and kissed her cheek. "I will be more careful."

She drew back to smile and thank him, and frowned when she found him with his eyes closed.

"Asmodeus?" She patted his cheek, afraid he had passed out again.

His lips parted on a snore.

Liora smiled, kissed his chin, and stood. She gathered the duvet and covered him as best she could while he was laying on top of it. "Pleasant dreams. Hope your first one is a doozy."

She turned to the two hellhounds and checked them over, taking note of any bad wounds. Remus licked a particularly nasty gash on Romulus's back while Romulus licked one on his left front leg. She patted Remus on his shoulders and he moved aside for her. She placed her hand over the cut on Romulus's back and focused there, watching the flesh knit back together. Once it was closed, she moved to the next wound, and then the next, until both hellhounds were healed.

She went to the door and opened it. Romulus curled up on the floor beside his master. Remus followed her out into the pale living room.

"He likes you," Serenity said, her French accent thick with her amusement.

Liora patted Remus on the head. "He's a sage seven hundred year old puppy and my hero. He woke me up before the dragon could eat us."

"May I stroke him?" Serenity didn't look certain.

Apollyon looked outraged by the request. "No."

"Yes." Liora frowned at him. He really needed to loosen up. Remus wouldn't bite Serenity's hand off. At least, she didn't think he would. She caught him under his jaw and turned his head towards her, staring deep into his red eyes. "No bitey."

His jaws parted, his tongue lolled and he began panting.

"That's a green light." She patted him between the ears and glanced at her cousin. Serenity nervously flicked her fair hair over her shoulders.

"He understands?"

"Sort of. He's better with that demon language. I don't speak it, but he always pants when he agrees to something." She approached Serenity, keeping her arm around Remus's neck. The hellhound made her feel small but Serenity looked even tinier next to him.

Her cousin bravely reached out.

Apollyon reached for the blade at his side.

Liora rolled her eyes and felt an incredible rush when Remus proved her faith in him to be right and didn't bite Serenity's arm off. Her cousin clumsily patted him between his ears.

Remus's left ear drooped.

"Oh!" Serenity said with a smile. "I broke him."

Liora fixed his ear for him, hiding her own smile. "We're working on that, but it does help me tell them apart."

"We're?" Apollyon said, his tone pure darkness. Now he sounded more evil than Asmodeus.

"Yes. We are. As in, me and Asmodeus." She gave him a fierce glare that challenged him to find a problem with that.

He muttered something beneath his breath and stalked into the kitchen. Liora was surprised he didn't drag Serenity with him. He was probably going in search of chocolate cake.

"How is Asmodeus?"

Liora's eyebrows rose and she looked back at her cousin. "At least you call him by his name. I appreciate that. He's asleep. His first dreams. I wished him doozies."

Serenity smiled.

"Even when they come and go between the mortal and other realms as frequently as Apollyon had, there are still things that are new to them." Her cousin sidled closer and dropped her voice to a whisper, "I, um… caffeine is new to him, no?"

Liora blushed. "Yes, and it is still new to him. You seriously could have warned me about the stamina thing."

Serenity turned beetroot red. "I was not expecting you to fall for an angel… you have fallen for him, haven't you?"

Liora didn't even try to deny that truth. Serenity sighed.

"Apollyon will fight you on this."

"It's none of his business… and you won't?" Liora couldn't believe what she was hearing. "You wanted him the hell away from me before."

"He protected you, and I have always been able to see when angels have found love, and he has found the deepest sort with you. I feel more good in him now."

She did too. It was growing, coming to the fore as he accepted it and didn't try to fight it.

"He struggles at times." Liora wanted to flop onto the couch and have a big girly chat but she was a complete mess and covered in black soot. She didn't think her cousin would appreciate her wrecking her nice cream furniture. At least they could wash the dirt out of the pale bedclothes.

Apollyon passed through from the kitchen, still grumbling under his breath, and headed into the other bedroom. Remus's sharp red eyes followed his every move, his ears pricked and body tensed. As soon as Apollyon disappeared, Remus's left ear flopped forwards and he began panting again.

Had the hellhounds known of Asmodeus's twin? They didn't seem to like him, but then he had threatened their master and he probably reeked of Heaven. She imagined that didn't go down well with any creature from Hell.

Liora leaned on Remus and he didn't budge, easily supporting her weight. She had never had a pet before, but she was beginning to think of him as hers too. She lazily stroked his sleek black fur.

"I need a glass of wine," Serenity said and those words were music to her ears. "You do too. Come on."

Liora followed Serenity into the small kitchen. Remus stuck to her like glue. Serenity poured two large glasses of white wine and handed one to her, and led her out on the balcony. Liora stepped out onto the terracotta tiles and sighed at the view. She never tired of looking out at the leafy park below her.

Remus shot to the balcony railings. His head darted around, his eyes scanning and ears pricked. If a canine could frown in concentration, he was doing it. He looked back at her and she detected a flicker of uncertainty, and then his thick whip-like tail thumped against the side wall of the terrace.

Liora sighed. "I don't think Asmodeus would be happy if we took you for your first walkies in the park without him."

She could just imagine the horror that would show on people's faces if they saw Remus galloping through the park with half a tree trailing behind him, bringing it to her to throw.

"Perhaps when it's dark?" Serenity put in and Liora nodded to back up the suggestion.

Remus whined and wagged harder, catching her in the side. She flinched and almost spilled her wine.

"You are hurt." Serenity set her glass down on the small round wrought metal table.

"Just a dragon bite. Nothing serious. It'll heal. I'll bandage it later when Asmodeus is awake." She lifted her crimson top to show her cousin the small wound. It had already stopped bleeding thanks to whatever Asmodeus had done and was looking less angry around the edges.

Liora lowered her top and stroked Remus again, trying to soothe him. He settled after a few minutes of petting, happily watching the people coming and going through the park. He ignored the dogs. Did he recognise the mortal realm variety of his breed?

Serenity picked up her glass and brought it up to her lips. Liora sipped her wine and relaxed into her chair.

A horse and rider passed along the path she could see through the trees.

Remus barked at ear-splitting volume. It echoed around the park like thunder. He shifted restlessly, bouncing up and down the length of the railing, watching the black horse. He barked again and dropped his front, sticking his backside high in the air and wagging his tail. Liora held her arm out in front of her, blocking it and avoiding being assaulted.

"Remus," she said and he ignored her, still intent on initiating play with a horse. "Remus!"

He shot up and knocked the glass of wine from Serenity's hand. It shattered on the terracotta. Serenity cursed. Apollyon's voice boomed from inside like the Devil himself and he appeared in the doorway, took one look at her cousin, saw the tiny cut on her palm and turned on Remus.

She wasn't sure what he said.

It sounded nasty though and Remus cowered, his ears flattening against his head.

Liora got to her feet and stood between Remus and Apollyon. "It was my fault. I shouted at him and he was just turning to look at me. He didn't mean to knock the glass."

"I want him out," Apollyon barked and she clutched Remus's scruff for support when Apollyon's power rose around her, pressing down on her. "Now!"

"No." Liora stood her ground, shielding Remus and weathering the force of Apollyon's power. It grew stronger, a heavy weight on her shoulders, driving her downwards. "If he goes, we all go. I go with them."

"No, Liora," Serenity said and turned to Apollyon. "Please, mon ange."

"Go where?" Apollyon snarled and Remus growled behind her. "Who in this world would take you in and have the power to protect you?"

Liora somehow managed to square her shoulders in spite of the oppressive force of Apollyon's power and realised she didn't have an answer to that question.

An arm shot across Apollyon's throat and Asmodeus loomed behind him, clutching his shoulder and grasping the back of his head with his other hand, pushing it forwards and choking him. The weight of his power decreased and she stared over his shoulder at Asmodeus.

His red eyes locked on her.

"The Devil's daughter would."

CHAPTER 16

Asmodeus's first dream was a nightmare. He saw Liora battling the dragon, bloodied and beaten, one arm hanging limp at her side. Remus and Romulus were beside her, trying to protect her, launching themselves at the immense beast whenever it dared to near her. He tried to intervene but Apollyon held him back, blue fire in his eyes, twisted amusement that showed the intense pleasure he took from seeing her fighting for her life.

Asmodeus had been like that once. Never again.

Liora needed him. He took no pleasure in her suffering. He wanted to make her feel safe again, protected. He wanted to protect her.

The scene whirled and he saw a closed white door, and then it shifted and he saw Serenity through a red haze. Liora was with him, standing above him. He looked up at her. He liked her. She was kind to him and his master. He had taken a vow to protect her together with his brother. He did not like when his master mated with her though. There were some things you could not unsee.

His master?

The Devil?

Asmodeus saw a park. Green. Bright. Colourful. Small furry demons escorted mortals through it. They did not interest him. A big black dog with a male on his back did interest him though. His heart lifted and beat harder, pumping excitement through him. He wanted to play with the big black dog.

Someone shouted at him and then someone called him a wretch that deserved to feel their wrath.

Sweet Liora protected him. Strange. She was still taller than he was.

Asmodeus bared his fangs at the other one, the one who looked like his master.

Not his master. Apollyon looked like him. Not the Devil.

Power. Pressing. Crushing. Protect Liora for his master.

Master?

Wake master.

Something wet slapped his cheek and Asmodeus shot up in bed. Romulus whined and nudged him towards the white door. Door.

Remus.

Liora.

Asmodeus burst from the room, his legs aching and protesting. He stumbled through the living room, looking for her. Remus had commanded Romulus to wake him. Apollyon had threatened Liora.

He spotted the bastard angel with his back to him, vulnerable, open to attack.

Saw Liora bravely facing him, holding out against his power and protecting Remus.

"If he goes, we all go… I go with them." Brave Liora. Sweet Liora.

His focus swam and he grabbed the doorframe of the kitchen to steady himself. Serenity said something he missed.

"Go where?" Apollyon snarled and Asmodeus heard Remus growl. "Who in this world would take you in and have the power to protect you?"

Liora tipped her head up and squared her shoulders. She had no answer. He could see it in her eyes. She didn't know what to say. She didn't have to know. He would speak for them. She had made her intentions clear. She wanted to leave with him and he had an idea about who might take them in.

He came up behind Apollyon, wrapped his arm around his throat before he could move, and shoved his other hand against the back of his head, choking him. The weight of Apollyon's power decreased and Asmodeus stared over his shoulder at Liora.

Her hazel eyes locked on his.

"The Devil's daughter would," he said and she frowned. Serenity stood. Apollyon chuckled at the suggestion. Asmodeus shoved him harder against his arm, killing that mocking laughter.

Erin was with child and the Devil had vowed to leave her and those who fell under her protection alone, unharmed, until she had given birth. It was a risk, but if he could convince her to extend her protection to him and Liora, she would be safe.

He was willing to bet that the Devil wouldn't dare launch a full-scale attack on Erin's location in order to get to him and Liora.

"Erin will take us in, and you know it." Asmodeus shoved Apollyon behind him and released him, swiftly moving in front of Liora and Remus to protect them. His head turned again. Not good. How long had he slept? It didn't feel like long enough.

Apollyon went to rush him but Serenity stepped between them, her hands on her hips. The blood drained from Apollyon's face. Scared of his petite witch?

Romulus growled from behind Apollyon, his fangs close to his neck and his nose against his ear.

Asmodeus smiled. It was nice to have the upper hand over his twin for once.

"We will take you to her and you can speak with her," Serenity said, the voice of reason. He appreciated her backing him up. It only added to his victory. Apollyon was alone. Asmodeus had everyone behind him. He could get used to this.

Apollyon looked as if he wanted to speak out against that idea and then folded his arms across his chest. His wings shrank into his back and his armour disappeared, a white linen shirt and black cut-off jeans shorts replacing them.

"Your mutts will have to stay." Apollyon shoved past Romulus and walked into the house.

"They're coming with us," Liora called after him. "I don't leave anyone behind."

Asmodeus wanted to kiss her for that. He looked over his shoulder at her and Serenity tiptoed away, leaving them alone.

Except for his hellhounds.

He spoke to them in the demon tongue, mentioning that they may see some more things they couldn't 'unsee' if they stuck around.

Remus whined and glanced longingly at the park.

Asmodeus added that it was a horse he had seen and while they were almost the same size, he did not think that the horse would play with him.

That only made him whine more. Asmodeus rubbed his ears, feeling sorry for him. "I will take you down when it is dark and cloak us and you can play with your brother."

"We will take you down," Liora said and hugged Remus. He wagged his tail and went inside, rubbing Romulus on his way past.

"Did I thank you for saving me and my hellhounds before we became toast?" Asmodeus turned to Liora and she scrunched her nose up, wriggled it and then shook her head.

"I remember you shouting at me about it."

"Ah." He shrugged, leaned against the railing beside her and nudged her with his hip. "Thank you for saving us."

She nudged him back and smiled up at him. "No problem. I hope you like sand, sea and stars."

He frowned. "Why?"

She stepped away from the railing and twirled to face him, a huge smile on her lips and a twinkle in her eye. "Erin lives on a tropical island. Margaritas! But not for you… because you're a shitty drunk."

Asmodeus growled and tried to grab her. She spun beyond his reach, giggling as she followed his hellhounds back inside. He stared after them and then sighed and looked over his shoulder at the park. If Remus was excited by a park, how was he going to take sand and surf? He was going to end up spoiled by this world, just like his master.

He followed them into the apartment and pretended not to see Apollyon in the kitchen or feel the force of his glare as he passed. He flipped him off over his shoulder at the doorway for good measure though.

"Asmodeus, wait."

He really wanted to pretend he hadn't heard that but the bastard angel had used his name and had spoken in a civilised tone. He turned around, leaned against the doorframe and folded his arms across his bare chest.

"You ever threaten my hellhounds again and I will sic them on you."

"Serenity ended up cut. Tell me, how would you have reacted if it had been Liora and my animals that had harmed her?" Apollyon rested his backside against the counter and his choice of clothing finally made sense to Asmodeus. Beachwear. He had zero experience of that but he would not dress like his twin.

Asmodeus hated himself for it but he said, "The same. The threat still stands though."

"Noted. Liora was injured during your escape from Hell. You need to do a better job of protecting her."

Asmodeus glared at him, holding his swirling blue gaze and refusing to back down. Apollyon unleashed a fraction of his power and he countered him, allowing his to rise to match it, keeping them equal.

"I did protect her. I shielded her from rock, fire and a fucking dragon." Asmodeus growled as his power rose further, slipping beyond his grasp, stirred by the anger pumping through his veins.

His claws extended and he flexed them, shoving his growing fatigue to the back of his mind together with the pain that still radiated through his bones. Pain that came from the injuries he had sustained while protecting Liora. He had done his best. He had saved his delicate mortal from being crushed by black stone and burned by dragon fire. How dare Apollyon overlook that in order to belittle him?

Apollyon tipped his chin up, his blue eyes brightening, the darker and paler flakes in them shifting and revealing his growing anger.

Asmodeus flexed his claws again. He wanted to beat his wings, shoot across the narrow room and rip his twin's jugular out with those claws.

"Do better," Apollyon said in a low, cold voice. "If you do not want me coming down on your head... do better. You know you could have."

Asmodeus bared his fangs. He did know that but he wasn't about to admit it. He should have cast a portal and pushed her through it together with Romulus and Remus, transporting them elsewhere within the castle. He had reacted on instinct though, and that instinct had demanded he shielded her fragile mortal body with his immortal one. He wasn't used to having to protect someone. This was new to him and he didn't want to make mistakes and place Liora in danger, but he was still learning. He would do better next time she was in danger. He knew without a doubt that there would be a next time. The Devil wasn't going to give up. He wanted Liora and he was going to keep coming at them until either he had her or Asmodeus had put him down.

Apollyon's power lowered, providing less resistance against his, and the angel relaxed against the counter in the small kitchen, looking very domesticated for a legendary angel of death and destruction. The Great Destroyer. Asmodeus could hardly believe that title applied to him as he stood there in the kitchen of his apartment, dressed in beachwear and giving him a pep talk on how to protect a woman.

He stared at Asmodeus in silence for long seconds until Asmodeus finally reined in his temper and his power with it.

"What will you do if Erin will not offer you protection?"

Asmodeus didn't want to think about that until after she had rejected his request. "Come up with another plan."

Apollyon's blue eyes mocked him. "It would be rather prudent to have a back-up plan before you are turned away."

Asmodeus averted his gaze to the counter beside him. His stomach rumbled. Cake. Not a chocolate one either. It was yellowish and had pale creamy topping and red glossy fruit on top that looked like strawberries.

"Liora says all angels are pigs," he said without thinking and Apollyon frowned at him. "She says we eat a lot."

He wasn't going to make it a question and give his twin the satisfaction of enlightening him.

"It is true. The more power we use in this world, the quicker we weaken and the more we need to eat." Apollyon slid the cake towards him.

"She says you can eat a whole chocolate cake in one go."

Apollyon huffed and tipped his chin up. "It was one time and I was annoyed."

"We eat more when annoyed?" Hell, a question. He cursed himself.

His twin shrugged. "I do. Serenity calls it comfort eating."

It was strange talking to his twin like this without either of them attempting to remove the other's head. He didn't even have the usual urge to at least maim him. He blamed his tiredness. He still wanted to sleep. Fighting Apollyon was a waste of his energy. He was too tired to play good twin versus evil twin today. He was too tired to be who everyone expected him to be and live up to those expectations.

He was too tired to do anything other than grab Liora, curl up on the bed behind her and sleep with his female. Sleeping with her would leave them both vulnerable though. They would have to take turns until they were away from Apollyon and Serenity, and he wasn't sure if they would be able to shake them now.

He knew Erin's location. He had felt it inside him like a beacon ever since he had met her in Hell all those months ago and realised what she was, and that they shared blood. He had never known what sort of place she had made into her home though. An island.

He could take Liora and his hellhounds there, leaving Serenity and Apollyon behind, getting a head start on them. A fragment of his heart, the good part growing inside him, warned not to leave them behind. As much as he hated being around Apollyon and didn't want to see him amongst his peers, admired and respected, adored, he had to allow the angel to take them to Erin. Erin knew Apollyon and Serenity. Their presence and introduction might increase the likelihood of them accepting him and Liora into the group and offering them protection.

Asmodeus needed to ensure that he could handle any situation that arose though. He needed to rest and regain his strength before they left, because he was still tired and weak even after his sleep.

"How long was I sleeping?" he said, too tired to even care that it was another question.

"Give or take twenty minutes." Apollyon cut himself a slice of the cake and set the knife back down on the plate beside it. Comfort eating? Because everyone had sided against him for once?

"How long do I need to sleep for? Liora sleeps for many hours."

"Many hours." Apollyon picked up the wedge of cake.

Asmodeus didn't have many hours in which to rest. It was imperative that they move Liora to the island and seek sanctuary there as soon as possible. He would have to settle for regaining only a fraction of his strength and hope it would be enough should problems arise.

Or when problems arose.

Erin was mated to Veiron. The only time he had met Veiron was on the plateau above the bottomless pit and the Hell's angel hadn't liked him very much. He had wanted to fight him. Asmodeus doubted that desire had faded in the past several months.

He definitely needed to bring Apollyon and Serenity with him to the island. Apollyon had convinced Veiron to leave him alone when they had met in Hell. His twin might be able to talk sense into the vengeful fallen angel for him and that would give him a chance to speak with Erin.

First, he needed to rest and regain his strength.

"Is it strawberry?" Asmodeus said with a jerk of his chin towards the cake and Apollyon stopped with the slice close to his mouth and nodded. Asmodeus swallowed his pride, snatched the remains of the cake and stalked away from Apollyon, waiting until he was close to the bedroom before quietly uttering, "Thank you."

"You are welcome," Apollyon shouted and Asmodeus cringed when Liora turned to face him inside the bedroom and gave him a questioning look.

"I thanked him for the cake," he snapped at her, daring her to smile. "That is all. It was on your behalf."

He offered the cake to her and her eyes lit up.

"I'll get fat if you keep feeding me sweet things." She took it anyway, slipped the short silver blade from the plate and cut a slice. She offered it to him and he stared at it. "I don't know what you're worried about. Angels don't get fat. Lucky sods."

"I know of interesting ways to burn calories." He took the piece of cake and devoured it.

"Does this involve coitus?" She grinned when he choked on crumbs and shook his head.

"Hunting is good. That used to make me feel as if I had worked out my body. Chasing the hellhounds is good. They are rather energetic." He tried to think of things other than ones involving being physical together in the bed behind her because she was on to him and had guessed what he had originally intended to suggest.

She had hunted demons. The thought of her taking on demons made him ill. She was powerful, but he found it hard to see past the delicate, petite female she was around him, laughing and teasing, showing him gentleness and affection. He couldn't help that whenever he looked at her, he saw a woman he wanted to protect from the dangers of the three realms. He saw a princess he wanted to place on a pedestal and would protect with his life, playing the role of her fairy tale knight.

A knight with only pieces of his armour and a tarnished heart.

How many demons had hurt his female? He touched the wound on her side, brushing his fingers over it. He had tried to protect her and she had still ended up hurt.

"That's a serious look." She set the cake down, took hold of his hand and lured him towards her, lifting his hand over her shoulder so he ended up right against her. She bit her lip, stroked her fingers over his bare chest, and flashed a saucy smile. "You need a shower. I need a shower. Water is a precious resource."

She flicked a glance behind her at another door in the wall beyond the double bed and then met his gaze again.

"Up for sharing a shower with me?"

That suggestion had him very definitely up in one department.

He was new to showers but he had a feeling that Liora would make his first experience of them one to remember forever.

He nodded and took the lead, earning a surprised look from his little mortal.

Asmodeus rounded the foot of the bed and looked back at her, narrowing his gaze on her body and growling low in this throat.

"Have you ever been washed by someone?" he husked and colour climbed her cheeks, a shy sparkle brightening her hazel eyes.

"No."

"Would you like me to wash you, Liora?"

She grinned naughtily.

"Hell, yes."

CHAPTER 17

Asmodeus tucked Liora close to him and drew in a slow deep breath to settle his nerves before the irritating angel and witch behind him picked up on them. He stared at the space they had cleared in the living room of Serenity and Apollyon's bright pale apartment. It would take him a lot of power to cast a portal large enough to allow all of them through, but they had discussed it and decided this was the best course of action. If they arrived together, Erin and Veiron, and the other residents of the island, were less likely to attack him and Liora or view them as intruders and a threat.

Liora pressed her front against Asmodeus's side, the feel of her hot soft body rubbing his wrecking his concentration. He could almost hear his hellhounds cringing and telepathically discussing how they hated the sight of them pressed together like this. That dreamlike intrusion into their minds had been one of the strangest things he had experienced in his long existence, and although he had very little desire to experience it again, it had been interesting to see things from his hellhounds' point of views and know how they felt about him and Liora.

At least they were clothed this time. Liora had lain naked with him like this, resting her head on his bare chest and using it as a pillow. She had detected his apprehension about sleeping and leaving them vulnerable, and had announced they were going to take shifts.

Asmodeus had agreed, based on the principle that she would be able to rest and regain her strength too. He had not expected that the moment he had awoken from a long restful slumber that she would tell him it was time to go. She had admitted with a blush of awkwardness colouring her cheeks that she had known only one of them would be able to sleep but that she had felt it best he be the one to rest because she needed him strong.

His anger had melted on hearing that, fading away, pushed from his mind by the fact that Liora needed him and had openly told him so.

It helped that she had changed into a short black flowing dress spotted with pale lilac flowers and looked delicious in it, distracting him from his darker thoughts.

She had tried to make him change into beachwear too, but he had insisted on remaining in what little armour he owned, unwilling to risk being caught without its protection. Apollyon didn't seem to think there would be any danger, or at least not to himself and Serenity. His twin still wore black shorts and a loose white shirt, and had tied his long black hair in a ponytail. Serenity had changed into a cream dress with small flowers branching across a strip of it around the hem near her knees.

Asmodeus still wasn't sure what he would choose to wear on a beach.

"Are we going, or not?" Apollyon said from behind him and Romulus growled, echoing Asmodeus's irritation.

Remus came up beside Liora and looked at him. Asmodeus drew in another deep breath, focused on the constant quiet hum in his blood that told him of Erin's location, and cast his free hand out before him. Black shadows grew from a spot in the centre of his focus, swirling outwards, rippling and growing until the vortex filled the room from ceiling to floor and almost across the width of it too.

Romulus flanked him and together with his trusted friends, he led Liora through the portal.

Cool black enveloped him.

Hot sun greeted him on the other side.

His senses blared in warning.

Asmodeus quickly shoved Liora behind him, pushing her under his black wings. He spread them to shield her, called both of his swords to his hands, and ducked backwards, avoiding the red blade that would have cut his throat open.

He swung upwards with one blade, knocking the long black engraved shaft of the weapon and lashed out with the other, driving the male away from Liora. Romulus and Remus snarled, hackles rising and heads lowering as they tensed, preparing to attack, ready to heed any command he gave them.

The male leaped backwards and growled right back at them, flashing rows of red sharp teeth. The skin around his flaming crimson eyes turned black and the warm breeze tousled his wild scarlet hair.

Veiron.

And he was about to go apocalyptic.

The portal behind them closed and Apollyon snapped something at Veiron, but neither Asmodeus nor the Hell's angel traitor were listening.

Veiron snarled, his big body turning black as it grew, muscles thickening and limbs stretching. His jeans shorts disappeared, the red-edged black armour of his kind replacing them, covering his broad chest and his forearms, shielding his hips and protecting his shins. His crimson wings shed their feathers and turned dragon-like and dark, the clawed tips flexing, speaking of the demonic angel's desire to rip into him.

Asmodeus stood his ground, flashing fangs at the male, refusing to back down even when the male finished his change and towered three feet taller than he was and far broader, his skin jet black and blazing red eyes shining with hunger for violence and bloodshed.

Liora gasped.

Veiron narrowed his gaze on her and bared his fangs.

Never.

Asmodeus would never allow this male near her.

"We mean you no harm," Asmodeus said, attempting diplomacy and peace talks even when his blood burned for violence. If he had ever needed proof of how much he had changed since meeting Liora, he had just had it. Before meeting her, he would have unleashed Hell on Veiron in an instant, going to war and seeking blood to satisfy his darkest desires. He would have killed Veiron on the spot for daring to disrespect him by challenging him.

Veiron ignored him and charged.

Asmodeus roared and slashed at Veiron, driving him further backwards on the sand. The footing was difficult, soft and hindering his movements. He wasn't used to fighting on this sort of terrain. He beat his black feathered wings, trying to keep himself upright and nimble, able to dodge the attacks that the Hell's angel threw at him, shoving forwards and jabbing with the long red curved blades of his double-ended spear. All the while, Asmodeus kept part of his focus on Liora behind him, ensuring that she didn't end up in the crossfire and was safe from the furious angel before him.

"Leave... I will not let you near her. Go back and tell the Devil I will kill him for this." Veiron snarled each word, his voice thick and gruff, as demonic and vicious as his appearance.

"I cannot leave." Asmodeus tried to keep him moving backwards, away from Liora, placing more distance between them.

The darker part of him demanded he give Veiron hell and teach him a lesson he would never forget.

The Hell's angel had been itching to fight him ever since they had first met, desperate to prove himself stronger. Asmodeus wanted to show the little wretch that he was insignificant, his power nothing compared with his own, and he would have if the situation had been different.

He had to hold back and weather the storm though, shielding Liora and playing nicely with the demonic angel, otherwise he would ruin the best chance he had of protecting her.

Asmodeus growled and struck the demonic angel's spear again, knocking it upwards. "I cannot let you defeat me. Listen to me. I am not here on my master's business."

Veiron countered Asmodeus's every thrust and slash, blocking his blades with skill that he admired. The male was wild, lost to his temper, but retained an incredible ability to fight and came close to breaking through Asmodeus's defence a few times, driving him backwards towards Liora.

Asmodeus blocked Veiron's spear with both blades, shoved upwards and then slashed at him, catching him on the thick breastplate of his obsidian and crimson armour. Veiron twisted out of the path of the remains of his blow, turned and battered him with his powerful wings before continuing in a full turn and bringing his spear down hard. Asmodeus bent at the knee to brace himself and blocked the black shaft of the spear. The spear hit hard, sending jarring vibrations down Asmodeus's arms. He growled and pushed forwards, knocking Veiron off balance, and shoved to his feet, preparing his next attack.

"Veiron!" A familiar female voice broke the tense silence and shadows swirled behind him.

Erin came rushing out of them, her short black hair blowing back from her tanned face and her black knee-length dress fluttering in the breeze.

Another female was before her in an instant, silvery feathered wings, chrome armour and long pale hair bright in the strong sunlight. She held Erin back so she couldn't leap into the fray.

A dark-haired male angel halted next to her, wearing silver and blue armour, his pale blue eyes locked on the battle. His gaze shifted beyond Asmodeus.

"Apollyon?"

Veiron roared and attacked harder, and Asmodeus almost lost his footing, each blow he blocked more powerful than the last. He couldn't go all out. He couldn't use his full strength to teach this pathetic male the lesson that he hungered to bestow upon his brutish head. He needed his assistance and he would never have it if he harmed him. Asmodeus wasn't used to having to hold back or ask anyone for help, and it was hard to ignore his desire to rip into the male and show him that he was weak, inferior, and foolish for challenging him.

"Veiron! Will you calm the hell down and let the guy speak? You're upsetting junior!" Erin pressed her hand to her stomach, rubbing her swollen belly. Asmodeus's lack of attention cost him.

Veiron slashed down his chest and Asmodeus roared in agony and stumbled backwards.

"Oh, I've had enough of this macho bullshit," Liora snapped from behind him.

Veiron went to cut him down and froze mid-swing. Asmodeus wrapped his arm across the long gash on his bare chest and growled at the male, bracing himself for his attack.

It didn't come.

Veiron's gaze inched downwards towards him and sweat broke out on his brow, as if just moving his eyes had taken incredible effort. What had happened to him?

Liora stepped into view beside Asmodeus, her hands held out before her. Black, red and purple ribbons shifted and danced around her fingers and forearms, and her eyes were darker than he had ever seen them, her expression fierce as she glared at Veiron.

"Liora," Serenity whispered and Liora tensed, blinked, and stared wide-eyed at her arms and then the demonic angel she had under her power.

She swallowed hard and stumbled backwards, lowering her hands at the same time. Veiron collapsed to his knees, shaking the island, bent over to clutch the sand and breathed hard.

Liora's hazel eyes grew even wider and Asmodeus sensed her panic. It flowed over him, beating in his veins and in his ears as her pulse accelerated and she breathed so fast he was sure she would pass out.

He shot to his feet and slipped his arm around her waist, supporting her as her knees gave out, keeping her upright. She turned wide eyes on him, her dark eyebrows furrowed, and pressed her trembling hands against his chest.

"Wow. That was pretty cool. You're either fearless or foolish to stop my man when he's in a rage... but it's nice that someone here was able to get him to cool off." Erin gave her sister, Amelia, the slip and walked up behind Veiron. She pushed him in the back of the head. "When I say you're upsetting junior, you're meant to stop fighting. This baby gives me hell when you're in danger and you know that, you big oaf."

Veiron growled and lumbered onto his feet, and his skin began to pale again, his body shrinking to its normal size. His armour disappeared, the black long shorts he had been wearing before replacing the pieces. He rolled his shoulders, twisted his neck and then checked himself over. Asmodeus wanted to slash the uninjured male across his chest, repaying him for the blow he had delivered while Asmodeus had been distracted.

Erin rubbed her stomach again and looked between Liora and Asmodeus. "Witch... and evil angel. I'm guessing you didn't come here to give my husband some exercise?"

Asmodeus shook his head. "I am not. I am here to request your help."

"Help?" Marcus, the male angel allied to Erin's sister, frowned at him, his blue eyes swirling silver. He looked beyond Asmodeus, no doubt seeing if Apollyon agreed with what he had said. Apollyon must have because Marcus looked annoyed and sheathed his silver blade at his waist.

"Why do you seek our help?" Erin said and Asmodeus braved a step forwards, ignoring how Veiron growled threateningly.

"I do not seek the help of all of you." He looked around at the four of them and then down into Erin's amber eyes. "I seek your help."

"My help?" She patted her stomach. "I don't know if you've noticed, but someone got me up the duff. I can't use my powers so I'm not sure what use I'll be to you."

"I do not need your power, and your pregnancy is the reason you are able to help me. The Devil has made a pact with you, yes?" Asmodeus sent one of his blades away but sheathed the other at his waist, keeping it close in case he needed it. Veiron looked ready to launch himself into another attack, regardless of what his female desired.

Erin nodded.

"I believe that the Devil will not dare start a war on your island and risk upsetting you, and therefore you are the only one able to protect Liora from your father." Asmodeus held his hand out to Liora and she came to him, slipped hers into it and stood beside him. "I am here to request that you offer us the same protection you give to the others."

"The Devil wants you?" Erin said to Liora and Liora nodded and wrapped her other hand around his, clutching it in both of hers. She was still trembling, weak from exerting so much power in order to freeze Veiron and shaken by how her magic had controlled her. "Do you know why?"

"No," Asmodeus answered for her and frowned. "I have tried to seek the reason but he refuses to give it, stating only that it is his business and that he believes Liora is dangerous in the wrong hands."

"What?" Liora gasped and he glanced at her, squeezed her hand, and smiled. It didn't erase the panic from her eyes. "You could have told me that before."

"I did not wish to frighten you."

"That's rich coming from a man who I distinctly recall enjoys scaring the shit out of people and torturing them for fun," Veiron growled and Asmodeus glared at him.

"Veiron, Gorgeous... you aren't really helping." Erin wrapped her arms around one of his and the Hell's angel moved behind her, enfolding her in his muscular arms.

He settled his hands on her stomach and sighed. "I did upset junior."

He pressed a kiss to her hair. She smiled and brushed her black hair from her face, hooking the thick red stripe down one side of it behind her ear.

"I do not trust him," Amelia said and furled her silver wings against her back. The wind tousled her long silvery ponytail and she closed ranks with Marcus, coming to stand beside him, her weapon at the ready. "Look what he did to Nevar. We have no reason to trust him or offer him any sort of protection. He's evil and dangerous, and for all we know, this could be a scam by the Devil to plant one of his men on the island so he can snatch the baby as soon as it's born."

"I second that." Marcus settled his hand on the hilt of his sword. "Is the female a relation of yours?"

The male looked beyond Liora to Serenity.

"Yes. She is my cousin."

"Asmodeus was sent to Paris to capture her and take her to the Devil," Apollyon said and Liora tossed him a scowl over her shoulder and then looked back at Erin.

"It's true that he was meant to take me to the Devil but he protected me instead. He killed a Hell's angel to keep me from the Devil's hands and he has risked everything to keep me safe. He's made an enemy of himself for my sake and the Devil won't stop until he has me now." Liora squeezed his hand again, tighter this time. "No matter what you think or what you know about him… he isn't here to harm anyone. He's here because he wants to protect me, and he believes you can help him do that."

Erin sighed, raked her gaze over Asmodeus, and then looked back at her sister and Marcus, and then up at Veiron. Seeking their input.

Asmodeus looked at the couple, feeling more than ever that his ability to protect Liora rested on their shoulders now. He had to convince them to offer them the protection they had given the others. Their friends.

How?

He was unaccustomed to acting kindly towards others and wasn't sure what the process of making friends involved, or whether he was even capable of convincing these people that he meant them no harm. He was sure that was the first step, and so far he had failed dismally at proving himself an ally.

In his defence, he had been attacked the second he had set foot on the island, before anyone had even asked him what he wanted.

Perhaps it was hopeless. If Apollyon and Serenity had brought Liora here without him, Erin probably would have granted her protection immediately. He was jeopardising everything by accompanying her.

"It is true that the Devil wants Liora," Apollyon said and Asmodeus growled, warning him not to intervene. He couldn't bear it if his twin was able to succeed where he could not, convincing Erin to give Liora the protection she needed from the Devil. "Asmodeus, this is not about us. This is about Liora… and Serenity."

"You speak perfect words, Brother, but forget I can feel your inner emotions. You desire to convince Erin to extend her protection to Liora and refuse it to me." Asmodeus's mood darkened, his hope draining away.

As it faded, the side of him that wanted blood on his hands and violence began to take control, growing within him, pushing down the good that Liora had nurtured.

These people before him had seen what he had done to Nevar, a guardian angel, on the plateau, battling him on his master's orders. Apollyon had been there and had fought him while Amelia, Marcus and Veiron had set Nevar free of his chains. He would play on that to turn them against him, if they needed any convincing. The three of them regarded him with cold, sharp eyes, all ready to cut him down if he said the wrong thing.

"Apollyon?" Liora looked behind them at the angel and Apollyon said nothing. At least the bastard didn't try to lie and defend himself. Asmodeus had known how it would be and had expected no more from his twin than this attempt to separate them.

"What would you do if I extended my protection to Liora and denied it where you were concerned?" Erin said and Asmodeus held his head high, masking the pain in his heart and crushing his desire to ask her not to do such a thing.

He released Liora's hand and stepped aside. "I would leave her under your protection. If you swear to keep her here and keep her safe… I will leave. I will do that for her."

Liora's heart picked up pace again and her anger flowed over him, laced with hurt. "I don't want to stay here without you."

The force behind those words warmed his heart.

Asmodeus turned to her and looked down into her hazel eyes, seeing the pain in them and wishing he could take it away. He raised his hand and cupped her cheek, holding her gaze and searching for the right words, the ones she wanted to hear. He couldn't say them. He couldn't lie to her.

"I am sorry, Liora," he whispered, low enough that she would know he spoke these words for her ears alone and meant every one of them. "I should leave. I want you to be safe, and you will be safe here if I go. I have no other course of action… no other way to protect you now. This is how it must be. Erin and everyone will protect you if I leave. I will do that for you. I would do anything to keep you safe."

"No," Liora murmured, lifted his other hand and pressed a kiss to it, closing her eyes at the same time.

Her fingers trembled against his, not from fatigue this time. She was on the verge of tears and he didn't want her to cry because of him and the decision that these people were forcing upon him. He didn't want to leave her but he had to do it, for her sake. His chest hurt, a dull heavy throb that beat in his blood, whispering a forceful demand to stay with this beautiful female because if he left, he would leave his heart behind and become empty, dead inside.

It pained him to see Liora, normally so strong and stubborn, standing before him with her head bowed in defeat. He wanted her to be strong again, to stand tall and face life with the determination and recklessness that he had come to admire in her. He wanted her to fight and be the woman he had fallen in love with.

Everyone fell silent and stared at them, and Asmodeus hated them for it. He wanted to be alone with Liora. He didn't want to leave her.

Liora raised her head, opened her eyes and looked up into his. Steely determination coloured her hazel irises. "We can go together. We can find somewhere else. Remus and Romulus can help you protect me. If we work together, we'll be okay."

Asmodeus cursed himself when tears lined her long dark lashes, each diamond drop cutting at him and making him bleed inside. He could feel her emotions, could sense her pain and suffering, and he found only pain in it himself. He didn't want her to hurt like this, as if he was breaking her heart. He wanted her safe and happy, and he couldn't achieve both of those things. If he made her stay and he left, she would be safe but not happy. If he let her leave with him and his hellhounds, she would be happy but not safe.

He cursed again, his head and heart aching as he tried to find a third way, the one that would fulfil both of his desires, and wouldn't end with them being separated.

"Please, Asmodeus," Liora whispered and squeezed his fingers. "I'll be safe with you."

Asmodeus did the hardest thing he had ever done in his life.

He released her and stepped back. "No. You will not. You will be safest here."

"And what will you do?" She frowned at him, her words harsh, and then understanding dawned in her eyes and she shook her head. "No, Asmodeus. No."

Romulus and Remus came to flank him and he silently thanked them for their support. He needed them now more than ever, needed to feel that someone was on his side, because he was on the edge, verging on doing something that he could see Liora believed was suicide.

"You are not fighting him alone." Liora lunged forwards and grabbed his wrist, her grip surprisingly tight. He looked down and saw ribbons of magic curling around his forearm, seeping into his flesh and squeezing it as firmly as her fingers were. "I won't let you fight him alone."

Asmodeus stared down at her, absorbing how beautiful she was when her eyes flashed with fire and she challenged him like this, ready to fight him if she had to in order to get her way and make him back down.

"You really expect me to separate them?" Erin said and Asmodeus caught her looking at Apollyon out of the corner of his eye. "How am I meant to do such a thing when I lived through the same hell as they are?"

The dark-haired woman looked around her, her gaze verging on golden now, seeking answers from everyone present.

"Apollyon, you can curse me to Hell… you can all shout at me about it later… but when it comes down to it, it is my decision, and I've made up my mind." Erin looked across at him. "I will give you the protection you desire, Asmodeus. I will give it to both of you. From now on, you fall under my protection. You are my friends."

The ground shook and Erin's face darkened, her eyes glowing gold.

"Yeah, you heard me. Bite me… no, I won't take it back… why don't you come up here and try it? Oh, that's right. You're stuck in Hell… Stick it. You heard. Stick it. I don't give a damn… I happened to have an opening for two new friends. Yeah, yeah. Nothing I haven't heard before. So he really is on your shit list?" Erin cast him a grim look and rolled her eyes, and continued her one-sided conversation. "No, I'm not listening. No. No means no... fine. Why do you want her so much? She doesn't look dangerous to me... well, she's pretty powerful, but... sorry to say that she's under my protection now... in my hands. Bored now. Really bored. Bite me, Pops. I hate you. Go to Hell... ah, you're already there. Burn in it. Ciao ciao!"

Liora stared at Erin and whispered out of the corner of her mouth, "Is she okay?"

"Telepathic communication with her father, I believe." At least, Asmodeus hoped it was and that she wasn't insane.

Erin brightened, her eyes losing their glow. "I got tired of walking around talking to him in my head when he bothers me. Veiron likes to know when my father is annoying me and that I'm verbally giving him the finger. One finger thoroughly given."

Erin smiled up at Veiron.

"Erin," Veiron whispered but Asmodeus sensed it wasn't anger or warning behind his softly spoken word. It was awe and admiration because she had accepted Asmodeus and Liora, and because she had stood up to her friends and her father, sticking to her guns and not letting them separate another couple she saw as similar to her and Veiron. Affection warmed the Hell's angel's black eyes and he drew Erin into his embrace and kissed her.

Amelia, Marcus and Apollyon cast Asmodeus dark looks that did warn him, telling him that if he stepped out of line, they would do all in their power to have him cast from the island and beyond Erin's sphere of protection.

Serenity smiled at him and then her hazel eyes shot wide with horror. "Ah... your... chiens!"

Asmodeus turned in time to see Romulus and Remus rolling down the sloping white sand, a furious tangle of black fur. The second they hit the shallow water lapping at the shore, they yelped, broke apart and growled at it.

He sighed and spoke to them in the demon tongue. "It did not attack you. It is water. Good for playing in and it will not harm you. Be aware there are creatures who make it their home, and some may bite back."

Remus eyed it warily and then bounded in ahead of Romulus. Romulus looked back at him, as if waiting for permission. Asmodeus waved him on.

"Cute dogs," Erin said and frowned up at Veiron, a slight edge of disappointment to her expression. "How come you don't have any?"

Veiron settled his arm around her shoulders and pinned her to his side. "Because hellhounds normally make a meal out of demons or angels. Having them for pets is one fucked up situation. I don't even want to know how he came to have tame hellhounds."

"He saved them as puppies."

Asmodeus cringed on hearing those words leaving Liora's lips. Everyone stared at him. Liora slowly turned to face him, a flicker of guilt flittering across her face.

He furled his black wings against his back and squared his jaw, fixing everyone with a hard look that dared them to make fun of him for having saved and raised the two hellhounds.

The sound of splashing and playful growls cut through the thick silence.

Erin looked him over, looked at the hellhounds playing in the shallows, and then her eyebrows slowly rose and disappeared beneath her straight fringe.

"Cool." Her amber gaze drifted back to him. "Are they the same sex?"

He nodded. "Males."

She looked disappointed. Why? He studied Romulus and Remus, and then Erin, catching the edge of excitement in her eyes as she watched them playing and stroked her belly.

"If they ever have puppies, sign me up for two, okay?" Erin said and the splashing stopped.

Romulus and Remus stared at her, looking as shocked as he felt. Clearly, they were beginning to grasp English and had understood enough of what she had said to know they didn't like the sound of it.

"I do not think they are ready to become fathers just yet." Asmodeus waved the two hellhounds on and they went back to playing in the water.

Veiron grunted and turned away, revealing the black and red tribal tattoos that curled around his biceps and deltoids, and over his shoulders and around his crimson feathered wings where they sprouted from his back. "I know how they feel."

Erin playfully slapped him on the backside. "Bastard."

Veiron growled, spun swiftly on the spot and went to grab her. She disappeared in black smoke and reappeared further up the beach, laughing at him when he stumbled forwards and almost fell into the sand. The big Hell's angel snarled, turned and beat his wings, shooting across the sand to her. He tackled her, scooped her up into his arms and carried her into one of the large green tents erected beneath the palm trees.

"That's them gone for hours. You'd think pregnancy would make them less like rabbits, not more," Amelia grumbled, brushed her silver hair from her face and flicked Asmodeus a glare. "Dinner's in an hour... if we can catch it."

Her wings shrank into her back, a long flowing white and blue dress replaced her silver armour and she walked back towards the camp. Marcus sent his armour away, changing into dark blue shorts with a silver stripe down the side, and an unbuttoned white linen shirt, and followed her, raking his fingers through his unruly dark hair at the same time.

"Erin seems nice," Liora said and the tense air hanging over them didn't improve. "Amelia seems a bit, um, protective?"

Serenity smiled at her. "You will get used to them. Amelia loves her sister very much. She only wants to keep her safe... like we want to with you."

The fair-haired petite witch held her hand out to Liora. Liora slipped hers into it.

"I know," she said and looked back at him, a smile curving her rosy lips. "We'll be alright here, Asmodeus. You'll see. It just takes time to make friends with new people."

He still wasn't sure how to make friends. Serenity and Apollyon led Liora towards the camp and Asmodeus watched them, and then Marcus and Amelia. The couple headed towards rocks that jutted out at the far end of the beach, two long sticks in their hands.

Dinner. If they could catch it.

He looked at the water to his right. Fish?

He had made friends with Liora by protecting her.

Was it possible to make friends with these people by supporting them in other ways? Could he convince them to trust him, and therefore Liora, by providing for them?

Asmodeus focused to send his wings away and then his armour, replacing the pieces with loose black linen trousers and leaving his feet bare.

He waded into the clear blue water until it reached his chest. Romulus and Remus swam over and both tried to get on him, pushing him under the surface. He shoved them off and broke it again, breathing hard. Water got in his eyes and stung. Salty.

He looked at his two hellhounds as they swam around him, clumsily kicking. Swimming didn't look very difficult and he had read about marine life in his books.

Romulus and Remus came back to him.

"I wish to provide sustenance for these people," he said in the demon tongue and both of the hellhounds looked confused. "We are to catch fish."

No luck. Remus bumped him and almost knocked him over again.

"Fish." Asmodeus flattened his palm, holding it vertical in line with his forearm, and moved his hand in a wriggling motion. With his other hand, he pointed to the water. "Marine life that is edible."

He didn't hold his breath.

Remus clambered on him, shoving him back underwater again, and he grasped hold of him, waded into shallower water and held him. The hellhound choked. Asmodeus held him closer, concern growing in his heart. Had he swallowed water?

Remus convulsed, every muscle in spasm, and then retched on Asmodeus's arm.

He pulled a face at the half-eaten something on his forearm and then grinned.

A fish, and by the looks of it, it had been large before Remus had chewed it up.

He looked at his two hellhounds.

If they could fish, then so could he. He had often hunted small demons that were quick. Fishing couldn't be harder than capturing them and it might turn out to be fun, and gain him the trust he desired.

He would provide for his female and these people. He would show them all that he was powerful and clever, and a good ally.

"Show me where and how to snare these creatures."

Remus kicked off him, scratching the wound on his chest and spilling his blood.

Asmodeus watched it trickle into the water and form a bloom.

Blood.

He lifted his gaze to the distance and a fin broke the surface a hundred yards out.

A big fish would provide enough sustenance for everyone.

He would impress his female and show her just how powerful her male was, and that he could protect her and provide for her.

A big fish needed bait to lure it to the hook. He rubbed his wound, spilling more blood.

The fin turned straight on to him and disappeared beneath the gentle waves.

His claws and fangs extended.

He could be both bait and hook.

Asmodeus grinned.

He would catch the biggest fish Liora had ever seen.

CHAPTER 18

Liora's heart almost stopped when she heard the struggle in the water. She turned in time to see Asmodeus go under together with Romulus and Remus, and shot to her feet. Her magic ran in violent spirals around her hands and she sprinted towards the sea.

She made it halfway there with Apollyon and Serenity hot on her heels before Asmodeus broke the surface and waded towards the shore.

With the biggest sea monster she had ever seen slung over his shoulder.

Romulus and Remus followed him out, fighting over a smaller fish.

Liora stared in stunned silence at her angel.

He sauntered along the beach towards her, one hand pinning his prize to his shoulder, the other flicking his black hair back from his face. Water ran down his bare chest and soaked his black linens, causing them to stick rather wickedly to his hips and legs, distracting her from the fact that he had apparently decided to take to fishing in his spare time.

"Is that a shark?" Liora didn't think she really needed an answer to that question to know that it was but she was having trouble believing what she was seeing.

Asmodeus grinned, bursting with pride, and held the seven-foot-long shark up by the base of its tail before her. She leaped back, bumping into Serenity, eyeing it with caution. It didn't move.

Remus sniffed it and went to take a bite but Asmodeus shoved him with his bare foot and growled. Remus snorted and then shook, spraying water all over Asmodeus, her and the others.

"You caught a shark… what the hell were you using as bai—" Her hazel gaze shot to his chest, she flew at him and slapped his shoulder as hard as she could. "You jerk! How could you risk yourself like that?"

He looked confused. Evidently, anger wasn't the reaction he had expected to get from her on presenting her with a dead shark.

"Wow, is that a shark? Did you kill it? Cool." Erin appeared beside her and Asmodeus's smile returned.

Clearly, that was the reaction he had expected.

He offered it to her again. Liora wasn't sure what to do with it. She stepped aside and waved towards Erin.

"I think it's for you," she said and Asmodeus growled at her, his eyes turning close to black but blazing red at the same time. Erin stepped forwards and he moved the shark away from her and bared his fangs.

"You are so like Veiron… all that smexy rolled into another hot package." Erin beamed at Asmodeus and Liora's gaze turned dark this time, jealousy making her want to growl. Erin slid her a knowing look. "I don't want him. I have my hands full with Veiron. He's a keeper though."

"Is that a shark?" Veiron appeared behind Erin and frowned at it, mild disgust in his eyes that Liora could see through. He was annoyed that Erin was impressed by Asmodeus's catch.

"What do you expect us to do with a shark?" Apollyon said and Asmodeus turned red eyes on him.

"It is a fish. Fish is a source of sustenance. I expect you to eat it." Asmodeus held the shark out to Liora again.

She really didn't want to be the one to raise this question because she knew it would hurt him when he only wanted to give her something to eat, and he hated it when anyone made him feel unsure of something in front of others, but someone had to ask it. Maybe she could word it in a way that didn't upset him or dent his pride.

"Does anyone know what shark tastes like?" she said, offering a bright smile at everyone. Amelia and Marcus had gathered too, lingering at the back, fishing rods in hand but no catch to show for their efforts.

That tense silence returned and she didn't like it.

Romulus and Remus bounded back into the water, snapping at each other. They both went under and then Romulus reappeared with a fish in his mouth, one that looked distinctly more edible than the one his master had caught.

"It tastes like fish." Veiron's deep voice broke the quiet and he jerked his chin towards the camp. "Come on, I'll show you how to gut the bloody thing and prep it. Erin loves shark. She says it tastes like chicken... don't believe her."

Veiron winked at his wife and led Asmodeus away, and Liora breathed a sigh of relief.

"It does taste like chicken," Erin said and smiled at her. "Everything tastes like chicken when Veiron cooks it. I don't know what he does. It's like a weird power he has. Wait and see. I think we still have some spice rub left over and some veggies. Should make a good meal... and can I just say that your slice of smexy is as crazy as mine. Who the hell uses themselves as bait for a shark?"

Liora smiled. A man who very much wanted to impress new people and make friends.

She had to admit, he had found a fantastic way of getting on the good side of Erin and her family. Nothing brought people together like food and full stomachs. He could have found a less life-threatening way of making friends though. She was going to have to have words with him later about what he had done. She was grateful for the meal but would rather he had chosen a more conventional way of fishing.

Apollyon muttered to Serenity, "He does not get this insane behaviour from my blood."

Liora frowned at his back as he led Serenity across the sand, towards the camp. Amelia and Marcus followed the couple, easily catching up and then falling into step with them, and they began to talk.

Erin moved up beside Liora and Liora glanced across at her and then her gaze caught movement. She looked back at the camp and smiled as Veiron kneeled by the dead shark laid out on a piece of blue tarp on the sand and Asmodeus mimicked him, resting his hands on his thighs.

Veiron grinned as he talked and Liora wished she could hear what they were discussing as the scarlet-haired Hell's angel took great pleasure in showing Asmodeus how to butcher a shark. Asmodeus frowned, his golden eyes intent on following every move Veiron made with the short blade, opening the shark's white belly. He pulled a face as the organs spilled out.

"Fish guts smell disgusting… and that's my cue!" Erin turned away from her, bent over and retched. Liora instinctively moved to her and rubbed her back as she dry heaved, clutching her belly. Erin bit out something harsh and then straightened. "Sorry. Junior is picky about some things. Loves the end result. Hates the method of getting there. I'll scoff the food when it's on my plate but throw up if I think about how it got there."

"Sounds like fun." Liora gave her a consolatory smile. "I thought angels couldn't get people pregnant."

"They can't, normally. It's because I share my father's blood… like Asmodeus does."

"He what?" Liora almost choked. "I thought he was created by the Devil from Apollyon's blood?"

"He was… but surely you've noticed he has certain attributes that Apollyon doesn't have?" Erin looked over at Asmodeus and she followed her gaze. Asmodeus looked up at her and Liora smiled when his expression turned concerned, showing him that she was alright. "Notice any similarities?"

Liora looked at Erin when she held her hands up, flashing a nasty set of claws that Liora didn't recall seeing before and then smiling to reveal short fangs.

Her claws shrank back into normal black painted nails.

Amber eyes. Black claws. Fangs.

"I've thought hard about it ever since I met him in Hell and it makes sense that the Devil would mix in a little of his own blood to ensure that Asmodeus was loyal to him and he could control him if he had to." Erin rubbed Liora's arm. "You look as though I just popped your favourite balloon."

Liora shook her head. "It's just… Apollyon and Asmodeus mentioned that the Devil has his men bringing all these women to Hell for him to seduce… and you're pregnant by an angel, which shouldn't be possible… and I guess… I…"

"You're thinking that Asmodeus's little swimmers might be firing on all cylinders?" Erin looped her arm around Liora's and squeezed. "My father has the power to plant life into a barren womb. I'm an… almost… perfect replica of his DNA. I have his powers, can contract with his angels, like Veiron, and can do everything he can. I'm like the female version of my father. That's the only reason I can take Veiron's, well, you know, and make a baby with it."

"Is that meant to be reassuring?" Liora looked across at her and Erin smiled brightly.

"I'm saying that I'm a complete replica of my father… and there's a vast difference between that and having a little of his blood in me. Asmodeus doesn't have the Devil's powers." Erin caught her under the jaw and turned her face away from him, towards Apollyon. "He shares his doppelganger's powers. Which would totally be a comfort if it weren't for the fact that Apollyon is some almighty angel of destruction. The Great Destroyer."

Erin's tone turned dramatic and histrionic for those final three words.

"Why did the Devil create Asmodeus?" Liora looked back at him and found herself smiling as he tackled chopping half of the shark into thick chunks, a look of fierce concentration on his face. He looked at ease around Veiron now, despite their earlier fight, and didn't seem to notice the wary looks that the male gave him from time to time. Did he feel more comfortable around someone from his own realm?

He probably felt as if he had an ally in Veiron.

"I don't know." Erin released her.

"I asked Apollyon when Asmodeus was sleeping and he said the same thing. He thinks that the Devil created him to be his right hand man, and I think that's what Asmodeus believes too."

"You don't believe that?" Erin said.

Liora shook her head. "I did before. I just thought the Devil had created him because he could and because he wanted someone strong on his side, a powerful being who could help him rule Hell. The longer we spend together, the more I fear the Devil had a reason for making him, and hearing you call Apollyon the Great Destroyer... what if the Devil created Asmodeus from his blood because of that? What if he had wanted his own Great Destroyer?"

"I wouldn't worry about it too much. Apollyon and Asmodeus have been around for thousands of years without being called upon for that purpose. My father likes insurance policies. He likes being in control. I would think that he made Asmodeus because he could and because his existence served as a sort of insurance policy—a way of protecting himself against Apollyon should the world go to hell." Erin patted her arm again. "Come on. It's getting dark and you really have to watch Veiron perform his miracle of turning fish into chicken."

Erin waddled up the beach and Veiron rose to his feet as she approached and opened his arms to her. She stepped into them and he wrapped them around her, lowered his head and kissed her. Asmodeus looked uncomfortable and his gaze roamed to Liora.

She smiled at him and then looked out to sea. The sun was setting, casting gold and pink in the sky that echoed on the crisp turquoise water. It was beautiful. She sighed and listened to the water lapping against the shore, letting it soothe away her worries. Romulus and Remus continued to frolic in the small waves, chasing each other. Asmodeus's gaze burned into her back, the intensity of it warming her right down to her bones, chasing away the last of her fears.

He wanted her to come to the group. She could almost feel it in her blood. He wanted her to return to him where she was safe and protected.

Liora's smile widened and she obeyed his silent command.

"Romulus. Remus," she called and the two hellhounds perked up, looked over at her and then came running full pelt towards her. She laughed as they rushed around her, springing at times, spraying her with water.

Liora turned towards Asmodeus. He was standing now, watching her, his broad bare chest bathed in golden light from the sunset and his long black linen trousers still damp and clinging to his thighs. Gorgeous. She would rather stare at him than the sunset behind her.

She walked towards him and Romulus and Remus rushed off in his direction.

Liora paused at a large piece of driftwood half-buried in the white sand. A mischievous smile tugged at her lips and she picked it up. It was too heavy for her to throw without assistance but that wasn't going to stop her.

She waggled it and whistled to get the attention of the two hellhounds, feeling Asmodeus watching her. She waited until Romulus and Remus were closing in on her again before focusing her magic on her arms and throwing the driftwood.

It flew through the air and Remus barked, the thunderous sound drawing a gasp from someone near the camp, and chased it with Romulus bounding behind him. They jostled for position, almost bouncing on top of each other. The huge stick came down over fifty yards along the beach and Romulus was first to reach it but Remus was right behind him.

She laughed again as they both grabbed an end and began tugging, fighting each other, and then tried to run back to her, both of them keeping hold of the stick.

"I like to watch you with my hellhounds," Asmodeus said from right beside her, making her jump and her heart leap into her throat. She hadn't felt him approach. She had been too lost in watching Romulus and Remus, playing with them.

"I never had a pet." Liora looked across her shoulder at him and smiled when she caught the warmth in his golden eyes as he looked down at her. "I'm thinking of adopting yours. What would you say to that?"

Asmodeus turned his profile to her and watched the two hellhounds, a faint smile on his firm sensual lips. "I would like that very much."

Liora looped her arms around his left one and squeezed. "Thank you for the shark."

Asmodeus slid his gaze to meet hers and smiled. "But if I ever use myself as bait again, you will kill me?"

Her own smile widened and she nodded. "Exactly. What happened to taking more care?"

"The shark was hardly a threat to me as the dragon was."

Her smile cracked into a grin. "So you admit that dragon was a threat to you?"

He huffed, slipped free of her and held his hand out. Romulus and Remus set the stick down in it and wagged their tails, eagerly waiting. Asmodeus brought the stick back behind him, spun on his heel and launched it down the full length of the beach in the other direction. Romulus and Remus shot off after it, kicking up sand as they raced past the camp. Erin laughed and watched them.

Apollyon looked thoroughly unimpressed.

Liora's smile faded and she looked back at Asmodeus, studying his eyes, his lips and then his fingernails.

"Your mood has changed abruptly. Did I do something wrong? Did you wish to throw the stick again?" Asmodeus said and turned to face her.

Liora shook her head, and then dragged her courage up and met his gaze. She touched the marks on her neck beneath her hair and felt the scabs.

"I was just thinking about something. You have fangs and claws, and golden eyes... like Erin... like the Devil."

He tipped his head back and smiled. "Ah, and you were wondering why I have these things? Erin has been putting thoughts in your pretty head. It is true that I have a drop of the Devil's blood in me."

"Why?"

He raised his hand, brushed his knuckles across her cheek and cleared the hair from the right side of her throat, hooking it behind her ear. He stroked the marks he had placed on her, his eyes darkening with desire that rippled through her too.

"To control me and make me obedient to him, and to ensure I would serve him and was everything he desired me to be... as evil as he is."

"But you're not as evil as he is. There's good in you." Liora placed her hand over his and flattened it, so the heel of his palm brushed the top of her breast.

Asmodeus stared at their joined hands, his pupils dilating further. "The Devil has... I lived with him for many centuries... I saw... Liora, there is a chance that this good in me did not come from Apollyon."

Her eyes went as round as the moon rising beyond the palm trees behind him. If Asmodeus was right, then that was a doozy of a secret he had just spilled to her. "Seriously?"

"I cannot be sure. I may be wrong but it is something that has plagued me for countless centuries. If I am right, then perhaps I am only as evil as the Devil is... but I am still evil. The bad in me outweighs the good."

"But there is good in you."

He sighed and looked over her head to the distant horizon and the sunset. It reflected in his eyes, turning them fierce and golden. She didn't expect him to answer. He didn't like it when she pushed and she was pushing, and he was going to stand firm and not give her what she wanted. She wanted to hear him admit that there was good in him but he couldn't bring himself to do that. It was easier for him to cling to the thought that there wasn't and that he was as evil as his master.

She looked beyond him to the group around the fire, took hold of his hand and began leading him towards them.

Serenity looked up and smiled as Liora settled herself on a thick log across the fire from her, close to Veiron where he was cooking on a grill over a smaller fire nearby. Erin stood beside him chatting about hellhounds and her father.

Asmodeus sat beside Liora when she patted the log and rested his forearms on his bent knees.

Apollyon and Serenity were still catching up with Amelia and Marcus. Liora's gaze fell on Apollyon and then returned to Asmodeus. She caught him staring at his twin, watching him, and kept still and silent. Apollyon laughed and talked with Marcus and the others, a completely different person to the one she was used to seeing. What was Asmodeus thinking as he watched his twin interacting with everyone?

His eyes were turning cold again, sharp and emotionless, and she could feel the distance growing between them. The evil she could always sense in him grew, battling the good and creating a struggle within him that made her want to rest her hand on his to reassure him that he didn't need to compare himself to Apollyon or think the things she could almost hear going around his head.

She wasn't very good at interacting with people and conversing easily either, and preferred to keep to herself most of the time. She wasn't like Serenity. Serenity could smile, laugh, and make friends so easily. Liora didn't have that talent.

Asmodeus didn't have to feel bad or that he was lacking because he didn't share Apollyon's ability to make easy conversation with these people. She opened her mouth to tell him that but Erin sat down on the other side of him, stealing his attention away from Apollyon.

"I've wanted to ask you this for months," Erin said and Liora leaned forwards so she could see the dark-haired woman, curious about what she wanted to know. "Did you mean to free me that day that you came to my cell or did you intend to torment me?"

Liora frowned at her, magic breaking to the surface of her hands, called forth by her anger over hearing Erin pose such a question to Asmodeus when he was in the grip of his emotions, struggling to find balance again.

"I desired to set you free." Asmodeus kept his voice low and she had the feeling he was trying to stop others from hearing their conversation. Angels had fantastic hearing though. She could tell that because a hush fell over the camp and suddenly everyone was looking her way.

"Why?" Erin said with a frown.

"Because I knew you were the Devil's daughter and I did not like how he was treating you. I felt it was... wrong." Asmodeus's dark eyebrows knitted together and Liora did settle her hand on his arm now, hoping it would offer him some strength and comfort in the wake of his minor epiphany. He knew right from wrong after all. He flexed his fingers and held Erin's gaze. "You have the Devil's blood in you, just as I do. I felt compelled to help you, but I am unable to breach the barrier around the prison without the Devil sensing it."

Erin smiled when Veiron rested his hand on her shoulder and she covered it with her own. "That makes us sound like we're sort of related... only you have two fathers. At the time, I thought you had wanted to help me. I'm glad I wasn't going crazy and was right, and you were looking out for me. You'd make one hell of a big brother. You have that leader vibe happening just like Apollyon."

Asmodeus stiffened and narrowed his gaze on her, and then glared daggers across the fire at Apollyon, daring him to speak. Liora pressed her hand more firmly on his arm, trying to stop what she could feel coming. Erin had meant her words kindly, but Asmodeus had grown to expect such words to be born of malice and spoken in an attempt to mock or belittle. He wasn't accustomed to kindness.

She could feel the tension in him cranking higher and blackening his mood. He didn't know what to make of what Erin had said, and the longer everyone stared at him, waiting for him to respond, the darker his feelings turned.

"Asmodeus," Liora whispered and he shot to his feet, knocking her hand off him, stepped over the log and strode away from the fire.

Erin blinked in confusion. Liora really didn't know what to say to explain everything. She gave up trying to think of something and went after Asmodeus, easily catching him before he went too far.

Liora slipped her fingers around his wrist.

He tensed and turned on her. "I need some peace and quiet."

"Stay." She stroked his arm and held his gaze, trying to soothe some of his tension away, and dropped her voice lower, so only he would hear her. She hoped. "Erin meant it in a nice way."

He flashed fangs and took his arm away, casting a black look over her head to the fire and everyone there.

"I need... I need to get away." He threw another look towards the fire and this one verged on panic. "I have to... I need a break."

"Why?" The reason dawned on her as his eyes flicked to her and then back to the others, darting over each of them in turn, and his irises burned red around the edges.

"I am not used to being around so many," he said quietly and she wanted to tell him that she had already figured that out for herself. He was fine when he was alone with her, and had seemed alright when helping Veiron, but being around the others set him on edge.

"I'll go with you—"

"No," he interjected harshly, and then his tone softened and he caressed her cheek, an affectionate edge to his golden eyes. "Remain with your cousin and the others. You must eat."

"So must you." She was sure he must be hungry after teleporting them all to the island, fighting Veiron and then wrestling with a shark.

"Save me some... just... give me five minutes." He cupped her cheek and looked torn between leaving and staying now, and she wished she could convince him to stay even when she knew he needed to go and would feel better for it. "I just need five minutes."

His unease returned when he looked beyond her. She could sense it in him and see it in his eyes, and she knew it stemmed from being around the others and Apollyon. He was trying to make friends, probably for her sake, so they could remain here and she would be safe from the Devil. He wanted to protect her but it was taking its toll on him. He felt he didn't fit in here.

She felt it too.

She felt as if strangers surrounded her and that she only truly knew Asmodeus. He was her haven, the one she felt safe around, protected and secure, and happy. She didn't want to let him go off alone and dwell on his dark thoughts, only making himself feel even more like he was out of place and evil, no good for her.

She didn't want him to leave her alone with these people.

But the look in his eyes spoke to her heart and told her that he really needed some time alone and she would never do anything to upset him, so she stroked the hand that lingered against her face and forced herself to nod.

A faint glimmer of relief flickered in his eyes and he tilted her head up, lowered his mouth to hers and kissed her softly. It reassured her more than words ever could, telling her that he appreciated this gift she had given him and that he wouldn't go far or leave the island. He would remain close because he wanted to protect her.

His fingers slipped from her cheek, he broke the kiss and turned his back on her.

Liora wrapped her arms around herself as cold stole into her veins and she watched him walk away.

Romulus bounded past her, following his master. Remus nudged her hand and she stroked him between his ears and looked down into his crimson eyes.

"Keep him safe," she whispered and gently tugged his left ear, propping it up.

Remus licked her hand and rushed after his master and brother.

Liora sighed and padded back to her seat near the fire, weary now and unable to shake the heavy feeling in her heart. No one closed in on her and she felt grateful for it, glad that they were giving her the space she needed too.

She glanced at Erin and caught the sympathy in her eyes. Maybe she and Asmodeus weren't as out of place in this group as they both had thought. Erin wore an expression that left Liora feeling that she knew what she was feeling and had been through it all with Veiron. A Hell's angel. One of the Devil's men, just like Asmodeus.

How long had it taken everyone to accept Veiron's presence in the group?

She could understand why Amelia, Marcus, and Apollyon looked at Asmodeus with darkness in their eyes. He hadn't proven himself to these people yet, not as he had proven himself to her. He hadn't earned their trust, and she had the feeling that part of him didn't want to either and he was only trying to make friends with them for her sake.

He didn't need them.

She could understand that too. He was used to being alone and doing as he pleased, just as she was. No close family ties. No one to answer to but himself. No friends. No hurt feelings when those friends turned on you and betrayed you. No broken heart when someone you loved died or was taken from you.

She got that.

Liora looked over her shoulder, watching him walking the shore with his hellhounds, alone again.

She felt sorry for him and she didn't like it because it made her feel sorry for herself too.

She had pushed away everyone except Serenity with her wild and dangerous behaviour, and how little she cared about anyone, including herself.

Liora looked across the fire at Serenity, watching her talking to Amelia, Marcus, and Apollyon, the centre of their attention again now. Serenity was all bright laughter and smiles, telling them about the trials she had gone through to become immortal together with a woman called Annelie, all so they could live forever with their angels.

"Annelie is immortal too now?" Amelia asked and Serenity nodded.

"She made it through by the skin of her teeth." Apollyon picked up a stick and poked the fire.

"And how is Lukas?" Marcus said and Liora eavesdropped. She didn't know much about Amelia or Marcus, or this Annelie and Lukas.

"He still works for Heaven." Apollyon tossed the stick onto the fire and watched it burn. "They call on him from time to time."

Marcus's expression darkened. "You think he reports on us?"

Apollyon shook his head, his look turning grave. "No, but I believe they may be able to monitor him somehow, and therefore us too."

Serenity said something in French and the darkness lifted from his face and he stroked her fair hair and settled his arm around her shoulders, drawing her close to him.

Serenity fell into conversation with Amelia again, sometimes answering questions Marcus posed too.

Liora felt as if she was standing on the outside and looking in, not part of the group at all. She had never felt more different to Serenity as she watched her cousin conversing easily with the group, part of it, at the centre of it with Apollyon.

She was just a shadow of Serenity.

Asmodeus was just a shadow of Apollyon.

Liora looked over her shoulder again, following his progress along the moonlit shore. She ached to go to him.

Veiron crouched beside her and handed her two plates of food, and dropped his voice to a whisper that felt as though it was for her ears only.

"Give him those five minutes and then go to him."

Liora looked into his dark eyes, surprised to hear support in his voice when he had been the one to attack Asmodeus on sight and only listen to reason once she had disabled him.

"I can't say I love the guy. I've got my reasons for the way I feel, but I'm man enough to admit that he's different now, and that... well, now I can see a little of myself in him." Veiron smiled at her and shrugged. "I was like that once... didn't play well with others... didn't belong here. Ask the missus. He wants you to go to him... he needs you to choose him over us."

Liora nodded, her heart feeling lighter when she realised that she and Asmodeus weren't the first to go through a rough start to a relationship and that it was more than possible to make it through and end up together. Erin and Veiron were proof of that. She glanced over at Erin and caught her smiling at Veiron, a touch of pride and love in her eyes.

"Erin saw the good in me once." Veiron held his hand out to Erin and she took hold of it, and settled her other hand on her belly. "And look at me now... about to become a daddy."

Veiron kneeled beside Erin and placed his hand over hers, holding her bump with her.

"And you'll be the best father in the three realms too." Erin kissed his cheek.

Liora smiled at them, remembering how her parents had been so filled with love and devotion too, and hoped that things turned out better for Erin and Veiron.

A prickle ran down her spine and her smile faded.

Someone was watching her.

She looked around the fire at everyone and found them looking at each other, and then over her shoulder. Asmodeus had his back to her still.

The feeling came again. She shivered as the intensity of the sensation increased and it felt darker this time and sinister, setting her on edge. The same feeling she'd had in Paris several times.

Was it the Devil watching her?
Or someone else?

CHAPTER 19

Liora left the fire and went in search of Asmodeus, wanting to be around him and needing to speak to him about the strange sensation of being watched that she'd had over the past few weeks.

She found him at the far end of the beach, staring at the dark water and the moonlight playing on it. Remus and Romulus were at the treeline, sniffing and investigating.

"Asmodeus?" she whispered as she rounded him and he didn't respond.

His glowing golden gaze remained locked on the water, no doubt fixed on a point deep below the waves.

She touched his arm and he tensed, his eyes snapping to her and the bright swirling fire in them fading.

"Your boss again?"

He nodded, closed his eyes and pinched the bridge of his nose. "He is getting persistent."

"Can you hear him like Erin can?" She hoped he said no, because the thought of the Devil pushing his voice into Asmodeus's mind and saying all manner of dark things put her on edge. She wrapped her arms around herself to keep the sudden chill off her skin.

"No. It is difficult to explain. I feel compelled to do something and I know it is not my own desire. In this case, I feel I must take you to Hell, to him." He sighed and opened his eyes to glare at the water. "I do not want to take you back to Hell. It is hard to refuse his orders but I will keep fighting him."

"Twice now I've... I..." Liora lost her nerve and focused, clinging to her courage again and telling herself that she could talk to Asmodeus about this. She didn't have to worry what he would think of her or that he might believe she was crazy. She could trust him with this and he would help her find an answer to the question that plagued her. "Someone is watching me."

Asmodeus immediately looked around them and pulled her into the protective circle of his arms, pinning her against his bare chest. She pressed her cheek to it and listened to his heart beating hard against her ear. He was so warm and the feel of his arms around her comforted her more than she had anticipated, chasing away her fears and leaving her relaxed and calm. He turned with her, scanning their surroundings.

"Do you know who?" He kept hold of her, one large hand against her shoulder and the other in the small of her back.

She shook her head. "I've never seen them. It started a few weeks back and since I met you, I've felt it twice more... both times you were being compelled by the Devil. Do you think it's the Devil watching me?"

Asmodeus ran his fingers through her hair, combing it back from her face, the motion soothing her further, until she melted into him and felt completely at ease. She was safe here in his arms. She had always taken care of herself, had never relied on anyone, not since her parents had died, but she found it easy to rely on him like this, letting him take care of her.

"Perhaps. It is possible he has been monitoring you. He cannot reach the pool I often use to see this world, but he has other methods at his disposal. Do not fear, Liora. He cannot set foot in this realm. You are safe here."

"With you." She burrowed into his embrace, pressing the full length of her body into his. His trousers were still damp, cold against her bare legs.

He brushed his hand down her face, drew her chin up and looked down at her, the fire in his golden eyes warming her and chasing the chill from her bones. She didn't care what everyone else on this island thought about him. They didn't know him as she did. They had never seen this side of Asmodeus, the one he only showed to her. He cared deeply about her and would fight the Devil alone to keep her safe from him. He would move Heaven, Hell and Earth for her sake.

Beneath his dark exterior and his vicious reputation beat the heart of a good man, one capable of beautiful feelings.

One who was looking at her with the deepest form of love in his eyes.

Liora pressed her hands against his chest, tiptoed and parted her lips.

Asmodeus took her invitation, dipping his head and bringing his mouth to hers.

He kissed her softly and slowly, turning the warmth he had awoken in her veins into fire that burned her and felt as if it would never die. She would always burn for Asmodeus like this, always warm whenever he was near and on fire whenever he touched her.

He angled his head and deepened the kiss, his sensual lips playing against hers, teasing her with their softness when she began to want more, craving the ferocity he had shown her in his castle. Part of her savoured this kiss though, enjoying the bliss that came from being with him like this, sharing a quiet intimate moment that relayed his feelings and drew hers to the surface, and reassured them both.

As the world melted away, the events of the past day began to catch up with her, running through her mind at warp speed. She longed to go back to the castle, even when she knew it wasn't safe for them there now. Her time there had been wonderful, bringing her closer to Asmodeus. She feared that if they stayed on this island, he would grow distant again, driven away from her by Apollyon and Serenity, and driven away from this place by the others.

Liora hooked her hands around his neck, holding on to him and swearing she would never let go. When he had threatened to leave her on the island, it had felt as though she would never see him again, as though they were saying goodbye.

She pressed her fingers into the back of his neck and he drew back. She fought him, desperately kissing him, trying to make him stay.

Asmodeus sighed, took hold of her wrists, and eased her hands away from his neck. He looked down at her, his face in shadow but his eyes glowing faintly, golden and intense, locked on her.

He released her left wrist and smoothed his palm across her cheek and into her hair, clearing it from her face. He hooked it behind her ear, settled his fingers beneath her chin and gently raised it so she was facing him.

"I did not want to leave you," he whispered, his deep voice husky and thick with the emotions that danced in his eyes, speaking silent words of reassurance and affection to her. "I never want to leave you."

Liora closed her eyes, swallowed, and then opened them again and held his gaze. She looked deep into his eyes, able to decipher his feelings now that she knew him better and had seen beyond the walls he had carefully constructed around his emotions, hiding them from everyone so they never saw who he really was or how he truly felt.

She could see the truth of him, the real Asmodeus that she had wanted to set eyes on and know, and it was because he was letting her in and letting her see him, and it touched her.

It had taken a lot for him to be like this with her, allowing his lighter emotions, the warmer ones, to come to the surface and blossom there, growing stronger each day they were together.

He had said that the evil in him outweighed the good and she wasn't going to fool herself by pretending that wasn't the case. There was evil in him, darkness that would always be there, but there was good in him too and it grew a little every hour they spent with each other, coming to the fore to offer some balance in his emotions, gently tipping the scales so evil no longer dominated his personality.

But regardless of the battle between good and evil in him, and regardless of what side might end up being his more dominant nature, she would always want to be in his arms and feel them holding her. She would always want to be with him.

Liora smiled and cupped his cheeks, keeping his eyes on her as she searched for the courage to be as open with her feelings as he was with his.

"I never want you to leave me," she whispered and the corners of his mouth edged into a smile that took her breath away.

It overflowed with happiness and love.

"Then I swear I will never leave your side." He gathered her back into his arms and kissed her again, harder this time, unleashing a fraction of his passion on her but still keeping it soft and light, filled with tenderness.

She slipped her hands along his jaw and around the back of his head again, and pushed her fingers into his short black hair. It was velvet beneath her fingertips, thick and luxurious. His hard body pressed into hers as he stepped closer to her, bringing them into full contact again. She trembled, a shiver of heat racing through her blood like a flash fire, and leaned into him, eager for more.

Asmodeus skimmed his hands down her back and clutched her bottom, and she smiled when claws pressed into her flesh. She probed his mouth with her tongue and found fangs. He groaned when she stroked one with the tip of her tongue and gathered her even closer, crushing her against his body as he took control of the kiss, bending her to his will.

The distant chatter of everyone else on the island drifted on the warm breeze teasing the white sand and she didn't care. Enveloped in darkness and Asmodeus's arms, she felt at peace with the world, safe and secure, alone with him.

"Make love to me, Asmodeus," she whispered against his lips and he groaned in response, clutching her to him, his claws digging into her backside.

She expected him to say something, to perhaps ask for a definition of making love or something equally as charming and innocent. He didn't.

He scooped her up into his arms, kneeled and laid her down on the warm sand. She moaned the moment he settled above her, his hard body pressing her into the soft sand, sending another hot shiver zinging through her, and wrapped her arms around his neck. He kissed her again, as maddeningly soft as before, and she wanted to spur him into unleashing his passion on her, but held herself back. She had asked him to make love with her, and this soft, tender, reverent kiss was just the beginning of a moment she knew would be one of the best in her life, even better than their first time together in his castle.

Asmodeus rocked his hips between hers, the feel of his hard length sending more shivers through her as it stroked her through her knickers. She struggled against the urge to kiss him harder, wrap her legs around his waist, and force him down onto her, and relaxed beneath him.

He pushed himself up onto one elbow and stroked his fingers over her neck, over the spot where he had bitten her.

"Do you want to do it again?" The look in his eyes said that he did and she wouldn't deny him if he admitted he desired to bite her again.

"Later," he husked and kissed her again, a brief fierce one that quickly subsided into something more intense and passionate as he rocked against her. He curled his fingers over her left shoulder and kissed down her jaw on the right side, trailing his lips all the way to where he had bitten her.

He licked the twin puncture marks and then continued downwards, kissing across her chest to the swell of her breasts.

Liora moaned as he carefully undid each small button that held her dress closed down the middle, teasing her with a mixture of kisses, licks and strokes of his fingers as he popped each one. She rubbed herself against him, shifting up and down his hard length, eliciting quiet grunts from him as he worked to free her breasts.

He stopped unbuttoning her dress when he reached her stomach, leaving the lower half of it done up.

Asmodeus drew back and groaned as he parted the two sides of her black summer dress, revealing her breasts to him. She joined him, moaning and tipping her head back as he dipped his head and claimed her right nipple, sucking it into his wicked mouth and swirling his tongue around the sensitive bud.

Liora tangled her fingers in the longer lengths of his black hair and held him to her, every nip of blunt teeth and swirl of his tongue sending her deeper into her desire, until she couldn't help herself. She began shifting her hips. He had moved beyond her reach and it drove her out of her mind. She needed to feel him between her thighs again, thrusting and rocking, filling her until she felt as if she would shatter around him.

"Asmodeus," she whispered and arched her back, thrusting her breasts upwards. He moaned and slipped one arm beneath her, holding her off the sand as he sucked her left nipple harder, the hint of pain only adding to her pleasure.

Liora stared up at the stars twinkling above her, losing herself in the feel of his hard body pressed against hers and his tongue and teeth teasing her. The stars shifted out of focus and she moaned again, tugging his hair and aching for something more. He took the hint and ventured further down, kissing between her breasts and thumbing her right nipple with his free hand. She swallowed hard when he traversed her stomach and slipped his hands down her body, settling them on her thighs.

He pushed her dress up and kissed her thighs. They quivered in response, trembling as he stroked them, his warm hands skimming softly over them and gently easing them apart. Liora brushed her hands over her breasts, teasing her own nipples.

Asmodeus growled.

His gaze bore into her, burning her, cranking up her temperature. She looked down the length of her body to him and teased him, toying with her nipples, tweaking them between her fingers and thumbs.

He growled lower.

Yanked her knickers down to her knees and off her feet.

Spread her thighs and stared at her.

Mother Earth, she wanted him when he looked ready to eat her whole.

She wriggled her hips, ripping another snarl from him, tempting him into taking her. His expression turned pained and he firmly settled his hands on her thighs, holding them apart. In the moonlight, she could see the hard outline of his cock as it strained against his linen trousers. He wanted her and she was teasing him into taking her as he had in his castle but she had demanded that he make love with her. It was cruel of her to try to push him over the edge when he wanted to fulfil her request, bringing things between them onto a deeper level.

Liora had just decided to behave when he rose to kneel between her thighs and undid his black trousers. He ran his right hand down his length, revealing the thick crown, and she pulsed with desire, quivering with the memory of how big he had been inside her, stretching and filling her, completing her.

Asmodeus slipped his other hand down her thigh and she moaned, shivering when his fingers brushed her curls and then he eased them between her plush petals. He dipped his fingers down to her core and drew them up again, spreading her moisture and eliciting another breathless moan from her. His gaze darkened, devouring her as he touched her, stroking her softly and taking her higher.

She bit her lip and cupped her breasts, squeezing them as he caressed her, swirling his fingers around her nub, sending sparks skittering outwards from her core. They lit her up inside, driving her to rock her hips, riding his fingers. He dipped them lower, stealing her breath as he eased them into her sheath and then withdrew again.

Liora groaned when he held her gaze and sucked his fingers clean, his gaze turning to molten gold as he tasted her. She licked her lips, thoughts of tasting him in return spinning through her mind. She wanted to wrap her lips around his thick hard shaft and suck him until he cried out her name and the whole island knew what they were doing here in the dark under the moon and the stars.

"You think wicked things," Asmodeus growled and she didn't blush.

She boldly held his gaze and wriggled her hips, earning a husky growl as her reward. "The wickedest."

He dropped forwards, coming to rest on his hands above her, pinning her beneath him again. His golden eyes held hers, captivating her, and she reminded herself that this wasn't about wicked things.

This was about making love and showing him that pleasure could be more than physical.

It could be emotional.

Liora brushed her knuckles across his cheek and he closed his eyes and leaned into her touch. It still amazed her that such a powerful, dark male could be like this with her and her alone, seeking her affection and enjoying it when she gave it to him.

She pushed her fingers into the shorter hair at the back of his head and slowly lured him down to her, bringing his mouth close to hers. His warm breath skated over her lips, unsteady and fast, revealing that he was on the edge too, feeling nervous about doing this. He hid it well, far better than she probably was.

She had always believed that the best way to overcome fear was to face it.

Liora reached between them with her other hand and wrapped it around his shaft. Asmodeus's hand covered hers, holding it against his flesh, and she thought he meant to stop her. There was resolve in his eyes though, passion that was breaking its restraints, coming to the surface. He held her hand to his flesh, shifted his hips back and guided himself to her with him.

She moaned as the crown nudged into her body and he eased forwards, slowly filling her. He took her hand from his and captured both of them, pressing his palms against hers and interlinking their fingers. Her breath left her on a sigh when he pinned her hands to the sand on either side of her head and eased into her, filling her completely, his gaze holding hers the whole time.

He lingered there, deep inside her in more than one way. She stared up into his golden eyes, drowning in them and the affection they showed her. He tightened his grip on her hands, holding on to her, and kissed her as he began to rock into her with long, slow strokes. She moaned into his mouth and closed her eyes, giving herself over to him, letting him have complete control as he made love with her.

Her chest tightened, her emotions running wild and consuming her as Asmodeus moved above her. More than their hands, bodies and lips were linked. It felt as if he had joined all of them, linking their souls and their hearts, moulding them into one being. Liora clutched his hands, her lips teasing his, brushing them lightly. She warmed all over, from her skin to her marrow, and deeper into her, until all of her burned for him and she felt sure that he burned for her too.

"Liora," he whispered against her mouth, stroking his lips over hers, and moved into her, slow and deep, taking all of her as pleasure rippled through her. She belonged to him now, body and soul, and he belonged to her.

She didn't care that he couldn't pledge himself to her as he wanted to. This was a pledge in her eyes, this moment where their hearts, bodies and souls met in union.

"Asmodeus," she echoed, breathless with pleasure and seeking more. He rocked deeper into her, tearing a soft moan from her throat, sending sparks of ecstasy chasing through her blood.

She undulated her hips, mimicking his actions, joining in as he gently quickened his pace. His fingers tightened, holding her hands, clutching them in a way that made her believe that he had truly meant his earlier words and would never let her go.

She searched for the courage to take things further, to show him that whatever he was feeling, she was right there with him, as lost as he felt.

Asmodeus drew back, breaking the kiss, and frowned down at her as he moved above her, pushing her closer to the fall into bliss. He searched her eyes, his intense, serious expression concerning her. He pushed her hands up, pinning them to the sand above her head, and pressed his forehead against hers. Their breath mingled, caressing her lips, and he thrust a few more times, taking her higher, before pulling back again and staring into her eyes, that same intense look in his. A flicker of fear lit their golden depths.

She was about to ask him what was wrong when he spoke.

"I love you, Liora," he whispered, low and breathless, his voice flooded with passion and adoration.

She only had one thing she could say in response to that heartfelt, beautiful and brave declaration.

"I love you too." She smiled and he caught it in a kiss, fiercer now, his passion flowing over her.

He released her hands and slid one beneath her back. The other claimed the nape of her neck. He kissed her harder, taking her mouth as he took her body, sending her rocketing higher until she couldn't stop herself from pouring out her desire and her feelings too. She met him thrust for thrust, wrapping her legs around his backside and rocking her body against his, moaning as he drove deeper into her. She kissed him fiercely, nipping at his lower lip between each one, ripping rumbling moans from him.

"Liora," he uttered, kissed down her jaw and buried his face in her neck. His hot breath sent shivery tingles racing over her skin with each panted exhalation.

Liora clung to him, moaning as he pumped into her, clutching her to him, holding on to her as tightly as she was holding on to him. She tipped her head back and stared up at the stars and the moon as her belly heated and tightened. Close. She groaned and grasped his hair, each hungry kiss he planted on her throat and each thrust of his steely hot length into her core driving her spiralling upwards. She clenched him and he unleashed a fierce growl and jerked hard inside her, thrusting deeper, his pelvis slamming against her sensitive flesh.

Liora bit back her cry of bliss and shattered, her body milking his and heat cascading over her flesh, running up and down her thighs and pumping through her blood, carrying ecstasy to every fibre of her being.

Asmodeus moaned huskily into her ear and drove harder into her, chasing his own pleasure and drawing hers out.

She flexed around him and raised her hips into his, and he grunted and slammed to a halt, his claws pressing into her back and her neck as he spilled himself inside her. He breathed hard against her throat, frozen and stiff above her, and then startled her by shifting quickly to her mouth and kissing her.

Instead of the hardness she wanted, he kissed her softly, sending more ripples of pleasure through her and heightening it, turning the ecstasy of making love with him into something more. Something divine.

She pressed her head back into the sand and he took the hint, drawing away from her.

Liora stared up into his eyes, seeing all of his feelings in them, every ounce of the love he had declared. It overwhelmed her and combined with all of her fears, everything from the past day crashing over her again.

She looked up at him and saw a man she couldn't live without.

A man she wanted to be with forever.

Liora stroked his cheek, wishing there was something she could do to make sure he would always be with her, fearing that the Devil would catch up with them and separate them, and that she would lose the forever she wanted with him.

There was something she could do.

"You think sorrowful things," he whispered, concern etched in his eyes. "Why? Tell me and I will find a way to bring back your smile."

She did think sorrowful things and it was beautiful of him to notice and to want to vanquish her dragons for her, freeing her of her fears.

Liora undid the clasp of her necklace and offered it to him. "I want you to have it."

Asmodeus stared at the pentagram in her palm. "Why?"

"Because it will protect you. It was my mother's and my grandmother's before that, and it goes back generations in my family. It has powerful magic. It will keep you safe. No one will be able to hurt you while you wear it." She moved it closer to him.

He placed his hand under hers, curled her fingers over the pendant and held on to her. "You need it more than I do. I cannot accept it."

Liora frowned. "I want you to have it, Asmodeus."

Asmodeus sighed, kissed her fingers, and then shook his head.

Liora wanted to force him to accept it but the steely look in his eyes said that he wouldn't budge, no matter how hard she pushed.

He took the pendant from her, placed it back around her neck and fastened it. He ran his fingers over the pentagram.

"Later, if you still want me to have it, I will accept it... when all this is over," he whispered and looked back into her eyes.

Liora nodded, hooked her hand around the back of his neck and lured him down to her. She kissed him, pushing her fear out of her mind.

Asmodeus loved her and was thinking in terms of success, planning a future with her, a future he believed they would have together.

She had to think that way too.

She had to believe that they would make it through whatever trials lay ahead for them.

They would have the future she wanted for them.

They would have forever.

CHAPTER 20

Liora smiled as Romulus bounded after Remus, chasing him along the white sandy beach. Turquoise water lapped the gently sloping shore to her left as she walked, watching the two hellhounds. A gentle breeze caught the skirt of her summer dress, causing the black material to flutter around her thighs. The sun played on her skin, warming it and chasing the chill of night from the island as dawn broke, painting the sky in hues of gold, pink and green. It was a beautiful place, idyllic and quiet, and she had grown used to life on the island during the week she had passed here with Asmodeus and the others.

She had spent every day with Asmodeus, settling into a routine that she looked forward to repeating every morning that she woke wrapped in his arms, snuggled up against him.

They would share breakfast with the others and then spend some time with his hellhounds, walking them around the island a few times in an attempt to wear them out. Normally, all it did was wear her and Asmodeus out instead. Romulus and Remus had boundless energy and found every inch of the island fascinating, and most days they had gone off alone to investigate it, returning every so often to steal food from plates and check on Asmodeus, and sometimes growl at Apollyon.

After their morning walk, Liora and Asmodeus would have another small meal, and then they would try to help the others with whatever work they had to do. It had been her idea and Asmodeus had been uncertain about it at first.

After the initial couple of days, the frequent arguments between him and Apollyon had subsided, and the two had formed an uneasy truce. Asmodeus had started working more with Veiron, leaving the others to work together. It wasn't the ideal solution, but Amelia and Marcus seemed to be finding it hard to trust Asmodeus.

Once they had done their work for the day, or Asmodeus had stormed off in a foul mood and she had gone after him, they would sit together on the sand, holding hands and watching the sun setting. Every evening had been beautiful, a colourful and vivid sunset that would stay with her forever.

Erin always called them over, labelling them as unsociable lovebirds. Asmodeus had bristled the first time she had called them that, until Erin had explained that she was teasing him. Veiron had said he didn't think Asmodeus knew what teasing was and her angel had informed him that he knew very well what it was, because Liora often teased him.

In the time they had been on the island, she had felt as if someone was watching her more than once. The latest time had been last night, when she had been showing Asmodeus how to cook the chicken and other items he had acquired during a mission he had volunteered for. The normal fishing trip had produced nothing, not even small ones, and Asmodeus had refused to allow her, and everyone else, to eat the remains of their scant vegetable supply as dinner.

He had disappeared before anyone could say anything, casting a portal and stepping through it. She had worried about him from the moment he had left to the second he returned, carrying two large green baskets that told her that he had visited the scene of his previous crime to re-enact it. Apollyon and some of the others had given her a look that suggested she correct his behaviour.

She knew that she should, but he had brought cakes and chocolate, and she was a sucker for the sweet things. Erin was too. She had almost snapped Asmodeus's arm off when he had taken three big bars of chocolate from a basket and held them out to Liora. Asmodeus had tried to resist her, but Erin had been vicious and merciless, not giving up and even resorting to flashing fangs and claws.

Liora had told him to let Erin have them, mostly because the poor woman was clearly craving chocolate and Veiron had had that edge about him that warned he was close to going demonic to ensure his female got the food she wanted.

Liora picked up a stick and dragged it behind her, scoring the sand with it.

This morning, Veiron and Erin had wanted to talk to Asmodeus about the Devil, and Romulus and Remus had decided that they didn't want to wait for their morning walk. She had offered to take them alone when they had growled at the couple who were responsible for the delay, and Asmodeus had reluctantly agreed, saying he would catch up with her.

Remus shot across the sand and into the wooded centre of the island, re-emerging with a huge stick. Romulus tried to snatch it from him and Remus growled, baring his fangs. Romulus uncharacteristically let him have his way and trotted along the edge of the palm trees, digging in places and burying his nose in the scrub.

It was the same every morning. She was sure that there wasn't an inch of the island that they hadn't turned over and investigated, but it didn't stop them from checking it out again. Liora didn't think that it could have changed much overnight.

Remus grew bored of his stick and went off to find Romulus, who had ventured deeper into the thick, lush green forest.

Liora wiggled her wrist so the stick trailing behind her caused waves like a snake on the sand and she basked in the sunlight as she walked. It was truly beautiful on the island.

How long was Asmodeus going to take to catch up with her?

She was already halfway around the island and was getting bored. She missed talking to him while they walked, sharing the sunrise with him.

A breeze blew against her back, the familiar sound of wings reaching her ears. She smiled and waited, knowing he would come up beside her soon and slip his hand into hers.

She felt his presence behind her and his eyes on her.

A prickle ran down her spine. Her blood chilled. She knew the feel of that gaze. Her heart stopped.

Black clawed fingers closed over her mouth, pulling her back against the hard body behind her. She grabbed her attacker's arm and yanked on it, lifting her legs and using all of her weight and her strength in an attempt to break free. Her magic rose to the fore to help her and she almost managed to pull the male hand away from her face. The man grabbed her with his other hand and covered her mouth again, silencing her before she could cry out for help. His finger and thumb pinched her nose, cutting off her air supply.

Liora panicked. Her magic burst out of control, lashing out at the man behind her and spilling his blood down his arms. He growled into her ear and she struggled, flailing wildly and kicking her legs. His grip on her tightened, his other arm moving to her chest to grab her arms. She fought him even as the world grew dim and her head spun, darkness encroaching and threatening to carry her away.

She couldn't pass out. She couldn't give in.

She lashed out and the man grabbed her arm, catching her necklace in the process. The chain snapped and Liora blindly grabbed for it, barely catching it. Remus barked. The man's grip on her mouth and nose tightened and she lost her fight against him and the darkness. It swallowed her.

Liora's head hurt. It felt as if someone was kicking it repeatedly, the rhythm of their assault leisurely but vicious, perfectly timed to keep her cringing with each thump.

"She wakes." The deep male voice roused her further. Her attacker?

She tried to open her eyes and failed. They hurt as much as her head and her lungs. Acrid air filled them, the disgusting smell telling her exactly where she was without her having to see her surroundings.

Hell.

Liora focused, calling her magic to her, wanting it readily available in case she had to fight.

Nothing happened.

She concentrated harder, trying to call it to her. It failed to respond and cold stole through her veins. It wasn't gone. She could feel it inside her. Deep inside her. It had never felt so distant to her.

The man moved closer, his gaze locked on her, intense and creepy. Not the gaze of the man who had attacked her on the island. This was someone else, someone infinitely more powerful and more evil.

Liora finally managed to open her eyes and looked up at the face of her captor. The Devil.

He preened black hair from his face and his golden eyes flashed with amusement, as if having her at his mercy entertained him.

"Having trouble with something?" he said, his voice curling around her and taunting her. It wasn't having her at his mercy that amused him. He was entertained by the fact that she had tried to call her power and it had failed to come, and that she had been dismayed to find it locked deep within her, beyond her reach. "The first rule of engagement is to disable your enemy's defensive line."

"I'm your enemy?" She looked around her at the elegant black room, cataloguing her surroundings. The first rule of being a captive was to know everything about your location, including the nearest available objects that could be used as a weapon.

Large mirrors took up most of the four walls, their decorative gold frames a decadent contrast against the black. Ebony cabinets lined the two walls on either side of her, their broad flat tops empty, and a fireplace stood behind the man before her.

Other than breaking the mirrors and using a shard of the glass as a knife, there was no weapon available to her if she had to defend herself or turned insane enough to launch an attack on the Devil.

"Indeed... although I would prefer to think of you as my guest. The choice is up to you." He looked her over and sighed emphatically. "It is a shame Asmodeus chose to disobey me. Things could have been far simpler, and better for all involved, had he carried out my commands."

His golden eyes roamed back to hers and she could see the similarities between him and Asmodeus, and Erin. He had built Asmodeus in his image, moulding him to be everything he was, but Asmodeus was so much more than this man before her. She couldn't believe what Asmodeus had told her about him. There was no good in him. Her senses were still online and all she could feel in him was pure evil and darkness.

"What do you want with me?" Liora went to stand and only then realised that she couldn't. Her eyes darted down to her wrists and she stared in horror at the thick black cuffs locked around her arms, pinning them to those of the gold chair she was sitting on. Her ankles felt similarly restrained. "I would hardly call this the behaviour of a good host."

The Devil smiled, flashing small fangs. "I told you. I had wanted us to meet on better terms. Asmodeus's behaviour means we cannot. He declared himself my enemy, and you are aligned with him, making you my enemy too. If I released you, you would seek to fight me, would you not?"

There was little point in lying to him. "I would seek to kick your arse."

He shook his head and sighed. "So many females in your world believe they can defeat me. I do wonder where you all get these ridiculous thoughts."

"Erin will kick your arse one day, and I will be there to lend her a hand."

He laughed now and did something that unsettled her even more.

He removed his crisp black jacket and set it down over the back of an elegant red padded armchair near the fire, and then undid the top button of his black shirt. He rolled the sleeves up his forearms as he moved towards her, his golden gaze boring into her, making her want to shrink back as he neared. His power washed over her, potent and dark, pressing down on her.

"How can you be there when you will be asleep?" He cocked his head to one side, his gaze gaining a twinkle she didn't like.

"Asleep... as in dead..." Liora swallowed hard. "You mean to kill me?"

He shook his head again. "No. Asleep as in unconscious. Killing you would defeat the purpose of having you in my care."

In his care.

A guest.

"What do you want with me?" she snapped, fear making her brave.

The Devil captured her jaw in one cold hand and shoved her chin up, forcing her to face him. He held her there, his claws pressing into her cheeks, and stared down at her.

"You are dangerous. I intend to render you safe."

Like a gun with the safety catch on?

"Why am I dangerous?"

He released her jaw and patted her cheek. "You do not need to know. All you need to know is that I will see to it that no harm befalls you while you sleep."

She wasn't taking that as an answer. She had a right to know why she was dangerous and why he wanted to flick her safety on.

"Is this because of my magic?"

He shook his head. "No, and that is the only question I will answer."

She wasn't taking that as an answer either. "Why do you want to protect me? I would have thought it would be easier to kill me if I'm so dangerous and you're so powerful."

"Why kill what I may one day have a use for?" The Devil turned away from her and waved his hand over the top of a small black table beside his chair. A silver knife appeared on it.

The Devil picked it up.

Liora swallowed hard, her gaze riveted on the dagger.

"What are you going to do with that?" she whispered, trembling as he advanced on her, toying with the delicate blade.

"This?" He pressed one finger on his left hand against the end of the hilt and one on his right against the point and turned them so the blade was vertical with its tip at the bottom. He released the hilt and the knife balanced on his fingertip. It stayed there, motionless and straight, not wobbling in the slightest. He smiled at her. "There is some truth in fairy tales. The myth of a prick of a poisoned needle sending someone into a deep, endless sleep in which they never age can easily come about from the truth of a prick of a special blade fed with powerful blood... and none come more powerful than mine."

Liora stared at his finger, watching it pale and turn bluish. He was feeding the blade. He was going to use it on her to send her into a timeless sleep.

"No." Liora struggled against her bonds, grimacing as they cut into her wrists.

The Devil frowned and flicked his other hand towards her, and she froze in her seat, crying out in frustration when she found she couldn't move.

"We cannot have you harming yourself now." He flipped the blade in his other hand and caught it. "I promise, dear child, that this will not hurt. I will not spill a drop of your blood."

Liora desperately called on her magic but it still didn't come. It lingered deep inside her and she realised that just as the Devil had trapped her within her own body, rendering her powerless to move, he had trapped her magic inside her blood.

"Please," she whispered, her heart calling out for Asmodeus to come, to burst into the room and stop this madman before he sent her into a sleep she feared she would never wake from.

She struggled again, her body not responding to her commands and her magic unable to help her break the spell the Devil had placed on it.

He kneeled before her, looking up at her, his amber eyes showing her no pity or remorse, and took hold of her left hand.

"You must sleep," he said in a low voice that sounded practiced to her ears, designed to soothe and placate, to calm and subdue.

She rallied and focused harder, calling on all of her strength and trying to force her body to move, to knock the blade away. He edged it towards her fingers and tears slipped down her cheeks as it pricked her skin.

Heat spread up her arm like fire and she cried out, screaming in agony as it burned her flesh and melted her bones. It hurt like a bitch.

Darkness loomed again, terrifying and crushing, endless.

She wouldn't have her forever that she wanted.

Everything ended here.

"Asmodeus," she whispered, hoarse and afraid as she sank into the gloom.

The Devil's voice echoed around her, soft and offering a strange comfort as oblivion claimed her.

"Sleep, Liora… the world will be safe then."

CHAPTER 21

The moment Asmodeus heard one of his hellhounds barking, he cast a portal and leaped into it, coming out on the other side of the island. Romulus bounded up to him, his red eyes glowing with fury. Asmodeus's heart pounded and he looked towards the shore and Remus, fearing what he would find. Remus pawed at something on the white sand and whined, the sound pained and heightening Asmodeus's fear. He sprinted to Remus and ground to a halt when he saw what it was on the sand.

Liora's pentagram.

He dropped to his knees and gathered the necklace into his fist, clutching it and using his senses to scour the island for her.

"What happened?" he said in the demon tongue to Remus and Romulus, his fear crushing his heart. Liora was gone. "Who took her?"

Remus whined and his left ear drooped. Romulus growled at something. A glassy strip across the sand.

Someone had opened a pathway to Hell here and had snatched Liora. Asmodeus touched the footprints in the sand. Liora's bare ones, delicate and small, and larger ones made by boots, distinctly male and definitely angelic.

A Hell's angel.

"Where's Liora?" The soft female voice came from behind him, her appearance made in silence. He had been so caught in the vicious storm of his emotions that he hadn't sensed her arrival.

Asmodeus glared up at Erin and she shook her head and then looked beyond him, seeing the same scar line that he had noticed.

"He wouldn't. My father is a bastard, but he wouldn't dare break the pact we have." Erin carefully crouched and touched the jagged glass fault line. "Still warm."

"I have to get her back." Asmodeus shot to his feet and gritted his teeth when he sensed the others coming towards them. He couldn't face them. Not when he was losing control, his emotions tearing him apart, pushing him towards the brink of unleashing his fury on the first person who looked at him the wrong way or said the wrong thing.

Liora had made friends on this island and he didn't want to give them reason to no longer trust her. She had been happy here, with them and with him. He wanted to make sure that when he brought her back, she would still have this place and these people, so she could be happy again.

Asmodeus threw his hand out and cast a portal, the black swirling vortex appearing between Erin and his hellhounds.

"Wait. We can think this through. We can all go together and bring her back, Asmodeus. You don't have to do this alone." Erin rose to her feet and he shook his head, refusing to heed her order.

They couldn't help him.

Erin and Veiron couldn't travel to Hell without risking their unborn child or falling into the Devil's hands.

Apollyon would only mock him, pointing out that he had again failed to protect Liora.

The others would follow Apollyon.

He had to do this alone.

Romulus and Remus whined, as if sensing his thoughts and knowing that included leaving them here. He couldn't bring himself to look at them as he spoke to them in the demon language.

"Remain here. I will bring her back. I swear it. We will all be together again." Asmodeus heard voices drawing closer and stepped into the portal. The darkness embraced him, a cool welcoming breeze over his flesh, and he changed into his armour as he travelled to the other side, deep into the bowels of Hell.

He stepped out on the main path between the lava river below the plateau and the Devil's obsidian fortress, and stared at it, knowing that the bastard held Liora there.

Asmodeus spread his black feathered wings and beat them, lifting off and flying over the inhospitable rocky terrain, heading towards the tall spires of black basalt that formed a semi-circle around the Devil's home.

It had been his home once.

When he had left it, the Devil had shown his disappointment and irritation by changing the enchantments on the entrances. They no longer opened to him as they used to, sensing his proximity and admitting him. He had tried several times to enter without the Devil's permission to attend a meeting with him and every time the doors had failed to open on his approach. He needed to find a way in.

Asmodeus's red gaze scanned the vast empty fields below him. Security was lacking today. Why?

He had expected the Devil to have at least a legion of Hell's angels ready to defend the fortress against him, ensuring that Liora remained locked within its walls. It was strange of his master to leave the fortress undefended.

He beat his wings and rose higher in the warm air, scouting further into the distance in case the Devil's men were lying in wait. He could see no one within at least a mile's radius, nor could he sense anyone.

Asmodeus flew over the huge spikes of black rock and swooped down into the fractured courtyard, landing near the steps that curved around the front of the fortress.

It was too quiet.

He placed Liora's pendant around his neck and its magic flowed over him, a cool sensation that felt like a gentle caress but was potent, as powerful as Liora believed it to be.

He took hold of the pentagram and looked down at it, studying the intricate star and the symbols engraved in the surface on both sides. It had been her mother's and her grandmother's before her. Passed down through generations in the female line to protect them.

She had wanted him to have it though, had desired he wear it so it would protect him. She had her wish in a way now, but he would return it to her the moment she was safe in his arms where she belonged.

Asmodeus curled his fingers around the star and approached the steps of the fortress, his gaze locked on the tall twin doors in the black forbidding façade.

"Open the doors and speak with me." Asmodeus's voice rang around the courtyard, echoing off the black spires of rock that surrounded him.

He waited, clutching Liora's pentagram, trying to steady his emotions so he could face whatever came next with a clear mind and heart, able to calculate the best moves and the quickest method of getting what he wanted. He wouldn't fail Liora. He would save her from his master and ensure the male never came after her again.

Nothing happened.

Asmodeus mounted the steps and his power began to rise, entwining with the magic contained within the pentagram. He swore he could feel Liora calling for him, her fear reaching out to him through the impenetrable black walls of his master's fortress.

"Liora," he whispered and tightened his grip on her pendant around his neck, his heart calling for her, his wretched soul desperate to see that she was safe and unharmed.

He released her pendant and called both of his swords to his hands. The curved golden blades gleamed wickedly in the dim glow of the lava pools dotted around the courtyard.

"Devil," Asmodeus commanded, his focus locked on his master now and the connection that existed between them in their blood. "Answer me. Show yourself. Give me back Liora."

The ground shook, bucking violently beneath his feet, but the doors remained closed to him.

Asmodeus held his twin golden and black blades out before him and crossed them, switching his focus to his power and his weapons, channelling his mounting fury into them. They began to glow, growing brighter with each second that he glared at the doors before him. He couldn't risk unleashing his power on the fortress, not while Liora was inside, but he could send the Devil a message, allowing him to sense his power.

Power that Asmodeus had never revealed to him before now.

He had always held back, only ever using a fraction of his true strength, never letting the Devil know just how strong he really was.

His power surpassed Apollyon's.

"Face me." Asmodeus switched the flow of his power, drawing it back into himself, absorbing it from his blades. They were key to Apollyon's power but the fool had never thought to awaken them and then take the power they held back into him, strengthening himself.

His claws grew, black and sharp, curling around the hilts of his blades. His fangs emerged, vicious and long, his lower canines sharpening to mirror them. His eyes burned red.

Shadows swirled around his feet, dancing and twisting, lashing out at his surroundings before playfully curling around his legs.

"Face me!" he roared and the ground shook again, harder this time.

A thick menacing snarl answered him, echoing in the hot acrid air.

Asmodeus grinned and cast his gaze to his right, up the height of the spires of rock that reached upwards to tower above him.

A huge clawed foot appeared, grasping one spire and smashing it into dust. A second mirrored it, breaking down another pinnacle, sending boulders bouncing down the curved wall. They tumbled towards him, each bigger than he was. The shadows at his feet raced towards them and lashed at them, cracking as they connected and the boulders exploded, raining dust down on the black pavement of the courtyard.

Smoke curled up from behind the wall and then an emerald green eye emerged from the darkness, the vertical slit of its pupil roving the land below and then narrowing when it locked on him. An unholy roar shook the land and the dragon rose up, beating enormous black leathery wings, blasting hot air and dust at him.

Asmodeus beat his own wings, keeping himself steady and keeping the dust at bay so it didn't steal his vision or choke his lungs.

The dragon landed on the broken section of wall. The basalt struggled to hold its immense weight, crumbling in places, causing the behemoth to stumble and fight for its footing. It beat its wings and cried out, its hooked beak opening to reveal rows of gleaming black teeth each longer than his blades.

Its skin turned black and eyes gradually melted into crimson.

Asmodeus welcomed the sign of its rage. Dragons fought best when angered and he wanted a good fight.

"Come." He crooked his blades, beckoning the beast to him.

It leaned forwards, setting its front feet onto the wall and digging vicious claws in for support, and hissed at him.

It was furious.

Asmodeus knew why. It was angry because they had escaped him before. There would be no escape this time.

There was only death or victory.

He refused to leave this place. Not without Liora.

The dragon shook its head, its curved black horns almost catching its wings, and then launched itself forwards.

Asmodeus grinned, kicked off the ground and rushed to meet it. He drew his right blade back and flapped his wings, shooting towards the dragon as it careened towards him, its own wings beating furiously. The second it was within reach, it slashed at him. He rolled over the top of the dragon's claws, barely missing them, pressed his left foot into them and pushed upwards, speeding towards the dragon's throat.

He roared and lashed out with his golden blade. The dragon snarled and twisted its head, unleashing a stream of fire from between its fangs. Asmodeus cast a portal and shot through it, narrowly avoiding the flames and coming out above the dragon.

The beast twisted to face him, slammed one clawed back foot in the ground, smashing the pavement, and snapped its jaws at him. Asmodeus tucked his wings back and dropped, dodging the dragon's teeth, and slashed across its left front leg. It hissed and swiped at him, catching his legs and sending him crashing into the ground.

The expected pain didn't come.

He rolled hard across the cracked pavement, came to his feet and quickly looked himself over before casting a portal and diving through it, coming out behind the dragon. There wasn't a scratch on him. Because of Liora's pentagram?

Asmodeus flung his left hand forwards, commanding his shadows. They twisted and rushed towards the dragon. It growled, jaws peeling back from its huge fangs, and its vicious barbed tail cut through the shadows, destroying most of them. Two of them sliced into the dragon's tail, spilling black blood and ripping an agonised roar from the beast.

It turned on him, each footfall shaking the ground, threatening to knock him off balance. Asmodeus beat his wings and took flight again, but didn't make it far. The dragon lunged, quicker than he had anticipated, and caught him hard with its right paw, sending him rocketing through the air and smashing into the wall at the far end of the courtyard.

Asmodeus tumbled down the jagged wall and landed in a heap on the ground. Unharmed. He was beginning to see why Liora liked this pendant so much, and why it was vital that he return it to her.

The dragon gave a frustrated shriek and charged.

Asmodeus picked himself up, beat his wings and ran up the curved wall. The dragon shifted course, coming for him, tracking his movements. He reached as far as he could run without flying, pushed off from the wall and flipped backwards. He spread his wings above the dragon's head and roared as he sent one blade away and clutched the other with both hands, bringing it down hard and pointed straight at his target between the dragon's horns.

It snarled and rose onto its hind legs, and Asmodeus growled as he overshot, ending up right in front of the dragon's head.

The dragon snapped at him, huge jaws coming close to claiming their prize. Liora's pentagram might protect him from injury but he wasn't sure whether it protected from death, and he was certain that being eaten whole by a dragon would result in that.

The beast's fangs caught his left wing and sent him spinning out of control. Asmodeus focused on his shadows, calling them to him, gathering them around him and twisting to face the dragon at the same time. He threw his hand towards it, sending the shadows streaming at the dragon, and then quickly cast a portal behind him and fell into it.

He came out above the dragon again and grinned as it swiped at the shadows, trying to clear them from its head so it could see where he had gone.

Asmodeus called his other blade to him, crossed them and snarled as he unleashed their power on the dragon. A shaft of red light shot down, blazing so brightly it almost blinded him. The dragon lumbered right, still swiping at the shadows mercilessly attacking it. Asmodeus huffed as the light tore through the dragon's left wing rather than its neck and cracked the ground, sending lava spewing upwards like a fountain.

The black dragon shrieked and lashed out blindly with its tail. Asmodeus beat his wings hard, trying to rise above the deadly obsidian barb on the end that was bigger than he was. It caught him across his shin, cutting into his gold-edged black greave but not his flesh beneath. One of the hooked spikes of the barb wedged into the metal and Asmodeus cried out as the dragon brought its tail down, dragging him with it. He tried to get his armour free but the ground came at him too quickly and he grunted as he hit it hard enough to fracture the pavement.

His ears rang. Not good.

He shook his head to stop it from spinning and then yelled as the dragon moved its tail again, pulling him back up into the air, leaving him dangling upside down.

Cursed beast.

It turned on him and growled, smoke curling from the nostrils in its beak and its red eyes glittering with victory.

Asmodeus stared death in the face.

He looked up at his snagged leg.

He really did hate losing pieces of his armour but desperate times meant desperate measures.

He just hoped that he couldn't injure himself while wearing Liora's pentagram.

The dragon's clawed right front paw shot towards him.

Asmodeus cried out and swung his blade at his own leg. It hit hard, easily cutting through the leather straps holding his greave in place, and he grimaced, expecting it to slice into his leg too. It didn't. His leg came free of his armour and he dropped.

Hard.

The dragon's paw shifted course, lowering to meet him. Asmodeus struggled to press his two blades together in front of him and focused everything he had on them. They glowed bright gold and red light blasted from where they crossed, shooting straight towards the dragon's paw.

It bellowed as the fiery light struck it, incinerating its claws, turning them into ash.

The beast lashed out with its tail, slamming it hard into the pavement below him. Asmodeus's greave came loose from the barbs and skittered across the black slabs.

Asmodeus hit the ground at an awkward angle, rolled and was on his feet a heartbeat later, racing towards the castle. He snagged his fallen greave on the way past and used a mental command to send it back to his castle in the wasteland. He didn't have time to repair it now.

The dragon beat its wings and came up beside him. Asmodeus sent another blast of light towards it. The beast rose above it and the beam hit the wall, blasting a huge hole in it and sending everything above it crashing down. He unleashed another beam at the dragon and it ducked, spiralling downwards. The light struck the spires of black rock nearest the right side of the fortress and clipped one of the towers. It crumbled and collapsed, sending a plume of black ash into the air.

His heart stopped.

The dragon landed between him and the fortress, its red eyes gleaming with victory again.

Bastard.

Asmodeus couldn't risk unleashing the power of his swords on the dragon while it stood between him and the fortress. Liora was in there. Even if the dragon failed to dodge the blast, it would cut straight through it into the building, destroying both of them.

He sent one of his blades away and curled his hand around the pentagram, searching for Liora, desperate to feel her and know she was still safe.

The dragon reared up, red shimmering across its scales. It was charging up, preparing to bake the entire courtyard with the inferno it held within. He couldn't let that happen.

Asmodeus furled his wings against his back and closed his eyes, drawing on all of his strength, channelling it into the shadows regrouping around his feet. Shadows that came from the Devil's blood in his veins. Darkness incarnate.

They would swallow the dragon whole given the chance.

He coaxed them, drawing them up to his hands, so they floated and danced around his clawed fingers and settled into his skin, rendering it black. The darkness flowed up his arms, cold and numbing, increasing his strength as it joined with him.

His blade turned black.

The gold on the remaining pieces of his armour melted into pure obsidian and then blazed purple.

The black feathers of his wings gained a violet shimmer.

Asmodeus embraced the darkness within him, pushing out the good, expelling it. It was the only way to stop the dragon. It was the only way to save Liora.

Good was his weakness.

Evil was his strength.

His black hair fluttered and shifted backwards, and black horns curled from behind his ears.

He opened his eyes, fixing his swirling purple gaze on the dragon, and bared his fangs as his teeth all sharpened and the darkness reached his chest and exploded outwards, turning all of his skin into the colour of the night.

The dragon hesitated.

Asmodeus couldn't blame it.

None saw the King of Demons in his true form and lived to tell others of his appearance.

Liora's pentagram burned into his chest and he growled as the power in it tried to repel him.

He called his other black blade, pressed his bare foot into the ground, and kicked off. He shot through the air towards the dragon and it threw its head back and unleashed hell on him. Fire as hot as the sun rocketed towards him.

Asmodeus grinned, pinned his wings back and locked his blades together before him, not slowing his ascent.

The inferno struck his black blades and they blazed violet. The fire bent around him, singeing his wings, and he endured it, gritting his teeth and growling as he thrust forwards. He burst through the other side and stared into the dragon's huge red eyes.

It lunged for him with its teeth.

Asmodeus launched the blade in his left hand, sending it spinning rapidly towards the dragon's neck. The beast reared back and shrieked as the black sword lodged deep between two of the thick bands of armour around the front of its throat.

Asmodeus's grin widened. He laughed as his boots hit the dragon's neck, he caught the blade and ran right, dragging it behind him, slicing across its throat. It desperately slashed at him and he swung his other blade, severing one of its claws, and then hacked at its throat. Black blood and red fire flowed from the ragged cuts, and the dragon lumbered forwards, trying to shake him. He dug his other black blade into the back of its neck and held on to it, riding each attempt to remove him.

He stabbed and slashed with his other blade, cutting through meat and bone, grinning the whole time as the beast began to weaken. Pathetic creature. It crashed into the ground and Asmodeus pulled his other blade out, brought them both back above his head and roared as he swung them down with all of his strength.

They sliced straight through the dragon's neck. Its head rolled across the courtyard and its body lurched, convulsing violently, its wings flapping. Blood and molten fire pumped from the ragged end of its neck, melting the black pavement beneath the dragon.

The dragon's body stumbled and crashed into the ground.

Asmodeus straightened to his full height on its shoulders and smiled as the dragon stilled.

Victory to the King of Demons.

He had told Liora that a dragon was no match for him.

The doors in the fortress behind him creaked open.

Asmodeus huffed as he sensed his master's gaze on him, feeling the full depth of his fury, and slowly turned to face him.

Standing on the dragon's corpse, he towered above the Devil, and for the first time in his life, his master had to look up at him.

Asmodeus grinned.

"Give her to me." He sent one sword away and held his black clawed hand out to the Devil. "You have what is mine."

"No, Asmodeus." The Devil rolled the sleeves of his black shirt down and buttoned them. "I cannot hand her over to you. She is safe. There is no need for us to quarrel."

"You speak so because you fear I will slay you as I slayed your dragon." Asmodeus beat his aching black wings and furled them against his back. He could feel cuts on his body. Wounds. It seemed Liora's pentagram refused to protect him when he was in this form.

The Devil flicked him a bored look. "I admit, I was surprised to discover this power in you... my power. It will not change anything, Asmodeus. Leave."

He felt the familiar tug behind his breastbone and growled. "No. I will not heed your commands. Give me Liora."

"Again… I cannot hand her over to you. She is safe and that is all you need to know."

"I want her back." The shadows slipped from his fingers, draining down from his chest to curl around them, eager for blood. He would give it to them if the Devil thought to keep refusing him. "She belongs to me. I demand to see her."

He needed to see her. His life and his sanity depended upon it. If he didn't see her in the next five minutes, he was going to go out of his mind and wreak havoc upon this entire realm until the Devil gave him what he wanted.

Liora.

"I cannot allow that." The Devil calmly moved forwards, to the edge of the curved steps. He frowned down at the courtyard as it bubbled and hissed, little more than a lake of lava and dragon's blood, and curled his lip. The fury Asmodeus could sense in him grew and shadows fluttered around the Devil's shoulders.

Asmodeus growled and tipped his chin up, the darkness flowing around his claws growing agitated, striking at the air in the Devil's direction.

"Give her to me," Asmodeus snarled and the pentagram burned him again, blistering his black flesh. It despised the evil in him. He could feel it. It wanted to be away from him and would burn through his body to achieve it. "I will not ask you again."

The Devil's eyes flashed red. "And I will not tell you again. She is safe with me."

"Let me see her."

"*No.*"

He growled in frustration. "Why not? Why have you taken her from me?"

"It is for the good of the world, Asmodeus. I cannot let you have her. She is dangerous in your hands."

"She belongs in these hands." He held them out to the Devil and then frowned at them, seeing what they had become.

Black.

Clawed.

Evil.

He flexed his fingers and curled them into fists. Liora would hate to see him as he was now. She wouldn't want to be in these arms that longed to hold her close to him, to shield her from the violence of the three realms and keep her safe.

She would see him as a monster.

Pure evil.

A true king of demons.

Just like his master.

The Devil straightened and tipped his chin up, holding Asmodeus's gaze. The shadows fluttering around his master's shoulders spread and grew, until they streamed from the back of his black shirt and flickered over his hands. Darkness shifted beneath his skin and his red eyes bore into Asmodeus, challenging him as his power flowed over him, pressing down despite the magnitude of Asmodeus's own power.

"I warn you… do not try to reach her, Asmodeus. Do not be a fool. I swear she is safe, unharmed, and she will remain that way. I do this for the good of the world."

"Good?" Asmodeus readied his blades and flashed his fangs. "You know nothing of good. What you do is evil… you seek to separate us… you seek to keep my Liora from me and I will not allow it. She is *mine*!"

The Devil's eyes blazed crimson and he growled, revealing his own vicious fangs.

"Try, Maggot. Only I can access the place where she resides and any who attempt to reach it will die."

His master cast his left hand out and Asmodeus roared at him as black tendrils shot around him, snaring his wrists and throat, choking him.

"For the good of the three realms, Asmodeus, do not be a fool."

Darkness swallowed him and then black slammed into him. He pressed his hands against the charred slabs, pushed himself onto his knees, and threw his head back and roared at the cavernous ceiling of Hell and the ruined castle before him.

His master would pay for daring to send him here, back to a place that only worsened his pain, heightening it until it ate away at him.

He lumbered onto his feet and breathed hard, trying to rein his anger in and subdue the darkness. The shadows slipped from his skin and his armour, and his horns shrank back into his head.

He had to look normal. He couldn't let them see him like this.

He couldn't let them see what was going to happen before it was too late.

He clutched the pentagram around his neck and grinned.

He needed to borrow something from his twin.

He needed to locate Liora within the fortress.

He needed a witch.

CHAPTER 22

Apollyon was growing tired of Asmodeus's behaviour. He checked his swords over and sheathed them at his waist, settling the curved golden blades against the pointed strips of armour that protected his hips. Everyone else on the island had already armoured up and were ready to leave as soon as he had retrieved Serenity from the other side of the island. She was trying to communicate with the idiot's two hellhounds, hoping to discover what he had told them about his plans, if anything.

He looked around him at the others, glad that they had agreed to come with him to Hell in search of Liora and Asmodeus. God only knew his twin didn't deserve their help after heading off alone like that, leaving Erin with his rabid dogs.

Erin paced near the fire, muttering dark things beneath her breath. The Devil had refused to respond when she had opened a line of communication with him and demanded to know whether he had sent his Hell's angels to snatch Liora, breaking the tentative truce between them. Since then, she had been detailing all the ways she was going to rip into her father and make him pay.

Veiron remained close to her, barely holding on to his more angelic form. Darkness ruled around his red eyes though, a warning that he could turn demonic at any moment. His gaze followed his female and from time to time he reached out and she would touch his hand as she passed. The act seemed to ground Erin, causing the shadows that constantly flickered around her hands to abate for a few minutes.

Amelia and Marcus were deep in conversation, strategizing and discussing how they were going to keep Erin from launching a dark unholy war on her father. She was in no state to fight, not without harming the baby. Everyone had silently agreed on that, exchanging looks that had created a pact. No matter what went down when they were in Hell, Erin was going to be surrounded at all times, held back from the fight and safe from danger. She would hate them for it, but she wasn't thinking straight. She was angry and wanted the Devil to pay, and everyone here knew where that would lead.

They were in no position to declare war on the Devil.

At least not while he had Liora.

Apollyon looked at the endless blue sky, charting the position of the sun. It had been hours since Asmodeus had gone off on a suicide mission. In a handful of minutes, he and the others would do the same, throwing themselves into Hell in order to take Liora back from the Devil.

How many times had he told Asmodeus to guard Liora more carefully, ensuring she was safe? The fool had let her go off alone and something had snatched her. He would be having words with the idiot when he reached him in Hell.

As soon as Serenity returned.

What was taking her so long?

Erin cast him a glance and then lingered, frowning at him. She ground to a halt on the white sand and brushed her jaw-length black hair back from her face.

"Holy fuck." Her amber eyes shot wide. "How long have the puppies been gone?"

"What do you mean?" Apollyon turned and stalked towards her. "The hellhounds are gone?"

She nodded. "I could feel them a minute ago... and now I can't. Veiron?"

The tall scarlet-haired Hell's angel shrugged his crimson wings. "Nope. You're right. They've popped off my radar. I could sort of sense them before."

"Serenity," Apollyon breathed and turned his focus to her, seeking her.

Normally there was a connection between them, a link between him and the witch who was his master. Now, there was nothing. He pressed his hands to his chest and closed his eyes, focusing harder and searching for her. A familiar tug behind his gold-edged black breastplate pulled him downwards, towards the sand.

Towards Hell.

Apollyon growled. "Asmodeus."

His twin was going to die for this.

He concentrated on the call Serenity was sending him.

It disappeared.

He gritted his teeth and curled his fingers into fists, clenching them tightly.

"He took Serenity?" Amelia said, her grey eyes beginning to turn silver and her emotions rising, tainting her power in a way that he could sense. "Why?"

"He has to have a reason," Erin piped in and ignored the scowl Amelia tossed her way. She settled her amber gaze on Apollyon and rubbed her belly, smoothing the black material of her dress over it. She was the only one not wearing armour, having complained that it hurt her baby and she didn't need it because she could teleport in a snap. "Maybe he wants Serenity to find Liora?"

A reasonable explanation. It would take a witch to find a witch. Apollyon was still going to kill him though.

The quiet voice at the back of his mind mocked him, pointing out that he had left his female alone and something had snatched her. He was no better than Asmodeus.

He let out a frustrated growl.

"We need to find them." He turned his focus towards Serenity again but felt nothing.

He had travelled in Hell for centuries and had heard rumours that Asmodeus held court in a distant region of the realm, having constructed himself a castle there that was fitting for the so-called King of Demons. None of the demons he had tortured for information had been able to give him a location though. They had only stammered that none went there. The King of Demons ruled a barren land and killed any who strayed into his realm.

He had never seen it for himself and didn't know where to begin looking. Hell was as vast as Earth and Heaven. Without a location, it would take months or years to track Asmodeus down, and he had a feeling that they had only hours.

"I cannot feel her. I do not know where Asmodeus has taken her." He looked to Erin. "Can you feel him?"

"I don't know how. I know he said that he could feel me... and I know he brought you here because he could sense my location... but I don't know how he does that, and I don't know if I can do it. I try to feel him and I get nothing back." Erin settled her hands on her stomach and looked to the others, her black eyebrows furrowing in frustration. "There has to be a way to find him before he does something insane... like that whole angel-bait incident with the shark."

"He does not get that from my blood," Apollyon muttered beneath his breath and frowned at the sand, his frustration mounting and getting the better of him. He needed Serenity back. He couldn't trust that Asmodeus would keep her safe in Hell. She was immortal now, but she could still be harmed. She could still die.

"There has to be a way to find him," Marcus said. "Can't we just head down to the plateau and await him? He is bound to go to the Devil's fortress."

"No. If we leave it that long... if we're late... Serenity might end up... well, you know." Amelia cast Apollyon an apologetic glance when he scowled at her, silently cursing her for voicing his innermost fears.

Veiron remained silent and still, his gaze locked on the charred black logs in the fire pit.

"Veiron?" Apollyon said and stepped forwards, coming to stand on the other side of the dead fire.

Veiron lifted his head, fixing crimson eyes on him that swirled with gold and black flakes. The gold began to dominate the red. Apollyon had seen his eyes do that before, when it had become apparent that he had formed a contract with Erin and he had been lost in a vicious temper, battling the Devil. Since then, his eyes had never turned golden. That they were doing so now unnerved Apollyon and put him on his guard.

"Nevar," Veiron growled.

"My guardian angel?" Erin said with a frown and Veiron nodded stiffly.

"He is obsessed with Asmodeus... he has been tracking him." Veiron turned his golden and crimson gaze back on the blackened driftwood. "If anyone knows where he is, it is Nevar... but... I do not want Erin to come with us."

"Why the hell not?" Erin planted her hands on her hips and glared at her male.

Veiron gently laid his hand on her swollen stomach and sighed down into her eyes, the gold in his fading. "Nevar is dangerous. Fucked up. I don't want you near him."

The last time Apollyon had seen the white-haired guardian angel, he had been intent on killing Asmodeus. Asmodeus had awakened evil in him, a terrible darkness that had fed Nevar's wrath and turned him on Asmodeus. He had still been recognisable as the male who had served Heaven, protecting Erin from a distance, but evil took hold quickly in angels with the capacity for it, dragging them swiftly down into the darkness.

"When did you see him last?" Apollyon looked across the fire pit to Veiron, fearing what his answer would be.

"A few weeks ago. Villandry called me to London... you remember?" He looked at Erin and she nodded, her amber eyes filling with concern. Veiron took her hand and squeezed it. "Nevar wanted nothing to do with me. He was… is… there's something very wrong with him. I barely recognised him."

Apollyon's black eyebrows met in a frown. "Evil. The darkness has him. Asmodeus awakened it in him."

"Well, it sank its claws pretty damn hard into the bloke. He is seriously messed up."

"But you think he will know where Asmodeus is?" Apollyon was willing to risk the wrath of a poisoned angel to find Serenity. He was strong enough to take down Nevar if he had to.

Probably.

Veiron nodded.

"Then I will pay him a visit. Where will I find him?" Apollyon stroked his blades and ignored the irritated and incredulous looks the others threw at him.

"*We* will pay him a visit. So where are we going?" Erin held her hand up when Veiron went to protest. He growled, his dark crimson eyebrows knitting hard above his red and gold eyes.

"Where would you find the damned?" Veiron gathered Erin into his arms, tucking her against his side, and held his hand out in front of him, his palm facing outwards. The air shimmered and the landscape beyond it distorted. Veiron grinned as curling black smoke formed and then a portal erupted in white fierce flames. "Cloud Nine."

He leaped into the portal and Apollyon followed him, landing in a grotty street outside a red brick building. There was a metal door with a neon sign above it. It was switched off.

A small black camera mounted on the wall above the door swivelled towards them.

Veiron saluted it with his middle finger.

The metal door creaked open and a huge shaven-headed man wearing worn black jeans and a charcoal grey t-shirt three sizes too small for his rotund stomach lumbered out. His gaze locked on each of them in turn and he pointed meaty fingers.

"No." Amelia. "No." Marcus. "No." Apollyon.

To Veiron and Erin, he grinned, flashing yellowing teeth, and jerked his thumb over his shoulder towards the dark room beyond the door.

Apollyon beat his black wings, shot across the narrow strip of grimy pavement between them, and grabbed him around the throat and slammed him against the door, bending it backwards until it smashed into the wall.

"You think to deny me?" Apollyon squeezed, digging his fingers into the male's chubby neck, until his flesh bulged from between them and his eyes watered. Veins popped out across his forehead and he turned red.

"I really wouldn't piss him off." Veiron sauntered past, guiding Erin into the building. "The Great Destroyer has anger management issues."

Amelia and Marcus sidled around them, giving him as wide a berth as possible, and followed Erin and Veiron into the dark club.

Apollyon leaned in, staring hard into the demon's eyes, his own swirling blue with his fury.

"You. Think. To. Deny. Me?" He spat each word, tightening his grip by degrees.

The demon tried to speak.

Apollyon loosened his fingers and waited.

"Mistake. Enter." The demon wheezed, his eyes watering and pleading him for mercy.

Apollyon tossed him across the narrow street, sending him crashing into a wall there, his anger getting the better of him. The male dropped to the ground, revealing an impact crater in the red brick, and landed in a puffing heap. He wisely remained there, even though Apollyon silently dared him to move so he could unleash some of his pent up fury on the worthless male.

"Demon filth." Apollyon swept into the building, his eyes quickly adjusting to the low light.

"I heard that," Veiron muttered from the shadows. "Play nice. The boss has a temper too, and she'll rip you a new one if you misbehave."

Apollyon scanned the club. This was pointless. It was dark, no one manned the bar, and the sign was off. It was evidently closed. Veiron was wasting his time.

Apollyon opened his mouth to demand they leave and search for Nevar elsewhere.

A feral growl came from the darkness ahead and vivid glowing purple eyes shone like jewels embraced in velvet.

Light streamed in from outside, chasing back the gloom a few metres into the expansive room, but beyond that was pitch black. Whatever the darkness concealed, it was angry, dangerous and wanted blood.

Apollyon could sense its evil slithering over him, power that challenged his own, bringing it to the surface to protect him from this creature's wrath and fury.

Black booted feet appeared from the gloom, pale light chasing up them as the male approached, revealing something that made Apollyon take a step back.

Armour.

Black greaves edged with violet.

No angels wore armour like that.

The male stalked forwards, the light racing up his bare thighs. His skin faded to black from just above his kneecaps down to his feet. A demonic angel like Veiron, in the midst of transformation?

Or something worse?

Hip armour was followed by a flash of bare stomach and black clawed fingers clutching a curved black and violet blade. The purple-edged black vambraces protecting his forearms bore a rampant violet dragon on each one.

What had Asmodeus done to him?

Nevar halted, his feet at the edge of the light, as if he didn't dare step into the sun's rays. The shadows barely touched his face, revealing it. He looked as Apollyon remembered, but in place of his normal jade eyes were fierce purple ones filled with twisted desires and vicious hungers, and his white hair looked as if he had cut it himself with a dull blade, hacking at the sides until they were tufted and messy but leaving it longer on top.

Nevar's top lip peeled back off his fangs and he narrowed his gaze on Apollyon.

"Die." He lifted his blade and Veiron was right in front of him, pressing his hands against his black breastplate and holding him back. Nevar snarled over Veiron's shoulder at Apollyon, his eyes flashing dangerously. "He must die."

"Not the right twin," Veiron said in a soft voice and held him firm. "See. Blue eyes. Long hair. Tendency to fall on the side of good over evil."

Nevar growled and breathed hard, lowering his blade with effort but not taking his eyes from Apollyon.

Veiron had been right.

Nevar was very screwed up indeed.

"Hungry," Nevar husked, bared his fangs and struck at Veiron's neck. Veiron braced his forearm against Nevar's throat, keeping him away, and growled at him.

"Not for eating, remember?" Veiron managed to shove him back and Nevar snarled, his face dark and filled with the hunger he had spoken of, thirst for blood.

"Veiron?" Erin whispered and Nevar's gaze fell on her, cleared and he shifted back into the shadows, sinking into them.

"Do not see... ward. Help me." He reached for her and Veiron swatted his clawed hand away, growling at him. He darkened again and snarled, baring his fangs at the Hell's angel, and then turned softer eyes on Erin, his pale silvery eyebrows furrowing as he gazed at her. His fingers flexed and voice dropped to a desperate whisper. "Help me."

Erin held her stomach and her own black eyebrows met in a look filled with pity. "I don't know how to help you. I wish I did."

Nevar growled and turned his back on them, heaving with each ragged breath he sucked down. His arms tensed, body going rigid, and he clenched his black fists. Blood dripped from between his tight fingers, evidence that he was harming himself with his claws.

"Leave," he snarled over his shoulder.

"We need you to tell us where to find Asmodeus." Apollyon stepped forwards before the angel could retreat into the darkness. Nevar's shoulders tensed further and a feral growl escaped him, rumbling through the pitch black room. His power rose, becoming stronger, laced with fury and entwined with rage. "Asmodeus has taken Serenity. You will help me find him. You will help me find her."

"And what is in it for me?" Nevar glared over his shoulder at Apollyon, the dark desires in his eyes informing Apollyon of exactly what he wanted in return for his assistance.

"I will let you deal with Asmodeus." He wouldn't let Nevar kill him but he would let the poisoned angel deal out some punishment for what Asmodeus had done to him.

Nevar grinned, blood staining his fangs and his lower lip. Had he been sucking on it? Was he so ravenous for blood that he would take his own to sustain him and satisfy his thirst?

"I do not feel like helping you." Nevar turned towards the bar and Apollyon realised that he was more than hungry as he stumbled towards it, one clawed hand out in front of him, reaching and stretching.

He was drunk.

The angel didn't stop when he reached the black bar. He hoisted himself up and leaned over it, fumbled around on the other side, and then straightened, holding a bottle of something. His boots hit the floor, he flicked the cap off with his thumb and chugged half of the colourful green bottle.

"You will help us," Apollyon said and braved a step closer.

"Will not." Nevar shook his head, causing the longer lengths of his white hair to fall down over his brow on one side.

He shoved it back out of his face, set the bottle down on the shiny black bar top and leaned heavily on it. He glared at each of them in turn, except Erin. To her, he gave another pained and longing look, and then bared his fangs and hissed, turning vicious again.

Veiron growled. "I warned you. I won't warn you again."

The big Hell's angel moved between Erin and Nevar, shielding her from the view of her former guardian. Losing sight of her seemed to pain Nevar and he quieted, staring at Veiron's chest, as if trying to see through the male to his ward.

"Help us," Erin said and touched Veiron's back, right between his large crimson-feathered wings, as she rounded him. The caress didn't soothe him as intended, at least not to the degree she was evidently expecting, because he moved with her, keeping one thickly muscled bare arm in front of her, holding her back and blocking her way to Nevar.

A wise move.

Nevar was unpredictable in his current state. There was every chance that he would attack Erin if she drew too close.

Nevar swigged from the bottle and Apollyon caught a flash of the label. Absinthe. A very potent alcoholic drink. Angels had incredible recuperative abilities though. Nevar would have to keep drinking to maintain even a tipsy state. The angel was beyond tipsy and deep into drunk and unruly territory, and something told Apollyon that it wasn't only alcohol this angel had been imbibing.

"Veiron, a word." Apollyon caught him by his left arm and pulled him towards the front of the club, feeling Nevar's gaze tracking him. Veiron pulled Erin with them, and Amelia and Marcus formed a defensive line.

Apollyon doubted it would stop Nevar if he wanted to get to him.

Nevar muttered black things beneath his breath, dark words that backed up the mixed and dangerous feelings that Apollyon could feel affecting his power. He wanted blood and sometimes he was finding it impossible to distinguish between Apollyon and the man he wanted to murder.

Apollyon pulled Veiron around to face him, keeping Nevar in view, and dropped his voice. "You may have warned me that Nevar's state was in part due to addiction."

"Addiction?" Erin whispered and edged closer, flicking a glance at Nevar. "To booze?"

"To Euphoria." Apollyon glared at Veiron and waited for him to deny ever knowing that fact. The Hell's angel didn't. He stared right back at him with jet black eyes that showed no glimmer of surprise or flicker of regret over not having informed him.

"He wasn't this far gone last time I saw him, alright?" Veiron hissed and slid his gaze towards his shoulder, towards Nevar where he propped up the bar behind him, drinking himself into oblivion. "Villandry has been trying to help him kick it."

Erin looked sceptical. "He's probably worsening things. That vampire is always mixed up in some bad shit."

Veiron shrugged. "He was the only one who wanted to do something about it… although I think that might be because he probably had something to do with it in the first place. Look, Nevar is still our only shot at finding out where Asmodeus—"

Nevar launched himself across the room and shoved Veiron to one side, pushing him into Erin and causing the Hell's angel to growl viciously as he quickly grabbed her to stop her from falling and harming her baby. Apollyon reacted immediately, drawing one blade and bringing it up in a fast arc, blocking the black sword coming straight for his throat.

"Die!" Nevar spun low and swiped at his legs and Apollyon beat his black wings, shot up and backwards, narrowly avoiding banging his head on the low ceiling. He unleashed more of his power, calling on it to give him strength and to issue a warning to Nevar too.

Even in this wretched state, the angel would be able to sense that he was up against a deadly foe, and liable to lose this fight as much as he was to win it.

Nevar flashed fangs and launched another attack, kicking off the tacky club floor and springing at him.

Apollyon dodged the weak attempt, twisted to let Nevar past, and brought the pommel of his sword down hard in the centre of Nevar's back plate, sending him stumbling forwards towards the open door.

Nevar turned wild purple eyes on him and the skin around them burned to ashes, the darkness curled up his arms to his elbows, and his claws lengthened.

"Evil." His voice thickened to a deep snarl and he breathed hard, chest heaving with each one, and flexed black claws around his sword hilt. "Put. This. In. Me… You. Pay."

"Not me." Apollyon drew his other sword and faced him, holding his ground and refusing to give in to the demented angel's threats. "Asmodeus did this to you. Recall the day he did… recall that I was fighting him, Nevar. You remember."

Nevar's face twisted and he slammed one hand against his mouth, his eyes widening. He growled into his palm and pressed his claws into his cheeks. The hand he held his sword with trembled and he stumbled backwards, towards the light.

The moment the full force of it hit him, he turned on it and snarled, slashing with his blade and rushing back into the shadows.

Apollyon had finally seen everything.

Nevar had horns.

They were small, but unmistakable, hidden beneath tufts of his white hair on the sides of his head.

The poisoned angel dropped his weapon and sank to his knees on the dirty floor of the club.

"I. Remember." He lowered his head, his air defeated, and held on to his knees. The longer lengths of his hair fell down and obscured his face. His shoulders shook and his knuckles blazed white from the force of his grip. He lifted his head and his gaze sought Erin through the pointed strands of his hair, and then roamed back to Apollyon. "You swear… swear I can make him pay."

Apollyon nodded without hesitation, his heart filled with pity for the male before him, unable to imagine what he had been through these past few months because of what Asmodeus had done to him.

But what had his twin done to Nevar?

Apollyon stared at Nevar as Veiron helped him onto his feet.

Was it possible these changes in the guardian angel were the result of a contract?

Nevar would never willingly go into a contract with the man who had tortured him and driven him to despair though. A contract was the only method of altering an angel's appearance that Apollyon knew of though, and the only answer that made any sense.

Asmodeus had the Devil's blood in him too. The Devil could contract with angels, turning them into his Hell's angels. He had passed that ability on to Erin. Was it possible that the Devil had unwittingly given Asmodeus that ability too and that the male was a true King of Demons, able to become a master to angels and turn them like him?

If it were possible, then this form that Nevar now had was one he shared with Asmodeus.

And Asmodeus would be able to command Nevar to do his bidding.

Nevar wouldn't be able to make Asmodeus pay because Asmodeus could order him to lay down his weapon.

Apollyon felt he should mention that but held his tongue. Nevar was his only lead and he needed him. If he revealed that he didn't believe Nevar would have the revenge he wanted if he could find Asmodeus, then the angel would revert to denying their request, leaving them without a guide and without a hope of finding Serenity.

"I swear, Nevar. You may make him pay for what he did to you." May, because he wasn't sure that he could or would have the vengeance he sought.

Nevar huffed and sheathed his sword, and the black around his eyes faded, the darkness retreating so it only covered his hands and from below his knees. His purple gaze slowly transformed, becoming frosty green again.

"What did Asmodeus do to you?" Erin whispered and he turned sorrowful eyes on her for a brief second before walking unsteadily back to the bar where he had left his bottle of absinthe.

Nevar raised it, eyed the scant remains, and then knocked it back. He tossed the bottle behind him and it smashed in the darkness.

"I would like to know the answer to that question myself… and I intend to ask Asmodeus when we reach the bastard's shitty castle." Nevar clawed back his silver-white hair.

"You know where this castle is?" Apollyon was more than intrigued as to how Nevar had come to know the location of Asmodeus's fortress but the steely look entering the angel's green eyes said he wouldn't tell him.

This man had secrets, dangerous ones, terrible ones.

"I have seen it with my own eyes... it lays in ruins." Nevar grinned wickedly. "I will take you there."

CHAPTER 23

Serenity was not pleased. The petite Parisian witch had sworn at him most shockingly in French, calling him a barrage of names he did understand and many he did not.

Asmodeus didn't care and had told her as much. She had huffed and sat down on one of the boulders in the ruined courtyard of his broken home.

Romulus and Remus lingered nearby, on edge and alert.

"Find her for me, Serenity," Asmodeus commanded and the fair-haired woman looked up at him, her hazel eyes bright with defiance. He sighed and did the only thing he could think of to win her over and convince her to do as he bid, more than willing to do this for Liora's sake. He went down on one knee before Serenity and rested his forearm on his bent leg. "The Devil has her... please, Serenity. Find her for me."

Serenity looked torn and then frowned at him. "Take me back to Apollyon. He won't understand... unless we explain. He will come after you."

She sounded concerned and he found that hard to swallow because it wasn't concern about her own welfare or Liora's, or even Apollyon's distress on finding her gone. It was concern for him. She didn't want her angel to discover her missing and come to Hell bent on revenge and filled with fury and unleash it all on Asmodeus.

Asmodeus rose to his feet and then sat on a black block of rock nearby, facing her. "I cannot take you back. Not until I know where she is in the Devil's fortress."

"We can find her together," Serenity said and he wanted to believe she sincerely meant that but he knew Apollyon and he knew the others.

They wouldn't help him. He had to do this alone.

Romulus and Remus came to flank him as they had so many times when he had sat on his throne in this fortress.

As they had when Liora had been here with him, part of his home, sharing it with him and his hellhounds.

He missed her.

Asmodeus growled and curled his fingers into fists, clenching them tightly enough that his bones ached and the points of his short black claws dug into his fleshy palms.

He didn't care if everyone came after him. Apollyon could lead a legion of angels to war with him and he wouldn't care. All that mattered to him now was finding Liora and having her back in his arms where she belonged, filling the hollow space in his chest that she had left behind.

He didn't care if everyone cursed him for taking Serenity either. Everyone thought him evil anyway. Only Liora had seen the good in him and only Liora mattered.

"Find her for me." Asmodeus left no room for argument in his tone this time. "Then you may go."

Serenity stared deep into his eyes, hers narrowing by degrees, and he felt as if she was trying to look through him, seeking out his feelings for Liora. She must have seen them and his desperation, because she nodded and held out her hand.

Asmodeus reluctantly removed the pentagram from around his neck, rose from his makeshift throne and placed it into her small palm. She closed her fingers over it, shut her eyes and held it close to her chest. Bright ribbons of red swirled around her hand, lighting her fair hair and pale face, and turning her cream dress crimson.

She was quiet for so long that he feared she was out to fool him, to keep him waiting until Apollyon tracked them down or the Devil sent another dragon to finish him. His patience trickled away, growing thinner by the second, and he began to pace. Remus sat up and watched him. Romulus took to pacing with him, keeping close to his side.

Finally, Serenity opened her eyes and looked up at him.

"She is in a fortress as you said. A great one with spires that melt into the darkness. She is deep beneath it... a small room... the floor is white crystal... it is bright and filled with light... she sleeps there."

Asmodeus growled. "Sleeps or lays dead?"

His heart couldn't bear the thought that it was the latter. It ached and stung fiercely, threatening to shatter and kill him.

Serenity frowned and clutched the pentagram harder, her gaze unfocused. She blinked.

"Sleeps." She lifted her gaze to his again and his relief echoed in her hazel eyes. "She sleeps."

Hope coursed through his blood, mending his aching heart, and he held his hand out to her.

Serenity went to place the pentagram into his palm and froze.

Asmodeus had felt it too.

A portal.

He swiftly turned to face the far end of the courtyard and growled as the fierce white portal shimmered, allowing Veiron and Erin to step through, followed by Apollyon, Amelia and Marcus. How had they found him so quickly?

The answer to that question stepped through the portal and then was right before him, a twisted grin playing on his lips and his eyes flashing violent purple.

Nevar.

Asmodeus turned to grab the pentagram from Serenity. Nevar saw and was there before him, snatching the pendant from her outstretched hand. Asmodeus roared at the male and he shot away from him, taking the precious necklace and grinning the whole time.

Asmodeus's heart pounded, adrenaline making it thunder against his chest, and his black claws sharpened.

"Give it back to me," Asmodeus snarled and lunged for Nevar. The angel leaped to one side, ending up closer to Apollyon, and Asmodeus foolishly hoped his twin would assist him and grab Nevar.

Apollyon let him pass without moving a muscle.

Asmodeus's fangs lengthened and he growled at Apollyon and then at Nevar. Nevar held the pentagram up. It swung from its silver chain, taunting him.

Asmodeus beat his large black feathered wings and shot towards Nevar. The wretched angel flashed him a wicked smile, dived to his right, rolled and came to his feet between Apollyon and the others where they had grouped together.

Apollyon ignored Nevar again and strolled towards Serenity. She was on her feet and in his arms a second later, and Asmodeus wanted to cry out his anguish and fury. He wanted Liora like that, tucked safely in his arms, not asleep and trapped in the Devil's fortress.

Nevar taunted him again with the pendant.

Asmodeus growled in frustration and called his blades to him. "Return it to me. Do not harm it. It is important. Please… give it back."

He focused on making those words into a command, an order that Nevar would have to obey. Nevar frowned and then his vicious smile returned, curving his lips. The angel had found a way to overcome his orders. He focused harder, trying to force Nevar's obedience.

He reached towards Nevar but the angel withdrew, keeping the distance between them steady, his twisted grin holding as he wound the chain around his fingers, drawing the pentagram up to his palm. Romulus and Remus growled, their hackles rising as they lowered their heads and bared their fangs, ready to attack if Asmodeus ordered it.

"Do give it back," Serenity said and Asmodeus caught the note of fear in her voice. It seemed Apollyon picked up on it too, because he looked down at her and smoothed his palm across her cheek. She lifted her eyes to meet his, her expression revealing the depth of her fear. "It protects Liora."

Apollyon's expression immediately darkened. "Give it back, Nevar."

Nevar shook his head and locked his purple gaze on Asmodeus. He held the pentagram up higher, so it dangled between them.

"Does this trinket have meaning to you? Do you value it?" Nevar's eyes shifted focus to the pentagram but Asmodeus didn't dare attempt to attack him. Nevar would see it coming. He glanced at Apollyon and then the others, silently pleading them to help him in retrieving Liora's pentagram.

Amelia had already drawn her silver blade and Marcus was ready beside her. Veiron was shielding Erin but the look in his swirling red-gold eyes said that he was with Asmodeus and would help take down Nevar if it came to it. Apollyon moved in front of Serenity and locked deadly blue eyes on Nevar, monitoring him closely.

"It means much to me, Nevar," Asmodeus admitted and didn't hide his feelings from his voice. He revealed all, every ounce of despair and fear, and every drop of hope that Nevar would do the right thing and return it safely to him.

"And what would you do to retrieve it?" Nevar flicked the star, making it spin, and his violet irises focused back on Asmodeus.

The bitterness in his voice and the anger in his expression didn't surprise Asmodeus. He had wronged Nevar and deserved his wrath, but the male was threatening Liora's safety and Liora's most precious possession, and he couldn't allow that.

"It means everything to Liora… and therefore it means everything to me," Asmodeus whispered and held his left hand out, keeping his right one around the hilt of one of his blades. "Please… return it to me."

Nevar shook his head again, twisted his hand to gather up the chain and opened it so the pentagram sat on his palm. He stared down at it, the cold edge of anger in his power rising. Asmodeus glanced at Apollyon. Apollyon nodded and he knew that as soon as he had an opening, his twin would attempt to retrieve the necklace. Asmodeus would do all that he could to make that opening happen.

Nevar looked up at Asmodeus through his lashes and narrowed his gaze on him. The area around his eyes bled into black. "Remove this darkness from me… this evil… and I will give you this item you value so much."

The angel lifted his head and pinned cold, empty eyes on him. The black around them began to spread and grew up his arms at the same time, reaching beyond the edge of his black and violet vambraces.

"I valued my life… my soul… and you destroyed it!" A blast of frigid cold shot out from Nevar and crashed into Asmodeus and his power rose to meet it, shielding him from the full force of Nevar's wrath.

"I cannot undo what was done." Asmodeus stepped towards him, losing all of his patience, unwilling to play anymore. He would take back the pentagram even if he had to kill Nevar in order to do it. Nevar had lost his mind, and the corruption in it wasn't born of anything Asmodeus had done. "Only you can overcome it because all I did was give your natural feelings a push. I did not plant evil inside you. It was already there."

Nevar growled and attacked him, lashing out with one blade. Asmodeus blocked it with his own golden curved sword and shoved him backwards. He stumbled, found his footing and snarled at him.

"You are lying!" Nevar closed his fingers over the pentagram. "I felt the evil enter me… placed there by you. You took something precious from me… and now I take something precious from you."

"No!" Asmodeus cried and lunged for Nevar at the same time as Veiron and Apollyon.

Nevar grinned and crushed the pentagram in his blackened fist. Bright purple and red light burst from between his clenched fingers. Asmodeus tackled him to the ground. Veiron collided with Apollyon.

Nevar laughed.

Asmodeus roared and grabbed him by the throat with his left hand, pinning him to the black ground, and grappled with his fist with his other one, trying to prise open his fingers.

Nevar opened them and fragments of Liora's pentagram spilled out onto the basalt.

"No," Asmodeus breathed and throttled Nevar, using both hands to crush his throat, his heart demanding the angel's life as recompense for what he had done to Liora. "Die… wretch… you will not live to see another day."

Apollyon grabbed him from behind, locking his arms under Asmodeus's and over his shoulders, and pulled him off Nevar. Veiron caught Nevar's arm and pulled him onto his feet. Nevar struggled and Veiron landed a hard blow on his jaw, knocking his head to one side.

"Settle down," Veiron growled, flashing red sharp teeth. Darkness encroached around his eyes. Asmodeus lashed out at Nevar with one leg, goading him, hoping to push Veiron into turning demonic and attacking him when he couldn't.

Nevar twisted violently in Veiron's arm and bit down hard on his left biceps. Veiron grunted in pain and Nevar broke free. The white-haired angel sprinted towards the edge of the courtyard and Romulus and Remus went after him, chasing him down. Nevar's black wings burst from his back and he launched himself over the edge. The hellhounds skidded to a halt, narrowly avoiding falling off the edge and dropping into the valley below.

"Bastard," Veiron muttered and pressed his hand to his arm. When he took it away, the wound had healed but the blood remained. "I'm going to kill him."

"Not if I get to him first," Asmodeus snarled and broke free of Apollyon's arms. He stumbled forwards, crashed onto his knees where Nevar had been, and carefully picked up the silver chain and every piece of the broken pentagram. He held them gently in his palm and looked up at Serenity as she stopped before him, concern shining in her hazel eyes. "Will it still work?"

Serenity crouched before him and placed her hand over his, covering the pieces. She closed her eyes briefly and then opened them, fixing them on his, and solemnly shook her head.

"The magic has been released. I am sorry." She pressed their palms together and curled her fingers around to hold his hand, and he wasn't sure what to do or how to respond. In the end, he closed his fingers over the back of her hand, taking the comfort she kindly offered him. "I can see how much it meant to you... how much Liora means to you."

Asmodeus lowered his eyes to their joined hands, his chest aching, and felt Apollyon's gaze on him, watching him closely. There was suspicion in his twin's feelings but also curiosity and a touch of what might have been concern.

Part of Asmodeus demanded he go after Nevar and make him pay in blood for what he had done. The greater part of him, the one that ruled his heart, said to focus on Liora and retrieving her. Nevar could wait.

This wasn't like him. Before meeting Liora, he would have gone after Nevar, making the angel pay for disrespecting and disobeying him, just like his master. He would have killed Nevar on sight and taken the pentagram from his cold, dead fingers before the light of Heaven could reclaim him.

Or at least held him and tortured him until he could no longer clutch the pentagram because he had no fingers in which to do so.

Now, all he could think about was Liora.

Asmodeus closed his eyes and held Serenity's hand, wishing it were Liora's delicate one warming his. He wanted her back. He needed to find her.

"Where is she?" The tremulous note in Erin's voice said that she already knew the answer to that question and didn't like it.

"He has her." Asmodeus opened his eyes, released Serenity's hand and got to his feet. He produced a small black leather pouch out of the air and carefully placed the pieces of Liora's pentagram into it, saving them. He would find a way to recreate it for her, and would make it even more powerful this time. Indestructible. "He is holding her beneath the fortress, in a room of crystal."

"She is alive?" Apollyon moved forwards, coming around him. He held his hand out to Serenity, who slipped hers into it, and helped her to her feet.

Asmodeus had expected his twin to erupt and attack him for taking Serenity from the island. The male seemed content with glaring at him. Because he had brought Nevar with him and Nevar had destroyed Liora's pentagram, not only upsetting Asmodeus but upsetting Serenity too?

It seemed that his twin wasn't immune to errors of judgement and mistakes.

That would have pleased Asmodeus once. Not now. Not while the Devil had Liora and it was his fault for letting her go off alone.

"She is sleeping, but unharmed," Serenity confirmed and Amelia and the others closed ranks, forming a tight group with him.

Romulus and Remus returned to his side, and Remus wagged his tail as Erin rubbed him between his ears, deep in thought.

"We have to get her back somehow," Erin murmured and then looked around them, the irritated edge to her expression conveying her feelings. She was annoyed that the Devil had taken Liora and was holding her at the fortress.

Apollyon looked equally displeased by the news, and Asmodeus knew why. Apollyon couldn't fight the Devil without risking losing and therefore releasing him from his captivity, giving him free rein to roam the mortal world.

"Erin," Asmodeus started and then caught the black warning look that Veiron tossed his way like a deadly blade, point first. He understood the Hell's angel's concerns but he couldn't do as he bid. He had to ask this of her. "If it were not important, I would not ask you this... but I need you to come with me. Only the Devil can access where he is holding Liora."

She smiled brightly and flicked her short black fringe from her eyes. "Then it won't be a problem. Consider me your skeleton key."

"No," Veiron snapped and grabbed her right forearm and she laid her hand over his. "I will not let you do this."

"You seem to be forgetting who the master is in this relationship." She stroked his hand and looked up at him, meeting his glowering gaze. "And I'm forgetting who the man is... come with me then. I'll be safe if you're around to scare away the big bad demons and my father."

He didn't look convinced. Asmodeus concluded that flattery did not get you everywhere.

"She is my only way in," Asmodeus said and Veiron shifted his crimson-edged black eyes to him. Fire burned like a corona around his pupils.

"She is our only way in." Apollyon stepped forwards and Serenity smiled and took hold of his hand. "If we do this, we do it together. No matter the risks or the consequences."

Asmodeus looked down at Erin's belly and ignored the voice that warned him not to speak the words forming in his head because everyone would think him weak if he did.

Good.

Not evil.

"Veiron." He waited for the scarlet-haired male's eyes to come back to him before he continued. "If it turns dangerous, you are to take Erin away. The moment we are in, you are to leave with her."

"We'll leave together." Veiron wrapped his left arm around Erin's slender shoulders and squeezed gently. "But if shit goes south, I'll get her away from there, kicking and screaming if it goes down that way."

"It wouldn't be the first time." Erin smiled up at him and then looked around at the others. "We're all in agreement on this then?"

Apollyon still looked wary.

"If you think about engaging him, I will take you down myself," Asmodeus said, shutting out the glares and angry words the others threw his way.

Apollyon held his hand up to silence them and then nodded. "I will leave him to you."

Asmodeus wasn't sure what to say in response to that. It was unlike Apollyon to show him any support or shred of positive feelings, and he had certainly never trusted Asmodeus.

He eyed him warily and nodded, part of him convinced that the angel was plotting his demise at the hands of his master and that was the only reason he had agreed to let him handle the Devil.

"We need a distraction." Asmodeus looked around at everyone, expecting them to throw him to the lions when he wanted to be the one to save Liora, not give them the chance to be her saviour.

Amelia twirled her silver sword in her hand as if it weighed nothing. "One distraction, guaranteed."

Marcus gave her a look that relayed how little he liked the mission she had just volunteered them for and then nodded in agreement.

"Give us a head start and you will have the distraction you need, although I will not guarantee how long it will last." Marcus rested his hand on the hilt of the blade sheathed at the waist of his blue-edged silver armour.

"No. It's too big a risk. We can't let you fight him." Erin shook her head and reached for her sister.

"I know you. If I don't do this… well, the alternative is you facing him, and I'm not about to let that happen. Don't worry." Amelia took her hand and squeezed it, her silvery eyes glittering with affection. "I won't let him take me from you. We'll make sure we keep our eyes on him and our backs together. You know Marcus will protect me."

Erin sighed, glanced at Marcus and met his determined pale ice-blue eyes, and then nodded.

"Be careful." She clutched Amelia's hand. "I know you're all super kick arse now and everything but you're playing with the Devil, and he won't play fair. Remember how we trained."

Erin had trained Amelia? She had fought the Devil in the past and knew his methods and some of his moves. It had been a sensible course of action to use her powers, the same as the Devil's, to teach her sibling and Marcus how to defend against him. Asmodeus admired her for it.

Veiron held his hand out and a flaming white portal appeared a short distance away from them. "It will take you to the plateau. Create havoc for as long as you can and then haul arse to the nearest gate. Marcus knows where it is."

Marcus nodded. "But it won't open without you."

"I'll be there." Veiron jerked his chin towards the portal he was holding open for them. "Now, go."

Amelia didn't hesitate. She tightened her grip on her silver blade and ran for the portal, the short white-to-blue dress beneath her chrome armour flowing around her thighs and her silver ponytail bouncing with each stride. She leaped through the portal and Marcus charged in behind her.

It shrank and disappeared.

Erin stared at the place where it had been, her fists clenched and black smoke fluttering around them. Veiron gently tugged her into his arms and pressed a kiss to her hair.

"She'll be alright. She's tough. Marcus will take care of her." He rubbed her back and she nodded.

Asmodeus felt another pang in his chest, an ache to leave now and find Liora. He had to wait. As much as he hated it, he was depending on the angelic female and her male to cause a big enough distraction that it would call the Devil out of his fortress. He wanted to fight the bastard for taking Liora and keeping her from him, but saving her was top priority. Once she was safe, he would come back and slay his master.

An enormous blue blast lit the sky in the distance and shook the ground beneath his feet. The tail end of a shockwave swept over him, powerful enough to knock everyone in the direction of it, and make his hellhounds whine.

"Amelia," Erin whispered, her eyes on the distance as the light flickered and faded and a noise like thunder rumbled over them.

Amelia was more powerful than he had expected and she had just got the Devil's attention. Asmodeus could feel the call go out, commanding all of his Hell's angels in the vicinity to attack the source of the explosion.

Only time would tell if the Devil would join them, leaving them able to sneak into his fortress.

Minutes ticked by and blue light lit the sky at intervals, the blasts weaker than the first but still incredibly powerful.

A black blast devoured a section of one of the huge blue orbs, clashing with it.

"Erin?" Veiron whispered and Asmodeus answered his silent question.

"My master has come out to play." He cast his hand before him and opened a black vortex there, large enough for all of them to travel through, including his hellhounds.

He would do as Liora had taught him and would leave no one behind.

Romulus and Remus leaped through first, leading the way. Apollyon followed with Serenity tucked close beside him, his large black wings partially curled around her. Veiron tried to do the same with Erin but she stormed forwards, her pretty face locked in lines of grim determination. Veiron followed close on her heels and Asmodeus brought up the rear, wishing once again that he had complete armour like the other angels in the group with him. Marcus had worn his blue and silver armour, Apollyon wore his gold-edged black armour, and Veiron had his crimson and black.

Asmodeus looked down at the gold-edged obsidian strips around his hips and his greaves. He had managed to fix the one that the dragon had damaged. It wouldn't offer him much protection though. He needed a chest and back plate, and vambraces. He needed complete armour.

And he had a feeling he needed it now more than ever.

He stepped into the portal and then out onto the courtyard of the Devil's fortress, close to the doors.

Someone gasped. It might have been Serenity, judging by how Apollyon held her closer to him. All of them were facing away from the fortress. Watching the battle raging on the plateau? Or did they already have company?

Asmodeus looked over his shoulder, following their gazes.

They were staring at the charred dragon carcass in the middle of the broken courtyard.

Apollyon raised a single black eyebrow at him.

"I was angry," Asmodeus said and stepped forwards, approaching the tall twin doors. "You would not like me when I am angry."

"Did he just make a funny?" Erin whispered to Veiron.

"I believe so." Veiron shielded her with his crimson wings and walked her towards the doors where Asmodeus waited, studying them.

He hoped this worked.

Erin reached him and the doors creaked and then eased open, parting to reveal the grand entrance hall.

She smiled. "Hey, presto! I'm so awesome doors open for me."

"That would be your father in you," Asmodeus reminded her and her look soured. He smiled at her reaction, amused by it. The more time he spent around the feisty female, the more he liked her.

She waltzed into the large room with Veiron hot on her heels and tipped her head back, her amber eyes growing enormous as they took in the height of the room. It reached up to over one hundred feet above them, with black stone staircases that joined the first five floors of the Devil's fortress. Hanging from the underside of the twisting staircases were elaborate chandeliers made of gilded demon bones, each holding over fifty candles that cast golden light over the room.

"We don't have to go up there, right, because the whole floating staircase without bannisters thing really creeps me out." She rubbed her stomach and he knew she was thinking about plummeting off the edge of one by mistake.

He was sure that Veiron would be close enough to her to catch her should that happen. The male seemed to grow anxious if he was more than two feet from her.

"We go down," Asmodeus said and stepped aside to allow Serenity to enter with Apollyon.

Apollyon slipped his fingers between hers and clutched her hand. "Can you locate her?"

She nodded. Asmodeus's heart beat a little faster and he drew his blades, keeping them at the ready. The castle was quiet except for the occasional quake caused by Amelia and Marcus's fight outside that shook the bone chandeliers.

Asmodeus felt certain that they wouldn't be alone for long. The Devil would grow suspicious and send his men to check the fortress, if he didn't come to check it himself.

He closed his eyes and focused, trying to sense whether his master had left anyone guarding the building and Liora. An unmistakable sensation spread through him, warning him that they weren't as alone as it appeared. There were Hell's angels in the fortress, lurking in the darkness, waiting for them. His heart told him to warn the others but his head supplied that if he did, there was a chance Veiron would insist on taking Erin away from the fortress, and he couldn't allow that. She was the Devil's daughter. His only way of opening the doors that stood between him and his love.

Romulus and Remus whined behind him and he looked back at them and spoke to them in the demon tongue. "Remain near the entrance and ensure nothing gets close to us. If my master returns, warn us. When you feel me call you, come as quickly as you can. Understand?"

They panted, their long tongues hanging out over their sharp black teeth.

Erin quietly whispered, "I am so tracking down a lady hellhound for you boys because I want me some puppies."

Romulus and Remus snapped their mouths shut and pinned her with sharp red eyes. Asmodeus raised an eyebrow at his hellhounds, impressed by how quickly they were coming to understand English. He was glad. He wanted Liora to be able to talk with them too.

Veiron shook his head and sighed. "You have a baby coming and that kid is going to be a handful. You don't need puppies on top of it."

She scowled at him. "*We* have a baby coming... and just for denying me puppies, you're getting all the late night wake up calls."

Serenity led them forwards, under the staircases, to a black door on the left of the room. Erin twisted the clawed hand that formed the knob and it swung open. It was dark beyond the door. Serenity held her hands out before her with her palms facing upwards and a red orb appeared. It twisted and turned, and began to glow more fiercely, turning golden as it grew in size. She walked forwards and it hovered ahead of her, lighting their way.

Asmodeus closed ranks with Veiron, keeping Erin between them, his senses on high alert as they reached the end of the corridor and began down twisting steps. The air was cooler and damp, cleaner than outside. Serenity bravely kept leading the way, Apollyon at her back, one hand on her shoulder to let her know that he was there with her.

Asmodeus's nerves threatened to rise and overwhelm him as they descended, winding ever deeper into the bowels of the castle. They came out on levels at intervals and Serenity always paused, closed her eyes, and then led them onwards, taking them to the next door, which Erin would open.

Each time, Asmodeus would hone his senses, searching for the Hell's angels he had felt.

Each time, he had the feeling that they were drawing closer to them.

He started counting the stairs to keep his nerves in check and give himself something to focus part of his mind on while the rest of him focused on sensing whether any dangers lurked in the darkness around them.

The battle above grew distant and then slipped beyond his senses.

Erin muttered something to Veiron, who stroked her hair.

"Your sister is still fighting and still safe. The Devil won't hurt her... he would break the pact if he did," Veiron whispered and she paused and looked up at him, her eyes bright gold in the low light.

"He wouldn't care... as far as we know, he's already broken the pact. He took Liora." Erin closed her eyes and hung her head. Her voice hitched. "If he resets the game, I'll be too weak to fight him and make him pay for everything he's done to me... for what he would have done to you... and to Amelia... and Marcus."

Veiron wrapped his arms around her and pressed his lips to the top of her head, closing his eyes at the same time.

"It'll be okay, Sweetheart. I swear it. No bad shit is going down on my watch. You'll see. We'll get Liora back and get the fuck out of this place, and I'll pick up Amelia and Marcus, and it'll all be good." Veiron sighed when her shoulders shook and a sob broke past her lips, and Asmodeus felt he was intruding on something very private.

He would give them a moment alone, but they were blocking the corridor.

Veiron rubbed her bare arms. "How about when we're all back together, we come back down and give your old man hell?"

Erin sniffed, lifted her head and brushed the backs of her hands across her cheeks. She gave Veiron a wobbly smile and nodded.

"You missed a tear." Veiron swept it away with his thumb. "Cry baby."

Erin shoved him in the chest. "It's these stupid hormones. I'm pissed as hell one minute and want to collapse in a puddle of tears the next. It's not easy being pregnant, you know? Especially with your kid. He's as temperamental as his father."

She rubbed her belly and Veiron placed his hand over hers, smiling down at the bump beneath her black dress.

"Hell boy junior likes it when you do that," she whispered and Veiron placed his arm around her shoulders, tucking her against his side, and began walking again.

"I'll just keep this hand here then," he said and she leaned her head on his chest as they walked. Veiron squeezed her shoulders and his voice dropped to an earnest whisper. "I swear, Erin, your sister and Marcus will be fine."

Asmodeus could understand her fear. While on the island, he had come to discover that Amelia was the original angel and the subject of a game between Heaven and Hell that Asmodeus had watched with curiosity since his creation.

Angels were eternal, and upon their death, they were reborn into their original forms but without their memories. In Amelia's case, she re-entered the world as a mortal baby and grew up hidden among the massive human population and the hunt for her began. One of Apollyon's duties was to kill her mortal form when the time was right and awaken her as an angel. Then, it was a race between Heaven, represented by Marcus, and Hell, represented by Veiron, to get their hands on her first and spill her blood on a sacred altar. Whoever spilled her blood sealed the other realm for centuries.

Amelia would then die.

So would Veiron and Marcus.

Erin had good reason to be concerned. If Amelia faltered, the Devil's men could kill her. The game would be reset. Even with the contract between Veiron and Erin, there was a chance she would lose her husband and he would be reborn as an angel of Heaven, unable to remember her and destined to fall and pledge himself to the Devil.

She would definitely lose her sister and Marcus.

Asmodeus found it hard to believe the lengths these people were going to in order to help Liora, risking their lives for her. Not just Liora though.

As much as he wanted to pretend they were doing it just for her, because she had gained their friendship and their trust, he knew deep inside that wasn't the whole truth.

They were doing this for him too.

Serenity wanted to reunite him with Liora as much as she wanted to save her cousin. He had caught the looks that Erin and Amelia had given him too, sympathetic glances that spoke of their desire to help him. Marcus seemed reluctant to get close to him, but was helping anyway. Veiron had clearly wanted to help him save Liora.

Apollyon.

The man who had sworn to kill him a thousand times over, who had battled him and come close to doing just that almost as many times, and who had always looked upon him with scorn and disgust, had looked upon him with concern and had chosen to assist him in his mission to save Liora.

Asmodeus still found that hard to digest.

They reached a level where there were no more steps or doors. Just endless maze-like corridors of black. The sensation of danger grew stronger. The Devil's men were waiting in the maze.

Asmodeus went against his better judgement. "We are not alone."

"You're telling me," Veiron whispered and stroked Erin's arm.

"How long have you known?" Asmodeus frowned and Erin looked over her shoulder at him.

"Since opening the main door of the fortress." She shrugged when his frown hardened, a ripple of shock racing through his blood, and then smiled. "You didn't expect me to run away from a couple of Hell's angels, did you?"

"No, I did not."

Her smile broadened, reaching her amber eyes. "Ah, you expected Hell boy to whisk me away. I know my husband. He's itching for a fight as much as I am. A few demonic angels? He won't even break a sweat."

"If he gets to fight one at all," Apollyon growled from ahead of them, his rich blue eyes burning in the darkness.

Veiron wasn't the only one itching for a fight.

Asmodeus called his curved golden blades to him. The weight of them in his palms felt good, reassuring. Whatever waited for them at the end of the maze, or even in the maze, was going to discover that he would allow nothing to stand between him and Liora.

Serenity took several wrong turns in the narrow alleyways, causing them to have to back up and try a different route. Each wrong turn and dead end worsened Asmodeus's temper and he was close to snapping by the time they finally reached a tall black room lit by torches cradled in the gilded bones of dragons' feet. The warm amber glow barely reached halfway up the towering height of the vaulted ceiling.

Asmodeus had the feeling they had found Liora.

Five Hell's angels in their demonic forms blocked the way to a single black stone door, their thickly muscled arms folded over their red-edged black breastplates and their crimson eyes glowing like hellfire against their black skin.

The one in the middle of the loose semicircle was far larger than the others, but all of them were bigger than normal Hell's angels, each standing over ten feet tall.

Veiron growled and shifted, rolling his shoulders. Black flowed over his skin and his muscles expanded, his limbs growing as he changed into his own demonic form. He pushed Erin behind him and Asmodeus did the same, forcing her behind him as he stepped forwards to form an offensive line with Veiron and Apollyon.

Erin huffed and Serenity muttered something about men.

His twin furled his large black-feathered wings against his back and tipped his chin up, his swirling blue gaze locked on the Hell's angel at the front of the group.

Asmodeus wouldn't grant him his wish. The biggest male was his.

He tightened his grip on his curved golden blades and launched himself with a roar at the male.

The large male sprang forwards and met him halfway, his red blade clashing with Asmodeus's golden one. Asmodeus surged onwards, driving the demonic angel backwards. Veiron and Apollyon joined the fight, tackling two of the angels each. Veiron's double-ended short spear was a blur as he dealt with his two foes, blocking and countering every attack they made. The vaulted room echoed with each clash of weapons, the strikes ringing out until it was a cacophony.

Asmodeus twirled beneath the path of one of this enemy's blades as the male struck at him and slashed at his shins with his own sword. The male beat his leathery wings, taking himself above the arc of Asmodeus's blow, and brought his other sword down.

A golden blade blocked the strike, causing sparks to shower over Asmodeus's bare back and wings, and Asmodeus rolled forwards and onto his feet. He flicked Apollyon a grateful glance and then growled as he attacked the large demonic angel from behind. The male whirled to face him and managed to block one of Asmodeus's blades. He surged upwards with the other one and grinned as it cut across the male's thick black biceps. Crimson spilled from the deep laceration, shining in the low light.

The demonic angel grunted, baring his sharp red teeth, and his eyes flashed.

He lunged for Asmodeus, claws swiping towards his wings.

The male meant to disable him.

Asmodeus dodged and ducked, and at the same time sent a mental command to his wings, forcing them to shrink into his back, removing a potential weakness. He rolled under the angel's outstretched arms, came to his knees, and brought his left blade around in a fast arc behind him. The male shrieked as the sword sliced into his right calf and Asmodeus shoved to his feet and twisted at the waist, lodging his other blade deep into the male's side.

He yanked it out. Blood sprayed from the wound, saturating the black tiled floor.

The demonic angel roared and turned on him, bringing twin blades down in a blur. Asmodeus sent one of his swords away and brought the other one up, and quickly shoved his palm against the flat edge of it, bracing himself for the blow. The male's twin blades struck his single one hard, the force of the strike almost driving Asmodeus to his knees.

He growled with effort and shoved upwards, knocking the angel's blades off his sword and sending the male stumbling backwards.

Bright light flashed off to his left.

Veiron had dispatched one of the five.

A second later, light burst closer to Apollyon.

Two down. Three to go.

The demonic angel before him grunted and bared his sharp teeth again, and Asmodeus swore he grew larger, his muscles expanding beneath his black skin. He had seen Hell's angels go into a rage, a fury so deep it made them crazed and increased their strength tenfold. If that happened, this male would prove himself a dangerous foe, one liable to break through Asmodeus and harm the females.

Asmodeus couldn't allow that.

He focused and began to circle the male, keeping the angel's attention rooted on him.

Shadows flickered around Asmodeus's feet and it took all of his effort to keep them there and stop them from covering him as he desired them to do. He didn't want the others to see his true form. They wouldn't understand. He needed the strength of his true form to give him the power to quickly defeat the angel though. Hopefully, the low level of light in the room would conceal his shadows from Apollyon and the others.

The demonic angel pushed off, coming straight at him.

Asmodeus flung his hand forwards and his shadows streamed towards the male, snapping at the black floor as they grew like an unstoppable wave. The male's crimson eyes widened as the first shadow reached him, curling around his shin and stopping him in his tracks, and then he unleashed an unholy scream as the rest lashed at him and burrowed into his flesh. The shadows dragged him down to his knees, the impact shaking the ground.

Asmodeus struck.

He clutched his sword in both hands and brought it down hard, cleaving the male's head from his shoulders.

It toppled and rolled across the tiles, coming to a halt by booted feet.

Asmodeus slid his golden gaze across to Erin. Serenity stood beside her, her focus on Apollyon. She hadn't seen his true power.

Erin stared down at the severed head by her feet and then raised her eyes to meet his. Unlike her friend, she had been watching him fight. She had seen that he too could command shadows, just as she could.

Light flashed, taking the body to Heaven.

Asmodeus pressed one finger against his lips.

Erin smiled, raised her hand, and pretended to zip her lips and lock them.

Asmodeus turned to assist Veiron with one of the remaining angels. Veiron skewered the male on the glowing red blade of his double-ended spear. Light burst across Asmodeus's eyes, temporarily blinding him. When his vision came back, the dead angel was gone.

A hand caught Asmodeus's bare shoulder.

He growled, grabbed the male by his wrist, and twisted downwards, using the sudden momentum to throw the male over his shoulder.

Apollyon landed on the ground with a grunt and a grimace.

Asmodeus quickly released him and Serenity rushed forwards, scowling at him as she passed.

When she looked at him like that, as if she wanted to fight him for some reason, she reminded him of Liora. They shared the same hazel eyes and the same slender build.

But Serenity couldn't come close to his female.

She was too wholesome and good. Too sweet.

Asmodeus sighed and looked off to his right, towards the door. His heart ached and he rubbed his chest. He hoped Liora was in there, only seconds away from him now. He needed her back in his arms where she belonged. He needed his wicked little witch with her mischievous smiles, playful teasing, and naughty streak.

He missed her.

Asmodeus turned away from the others and walked to the black stone door. His gaze took in every inch of the carved surface. It depicted dragons and a monster far larger than they were ravaging lands and devouring mortal, demon and angel alike.

Erin moved past Serenity, slowly lifting her hand as she approached the door. It didn't open. Asmodeus growled and Erin cast him an apologetic look, and then looked at the carving on the door. She ran her gaze over it and lingered in one spot. Her gaze brightened, glowing gold, and lost its focus, as if she was slipping into a daze, the sort he fell into when the Devil was commanding him.

Asmodeus peered past her at the figure of an angel being crushed under the foot of the gigantic dragon-like monster and the other figure it clutched in its claws.

She touched them both and the door creaked open.

Serenity's power spiked and she rushed into the room. Apollyon grabbed her and froze as he went to pull her back to him, his gaze fixed beyond her. Asmodeus was ahead of him, his heart jackhammering in his chest, driving his blood to a wild beat. He pushed past them, raced to the dais in the centre of the glowing white room and pulled Liora into his arms.

She didn't respond.

He clutched her limp body to him, supporting her head as it lolled, tangling his fingers in her chestnut hair. She was cold. He rubbed her bare arm with his other hand, trying to warm her and hoping it would wake her. The room was chilly and she wore only her short black dress. It was the only reason she slept so soundly. If he could get her warm, she would surely wake.

She had to wake.

"Liora," he whispered close to her ear, his heart clenching like a vice behind his ribs, turning as icy as she felt beneath his fingers. "Wake up."

Serenity came to them and he loosened his grip on Liora, letting the witch near her, silently pleading her to wake her cousin somehow. She bent close to Liora and placed her hands on her chest. Crimson magic spiralled around her arms and flowed over her hands, seeping into Liora, but she still didn't wake.

Asmodeus's heart fractured, the pain so intense he couldn't breathe.

Erin's voice broke the tense silence. "You said only the Devil can get to this point... then maybe only the Devil can wake her."

Serenity moved aside to let Erin near to Liora. Erin looked her over, her amber eyes glowing faintly, and then rested her hand on Liora's chest, right over her heart. She closed her eyes and frowned, and Asmodeus teetered on the edge of despair, his life draining away as he looked down at Liora's ashen face and pale lips and begged her to wake.

Erin wavered and Veiron came forwards, and Asmodeus snarled at him, warning him not to pull her away.

Not yet.

He searched Liora's face, desperate for a sign of life, something to give him hope.

Her lips darkened.

Her cheeks grew pinker.

"Wake, damn you... wake... I will not live without you," Asmodeus whispered and brushed his knuckles across her cheek.

Erin paled.

Veiron pulled her away, flashing red sharp teeth and growling at Asmodeus when he released Liora and moved to stop him. Asmodeus looked back at his little mortal. She lay on the crystal, still and lifeless.

"Come back to me," he whispered in the demon tongue and clenched his fists at his sides, digging his claws into his palms. "You said you wanted me to never leave you... so don't you dare leave me now."

Liora's eyes burst open and she shot up into a sitting position, gasping at air.

Asmodeus was by her in an instant, pulling her into his arms. She flung hers around him and clung to him, burying her face against his neck. He wanted to stay here like this with her for a while, savouring the feel of her in his arms and giving her comfort, bathing in the joy of having her close to him again, back where she belonged, but he couldn't risk it.

"Come, little witch, we must leave this wretched place." He pressed kisses to her hair and smoothed it from her brow, and she nodded, trembling in his arms. He could feel her fear and her pain, and he wanted to take it all away.

He would take it all away.

He would take her back to the island, to her newfound friends, and would protect her and make sure no one ever took her from him again.

He stood and lifted her from the dais, setting her down before him and holding her while she found her balance again.

Liora slowly lifted her gaze to meet his. "I knew you would come for me."

He smiled and stroked her cheek, and then frowned as a noise like thunder echoed from the room behind him. Remus and Romulus. They had come to him and he hadn't called.

There was a commotion near the door, a cacophony of shouts, growls and snarls, and he turned on his heel to face the intruder. The tip of a blade came at him and then Liora was before him, her small body shielding his, and he roared his fury as the black sword punctured her back, came out through her stomach and stabbed into his chest.

Liora's hazel eyes went wide and she coughed up blood.

Asmodeus pulled himself from the blade and caught her as she fell. Blood streamed from the wound and saturated her black dress. It dripped and pooled on the floor together with his, soaking into the crystal and turning it scarlet.

His knees gave out and hit the floor hard, but he didn't feel the impact. He didn't feel anything as he stared down at Liora where she lay in his arms, a sword skewering her, her life slipping away.

She couldn't leave him.

She had promised.

They both had promised.

Veiron came to kneel before him and carefully pulled the sword from Liora's back. She cried out, the sound of her pain tearing at his heart and driving his own to the back of his mind. Asmodeus smoothed his hand across her damp brow and let Veiron take her from him. He silently begged the Hell's angel to forget the bad blood between them and save her, because he was already paying for what he had done.

Asmodeus growled and fixed his eyes on Nevar.

"You die for this," he said and Apollyon grabbed him from behind, holding him back and refusing to give him even an inch in which to move. Asmodeus snarled and struggled against him, his knees slipping around in the blood leaking from his chest, weakening him. "Heal me... I want to kill him!"

Veiron ignored him and focused on healing Liora instead, and his heart thanked him for it. She deserved the Hell's angel's attention more than he did. She had shielded him from a blow meant to kill him. She had taken that pain on herself and possibly that fate too. He looked down at her, his breathing turning as shallow as hers was, pleading whatever higher power would listen to him to deliver her from the arms of death and back into his. He couldn't lose her.

Nevar drew another blade out of the air.

"I don't bloody think so." Erin held her hands out and blasted him, sending him crashing into the crystal wall with enough force to leave an impact crater.

Nevar slumped to the ground unconscious but Erin moved to stand over him, keeping her right hand extended and her eyes on him.

"If he moves, I'm hitting him again, and I'm taking my phasers off stun."
Black ribbons of fire flickered around her fingers.

Asmodeus wasn't sure what a phaser was and he definitely wasn't going to let
Erin kill Nevar. That pleasure was his.

Liora moaned, recapturing his attention, and he stopped struggling against
Apollyon and stared at her as Veiron held his hand over her stomach. He sagged,
giving up his fight and willing her not to do the same. She had to live.

"Tell me she will live," Asmodeus said and frowned as the room grew dimmer
and colder.

Veiron glanced at him and then down at his chest, his scarlet eyebrows knitting
tightly.

"Serenity, you need to take over here." Veiron looked at her and she rushed to
kneel beside her cousin, red magic spiralling into life around her hands. The Hell's
angel moved to him and he shook his head.

"No... take care of her... she has to live." Asmodeus wavered and his head
dropped forwards and he couldn't lift it for some reason. He looked down at the
pool of blood growing beneath him and blossoming as it soaked into the crystal. It
swirled within it and the room twirled with it, going out of focus.

"Sorry, but you have to live too," Veiron whispered and placed his hand
against Asmodeus's bare chest.

Fire shot into his heart and Asmodeus arched forwards, flung his head back
and growled through his gritted teeth.

The room blazed so bright it blinded him and then darkness embraced him.

CHAPTER 24

Liora felt terrible. Her mouth was bone dry. Her body ached all over, stiff and sore, as if she had gone ten rounds with a demon horde. Her eyes were sticky and stinging. What had happened to her?

She lay still, a warm breeze caressing her skin and sweeping away some of her aches, relaxing her. It didn't carry the acrid stench of Hell. It smelled like saltwater and sand.

The island.

She remembered Asmodeus coming for her. She remembered waking and seeing him standing over her, the others around him.

She remembered a man coming at him with a sword and then incredible pain.

Liora slowly lifted her hand, the action making her wince as her muscles protested, and touched her throat. Her necklace was gone. It explained why the sword had penetrated her. She had reacted on instinct, used to it protecting her, forgetting that she had lost it when someone had snatched her from this island.

She cracked her eyes open and squinted. The light made them water, giving her some relief from the gritty dry scraping of her eyelids as she blinked, trying to clear her vision.

The green roof of a tent came into focus and another breeze blew in through the open flaps. She sighed and touched her throat, feeling the marks that Asmodeus had placed on her, and then inched her way downwards to the point on her stomach where the sword had penetrated her.

She was dressed, the fabric soft beneath her fingers.

Liora pushed herself onto her right elbow, grimacing as the effort drained her and caused her insides to ache along the path the blade had taken through her body.

She looked down at the black tank and shorts she wore. If she had to guess, she would say they were Erin's clothes. Serenity didn't own anything this dark and sombre, and she couldn't imagine Amelia lending her clothes.

A noise outside caught her attention, the feral wild snarling setting her heart racing.

Was there some sort of beast out there?

It sounded furious and dangerous, and pained.

Liora managed to make it onto her knees and crawled out of the tent onto the warm white sand. The first touch of sunlight on her skin was bliss and she breathed deep, savouring the clean air. She had thought she would never see this again, never gaze upon the glittering turquoise sea and the endless rich blue sky, or hear the palm trees swaying in the gentle breeze and the waves steadily breaking against the shore.

She scouted the area, spotting everyone at the far end of the beach on her left, and then frowned when she saw Romulus and Remus closer to her on her right, guarding a square, steel cage in the shade of the palm trees.

The beast?

Remus perked up when he noticed her, shifting to stand and wagging his tail. His movement revealed that it wasn't a beast in the eight-foot-square cage he guarded.

It was a man.

The one who had tried to kill Asmodeus.

Liora pulled herself to her feet using the tent poles, anger giving her strength and making her forget her desire to see her angel and the others. She needed to know why this man had wanted to kill Asmodeus.

She walked slowly to the cage, her pain fading with each step, obliterated by the turbulent emotions lashing at her as she stared at the white-haired man.

As she drew closer, she could feel the power in the cage. Enchanted. Serenity had cast a spell upon it to make it impossible for the man to escape. She would thank her cousin later, after she had discovered why this man had wanted to kill Asmodeus.

He spotted her and his pale green eyes turned stormy violet, his meagre clothing disappeared, replaced with purple-edged black armour, and he snarled, flashing fangs at her.

An angel?

Or a demon?

He tried to stand and wavered, collapsing onto his knees and growling. Not in warning or fury this time. There was pain in it and despair. Sweat broke out across his pale brow and he breathed hard, his arms trembling as he grasped the bars, clinging to them as if he would crumple completely if he let go.

The man lifted his gaze to hers, green spreading through the violet of his irises, and his silvery eyebrows furrowed. His cracked lips parted and he looked so filled with despair and suffering that for a moment she forgot what he had done to her and tried to do to Asmodeus.

She edged a step closer and Remus came to her, nudging her back, away from the man. Liora petted the big black hellhound to reassure him, rested her cheek against his thick neck, and then wrapped her arm around him for support. She moved forwards again, closing in on the cage, Remus acting as her crutch once again.

The man's eyes turned violet and he snarled as he launched himself at the bars, rattling the cage. He smashed his fists against them one moment and clawed at her through them the next, growling and glaring at her, his aura filled with darkness and infinite rage.

Romulus bared his black fangs and growled.

The man swiped at her again and then collapsed, leaning against the bars with his forehead pressed hard against one of them. He breathed heavily and muttered things to himself, things that sounded sinister and she didn't understand. A demon language.

His shoulders shook and he laughed, and then his face screwed up and he curled clawed fingers around the bars and looked at her with eyes flooded with fear and sorrow. She could feel the emotions emanating from him. They were strong, violent, clashing with each other and driving him between fury and despair.

His gaze flickered beyond her, towards the end of the beach where the others were, and flashed violet again. He snarled and grasped the bars, pulling and straining in an attempt to bend them, desperation etched on his face.

She didn't need to look to see who had the focus of his attention and his rage. Asmodeus.

He still wanted to kill him.

Why?

Liora leaned on Remus and studied the man in the cage. A lost soul. She wanted to hate him but couldn't help feeling sorry for him.

His eyes darted back and he stared at her. A familiar sensation went through her and she frowned at him.

"You were the one watching me," she whispered, not expecting him to respond. Whatever had happened to him, he was beyond speech right now, lost in his emotions and his pain, drowning in despair.

She wanted to be angry with him, both for what he had tried to do to Asmodeus and what he had done to her. He had kidnapped her from this island. He had handed her over to the Devil. He had almost killed her.

She wanted it, but she found herself pitying him as she watched him talking to himself and shaking all over, feverish and delirious.

His eyes went back to Asmodeus and he attacked the cage again, clawing the air in his direction, snarling and growling.

Romulus growled back at him and he quieted again, shrinking back into the cage, as far as he could get from the hellhound. The man huddled into the corner there, his arms wrapped around his knees.

Liora released Remus and kneeled in the sand a few feet from the cage and the man, keeping herself beyond his reach.

He looked at her out of the corner of his eye, his irises jade again but shot through with black and purple.

"Did Asmodeus have anything to do with your condition?" she said, not believing he would understand her in his current state, but needing to ask him anyway.

"Die!" The man hurled himself at the cage and shot his arms between the bars, clawing at her.

Wind blasted against her and Asmodeus was beside her. He drew his leg back and she saw his intention to kick the cage.

"No," Liora snapped and held her arm out, stopping him from striking the man.

He lowered his leg, turned to her, and held his hand out for her to take. She slipped hers into it and he pulled her into his arms, holding her close to him. Liora allowed herself a few seconds in which she pressed her ear to his chest, listened to his heart beating strong, and savoured how good it felt to be in his arms again.

She pushed her hands against his chest to make him release her and he frowned down at her, tightening his grip at the same time.

Liora looked up into his golden eyes and resisted her desire to brush her fingers through the wild black lengths of his hair, feeling its softness beneath their tips, and step back into the shelter of his embrace.

She couldn't. She had to ask him something and she knew that when she did, the gentle caring man before her would disappear and he would distance himself. She could understand why even as she didn't want him to do it. He would want to protect himself. He would think she was out to hurt him.

She wasn't but she had to know.

"Asmodeus... did you have anything to do with this man's suffering?"

His eyes turned cold, his anger rising in them and in his power on her senses. She swallowed hard and held her ground, refusing to let his icy glare or his feelings scare her away from finding out why this man had been following her, why he had handed her to the Devil, and why he wanted to kill Asmodeus.

Something told her they were all connected to something Asmodeus had done to him.

He wanted revenge.

Asmodeus released her and stepped back, placing a small distance between them that felt vast, frigid, and impassable.

He shifted his cruel gaze to the man. "Nevar is addicted to Euphoria and in withdrawal."

Euphoria. She had heard of it a few years ago, during research she had been conducting on a small group of demons in London. It was the name for a drink made of alcohol and a drop of demon toxin. When combined with a demon's blood and given to a mortal, it would give the mortal a serious high in which they had zero inhibitions, and would also give the demon control over them, a free pass to do whatever they wanted with the drugged mortal.

This man before her wasn't mortal though.

"He's an angel, isn't he?" Liora looked down at him. "He doesn't look like an angel should... Euphoria isn't responsible for his darkness and appearance, or all of his suffering."

He locked his pale green eyes on her and Asmodeus growled. The man snarled back, purple obliterating the green in his irises again.

Nevar.

She had heard that name before. Amelia had mentioned him when they had first come to the island. She had told the others not to trust Asmodeus because of something he had done to Nevar. Liora stared at the male in the cage and knew that Asmodeus was responsible for his plight even when she didn't want to believe it.

Liora turned back to Asmodeus and squared her shoulders.

"I will not ask again. Did you do this to him?"

Asmodeus averted his gaze and it was all the answer she needed.

"Why?" she said softly, her shoulders slumping, and her eyes wandered back to the man in the cage. An angel with terrible evil within him, far stronger than what she had felt in Asmodeus when they had first met. He was lost to it, revelling in the darkness within even as it tormented him.

"I have no reason. No excuse," Asmodeus said and she felt his gaze return to her, and knew he wanted her to look at him with forgiveness and understanding. She couldn't right now. He had done something terrible to this man and it had resulted in her being pulled into his vendetta and into danger. Asmodeus heaved a sigh. "I only gave the darkness within him a push. He was already different to others. He would have become this sooner or later."

Liora turned on him. "You can't know that. There's darkness and light in all of us and many maintain the balance. Why did you do it?"

Asmodeus tipped his head back and jammed his hands into the pockets of his long black linen trousers, the action causing the muscles of his bare torso to tighten and distract her for a second. She shoved her desire to the back of her mind, bringing her focus back to what Asmodeus had done to the man in the cage. Nevar.

"I wanted to use Nevar to shake Heaven. He refused my orders and fought me."

"You forced Nevar's darkness to take hold of him, condemning him to suffer as the evil within him grew, because you wanted to shake Heaven?" She couldn't believe what she was hearing.

She took a step backwards, away from him, and he dropped his gaze and reached for her, a pleading look flittering across his face before he got the better of himself and scowled at her. She didn't want to hurt him, but she was finding it hard to take in what he had done and overcome it.

Asmodeus lowered his hand to his side.

"It was a selfish and cruel thing you did... and I can't blame this man for wanting vengeance." Liora turned her back on him and crouched near the cage, eye-level with Nevar. The man watched her closely, a flicker of wariness in his eyes, as if he expected her to lash out at him. "Look at what you've done to this soul, Asmodeus. Are you proud of yourself?"

She glanced over her shoulder at him.

Asmodeus stared at Nevar.

"No." He looked away again, gazing at the ocean to his left.

Liora reached towards the bars.

"Do not do that!" Asmodeus was beside her in a heartbeat, grabbing her shoulder and pulling her back.

She shrugged free and ignored him, bravely reaching through the bars with her right hand. She laid her palm on Nevar's damp pale cheek, feeling him trembling and how fiercely the fever gripped him. Nevar lowered his head and closed his eyes.

Liora sighed.

"Are you pleased with your work, Asmodeus?" she whispered and stroked Nevar's cheek, focusing on her fingertips and her magic, letting it flow from her and into him. She couldn't heal him, not when his suffering stemmed from an addiction, but she could soothe his fever and hopefully take away his deliriousness. "You destroyed this man and made him into a monster."

Liora looked up at Asmodeus where he stood over her, pain shining in his eyes, combining with the fear she could feel growing within his power, flowing around her.

"I never believed you capable of such cruelty and evil, but perhaps the others are right and there is no good in you." Liora felt horrible the moment the words left her lips because she knew there was more good in him now than when they had met, and she knew he was trying to be good and grasp how people behaved in her world.

Asmodeus's eyes verged on red, a warning of the anger and hurt she could feel rising within him like a tide. Tears lined his lashes and he gritted his teeth, his jaw muscles tensing in response, and his nostrils flared.

"There is... I swear it, Liora," he bit out and clenched his fists at his sides. "Do not listen to them. I did this... but I was a different man. You changed me. If I could undo what I have done... I would."

Liora took her hand away from Nevar's face, stood and took a step towards Asmodeus.

His expression turned wild and dangerous, and he spread his enormous black-feathered wings, blocking her way.

"I will not let you leave me." He ground the words out, his voice thick with pain and emotion but dark with anger and commanding too. She wanted to tell him that she hadn't intended to leave him. She had only been coming to him to soothe his pain. He didn't give her a chance to speak. He grabbed her shoulders and held her tightly, his claws pressing into her bare skin. "I have done my best to be good for you. I want to be good... but there is evil in me. It is the way I was created."

She knew that.

"I admit that I am shocked by what you've done to Nevar," she said and his grip on her arms tightened, the darkness she could feel in him growing and beginning to obliterate the good. She wasn't out to hurt him and wasn't going to say anything that would make him feel wretched. She only wanted to make him feel better. "But I have also seen the realm you have spent thousands of years in and met the man who is your master, and therefore I know that your behaviour is the result of your upbringing."

He tried to pull away but she grabbed his wrists and held him fast.

"You've lacked friends, Asmodeus... exposure to good things and seeing how people in this world act, and how we interact with each other. Your world is nothing like mine. What you did while down there was what is acceptable and normal in that place."

Asmodeus closed his eyes and whispered, "But not acceptable and normal in this place... not acceptable to you."

Liora sighed. "No. I would never do the things you've done, but then I didn't grow up in Hell. If I had, I probably would have done terrible things too, without thinking there was anything wrong with it... and without remorse."

"I do regret what I did to Nevar," he snapped and twisted his hands in hers, coming to hold her wrists as if he feared she would try to pull away from him now. "I am sorry that I did such a thing to him. You are right and it was cruel and wrong. I can see that now."

Nevar snorted and Asmodeus growled at him, baring his fangs.

Liora felt for Asmodeus because she knew it was true. He shouldn't have any good in him but there was some, and she could still see it, and she could see in his eyes and hear in his voice that he was sorry for what he had done. He regretted it now and wouldn't do such a terrible thing again. It was hard for him to go against his nature but he was trying to do just that so he could be a better man.

She sighed. Her heart ached for him as she thought about everything they had been through. Asmodeus had struggled throughout it all, fighting his instincts and battling to overcome the darkness within his soul, doing his best to learn quickly about her world and how things worked here, and to accept others into his life, all so he could be a good man for her.

All so she would love him.

He didn't need to change for that to happen. She loved him with every fibre of her being, every drop of blood in her body and every ounce of her soul.

"Liora?" Asmodeus whispered, his eyebrows furrowing. He dropped his gaze to her arms, released her and hastily brushed his fingers over her skin, over the points where his claws had dug into her. Remorse filled his eyes. "I did not mean to harm you."

Liora caught his right wrist and shifted her hand to his, capturing it and holding it, stopping him from fussing over a few cuts that had barely stung. If anyone was hurting, it was Asmodeus, and it was because of her.

She raised her other hand to his face and cupped his jaw, and he instantly leaned into her touch, closing his eyes and sighing out his breath.

"I didn't mean to hurt you," she whispered and he looked down at her, a beautiful flicker of relief in his eyes that spoke to her heart and made her want to kiss him.

Nevar growled and Asmodeus cast him a black look. Liora turned her head, looked over her shoulder at Nevar, and then shifted to face him.

His eyes were half-purple and narrowed on Asmodeus. He bared his fangs and curled long black clawed fingers around the bars of his prison.

"We must be able to do something for him. What does he need?" She pitied the angel as he muttered things to himself, his skin paling, the effect of her magic already fading and letting the fever take hold of him again.

Asmodeus came up beside her, his right wing tickling the backs of her legs. "He needs Euphoria."

"That won't break his addiction though." It would only make it worse, giving it a new, firmer grip on him.

Asmodeus stared at the angel for long, tense minutes in which Nevar growled at him, constantly flashing fangs, his steady gaze turning purple and filling with dark, violent thoughts that she could almost hear. He still wanted to kill Asmodeus.

Asmodeus would want to kill him in return if she told him what she had realised, that he was the one who had been watching her and who had taken her from him, delivering her to the Devil. She glanced up at Asmodeus, studying his noble profile. He was beautiful when lost in thought, seeking an answer that would please her.

His amber gaze slid to her and his expression softened, affection filling it and warming her. She liked it when he looked at her like that, as if she was his whole world and the only thing that mattered to him.

"It is possible he could wean himself off on normal, non-demon blood." Asmodeus didn't sound particularly sure but at least he had found a potential solution to Nevar's terrible addiction.

"How did you awaken the darkness within him?" she said and he frowned at his feet. "I won't be angry with you."

"I formed a contract between us, forcibly. I spilled his blood and gave him mine, mingling them in a wound I had placed on his chest."

Liora gazed down at Nevar. He had looked wild in the crystal room, verging on demonic, with his arms and legs covered in black skin. He had fangs like Asmodeus now. She glanced up at Asmodeus.

"Did the contract change his appearance?"

He nodded. "As the darkness within him took hold and the contract between us strengthened, his appearance altered."

"Altered to mirror his master's?" She held his gaze and he didn't look away. He nodded again but it was smaller this time, speaking of the wariness she could see in his eyes. He didn't want her to question him about this, but she needed to know. She wanted to know all of Asmodeus. The good and the bad. The angelic and the demonic. "So... there is a side of you like this?"

"My true appearance is closer to the Devil's... I am darkness incarnate, as he is. I..." He raised his right hand with his palm facing upwards and stared at it. It began to change, his black claws growing thicker and longer, sharper. The darkness bled from them onto his skin, turning it to the colour of night, and crept up his fingers and over his hand to his wrist. Like Nevar's hands were. Asmodeus closed his eyes and lowered his head. "I do not want you to see me like that... ever."

"Why not?" Liora moved closer to him and touched his black hand, marvelling at how rough his claws were beneath her touch but how smooth his skin was. She had expected it to be as rough as the basalt of Hell.

"Because you would think me a monster too." He took his hand away and she caught it before he could completely withdraw, holding it gently in both of hers.

She had called Nevar a monster. It was understandable that Asmodeus would think she would view him as the same if she saw what he had called his true appearance.

"You would think me evil." He slipped his hand free of hers and turned his face to one side, away from her.

"I don't think Veiron evil and he's gone big and black and completely weird a few times since I've known him." She paused and frowned at Asmodeus. "Do you turn like him?"

"No... I am... different."

"Different how? I want to know." She held his gaze when he looked at her, showing him that she was telling the truth and wasn't saying these things just to make him feel better. She really did want to see him in his true form.

"Different... like this..." Asmodeus closed his eyes and she tensed when black shadows loomed around his feet and fluttered there, striking at the sand like vipers. They avoided her and she knew it was because of Asmodeus's feelings for her. He didn't want to harm her.

Asmodeus drew in a deep breath, his bare chest expanding with it, and the shadows swirled up his legs and danced around his clawed fingers. They settled onto his skin, turning it black, and flowed up his arms.

His black trousers disappeared, replaced by his greaves and boots, and his loincloth and the strips of armour around his hips. One of his greaves had a long slash in it that hadn't been there before. Had he been fighting again?

The gold on his armour melted into pure obsidian and then blazed violet, matching Nevar's.

The black feathers of his wings gained a purple shimmer in the sunlight, reflecting brightly.

His black hair fluttered against the breeze and shifted backwards, and small obsidian horns curled from behind his ears.

He opened his eyes, fixing his swirling purple gaze on her. He snarled, flashing his fangs, and all of his teeth sharpened. The darkness reached his chest and exploded outwards, turning his skin into the colour of the night.

Nevar growled and attacked the cage.

Asmodeus roared at him and the angel shrank back into the corner, huddling there. A male put firmly in his place by his master.

"I knew it." The deep male voice came from behind Asmodeus and Liora looked across at Apollyon as he stared at Asmodeus, a grim edge to his blue eyes. "You contracted with him."

Asmodeus nodded, drew in another deep breath, and the transformation reversed, leaving his skin as golden as his eyes. Liora mourned the loss of his little horns. They were sort of sexy and she had wanted to tiptoe and stroke them.

If she told Asmodeus that, he would probably choke on something.

His gaze flickered to her, the wary edge back in it, and then away to Apollyon.

"We were discussing Nevar's rehabilitation." Asmodeus furled his black wings against his back and it was weird hearing him talking to Apollyon in a civil tone, and doubly weird when Apollyon responded in kind.

"I think it will be long and troublesome. Have you come up with any possible solutions?"

Asmodeus nodded again. "Blood. It is possible that given blood of a non-demonic source over a period of months that Nevar will be able to overcome his addiction."

"But that would leave him addicted to blood, right?" Liora hadn't thought about it earlier when Asmodeus had suggested it but if they gave Nevar blood for months on end, they were only shifting his addiction from Euphoria to something else, and probably making him more dangerous to mortals.

He was hungry for a fix of demon toxin and blood right now.

Making him hungry for mortal blood sounded very bad to her.

"We will make sure that he is weaned off blood too." Apollyon sounded confident enough and she felt better knowing that it wasn't just Asmodeus who would be handling Nevar's trip to rehab.

Liora touched the marks on her throat and then looked down at her wrist. "So he needs regular doses, right?"

Asmodeus's fingers curled around her wrist. "Not of your blood, little mortal. Witch blood will only get him addicted to the power that flows within your veins."

She blushed at the flash of a memory. Asmodeus biting her. Tasting her. He knew first-hand the power in her blood and she wanted him to know it again.

He frowned at her and lifted his free hand as if to touch her face. She cleared her throat and glanced away, but caught the wicked tilt of his lips. He was on to her. He knew she was thinking naughty things.

She coughed again and tried to sound as if her mind was on the important business of rehabilitating Nevar and wasn't replaying Asmodeus biting her on repeat.

"But we need to start feeding him now, to help him through the withdrawal."

"If you insist we begin now, it will be my blood he will have. Technically, I am not demonic, and it is possible that my blood would be the best choice, given that I am his master." Asmodeus released her and crouched beside the cage.

Nevar hissed at him and pressed back into the corner, trying to get away.

The second Asmodeus placed his arm through the bars, Nevar changed abruptly. He lunged forwards, grabbed Asmodeus's wrist and pulled, slamming Asmodeus against the bars of the cage.

Nevar viciously sank his fangs into Asmodeus's arm, clutching it with both hands, and curled his claws around, pressing them into his flesh and ripping at his skin. Asmodeus grunted and gritted his teeth, wincing as Nevar drank, making wet greedy sucking noises and cutting at Asmodeus with his claws.

Asmodeus paled.

"Stop," Liora snapped and Asmodeus ignored her. She slammed her hands against the bars of the cage near Nevar. "Stop!"

Nevar blinked and looked around himself, an air of confusion in his green eyes. They widened and he released Asmodeus's arm and shot backwards. Asmodeus stumbled to his feet and she ducked beneath his arm and caught hold of him, steadying him as he spread his wings and fought to remain standing.

Nevar stared at her, blood saturating his face and his hands. He kept blinking, staring, breathing faster and faster, and she could sense the panic rising within him, bringing fear and anger in its wake.

He snarled and launched himself at the bars, slashing at Asmodeus with his black claws. "What did you do to me this time?"

Liora held on to Asmodeus, pressing one hand against his chest and one against his back, holding him upright but struggling beneath his weight.

"Asmodeus did nothing bad to you," she said and Apollyon came to her, taking hold of his twin for her. "You needed blood to help you fight your addiction and that was all he gave to you."

Asmodeus found his balance at last and some of the colour returned to his skin.

Nevar spat onto the sand beneath his cage. "You taste disgusting."

"Why thank you," Asmodeus snarled, lifted his arm to his face and licked the cuts, cleaning the blood away.

Liora couldn't miss the blatant hunger in Nevar's green-to-purple eyes as he watched Asmodeus.

He wasn't satisfied even though he had called Asmodeus's blood disgusting. He lusted after more.

Nevar flicked her a look of revulsion and then huddled back into his corner, muttering in the demon tongue. Asmodeus frowned at him and she was tempted to ask what Nevar was saying, but he didn't look as if he would tell her.

He placed his arm around her shoulders and led her away from the cage, leaving Nevar mumbling to himself, guarded by the hellhounds.

"What happened to your armour?" She pointed at the greave with a slash in it and then looked up into Asmodeus's eyes.

"Dragon," he said and she smiled. "The Devil sent it to deal with me when I came to take you back from him. I did tell you that I could defeat it."

He had, and she was glad that she hadn't been around while he had been battling the enormous beast. She didn't want to see him fighting such a dangerous creature. Her magic was threatening to take control of her right now, when she was only imagining it happening. If she ever saw Asmodeus locked in such a battle, his life on the line, she would completely lose control and become a slave to her power, stopping at nothing to protect him. There was a chance she would destroy everything in her path.

"Some people would like to see you," he said and she nodded, pushing her dark thoughts away and taking a deep breath to bring her magic back under her control.

She wanted to see them too.

He paused halfway to the group, released her and looked out to sea.

Liora could feel him pulling away and distancing himself, and it left her cold inside.

She caught hold of his left wrist and he tried to twist free but she held on to it, refusing to let him go. She stared down at the bloody welts on his arm and tried to search for the right words, the ones that would make everything better.

Nevar had sliced into Asmodeus's flesh with his claws and the bite wound was ragged, as if he had buried his fangs in Asmodeus several times while feeding.

"Do they hurt?" She lifted her gaze to his.

He looked uneasy. "No."

Liora smiled sadly. He was being guarded again. It upset her but she understood why he wasn't willing to drop his guard around her right now. He still couldn't decide whether she was going to leave him or not and she was doing a terrible job of showing him that she was sorry about what she had said and that she should never have said it in the first place, and that she wanted to be with him still.

She kept hold of his hand. "They must sting at least."

Liora placed her other hand over the wounds and focused on her power, calling it forth. It swirled purple and red around her fingertips and she channelled it into his arm, healing the slashes and deep punctures. He shook beneath her hands and she could sense his uncertainty.

When the wounds had healed, she lifted his arm and pressed gentle kisses to every red mark that remained, lavishing them with affection. His trembling ceased and uncertainty became something else.

Liora drew back and gazed up into his dark amber eyes, the hunger in them calling her to action, demanding she give him what he wanted.

She tiptoed to kiss him and he hesitated and then pulled away from her, breaking free of her grip.

He looked beyond her to the camp, down into her eyes, opened his mouth and then turned and walked away.

Liora blinked, numb and cold, shaking inside.

She stared after him as he walked towards the sea, his hands in the pockets of the black linen trousers he now wore and his wings shrinking into his back.

She wanted to go to him and tell him again that she was sorry, to apologise properly this time and not dance around it, but she held back, resisting the urge to follow him. It wasn't just the things she had said that were making him draw away from her again. He was thinking about what he had done to Nevar too and struggling with his feelings, and he needed space. If she went to him now, she would be pushing him again and that was the last thing she wanted to do. She wanted to make him feel better, not make him feel crowded and cornered.

He tipped his head back and looked up at the sky.

Serenity rushed over to her, dragging her attention away from Asmodeus. She hugged her cousin and closed her eyes, drawing comfort from Serenity's warm embrace. It lifted her heart.

Her cousin led her to the group gathering around the fire and Liora glanced back at her angel.

She would give him five minutes.

Then she would introduce him to something new.

Make up sex.

The ground trembled beneath her feet.

Fiery streaks appeared on the white sand close to Asmodeus and Nevar.

CHAPTER 25

Asmodeus called one of his curved blades to him the moment the first tremor shook the sand and was racing for Liora when a jagged fault line cut across his path, shooting thirty feet wide in less than a heartbeat. The water to his right hissed as the fiery line rocketed into the sea, sending salty steam up into the air.

Something growled off to his left.

His head whipped that way, causing the longer lengths of his black hair to caress his brow.

Nevar was halfway to demonic and hurling himself against the bars of his cage, his gaze fixed with deadly intent on something ahead of him, towards the camp.

Asmodeus's golden eyes leaped there and caught on the three Hell's angels standing before the cage in their true forms, their leathery wings furled against their immense black bodies and their eyes glowing crimson. The leader of the group bared red sharp teeth at Nevar and motioned to his comrades, grunting dark words in the demon tongue.

They meant to take him.

Asmodeus leaped over the fault line before him as it widened, unwilling to wait for the Devil's men to appear. They were coming for him too. He had to reach Nevar and drive the Hell's angels away before they could take him down to Hell. He had put the male in the cage and had commanded Serenity to place her most powerful enchantment on it so he couldn't escape, and had kept him there in a weakened state. Nevar was in no condition to fight and, as much as he wanted the angel to pay for what he had done to Liora, he couldn't stand by and let the Hell's angels take him. He had made a vow to see to Nevar's rehabilitation and to help him. He meant to keep that vow.

He never broke his word.

Claws snagged his left ankle and tugged hard, sending him slamming face first into the white sand. He gasped for air and got a lungful of sand instead.

Asmodeus choked on it and pushed himself up at the same time as he kicked out at the Hell's angel who had grabbed him. His boot connected hard with the demonic angel's face and he grinned as the male grunted in pain and released his other leg. Asmodeus leaped to his feet, called his second blade to him, and attacked, not giving the male a chance to shake off the blow.

Nevar shrieked, the sound born of fury, and a sharp snarl followed it together with the scent of blood. One of the Hell's angels had come too close to Nevar's claws. Asmodeus kicked off, the soft sand hindering his movements, and made a break for Nevar. The cage was in pieces behind Nevar, ripped apart from the outside. It was pandemonium as the male faced off against the three Hell's angels, using his black claws against them, fighting like a mad fool even though he was outnumbered and outgunned. The three demonic angels had their red-bladed spears drawn and had already landed blows on Nevar, cutting across his thighs and upper arms.

They were pulling their punches though. Why?

Shouts came from the camp and then Veiron was in the thick of the fray in his true form, his meaty black fists smashing faces and cracking bones. He flashed twin rows of vicious red teeth at the other Hell's angels.

"You seriously want to tangle with me?" Veiron growled, his voice rumbling and deeper than normal, and grabbed the Hell's angel that had attacked Asmodeus. He launched the male into the three battling Nevar. The leader dodged him but he crashed into the other two, taking them down into a heap.

Asmodeus had made it halfway to Nevar when a portal opened right in front of him, exploding in white-hot flames, an arm shot out and dragged him inside. He hit the rough black ground on the other side and, the moment he stopped rolling, pushed onto his feet and called his blades and his limited armour.

The Devil stood before him, his towering black fortress as his backdrop and his eyes bright crimson. He folded his arms across his chest, the action causing his black tailored suit jacket to tighten around his muscles.

A wave of power washed over Asmodeus and drove him to his knees before he could even brace himself against it.

The Devil was what Liora had once termed 'pissed'.

Another portal opened and Nevar fell through it, landing hard on his face and growling into the cracked pavement. He pressed his palms into the slabs and tried to push himself up. His arms strained, muscles bunching and tensing, but he didn't manage to move an inch. It wasn't his weakened state stopping him from righting himself. It was the force of the power pressing down on him. The Devil was extremely pissed at Nevar. Why?

Asmodeus felt a portal open a few metres behind him and then heard bickering.

Erin's voice became clearer, ringing out around the courtyard.

"I don't care, Veiron… he broke the rules and he'll bloody well pay." She stormed past Asmodeus and he raised an eyebrow at her.

She walked unhindered, as if the Devil wasn't exerting all of his power and fury on the area.

Was he directing it only at him and Nevar?

Asmodeus inched his eyes left. He couldn't see the others. He focused on his breathing and his power, willing his body to obey him and move. His head shifted a few inches. Veiron and the others were behind him, all of them on their knees, the rotting carcass of the dragon beyond them. Amelia and all of the males wore their armour and had their weapons drawn.

Liora.

Anger emanated from her in powerful waves.

She knelt beside Apollyon and Serenity, breathing hard and fast, stilted ribbons of magic encircling her hands. Her eyebrows knitted and her jaw tensed, her steely hazel gaze locked on him.

He hoped that the fury he could feel in her wasn't directed at him and that she had moved past how she had felt on the beach, coming to terms with the things he had done and seeing that he truly did regret his actions now. At the same time, he felt he deserved her wrath for dragging her into this.

She had been through one ordeal after another since meeting him, and the worst of them were completely his fault, the result of what he had done to Nevar.

Asmodeus stared into her eyes and silently apologised to her, hoping she would see that he was sorry.

The hard lines of her face softened and relaxed, and then her gaze shifted and fixed on the Devil, gaining a dark edge again. It gave him the answer he needed and eased his troubled heart. She was angry with the Devil for taking him and wanted to make him pay.

Asmodeus could feel her desire to come to him and could sense her need to fight his master, and wished that she could move even as he was glad that she couldn't.

Her magic was at the ready but she was still weak, recovering from the wound Nevar had dealt her and what the Devil had done to her.

She wasn't strong enough to fight his master and he feared that if she somehow broke free of the Devil's power, she would try to attack him and would get herself killed. He couldn't go through that again. He had come close to losing her once and the pain of seeing her fade away, seeing her standing on the brink of death, had almost killed him. He couldn't lose her. He would die without her.

Every fibre of his being cried out to have her close to him, tucked safely in his arms. He needed to feel her in his embrace and whisper to her that he would never let the Devil hurt her.

He would do better.

He would keep her safe and be a good man for her if she would have him.

Apollyon was beside her, glaring at the Devil with violence swirling in his blue eyes. The Devil's power was holding him for now, but it wouldn't for long. Asmodeus could feel Apollyon's power rising, pushing against the force of the Devil's and slowly shoving it back from his twin and those close to him.

Erin halted in front of the Devil, planted her hands on her hips, and huffed.

"You broke the pact!" Black flames licked up her arms and danced around her fingers, and shadows flickered above her shoulder blades.

She was the spitting image of her father. A mistress of darkness bent on bestowing a hard lesson upon the head of her enemy. Possibly by removing it. It was Asmodeus's preferred method.

"I did no such thing." The Devil calmly stood his ground, his red gaze dropping to her.

"You hurt my friends," she said and he shook his head. Erin's frown hardened. "You did. For starters, you took Liora from the island and you hurt her."

"I did not take her from the island."

"Fine. Semantics. Your minions took her from the island. It still counts as breaking the pact."

The Devil picked his black claws and then lifted a bored gaze to her. "My minions did not break the covenant and I did not harm Liora."

The shadows emanating from Erin's back grew larger, flickering on an unknown breeze, and Asmodeus could feel her power rising with her anger. "Liar. If you didn't take her and your men didn't take her, then who did? There was evidence, you bastard. A bloody big fault line like Hell's angels make."

The Devil's red eyes shifted down to Asmodeus. "I recall other beings having the ability to create such a rift."

Asmodeus frowned. It was true that he had that ability, but he hadn't taken Liora. The Devil had commanded him to bring her to him, but he had resisted. He hadn't succumbed to his master's order. He would remember if he had done such a thing against his will.

If he hadn't taken her and Hell's angels hadn't taken her, then who else had the power to create a rift?

Apollyon did.

Asmodeus's eyes narrowed and switched, burning crimson as it dawned on him. His fangs lengthened, pressing hard against his compressed lips.

"You," Asmodeus ground out and stared at Nevar where he lay face down beside him, still struggling against the pressing weight of the Devil's power. The abilities of the master were often passed to servants. "You took Liora."

Guilt flickered in Nevar's violet irises.

"You!" Asmodeus growled and jerked towards him, and roared when he couldn't break the hold of the Devil's power. He wanted to rip into Nevar.

He had orchestrated the whole thing.

Nevar had taken his precious Liora from the island and delivered her to the Devil, knowing it would hurt him and make him desperate.

Nevar had then led Apollyon to him, giving him a chance to confront him with would-be allies around who could protect him. When that confrontation had failed to provide the result the angel wanted, he had taken drastic measures to hurt Asmodeus. He had crushed the one accessible thing he held dear.

Liora's pentagram.

He had then tracked them to where Liora rested and had waited until Asmodeus was vulnerable and distracted before delivering the final blow. Only it had gone wrong. Liora had protected Asmodeus, wrecking Nevar's chance to kill him.

All this to have revenge on him?

"Why?" Asmodeus croaked and his shoulders slumped. "You hurt me as I have hurt you... but you hurt others too. You hurt Liora. She was innocent in all this."

"You love her," Nevar growled into the basalt beneath him. "I wanted to hurt you. I still want to hurt you. I want to rip out your heart... she is your heart."

"I will rip out your heart," Asmodeus growled and tried to attack him again. The Devil's power held him fast. He snarled and bared his fangs at the dark male on the steps above him, earning a glare and an increase in the power pressing down on him as his reward. Asmodeus fought it. "Release me."

"I swear, Nevar... you lay a hand on Asmodeus and I will end you. Release me," Liora barked from behind him and he sensed her power rising, her fury coming to the fore and bringing her magic with it. It pushed against the Devil's power and his own, a powerful tempest that physically rocked him forwards. "Release me, you bastard!"

The Devil raised his hand and glared at Liora, his eyes burning crimson. The strength of her power instantly diminished.

"Damn you! I won't let you lock down my magic again." Her words were a black snarl and Asmodeus managed to look over his shoulder at her.

Purple and black magic crackled around her hands where they clutched her bare knees, intermittent and weak. Her arms trembled and her knuckles were white. The Devil was exerting incredible power on her and his little witch was fighting it, determined not to let his master force her to the ground. Beads of sweat dotted her brow and she struggled to breathe. Her hazel eyes turned wild, her pulse raced and her panic washed over him.

The Devil was choking her.

"Stop it. You are hurting her," Asmodeus snapped and turned on his master. "Harm her and I swear I will make you pay for your mistake."

The Devil sighed and lowered his hand, and Liora gasped at air. "Fine, but if she even thinks about raising a single finger against me, I will not hesitate to make an example out of her."

Asmodeus growled and bared his fangs, and the Devil raised a single black eyebrow at him.

"Do not threaten me, Asmodeus. It is tiresome."

"Then release me." Because he still meant to break Nevar's neck and send the twisted male back to Heaven and to a nightmare. Nevar didn't want to die. He didn't want to forget everything that Heaven had done to him and become an obedient sheep again.

Nevar snarled at him.

"No. It would not be wise. We need him alive." The Devil turned away from him, focusing back on Erin.

We? Asmodeus frowned. He had never heard his master speak in such terms before. The Devil only ever cared about what he wanted. Why did he suddenly want to protect Nevar?

His master held Erin's gaze. "So you see, Daughter, I did not break the pact. Nevar delivered Liora to me so I might protect her. She needed my protection."

"You hurt her. You made her sleep." Asmodeus struggled against his invisible bonds, every muscle tensing until he felt as if they would burst from the exertion.

Nothing happened.

He growled again and breathed hard, fighting to keep his frustration and fury in check so he could talk to his master without resorting to threatening him. Upsetting him further would only result in casualties. Asmodeus had no love for many of the people gathered around him, but Liora did, and he loved her, so he would protect them too.

"I warned you, Asmodeus. She is dangerous in the wrong hands. I sent her to sleep to protect her." The Devil moved to the edge of the steps and stared down at him, his eyes swirling fire.

"Liar," Erin muttered and squared her shoulders. Her black dress fluttered around her thighs and a breeze tousled her short black hair and the shadow wings growing from her back. "You forget I know when you're lying, Pops. You might have sent her to sleep to protect her, but that isn't the only reason you wanted her out of commission but in your hands."

"True." The Devil regally waved his hand and a tall-backed black stone throne appeared behind him.

"And, you did break the pact. You sent your thugs to take Asmodeus and Nevar from my island. Asmodeus is my friend. Nevar is sort of a work in progress. You can work your way out of what happened with Liora, but you cannot get out of that one." Erin tipped her chin up and glared at her father.

Asmodeus stared at her. She thought of him as a friend?

Erin glanced his way and winked at him. "You look like you just got the shock of your eternal life."

Asmodeus snapped his mouth shut and frowned. She sounded like Liora when she teased him.

"Also true, Daughter. I did take Asmodeus and Nevar, but they left me little choice." The Devil seated himself and sighed as his gaze drifted from Erin to Asmodeus and then Liora, and finally settled on Nevar.

The angel grunted and flattened further against the broken pavement, his eyes watering as he gritted his teeth. The Devil was forcing more pressure onto him and less on Asmodeus. He tried to move but failed to make any significant progress.

The Devil shook his head. "Do behave, Asmodeus. I need you alive but if you do something foolish, I may forget that and kill you… and then your precious love."

Asmodeus flashed his fangs and growled. He wouldn't let this male near Liora. Never again.

The Devil's eyes settled back on Nevar. "I thought you would be useful, but it turns out that you are yet another disappointment. Do you know what you have done?"

Nevar didn't look as though he did and Asmodeus didn't know either. The expression on Erin's face warned that she was losing patience fast and that the Devil had better explain himself soon, or she was going to act out her retribution for him breaking the pact.

"I did not think so. Come and I will explain." The Devil crossed his legs, leaned back into his chair and crooked his finger.

Someone shifted behind Asmodeus.

Liora stepped into view and slowly approached the Devil. Her lips compressed into a thin line and her eyebrows married, and her hazel gaze darkened. Magic flickered around her hands, coming in bursts that lasted barely a second before they disappeared again, subdued by his master. She was fighting but she wasn't strong enough to break free of the Devil's power.

She couldn't protect herself.

Asmodeus would do it for her.

He growled and fought with every ounce of his strength. When that failed, he gritted his teeth and called on his darker nature, the side he had tried so hard to hide from her, the one she had asked to see. She hadn't looked at him as if he was a monster. There had been only affection, curiosity, and a touch of desire colouring her hazel eyes. That knowledge gave him the strength to use that side of himself again now.

Shadows burst from beneath his knees, snapping at Nevar and striking at the ground around Asmodeus. Nevar growled at him, baring his fangs. Asmodeus stared him down and flashed his own canines, driving Nevar into submission as his power rose, battling against the Devil's. The darkness curled over his hands, turning his nails to claws and cascading upwards until it had reached his shoulders. The shadows around his feet burrowed into his legs, swirled over his thighs and banded around his stomach, turning his skin black as night.

The weight of the Devil's power lessened as his own power rose to the fore, pushing it back. He focused and growled, forcing the Devil's power back, and stumbled to his feet.

The Devil shot him a black look and raised his hand. Liora stopped. The force of his power increased in strength again, shoving at Asmodeus, landing hard on his shoulders and driving him back down. He refused to kneel again, standing his ground on trembling legs, battling the immense force of the Devil's power.

"You will not touch her. Never again," he growled and rose to his full height against the overwhelming weight of the Devil's power. "I will not let you!"

The shadows exploded over his chest, his wings shot from his back, and his horns curled from behind his ears. He launched forwards and was in front of the Devil before the male could move to defend himself, sweeping Liora behind him and shielding her within the cocoon of power around him.

Hot palms pressed against Asmodeus's sides and then she rested her head between his wings. Her warm breath teased his flesh and he trembled as he clutched her close to him with one hand. In his other, his sword appeared, flashing violet and black.

"For once, you do not disappoint me, Asmodeus." The Devil casually crossed his legs the other way and the corners of his wicked lips tilted into a half-smile. "You will need this ferocity to protect what you have awakened."

"Awakened?" He faltered and frowned at the male before him. What was he talking about?

The Devil's gaze slid down to Nevar again and narrowed on him, burning red with furious fire. "Or should I say… what *he* has awakened."

"Asmodeus?" Liora whispered and he looked over his wing at her.

He pulled her around to his front and tucked her against his side, curling one wing around her to keep the Devil's eyes off her bare legs. He had asked Erin to dress her after they had tended to her wounds and had bathed the blood from her skin, and the female had lent her the sexiest black shorts and top Asmodeus had ever seen. He wanted to growl at any male who dared look upon his female when she was dressed this way.

Liora looked up at him, her eyes speaking to his heart, relaying her emotions. "I feel strange."

"Shh, my sweet little mortal." He sent his sword away and stroked her cheek, hoping to soothe her fear.

She wasn't the only one who felt different. He had thought it was the Devil's power but within the shield of his own, he still felt strange, as if his body knew something his mind did not. Something was wrong.

Now that he was thinking about it, he had felt this way since the crystal room.

Since the moment Nevar had skewered them on his sword.

Ever since then, he'd had a sense that he was being watched or was linked to someone, like when the Devil called him.

The feeling had been subtle at first, but now it was strong and compelling him.

He felt as if he needed to return to the chamber.

Awakened.

Asmodeus recalled the carvings on the door. The dragons and the behemoth amongst them, devouring angel, demon and mortal alike.

He looked down at Nevar and then to the Devil. "What has he done?"

"He has ended the game," the deep voice came from behind him and he turned to look at Apollyon. The male's eyes swirled blue fire and he grasped his twin golden blades. His power rose, pushing against Asmodeus's, and he strained as he slowly got to his feet, stumbling as he fought the Devil's power.

"How?" Amelia said from beside him, her grey eyes filled with disbelief. "The game is eternal. That pretty much means there is no end to it… so how the heck can he have ended the game?"

Apollyon looked into Asmodeus's eyes and a chill went through him, his sense that something was wrong gaining clarity and form in his mind.

Asmodeus whispered, "Because everything is about to be destroyed."

"Wait a minute." Liora pushed away from him, bringing his focus down to her. The wild edge to her hazel eyes told him that she was afraid, that he was frightening her, but her heart was steady, speaking to him and telling him that she knew he was voicing the truth.

The Devil clapped. "Brains and brawn. I had hoped you would serve your purpose one day, but I had not planned that it would be this day."

Asmodeus released Liora and faced his master. "You created me because you needed Apollyon's blood… the blood of the Great Destroyer."

"You are not the Great Destroyer." The Devil stood and looked back at the fortress, and then at Apollyon. "And neither are you. The true destroyer slumbers still, but it will awaken, given life and form by the power of the blood of Apollyon and the sacred blood carried in the veins of the mortal female."

"You said you didn't want to spill my blood," Liora whispered, her eyes growing larger, staring blankly at the Devil. Asmodeus could feel her emotions, could sense the turmoil and pain inside her. Tears lined her dark lashes. She shook her head as her heart steadied and her emotions changed, fury burning her softer ones to ashes. "You sent the demons… you sent them for my mother. You bastard!"

Asmodeus caught her arms before she could launch herself at the Devil and pulled her back into his embrace. She slammed her fists against his bare chest, each blow harder than the last, the threads of purple and black magic chasing around her hands giving them force beyond mortal strength. He weathered them and struggled to hold on to her, refusing to let her go.

The Devil would kill her if he did.

He wanted to make the bastard pay for what he had done to her family too, but keeping her safe and alive was more important. He had to protect her.

He managed to get his arms around her and pinned her to his chest. She pushed her palms against him and her magic struck at his flesh, burrowing deep and stinging him. Each lash drained his strength and increased hers. She was absorbing his power, strengthening herself so she could break free of his arms and fight. He couldn't let that happen.

"Did you take Liora's family from her?" Asmodeus said and she stiffened in his arms, her palms pressing against his chest and her magic halting its attack.

She wanted to hear the Devil's reply.

"I did." The Devil stepped towards them and Asmodeus drew Liora closer, expecting her to begin fighting him again.

She didn't. She trembled in his arms, her forehead resting against his chest and heart pounding in his ears. Asmodeus stroked her hair, needing to comfort her, wanting her to know that he was here for her and he would never leave her. She had lost her parents because of his master but she would never lose him.

"Why?" Liora whispered against his chest.

The Devil huffed. "They were not meant to die. I dealt with the fools who disobeyed my orders and killed them. I had foreseen that her mother would pass the pentagram to her, allowing my men to capture her."

Asmodeus's eyes widened as he recalled how the pentagram had reacted to him when he had unleashed his true nature, changing into his kingly form. It had tried to reject him.

"It repels evil." Asmodeus stared at the ground by the Devil's feet, lost in his thoughts. "The pentagram had protected the female line for generations, making it impossible for a being with evil intentions in its heart to harm them, keeping them out of your claws and those of your men. Her mother gave it to her in order to keep her safe from you and then sacrificed herself so you couldn't get your hands on her and the power locked within her blood."

Liora shifted in his arms and he looked down at her. Tears sparkled in her hazel eyes and he could feel the pain beating in her heart. She touched the spot over it where her pentagram belonged. It was gone forever, taken from her by Nevar. It could no longer protect her, but Asmodeus would keep her safe in its stead. He would repel all who would mean her harm with his blades and his claws.

Asmodeus gently brushed a tear from her cheek and she closed her eyes and leaned into his touch. He lingered with his hand against her face, giving her time to absorb the comfort she needed from him, wanting to soothe her pain. If he could, he would take the Devil's life in payment for the lives the male had taken from her.

If he could.

"I only desired to send her mother to sleep, keeping her safe in the chamber," the Devil said.

"On hand in case you needed to awaken the Great Destroyer… just as you kept me close by… a sacrificial lamb that you created for one purpose. I was never meant to be your second in command. I was only ever meant to be another pawn in your twisted games." Asmodeus tightened his grip on Liora, clutching the one good thing in his life, the one thing that had given it purpose. Everything else had been a lie. Centuries of existence. Centuries of the Devil praising him and encouraging him, giving him free run of the realm, playing on his desire for power.

All along, the Devil had been manipulating him, honing him for this purpose.

He had wanted him to bring Liora to Hell, to him, so he could place her in that chamber and spill their blood.

He looked at his master, seeing only seething anger in his red gaze. No twisted smile of satisfaction. No glimmer of sick happiness.

Something was very wrong.

Asmodeus stared at him and he stared right back.

"You did not want to spill her blood or mine… you truly wanted to keep her safe."

The Devil inched his head downwards. "I never intended to awaken the destroyer, unless I was forced to by Heaven."

"It was another bloody insurance policy. I was right." Erin clenched her fists at her side. "I said that you must have created Asmodeus as a sort of insurance policy and I was bloody right. You wanted to wield the threat of awakening this destroyer… this monster. Now that it's happened, you're all miffed about it… why?"

Nevar shot to his knees, arched backwards and roared at the cavernous black ceiling of Hell. He snarled, fangs sharp between his lips as they peeled back, and clawed at his violet-edged black chest plate.

"Nevar?" Liora went to reach for him and Asmodeus pulled her back against his front. She turned on him. "He's hurting."

Asmodeus could feel it too, and admired her compassion after everything Nevar had done to her, but he wasn't sure it was Nevar's pain he was experiencing.

The ground shook violently and Asmodeus drew Liora closer, fighting to keep his balance as the basalt bucked beneath them. It ended as quickly as it had started and ominous silence settled over Hell.

Nevar ripped his breastplate off, sending it clattering across the black basalt. The back plate dropped behind him.

Violet light burst from his chest, blinding Asmodeus, and then winked out again.

Nevar breathed hard, still arching backwards, his hands shaking viciously against the sides of his head, his fingers clawing his white hair back with such force that it pulled at his skin.

Asmodeus stared.

Purple spots of light chased over Nevar's bare chest above his heart, smoke curling from them as they marked his pale skin, carving a shape into it. It began to take form. A reptilian head armed with sharp fangs and six curved horns. Wings that followed the sweeping arc of its scaly body. Clawed feet. A long barbed tail. It formed a circle on his chest the size of Asmodeus's palm. In the centre of the beast, a perfect replica of Liora's pentagram appeared. The dragon shifted and Nevar cried out again, the sound echoing around the curved courtyard. The beast clutched the pentagram in its claws and settled.

The light faded.

The sense of pain in Asmodeus faded too and Liora sagged against him. Her magic curled around her hands in black, red and purple ribbons of light. Had it come to protect her or was she intending to launch an attack? Her heart was steady again, her emotions verging on dark, and her eyes slid towards the Devil.

Asmodeus drew her closer and she flicked a glance up at him. He shook his head slightly, silently warning her not to attack the Devil. They were in no position to fight him right now, not with Erin in the firing line and with Apollyon present. It was too risky. Liora frowned and then finally nodded, and he could see in her eyes that she was only putting her plans on hold and not giving up completely. She wanted the Devil to pay for what he had done and when the day came, Asmodeus would be there by her side.

She looked over at Nevar and Asmodeus followed her gaze.

The Devil pointed a single clawed finger at Nevar's chest. "That would be why I am annoyed… and why I am not killing him, and would suggest none of you do either. In fact, I would suggest you do your best to keep the wretched maggot alive."

"Why?" Asmodeus had vowed to keep Nevar alive and help him rehabilitate, but that had been before he had realised the extent of what Nevar had done to him and to Liora. Now, he wanted the bastard's blood on his hands.

"Because the fate of the world depends on him." The Devil turned away from them, waved his hand so his throne disappeared, and began walking back towards his fortress. "He awakened the Great Destroyer. He must deal with the consequences."

"Enough with the cryptic bullshit," Erin snapped and the Devil glanced over his shoulder at her, one eyebrow cocked high. "Are you telling us that Nevar is somehow connected to the destroyer?"

The Devil smiled wickedly. "Not somehow. Nevar is the creature's master."

His fiery gaze shifted slowly to Asmodeus and Liora, and Asmodeus pulled her closer, unwilling to allow her out of his arms while the Devil was around and looking as though he needed someone to take out his anger on, and while Liora was still having thoughts about fighting him.

"And you two are the creature's guardians. I will expect you to be here to do your duty, Asmodeus. It might be one hour or one century before the beast awakens. That is one hour or one century in which you will guard the chamber. I command you to remain here in Hell until the time when the Great Destroyer awakens and your…" He flicked Nevar a glare and his voice dripped with venom. "*Pet… will remain here with you.*"

The Devil was ordering him to remain in Hell?

"I cannot." Asmodeus released Liora and felt her gaze on him.

She would never consent to living in Hell with him, not after everything she had been through in this realm. She hated this place and his master. She hated the things Asmodeus had done while here and the sort of man it had made him.

If he had to remain here to watch over the destroyer, he would have to do it with only Nevar for company.

But he didn't want to lose Liora.

"You can and you will. End of discussion. You will obey me, Asmodeus." The Devil stalked away from him and Asmodeus wanted to hurl himself up the steps, grab his shoulder and force the male to rescind his command.

It was already flowing through him, tugging him into obeying, the power of it stronger than any order the Devil had issued to him before. He wouldn't be able to resist this one. The Devil had placed all of his power into it and Asmodeus was his unwilling servant. He had to carry out this command.

"Asmodeus?" Liora whispered and he couldn't bring himself to look at her.

The Devil hadn't mentioned her. He hadn't demanded that she stay in Hell. Could Asmodeus demand such a thing of her?

Would she want to live with him?

On the beach, she had been quick to show her disappointment and disapproval. She hated what he had done to Nevar and so did he, because it had made her see the evil in him, the extent of the darkness he held within his heart, and there was nothing he could do to make her forget that, especially not while Nevar was around.

The male curled over on his knees, rocking back and forth, clutching his chest and muttering black things in the demon language. He wanted blood.

Asmodeus closed his eyes and his horns shrank into his head, his shadows slipped away, and his fangs ascended.

"What happens now?" Liora said and Asmodeus tried to look at her but his gaze refused to settle on her. He stared off to her left, at Nevar.

He wanted to tell her that she would live with him in Hell. He needed her to stay, wanted them to be together because he couldn't live without her now, but how could he convince her to remain in Hell with him when what he wanted most of all was for her to be happy and safe?

She would be neither of those things in this realm.

"I will take you back to the island and then I will return here with Nevar." He couldn't bring himself to say more than that, to voice what he knew he had to do, because he didn't want it to become real.

He didn't want to let Liora go, even when he knew he must.

"Oh," she said in a small voice and cast her gaze down at her feet. "I see."

Asmodeus cursed beneath his breath. He didn't want her to see. He wanted her to tell him he was crazy and being a fool. He wanted her to tell him that he was being beta again when she liked him alpha. He wanted her to give him a sign.

He wanted her to fight for him just as he wanted to fight for her.

He needed her to stay with him.

She would.

He would do all in his power to convince her that they belonged together and that he could keep her safe and make her happy if she lived in Hell with him.

He refused to let her go because she belonged to him now and he belonged to her.

Forever.

CHAPTER 26

Liora left the group by the fire as the sky changed, turning gold and pink. The gentle swaying of the palm trees in the warm breeze and the swish of the water against the shore didn't soothe her in the slightest this evening.

Asmodeus was leaving.

He was going to follow orders and return to Hell with Nevar and his hellhounds, and she would never see him again. She had gone through one feeling after the other since he had announced his intent in Hell. Bitterness and disappointment. Anger and resentment. Misery and heartache.

Now, she was feeling so many conflicting emotions that she wasn't sure what she was doing. She couldn't focus, couldn't think, and couldn't function, but she knew there was something she definitely couldn't do.

She couldn't let Asmodeus leave.

He had changed back into his black linen trousers after they had arrived on the island and they had discussed everything they had learned with Apollyon and the others, formulating a sort of plan. Liora hadn't listened to half of it. She had spent most of the hour staring at Asmodeus, wondering why he was intent on leaving her behind.

It had been at the end of that hour when she had realised she was the reason why he hadn't mentioned taking her with him to Hell.

In the midst of the terrifying revelation that her blood combined with Asmodeus's had awakened some sort of primordial monster and that the end of the world was either potentially nigh or a long way off, she had forgotten all the terrible things she had said to Asmodeus. She had forgotten how things had been between them before Hell's angels had snatched him from the island.

Asmodeus had turned to leave with his two hellhounds as his only company and she had tried to stop him. He had squeezed her hand and given her an empty smile, and told her that he needed a minute alone. She had given him five because she had seen in his beautiful eyes that he needed every second of them. He was fighting himself again, torn in two because of the orders his master had given him.

And because of the things she had said.

That little revelation was the reason she was moving at an ever-increasing pace across the warm sand, trying to catch up with him before he did something stupid like leaving without saying goodbye. She had to explain and apologise, and make him see that she hadn't really meant what she had said.

She needed him.

He couldn't leave her.

He had promised.

He reached the far end of the beach. Romulus and Remus stopped playing in the water and raced to him. He held his hands out to them and her heart clenched when he rubbed them between their ears and heaved a sigh. She hurried along the firm white sand, running now, the water splashing over her bare feet as the small waves rolled in.

She managed to catch up with him at a spur of rocks that curved outwards into the water, sheltering the bay.

"Asmodeus?" she said and he stopped with his back to her and raked his fingers over his black hair, drawing it tight between them.

He sighed but didn't turn to face her. He waved his hand and Romulus and Remus took off again, bounding back into the water.

She edged closer to him, wanting to be near him, needing it. When the Devil had captured her and sent her to sleep, she had thought she would never see him again and it had hit home just how much she loved him, just as seeing Nevar had made her acknowledge the terrible things he had done.

And something told her that it had made that hit home for Asmodeus too.

"You're thinking about what you did to Nevar, aren't you? And the things that I said to you," she whispered and he lowered his head a fraction of a degree and then looked out to sea at the sunset.

"I regret what I did to him now... and I know you are struggling with your feelings about it and about me." He looked over his broad shoulders at her, the regret he spoke of in his golden eyes, calling her to go to him and comfort him, and tell him everything he needed to hear so his pain would fade away. "I do not want you to think me evil when I have tried so hard to be good. I would hate to be alive knowing that you despised me because of the things I have done in the past."

She knew that. He had changed so much since she had met him, but even back then she had seen good in him and had felt attracted to him. Part of her believed that this revelation and seeing the extent of his wickedness and how cruel he could be should change her feelings for him but it hadn't. She still loved him.

She still wanted to be with him, even if that meant living in Hell.

He swiftly turned and caught her hands, clutching them in his, holding them with such force that she couldn't move her arms. She couldn't take her eyes away from his, couldn't speak to alleviate the nerves she could feel in him and the desperation she could see in his eyes. That desperation quickly became resolve, beautiful and fierce, lightening her heart and giving her hope.

"Do not give up on me, Liora. I could not bear it. I have sought to protect you but in the end it was the result of my own foolish actions that placed you in the most danger and took you from me." Asmodeus looked down at their hands and then back into her eyes, and his gaze flickered beyond her shoulder, darkening as it landed on the area around the camp, most likely settled on Nevar. Asmodeus raised one of his hands and brushed her throat, his focus lingering there and his voice dropping to a soft whisper. "And my actions have taken something of value from you... something precious to you... and I cannot give it back."

"What happened to it?" She had thought that it was missing, not that it was gone.

"Nevar crushed it. He was angry with me. I am sorry, Liora. I failed you once again. I tried to take it back but I could only do so by taking Nevar down, and I..." Asmodeus pressed his palm to her chest, his fingers stroking her throat.

"You didn't want to kill him… because of me." She could see it all playing out in his eyes. He had held back because he had thought of her and what she would think of him if he killed Nevar. What had she done to her proud, beautiful, wicked angel? Liora took her hands from his and cupped his cheeks, bringing his gaze to meet hers. "I don't think you're evil, Asmodeus, and nothing you could ever do would change my feelings for you. I don't want you to live in fear of that happening… believing that any action you take would make me leave you. I'm not condoning you killing without reason, but, well… if there's need… I mean, if I'd had my faculties about me a little more in that crystal room, I would have killed Nevar not just jumped on his sword."

Asmodeus frowned and lowered his hand to her stomach, brushing his fingers over the black material of her tank top. "I wish you had not done that."

"In my defence, I thought I had my pentagram on, but I don't regret what I did because if I hadn't… I don't want to think about what would have happened." Liora swallowed, trying to ease the tightness in her throat and fighting her tears.

She didn't want to cry. She wanted to be happy. Asmodeus was safe and alive, and so was she, and that was all that truly mattered.

Asmodeus tunnelled his fingers into her hair, drew her to him and pressed a kiss to her forehead, lingering there with his lips against her. She closed her eyes and absorbed the love in his kiss, the tenderness and affection she could feel in it, and the relief too. She couldn't imagine what he must have gone through or felt after discovering she was gone, and after hearing the reason why the Devil had created him.

Liora settled her hands against his chest, feeling his heart thumping against them and sensing his confusion and pain. He had been as hurt as she had over the past day. No, he had been through worse. She had turned on him and the Devil had done the same, and now he was talking of leaving her and going back to Hell, with only Nevar for company.

No good would come of that.

He needed someone to help him with Nevar.

He needed her.

He looked down into her eyes with ones that were pure gold in the light of the sunset, filled with deep longing that she wanted to satisfy. He needed her and she needed him, and if he asked it of her, she would go to Hell to be with him.

Screw waiting for him to ask her. She was going with him whether he liked it or not.

She straightened and locked eyes with him, shoving her fears away and embracing her love for him.

"You swore to me… Asmodeus. You said you would never leave me… I won't let you leave me." She was beginning to ramble but she didn't care. She couldn't stop herself even if she tried. Her mouth was in control now, voicing everything in her heart. "I know we've had our ups and downs, and I haven't been the best girlfriend a wicked angel could want… and I wish I could take back what I said… but I can only try to make things better…"

"Liora," Asmodeus interjected, but she couldn't stop her mouth from running.

"I swear that things will be different. That whole thing with Nevar just shocked me and caught me off guard, and now that I look back… well, he's sort of an arsehole. I mean, he still wants to kill you even though you said that you'd help him…"

Asmodeus grabbed her upper arms and frowned at her. "Liora—"

"We said that we'd help him." She spoke over him and he growled at her. She told herself to shut up, that he wanted her to be quiet for five seconds and let him speak. Her mouth didn't get the message. She had to keep speaking. She had to get everything out in the open and apologise and make him see that he was wrong about her. She could deal with everything that lay ahead for them, including moving to Hell. "That's another reason I can't let you leave. You hear me? I know I said some bad shit and I'm sorry… I'm sorry about what I said. I shouldn't have said—"

Asmodeus snarled, tugged her against him and kissed her hard. Liora's eyes shot wide and then fell to half-mast and she melted under the heat of his kiss, forgetting everything she had been about to say and savouring how good it felt to have his lips on hers again. It reassured her, soothing her hurt and chasing her fears away.

He tightened his grip on her arms and kissed her harder, his mouth claiming hers and his tongue thrusting past her lips. She tackled it with her own and pressed her palms against his chest, digging her fingers into his warm flesh. He groaned and shifted one hand to her backside, cupped her right cheek and clutched it as he devoured her. Liora moaned and tilted her head back, giving herself over to him. She flicked her tongue over one of his short fangs and he grunted, growled and yanked her closer, until every hard inch of his body pressed into hers and she burned for him.

She whined when he pushed her back, breaking contact between them.

"I will have to remember that kissing you is the most effective way to shut you up." The corners of his kiss-swollen lips curved into a wicked smile. "Will you listen to me now, little mortal?"

She nodded dumbly, trying to get her faculties in order, her head still spinning from the kiss.

If he was going to kiss her like that every time her mouth started running and she couldn't stop it, she might just let it happen more often.

Wait.

He was talking about the future?

Asmodeus sighed, his broad chest expanding deliciously with it and tempting her into running her short nails down it, and then brushed his knuckles across her left cheek. He stared down into her eyes, an earnest and beautiful look in his golden ones.

"I must go to Hell… and I know how you must feel about that realm and you must think I am evil now that you have seen what I am capable of—"

Liora grabbed him around the back of his neck, pulled him down to her and shut him up with a fierce kiss. He wasn't evil. There was darkness in him, and it did outweigh the good, but that didn't make him evil.

She pushed him back and frowned up at him. "I told you… I don't think you're evil. Now what were you saying about going to Hell?"

He huffed. "I must go. I cannot ignore my master's order. After everything you have been through because of me—no, I swear to you, Liora, I will never let anything happen to you ever again. I will protect you. I will do better. I will be a good man for you… the only man that you need."

Liora smiled. "I know you will, Asmodeus… but if this is how you feel… why have you been so quiet and distant, so troubled?"

His gaze shifted back to the water and the sunset. "I was thinking about our situation and trying to find a suitable solution."

"And what did you come up with?" Liora sidled closer, keeping her gaze on his noble profile, waiting for him to tell her that he would take her to Hell with him.

"I will not force you to come with me to Hell. I will petition the Devil and see that he grants me leave so I may visit you."

Her heart fell.

Asmodeus frowned and turned his golden gaze on her. "Your emotions changed abruptly. Why? Do you not wish me to visit you?"

Silly male. He always looked for the negative and never the positive.

He moved to face her, lifted his hand as if to touch her cheek and then lowered it back to his side. "I only desire to keep you safe and happy. It is all I have ever desired. I am trying to do what is right for you, Liora… to find a way that we can be together still."

She dropped her gaze to his bare feet and hers, hating the tiny distance between them. She wanted to be in his arms again. She wanted to tell him that he was a fool. She wanted to tell him that he was breaking her heart.

"I'll hardly see you," she said to their feet.

Asmodeus fell quiet and she could sense his struggle, knew without looking that he was staring at their feet too, his handsome face locked in a pensive expression as he tried to find a solution that would please her.

"You said you wanted me to be happy and safe. I won't be happy if I only see you once in a blue moon, Asmodeus." She looked up at him and his gaze shifted back to hers. "You made a promise to me and now you have to keep it."

"I am trying to keep it." The sharp edge to his tone echoed the turbulent emotions colouring his eyes, making the amber and black flakes dance among the gold. "I will do my best to visit you as often as I can. I wish there were another way… but I have run all the scenarios and this is the best solution."

She shook her head and he frowned at her.

"There is another scenario where we can be together."

Asmodeus tipped his head back, growled in frustration, and then looked back down into her eyes. "I cannot live in this realm. I do not want to part from you for a minute… not a second… but I must."

"No," Liora said and slipped her right hand into his left one, holding it gently. "Not you living here, Asmodeus. I'm talking about me living in Hell."

"Liora," he started, his shock rippling through the point where they touched, and then sighed and opened his mouth to speak again.

He was going to protest and shoot down her suggestion.

She brushed her palms over his bare chest, skimmed them across his broad shoulders and then up his neck. She buried her fingers into the shorter hair at the back of his head and lured him down to her, marvelling that such a powerful male could be so compliant in her hands, bending easily to her will.

When he was close, she tiptoed and swept her lips across his. He didn't respond at first and his body remained rigid and tense beneath her hands. Liora closed her eyes and kept kissing him, refusing to give in and not wanting him to speak until she had melted his resolve and had won.

He snaked his arms around her waist, pulled her flush against him and deepened their kiss, claiming her mouth fully and making her melt inside.

A second later, he broke away and pressed his forehead to hers.

"I thought I had lost you," he whispered, husky and gruff, his hands clutching her sides.

"I'm right here," Liora murmured and tipped her head up, bringing their noses together. "Not going anywhere. Not letting you go anywhere either."

His hands trembled against her waist and then flexed and steadied, as if he had fought his overwhelming emotions and had won, finding solid ground again. He shifted one, brushing his fingers across the point on her stomach where Nevar's sword had punched through her.

Liora realised that he wasn't just talking about her leaving him because of things he had done or them being separated because of his orders to remain in Hell. He had thought she was going to die.

"I thought I had lost you too." She stroked the pale scar on his chest, directly over his heart, her throat closing and tears threatening to line her lashes again.

Remembering that cold terrifying moment chilled her blood and sent a shiver through her. She had been so afraid that Nevar had been about to strike Asmodeus down and that she would lose him forever. She had wanted to save him.

When Nevar's sword had gone right through her, she had been afraid for other reasons, feeling her life slipping away and the world growing hazy.

She had thought that fate was going to keep separating them no matter what they did and that they would never have the ending she wanted for them. Now it was trying to separate them again, taking Asmodeus back to Hell and leaving her alone in the mortal realm.

She wouldn't let that happen and she finally felt as if Asmodeus wouldn't let it happen either.

They would never be alone again. They would always have each other.

Liora pulled Asmodeus down to her and kissed him hard, a slave to her emotions. They were raw, fierce and demanding, pushing her to feel him in her arms and his lips on hers, to know his touch and that it was real.

They were alive and together, and nothing would change that.

They would have their happily forever after now.

Asmodeus broke the kiss and pressed his cheek to hers, his warm breath tickling her throat.

"Will you stay with me, Liora?" he whispered into her ear and she shivered in response, clutched his head and nodded.

"You can't get rid of me that easily," she murmured against his cheek and softly kissed it. "Someone has to help you with Nevar, and your duties, and the hellhounds, and then there's rebuilding our castle. I can really help with that. Magic is very good for lifting heavy objects—"

Asmodeus shot backwards, grasping her hips and holding her at arm's length. "*Our* castle?"

She couldn't help but smile at the wonderfully startled edge to his golden eyes and the way the flakes in them swirled, betraying the emotions she could feel in him. She had made him happy at last.

"Our castle." Her smile broadened when the corners of his lips tilted upwards. "I did tell you that I was adopting your hellhounds and that I was going to help you with Nevar, and technically I am one of the guardians of this… whatever it is… that Nevar woke up."

She didn't want to think about that part. Whatever it was that was stirring beneath the Devil's fortress, they could deal with it. The Devil had promised to aid them. Heaven had sent a message via Apollyon to say they would have all the angels they needed when the time came. Everyone on the island had agreed they would fight.

Three realms working as one. Together, they would stop the Great Destroyer.

"You will come to Hell with me. You will stay with me," Asmodeus said, his luscious deep baritone sending a hot shiver through her. There was a command in those words. An order that she was all too happy to obey. It felt good to see him finding his confidence again. There truly was nothing sexier than Asmodeus when he was king. "I will not leave you behind."

"Leave no one behind. A good motto to live by," she whispered, slipped her hands over his forearms, and caught his elbows. She drew him back to her, her gaze falling down the slope of his nose to his wicked mouth. "Now, does that mean we just moved past the casual boyfriend-girlfriend status and you're asking me to move in with you? Because I didn't hear that question leaving your lips and I know guys like you don't like commitment. It's cool. I can always make a little house of my own in Hell and just drop by to visit your castle from time to time."

Asmodeus grinned, slid his arms around her waist and tugged her hard against his body.

"I do not fear commitment. I have been committed to you since the moment you placed me under your spell and stole my heart in Paris, little witch. These are strange words for me to say, but I believe I will like the result." He raised one arm, smoothed his hand along her jaw, and tilted her head back.

She stared into his eyes, caught in them and breathless, struck silent by how they swirled with his emotions, drawing her deeper into them and making the world fall away until all she knew was her beautiful wicked angel.

He had said she had placed him under her spell. She was firmly under his and had been for what felt like a long time, and she hoped it never broke.

He took his hand from her face and a black rose appeared in his fingers. He tipped it towards her, his expression solemn and serious. "I do not have much to offer you… a broken castle… a black heart… two hellhounds who will drive you crazy… but I swear to provide for you and protect you. I will do all in my power to make your life with me comfortable and as normal as possible. Will you move in with me, Liora?"

She feigned thinking, barely holding back her smile. The smile that had curved Asmodeus's lips faded as seconds ticked by and his eyes darkened.

"Will you let me read all the books I want and help me translate the spells?"

He nodded. "Of course. We will make you the most powerful witch in the three realms."

She liked the way he said that, as if he was imagining forging himself a queen to suit the King of Demons.

She guessed if she lived in a castle and was in a steady relationship with the king, she could consider herself his queen. It was certainly a step up from rogue demon hunting witch with a bad reputation amongst her kind for being rebellious, vicious and a bit wicked.

Her King of Demons was a perfect match for her and she had known it from the moment she had set eyes on him. He wasn't the only one who had lost their heart in Paris.

"And you'll see to my needs?" she said, her eyebrows rising expectantly.

His eyes darkened for a different reason, desire dilating his pupils. He growled, "All of your needs."

She tapped her finger against her chin and wriggled her nose in thought, fighting the urge to give in to her desire to kiss him. He was too sexy for his own good when he growled things at her. Her gaze flicked to his ears. She really wanted to see those little horns of his again.

"Say yes," he husked and she was powerless to resist his demand.

"Yes," she whispered and he grasped the back of her neck, dropped his head and claimed her lips in a soul-searing kiss.

Liora leaned into him, clutching him to her and savouring every sweep and stroke of his lips against hers. In his arms like this, held close to him, she felt cherished and loved, and as if she had found her perfect man. She had found someone she could depend on and could lean on in times when she needed his strength, and she knew in her heart that Asmodeus felt the same.

She drew back and stared up into his mesmerising eyes, picking out every dancing fleck of black and amber amidst swirling gold. She loved it when he looked at her like that, as if she was the centre of his world. She reached up and twirled his black hair around her fingertips, and smiled wickedly.

"We had our first proper argument," she said and he frowned at her, canting his head to one side at the same time. "You know what that means."

He shook his head.

"Make up sex!" She waited but he didn't choke.

His eyes darkened, his pupils devouring the gold fire.

Liora frowned, a touch of disappointment flowing through her. She had expected a more satisfying reaction. She grinned as an idea dawned on her, tiptoed and stroked her fingers through his wild black hair, settling them just behind his ears.

She brought her lips to his left ear and breathed into it, "I want to tug your sexy little horns while you fu—"

Asmodeus choked.

Growled.

Grabbed her.

Liora squealed as he twisted her into his arms, enfolding her in his black-feathered wings, and cast a swirling shadowy portal on the sand beneath them, sending them plummeting into Hell.

His curved obsidian horns sprouted beneath her fingers.

Warmth spread through her as he beat his wings and they glided towards his castle. Their castle.

Liora leaned in and kissed him, stroking his horns at the same time and earning a husky growl as her reward.

Not even fate could part them now.

They wouldn't let it.

Together, they were stronger.

Together, they could take on the world.

Or at least save it from destruction.

Nothing would stand in the way of their forever.

The wicked King of Demons.

And his witch queen.

The End

ABOUT THE AUTHOR

Felicity Heaton writes passionate paranormal romance books as Felicity Heaton and F E Heaton. In her books she creates detailed worlds, twisting plots, mind-blowing action, intense emotion and heart-stopping romances with leading men that vary from dark deadly vampires to sexy shape-shifters and wicked werewolves, to sinful angels and hot demons!

If you're a fan of paranormal romance authors Lara Adrian, J R Ward, Sherrilyn Kenyon, Gena Showalter and Christine Feehan then you will enjoy her books too.

If you love your angels a little dark and wicked, Felicity Heaton's best selling Her Angel series is for you. If you like strong, powerful, and dark vampires then try the Vampires Realm series she writes as F E Heaton or any of her stand alone vampire romance books she writes as Felicity Heaton. Or if you're looking for vampire romances that are sinful, passionate and erotic then try Felicity Heaton's new Vampire Erotic Theatre series.

In 2011, four of her six paranormal romance books received Top Pick awards from Night Owl Reviews, Forbidden Blood was nominated as Best PNR Vampire Romance 2011 at The Romance Reviews, and many of her releases received five star reviews from numerous websites.

To see her other novels, visit: **http://www.felicityheaton.co.uk**

If you have enjoyed this story, please take a moment to contact the author at **author@felicityheaton.co.uk** or to post a review of the book online

Follow the author on:
Her blog – http://www.felicityheaton.co.uk/blog/
Twitter – http://twitter.com/felicityheaton
Facebook – http://www.facebook.com/felicityheaton

FIND OUT MORE ABOUT THE HER ANGEL SERIES AT:
http://www.felicityheaton.co.uk

CPSIA information can be obtained at www.ICGtesting.com
Printed in the USA
LVOW11s1018231013

358229LV00001B/22/P